FRACTAL MODE

BOOK TWO OF THE MODE SERIES

PIERS ANTHONY

ACE BOOKS, NEW YORK

This Ace Book contains the complete
text of the original hardcover edition.
It has been completely reset in a typeface
designed for easy reading, and was printed
from new film.

FRACTAL MODE

An Ace Book/published by arrangement with
the author

PRINTING HISTORY
Ace/Putnam hardcover edition/January 1992
Ace paperback edition/December 1992

ISBN: 0-441-25126-9

Ace Books are published by The Berkley Publishing Group,
200 Madison Avenue, New York, New York 10016.
The name "ACE" and the "A" logo are trademarks
belonging to Charter Communications, Inc.

PRINTED IN THE UNITED STATES OF AMERICA

10 9 8 7 6 5 4 3 2 1

CONTENTS

THE child was clumsy and rebellious. This was the remedial class, and he had no taste or talent for music. He wanted to be outside playing tag-ball. Still, Nona had never expected him to bite her.

Music was fundamental to the culture of Oria, and every child had to learn at least one instrument. This one would never be proficient, but he had to master the basics, or suffer consequences. The teacher did not want to call on a despot for punitive magic, so she tried kindness first. She assigned the prettiest and most talented music assistant to this difficult case. "If you can't do it, no one can, Ana," she murmured. She used Nona's pseudo name, not knowing her real one; only one other living person knew that. Well, perhaps another knew it, but that one would never tell.

Nona smiled. The boy was only nine, the required age for the onset of musical training, but even at that age they could be moved by an attractive woman. She was two months shy of her second nine, in the interim between the completion of her training and the onset of legal maturity. Everyone assumed that she would become a music teacher, but she had serious private doubts. She dared not express those doubts, for if the despots learned her secret they would destroy her.

She approached the boy. "Hello, Jick," she said pleasantly. "Why did you choose to play the lute?"

"I didn't," he said. "I don't want to. I hate it."

So his parents had required him to use this instrument. It was not her place to second-guess them. "Well, perhaps you will like it better when you get to know it," she said with careful cheer. "Let me help you get set."

She set his left hand on the stem of the junior instrument, his fingers on the frets. She guided the other hand to the body of it. "You hold it before you, like this," she explained, getting it into the right position for playing. "With this hand you pluck the strings, and with this one you adjust their tones. See, you can make several notes from a single string." She pressed on his left forefinger with her right forefinger, on the string, to demonstrate the effect.

Instead of moving as she indicated, he jerked his head suddenly forward and bit her finger, hard.

Nona shrieked, wrenching her hand away. The flesh tore and blood welled out.

The headmaster appeared. He snapped his fingers. The pain abruptly abated—and the boy screamed. The man had performed an instant transfer spell, causing Jick to suffer Nona's pain. There was a muffled titter from others in the class; they knew it served him right.

But in his agony, the boy threw down the lute, smashing it. Nona was busy inspecting her hand, trying to assess the damage, but she knew that this incident had already escalated dangerously. She was apt to get the blame for letting it happen.

"Go home and have your mother tend that," the headmaster said with a deceptively gentle voice. "I'll deal with this." His expression turned ugly as he faced the boy.

Then Nona knew that the man had been watching, probably by means of an illusion in another room, and knew exactly what had happened. He was technically a theow, but had a despot ancestor, and so had more magic than was normal for a theow. That was why he was in charge of the school: he could enforce discipline. She put her finger to her mouth, licking off the blood, and hurried out, relieved.

As she walked down the road from the school, she concentrated on her injured finger. The pain was returning as she got out of range of the transfer spell, but she should be able to craft an illusion of healing that would help.

Under her gaze the torn flesh knitted itself back together, and the color became normal. The pain faded, and her finger looked whole. But of course that was only the way it seemed; the damage remained, under the spell. Only the despots could do the potent magic.

She walked on out of the village and up the path to her house, which was nestled a bit apart. At first she had not understood why, but later she had learned: it was because of the secret. Her folks had made this isolated house and moved here twenty years ago, in anticipation of her presence. Now she understood how wise a decision that had been.

Her mother was weeding beans in the garden beyond the house. Nona realized with a small shock that the woman looked old. She was in her fifties, having gotten Nona late, and now seemed to be aging more rapidly than she should. Nona felt a pang of guilt, suspecting why that would be. Stooped shoulders, gray hair, deep facial lines—yet the goodness of her shone through the fading shell of her body.

Nona hurried out to her. "A boy bit my finger," she explained as she approached. "The headmaster sent me home to get it tended. I made a spell to hide it."

The woman took the proffered hand. She touched the finger, and there was no pain. She had no magic of this sort, but much experience of the natural kind. "This one?" she inquired with a lift of one brow.

"Yes. He bit so hard he tore my flesh. The headmaster made a transfer spell, so the brat got the pain instead of me, but I still have the injury. I hope it won't hurt my playing!"

"Child, this finger is not injured," the woman said.

"I covered it with illusion," Nona reminded her.

"I think you did more than that."

Startled, Nona looked at her finger. She flexed it. There was no discomfort. She touched it with her other hand, and found no injury. She lifted her eyes to meet her mother's gaze. "But—"

"I believe you," her mother said. "You are maturing."

Nona fell in beside her and helped pull weeds. They did not speak much, because it was never possible to be certain that a despot wasn't magically listening, but they had long experience at communication with minimal speech.

Nona remembered how her magic had gradually come upon her. As a child she had learned to convert her pease porridge to sweet pudding, and thought that others did the same. Later she learned that their conversions were mere illusion, while hers were actual. Similarly, when she conjured a living bird to her hand, it was real, while others fashioned only the semblance.

Her mother had cautioned her to restrict herself to illusion whenever in company, and not to tell anyone of her abilities. This was because only the despots were supposed to practice significant magic, and a theow who did it would be in peril. The despots used magic to suppress the theows, and reacted fiercely to any conceivable challenge.

So it was that Nona had lived, if not a lie, a charade. She could do significant magic, but no one knew. No one except her mother. Not even her father, though perhaps he suspected.

Actually they were not her birth parents. They had somehow known that they would have a changeling, and had prepared for it. When their only baby was born, they had taken him out at night to the town meetinghouse and left him. Before dawn they had returned and taken the changeling: Nona.

Who were her natural parents? Nona did not know. But she did know this: she was the ninth born of the ninth generation. The ninth of the ninth. That was what accounted for her magic.

And she was the one who might have the power to rid fair Oria of the despots, according to the legend. If she could only discover how.

That was why she had had to be hidden. Had the despots known there was a ninth of a ninth, they would have razed whole villages to destroy that baby. So her natural parents had given away an early baby, hiding the fact that it had ever been born, in this manner reducing the count. Then when they birthed the ninth, it was reckoned as the eighth, and they did not have a ninth. That eighth was then exchanged for another, so that if the despots became suspicious, they could verify that there was no special magic in that boy. The magic was in the lost one, Nona. Nona, called Ana, so that the significance of her real name would not give her nature away. For her name meant "ninthborn." The people did not know, but the body did; the magic was in her, and it was growing. To all others, she seemed to be the first and only child of her mother, who had had difficulties in her birthing and could not bear another. There was no magical threat in a firstborn theow, and little in a female, so her concealment was effective.

Now she had manifested another ability: healing. She

had cured herself of a troublesome injury, without even realizing. Illusion could be marvelous, but in the end it was transitory. Real magic lasted. Her healing, supposedly a mask over injury, had eliminated the injury itself.

They came to the end of the row. "Come inside," her mother said. "I will bandage your hand."

Because they could not let it be known that the healing had taken place. After a week, yes, but not after a day. After less than an hour, actually.

Nona followed her mother to the house.

A week later the bandage was reduced to a thin wrapping around the finger, and that was masked by a spot illusion. Only those who actually touched her hand sensed the bandage. In a few more days she would remove that, and wear only a small scar—which would actually be illusion, because her finger had healed scarlessly.

The errant boy, Jick, had been severely disciplined. He now wore a muzzle. It would be long before he bit another person—and if he did, he might be subject to the discipline of the despots, who well might conjure away his teeth. Nona had been relieved of her assisting, not because they thought her injured or culpable, but because it was policy to let things settle after an incident.

She used the time to query her mother, when they could converse with minimal risk. Her father worked at the castle as a horse trainer, so was no problem in the day. It was not that he would willingly betray her secret, but that the despots could use their terrible magic to get anything from anyone who knew anything. Only complete lack of suspicion protected her. So she acted like a somewhat spoiled juvenile, sleeping late, until her mother hinted strenuously that she should help with the fieldwork. Then, grudgingly, she went out to tackle the relentless weeds beside her mother, and only then, their real purpose masked by the charade, did they talk. Even so, it was in interrupted segments, so that any magical eavesdropping would pick up only an innocuous fragment.

Nona would soon be eighteen. If she did not find out how to save Oria before then, she might not be able to thereafter. She was the only one of all the theows who could do it. This was her window of opportunity.

"But why not longer?" she asked.

Because, her mother clarified in snatches between weeds, a woman's magic came to her through her ancestry, and departed through her babies. With each baby she had, she would lose part of her power, until the ninth would take the last of it, and she would be no more than an ordinary caretaker. In addition, she would have to care for the children, and that would anchor her to her house. She could not afford to marry, or if she did, she could not afford to have children.

"But I don't want to anyway," Nona protested. Indeed, whether because of her raising or her nature, she was appalled by the prospect of becoming a brood mare. Romance she could handle, but that notion stopped short of baby birthing.

Her mother only smiled sadly. Marriage and babies and deepening poverty were a theow woman's destiny; everyone knew that. It was an aspect of the system. Only those who had significant magic lived well; the others got along as well as they could. Those who became too poor to sustain themselves, whether because of age or depletion, disappeared: the despots had little tolerance for burdens.

"But how?" she asked.

That was the key question. She had more or less understood the answers to the others, for they were common knowledge. But since the magic power Nona had was no more than that possessed by the despots, that was not enough to oppose them. It merely signaled her nature. Perhaps it would continue to grow as she aged—but not if she started having babies. Since it would be hard to avoid having babies if the despots remained in power, that prospect seemed insufficient.

"You must ask the Megaplayers," her mother murmured, hardly loud enough to be heard.

The Megaplayers! But they were long gone, now hardly more than a memory. Only their giant stone instruments remained, weathering at the brink of the sea, awesome monuments to the greatness of the past. Of course the despots would not have a chance if the Players returned! Yet surely the Megaplayers were dead.

Her mother shook her head. "They live."

How could she know that? But Nona trusted her. The Players lived.

Still, how could she find the Players, to ask them anything? And if she did, why would they pay any attention to her? She was only a lowly theow woman.

Her mother smiled. "Music."

If there was one thing Nona excelled at, it was music. She had a natural talent for it, enhanced by her magic, which sublimated in this expression. Now she realized that the Mega-players had to be musical. Consider their instruments!

So she had her answer. She would have to seek the Players where their instruments lay. She would have to appeal to them, and if they responded, they might act to abolish the despots. It would be easy, for them, for the magic of the Mega-players was like none known since.

Yet what had banished the Players, long ago? Surely it could only have been some power even greater than they. Where was that power now?

Nona shook her head. Whatever the answers were, she had perhaps two months to find them. Then she would be eighteen, and her fate would pursue her.

SHE could not risk a trip alone to the instruments. This was not because there was physical danger, for the region was sanguine. It was because it might alert the suspicion of the despots. She had to have a seemingly unrelated pretext to go there.

So she did the obvious: she made a date with Stave to view the sea. The fact was that the place of the instruments was a rendezvous for lovers, because of the bracing sea air and the lingering magic of the region. But she specified afternoon, thus signaling that the prospects for romantic involvement were limited. He, however, was free to hope that if the afternoon excursion turned out to be successful, there would be an evening liaison on another occasion. He was happy to agree to the date.

The day was beautiful. There had been recent rain, and the meadows were greening. Even the dread castle of the despots, at the crest of the highest hill, looked almost pretty. Of course it had not been built by the despots; they had merely moved in after the Megaplayers left. So whatever beauty it possessed was what lingered despite its present occupancy.

She wore her best red theow tunic with the matching slippers. Stave, more sensibly garbed in his dull blue work tunic, was taken aback. "You'll soil it on the grass!" he protested.

"Not if I don't sit," she replied.

"Of course," he agreed, politely masking his disappointment. Couples normally sat near the brink of the cliffs, looking out over the waves, and drew close when the sea winds were chill. It was a most seductive pretext. Hands could stray as far as desired or tolerated, concealed under those tunics. In fact, almost anything could be done under tunics, when both parties wished.

She did not want to turn him off, however. She had no intention of getting serious, but Stave was a decent young man who deserved decent treatment. Had she desired a settled life and babies, he would have been as good a choice to share them with as any. "If I do sit, it will be on you," she said. "So that my tunic will not touch the ground."

He pondered that as they walked. There were ways and ways to interpret it, and some of them were intriguing. His disappointment faded.

There was a bark to the side, and a blur of white. Cougar had spied them, and was running to join them. He was the village dog, of mixed breed, not at all like a cougar, but somehow he had acquired that name. Normally only the despots kept animals, but sometimes they allowed one to wander unattached. Cougar loved adventure, and a trip to the instruments was that, by his definition. Indeed, it was said that a tryst wasn't complete without the dog.

Stave picked up a stick. "Fetch, Cougar!" he cried, hurling it ahead of them.

The dog launched himself in pursuit, joyfully. But as the stick landed, it assumed the likeness of a skunk. As the dog caught up, the skunk turned tail, making ready to spray.

"You shouldn't tease him," Nona murmured.

"He's too smart to tease," Stave replied.

Sure enough, Cougar charged right in and caught the skunk in his jaws. He had not been fooled by the illusion. But, in a seeming act of retribution, he brought the stick back not to Stave but to Nona.

She reached down to take it, using her own illusion to convert the skunk into a bouquet of flowers. "Thank you, Cougar," she said, patting him on the head.

"You're welcome, lass," the dog replied.

She elbowed Stave in the ribs. "Watch you don't get bitten in the hind pocket!" the dog said in a more feminine voice.

Cougar wagged his tail. He enjoyed being part of an illusion.

There was a rumble of thunder. They looked, and there beyond the castle a storm was building, appropriately sinister. However, it was unlikely to come in this direction, and if it did, they would have time to return to the village before it struck. There was even a rainbow, probably the work of an idle villager, because the angle was wrong for it to be natural.

They reached the place of the instruments. Nona handed Stave the bouquet, which became the skunk again as he took it. She ran ahead, up to the very brink, and stood looking out. Cougar did the same, to the right, sharing her spirit.

The sea wind sought her out and tugged at her hair and the skirt of her tunic. Both material and hair flowed to her left, and the air stroked every part of her body with an intimacy she would not have permitted in anything else. She was exhilarated. She shaded her eyes with her left hand and waved to the sea with her right. She wished she could be here forever.

Then she looked down. The cliff at whose brink she stood was no ordinary work of nature. It was a monstrous stone musical instrument, a hammered dulcimer without its strings, rising five body lengths above the heaving surface of the water. Two giant stone roses were set in it, red with green leaves despite the weathering of the stone. In these alone the old magic lingered. The rest of the instrument was scarred with cracks and chips, and the top was overgrown with moss and grass.

How long had it been since the Players left? No theow seemed to know, and if the despots knew they did not tell. How long did it take for waves and weather to make stone crumble? Nona shivered. Longer than the time required for nine generations, obviously. Far longer, surely.

She looked to her left. There was a giant mandolin, its stone also cracking apart. The grass and moss outlined its entire top surface in green, and its hole was a dark cave into which the waves crashed. To her right was a great fiddle, in similar ruin.

These had been the possessions of the Megaplayers, even in their destruction suggesting the immense power of that lost age. What giants had wielded these mighty instruments? What could their music have been like? What could have caused these beings to depart, not only leaving their music behind but dumping their treasures into the sea?

Nona tried to imagine the Players, and could not. She tried to fathom the playing of the instruments, and could not. It was all too far beyond her. Yet somehow she had to find the Megaplayers and call on them to return. To deliver her people from near slavery. If only she could!

She stepped to the side, then back. She hopped. She shifted her weight and turned her body to an imaginary rhythm. She spun about, her skirt flaring out, her brown hair wrapping around her face. She felt a faint beat, as of distant marching or a baby's heart. She heard a faint sound, as of a delicate melody hidden behind crashing waves.

In a moment she was dancing. At first she set her feet deliberately in the patterns of the dance. Then something took them, and she abandoned herself to it. She stepped and whirled, kicked and leaped. The beat intensified, carrying her with it. She saw the world turning around her, the sky above, the sea below, and she was not in it but *of* it. She floated, she soared!

"Ana!"

She fell, abruptly released from the spell. Stave caught her, his strong arms bearing her back from the brink. "You were going to leap!" he exclaimed apologetically.

She realized that it could be true. Something had imbued her, and she had let go of her own will. It had been glorious— but now she realized how readily that possession could have swept her over the cliff and into the surging sea. Actually that would not have meant her death, because she had developed the power to fly, or at least to float in the air and to propel herself by attempting to conjure heavy objects to her. But if she had gone over the cliff, and fallen, and used that power to save herself, her secret would have been out, and that would have meant her death at the hands of the despots.

"Thank you," she panted. "I—I lost control."

"I never saw anything so beautiful," he said. "You danced as if the Players had taken your feet! Your legs were so lovely when your skirt floated up. Where did you learn those steps?"

The Players . . . Could it be? Had she made contact? The prospect awed her. But what could she say to Stave?

For a moment she was nonplussed, knowing that she

could not afford to have him guess that she was tuning in on the music of the Megaplayers, but also that it would not be right to lie about it. The magic she sought was the essence of truth; a lie would taint and perhaps nullify it. Yet if she distracted him by waxing romantic, she would be deceiving him in another way. She had no intention of marrying him.

"Just how far did my skirt rise?" she inquired, forcing a blush. This was about as much of a ploy as she cared to try: diverting him to a minor matter.

"Oh, not that far!" he said quickly. But it was obvious from the dilation of his pupils that it had been too far. Yet maybe that had solved her problem: he had already been distracted. It was not the way she would have chosen, but perhaps it was just as well.

"I tell you, Ana," he said as she hesitated. "I always thought you were, well, distant. Not the sort of girl to take on a date. I came here with you mainly from curiosity. But when you danced—you are a truly comely woman—it would be easy to love you."

"Don't do that!" she exclaimed. Then she had to laugh. "I mean, I didn't mean to—"

She saw him grow subtly tense. He felt rebuffed. "You just wanted to see what kind of impression you could make on a man when you tried?"

"No, I—"

"Well, I'll tell you: you made an impression on me!"

This was getting worse. "Stave, I'm sorry. I shouldn't have—"

He smiled, not comfortably. "You're trying to say that you didn't know how well it would work, or if it would work at all, and it worked too well? I understand. You had no more interest in me than I had in you. You just wanted to try the dance and see. Now you know: it works. So it's time to fetch whoever it is you're really interested in, and make your skirt flare up for him, so—"

"Stave, no!" she cried, chagrined.

"It's all right. There's someone I'd like to impress too. Can you show me how to do that dance?"

She stared at him. She had not tried to deceive him; he had deceived himself. But she had to accept it. If he took the dance as a romantic prelude, instead of a connection to the Players, there would be no suspicion.

"I can try," she said. "But it isn't something I learned. It just happened."

"Let's make it happen again." He set down the skunk, which became a stick as his hand left it. "You did a side step, like this, and back. Then you hopped." He did these motions and he talked. He was nimble on his feet; he knew how to dance. "Then something happened."

She had heard the distant rhythm of the Megaplayers! But she doubted that he would be able to hear it too; he was not ninthborn. Could she duplicate the dance without that music?

She tried. She set her feet in the remembered pattern, and her body moved, but the magic was not there.

"No, that's not it," Stave said, following her perfectly. "But the wind was taking your hair and skirt. Maybe if I try it up at the brink." He walked to the verge, faced out as she had, and tried the steps again.

The wind caught at him, as it had at her, and the sound of the sea seemed to grow louder. Stave danced—and it seemed almost that he was getting it. Certainly his tunic was flaring; if it went any higher she would have to avert her gaze. Then he misstepped, and teetered on the brink.

Nona screamed, and Cougar barked. At the same time, she exerted her magic, drawing him to her by a spell of attraction. Just enough to prevent him from falling outward. Stave caught himself, and dropped to the ground, catching his fingers in the sod for support.

Nona ran up, her heart pounding. "I thought you were going over!" she said, dropping to her knees beside him.

"So did I," he confessed. "I almost got it, but then—"

"Enough! Get away from the edge. Don't dance any more. If—if you want something of me—"

He glanced into her décolletage as she leaned toward him. "I do. There is no other woman I wish to impress. But I think—I think it is forbidden. Get your bosom out of my face before I forget."

She straightened up, smiling contritely. She had come to him in genuine alarm, thoughtless of her appearance. The tunics of the theows tended to be too large in the neck region, so that women normally held them closed with one hand when bending forward. Certainly she had given him something to see! She was no longer embarrassed; the horror of his near fall over the brink had banished that. But she played the innocent. "Forbidden?"

He got up and dusted himself off, then extended a hand to help her up. "Will you answer one question?"

Had he felt the faint presence of the Players? Suddenly she feared that he had. He might not have been able to attune well enough to dance, but he might realize that something was there. She didn't want that. Neither did she want to discuss it, because the despots could be eavesdropping with their magic.

So she did not answer. Instead she stepped up close and drew his head down for a kiss.

She could tell by the way his body didn't give that she wasn't fooling him. He *did* suspect.

Then he put his mouth down by her ear. "I felt it," he breathed, his moving lips actually touching her ear. "I felt your magic save me. You can trust me."

Could she? He had made it seem like an endearment, as if kissing her ear. In the process he had eliminated both sight and sound, because not even a magic spy could hear such a faint sound beyond her ear or see the motions of his lips against it. Yet suppose he merely wanted to learn something about her, so as to curry favor with the despots by telling them? She could not risk it.

"Nona," he breathed.

She jumped. *He had spoken her true name!* But no villager knew that. Not even her father knew it, and if he suspected, he would never have told.

Then, to cover her reaction, she spoke. "You bit my ear!"

"A love bite," he said. "Isn't this what we came here for?"

"I'm not sure." Indeed, she was in doubt. Was he going to require her favor, in return for his silence? She did not see him as that type of man, but he had already expressed interest in her body. This could be a dangerous game.

He drew her slowly in, and kissed her. This time she was the unresponsive one. He pretended not to notice, then moved back to her ear. "Can you hear me?"

That much she could admit to. She tightened her arms around him, once.

"Then listen," his lips said almost soundlessly into her ear. "I am the other changeling."

Again she jumped. "Will you stop that?" she said aloud. "I need that ear." *The other changeling? The baby they switched with her? The true child of her parents?*

"But it tastes so good," he protested in his normal voice.

They kissed and clinched a third time. This time she held herself still for the whole of what he had to say.

"I thought I was the eighth and last child in my family," he continued into her ear. "But my mother let slip once that she had lost one. I thought she meant the baby had died. But later I learned from another slip that it had been given away to skew the count. For my mother was the eighth child of her family, and had been required to marry young, lest she have magic. She was the eighth generation. That meant I was the ninth of the ninth, masked as the eighth to save my life from the despots. It applies only to females, but the despots tend to act first if there is any doubt."

They changed position, and kissed a few times in case there were watchers. Cougar settled down a short distance away; he did not find kissing as much fun as fetching, but he could tolerate it. The dog had learned that sometimes kissing led to more interesting activity. Then Stave sat on the ground and she joined him, pulling up her tunic so as not to soil it, though this meant that her bare bottom was on his lap. Had he drawn up his own tunic—but fortunately he did not. He was after all not pursuing her that way, though at this point that was a mixed relief. He ran one hand along her bare leg while he nuzzled her ear again, and she had to tolerate this for the sake of the appearance they had to make. He had abruptly become most intriguing, in an entirely different way.

"But I had no special magic," he continued. "Only the skill of illusion we all share. And my parents did not seem to expect more of me. How could that be, if I was the ninth? This concerned me. I did not at first understand that the effect is limited to the female line. Then I realized that there could have been a double mask. I did not closely resemble my siblings, though none ever teased me about it; indeed they helped me to be more like them. I could have been from another family—exchanged for the true ninth."

His hand was resting high on her leg, but he was not moving it now. His interest was only for show. She, in contrast, was far more interested than she had been. Stave was after all no ordinary young man; he was bound to her in the most special way. He was in a sense her brother, and in a sense her protector.

She moved to put her mouth at his ear. "I never guessed!" she breathed. Then she touched her teeth lightly to his lobe.

"Hey, now *you're* biting!" he protested.

She mussed his hair. It was fun flirting, now that she knew it would lead nowhere. "You are getting fresh for a first date. Get your hand off my leg."

He looked regretful. "Oh." He removed his hand.

She embraced him. "You should not be too quick to believe what a woman says."

He held her close and breathed into her ear again. "So when I came of age to wander, I walked from village to village, staying only long enough to see every person who was my age. When I came to this one, and saw you, I knew. You could have been one of my foster sisters. Then I looked at your parents, and they were fair like me. And your father—"

He paused. He brought his right hand around and turned so that his wrist was before her eyes. There was a small wine-colored stain—exactly like the one on her father's wrist. There was no doubt of it: he was the son of her parents.

He had had as much reason to come here with her as she had with him. She had been looking for the Megaplayers; he had been looking for his alternate. His expression of diffidence had been only a cover.

Now she knew his question, and she trusted him with the answer. She glanced around, and spied a dry stem of grass. She picked it up. "I will give you an illusion," she said. In her hand it became a rose, its hue matching her dress, its bud just opening. She handed it to him.

He took it by the stem and brought it to his nose, pretending to smell its perfume. Then he froze, for just a moment. He brought it closer and actually touched his nose to it. A subtle shudder went through him; had she not been sitting on him she would not have known. She had answered his question.

For it really did smell like a rose. Because it *was* a rose, not a mere illusion. She had transformed it: sight, feel, smell. But he knew the difference between the semblance of a rose and a real one, for he could not nullify it.

He handed it back to her. She flipped it away, and it

became the grass again, reverting in the manner of illusion when it left the hand of its creator. She had changed it back; had she not done so, the rose would have remained.

Stave drew her close again. He was shivering, though the day was warm. "How may I help you, my sister?" he whispered.

She took her turn at his ear. "Date me again. Let me dance with the Players. I must find them if I can. Tell no one."

"I will tell others I touched your body," he breathed back in due course. "I will touch it more each time." He put his hand on her leg again, at the exact place it had been before, just above the knee. There remained some distance to go before such touches got serious.

She nodded. They would have to appear to be getting quite intimate, so that no spy could doubt the nature of their interest in each other. It would be a perfect cover, much better with his cooperation. "Thank you," she whispered.

Then they kissed once more, and she protested that it was getting late, and he protested that there was still plenty of time in the day, and she pointed to the storm which was expanding toward them, and he suggested that they could take off their tunics and roll them up to keep them dry, and she suggested that he take off his head and roll it up instead, and he finally agreed that they would return to the village. He evinced silent disappointment that he had not been able to make more progress with her, and she evinced silent relief that she had managed to restrict his ambition, this time.

Yet behind the act was something else. They had found a bond, and they were in a manner brother and sister. But they were not related, and they did like each other. The romance they were pretending was not fully pretense. She had come to understand, in the course of their close contact, that he really was interested in her body as well as her nature, and she was becoming interested in his interest.

IN the following month they came many times to associate near the instruments. Nona would dance and Stave would watch, and then they would get together and become increasingly affectionate. Sometimes there were other couples there. It didn't matter. Stave and Nona were now known as a couple, and it was thought they might marry.

Indeed, the notion of marrying Stave was growing in her.

She wondered whether her destiny could be truly worth it, if it took her away from him. She liked his kisses, and the touches of his hands on her body. When he reached the permissible limits, she took his hand and guided it to more intimate regions than she would have tolerated had she not had control of it. It was both game and not-game, at the verge of loss of control. She wanted to stop teasing him and being teased by him, and to let nature take its course beyond. But that would be tantamount to commitment, and she couldn't afford it. Never before this series of dates had she truly understood how a girl could actually come to desire what it seemed every young man did.

Meanwhile she was definitely getting closer to the Megaplayers. She felt them more perfectly each time she danced. But they remained distant. Their music was there, capable of being evoked in her mind, and the beat of it grew stronger, but that was all. The Players themselves were somewhere else.

How was she to reach them? She had only one more month before her birthday. Then she would have to marry Stave, or risk the alternative. They discussed this openly, for it was independent of her quest.

"If we go to work for the despots," he said, "I will become a carpenter like my father and build shelves. That is my training. But though you are trained in music, you may not be sent to teach it. You are too beautiful."

"I know," she agreed.

"If we marry, I will still be a carpenter, but you will not be the plaything of your employer. They will let you teach music."

"Until I begin having children," she finished. There was the crux of it. When she began bearing babies, her magic would diminish, and her chance to find the Megaplayers would be gone. She had to find them *now*—and was not succeeding.

There had to be some way to reach them. Dancing wasn't enough; it only verified the presence of their lingering magic. But what else could she do?

There had to be a way! Tomorrow she would find it. Somehow. Her magic sense was tingling; she could not actually foresee the future, but she could tell when something important was about to happen.

•   •   •

THE day was much like the one when she and Stave had first come here, except that there was no storm forming in the distance. There were no other couples, but Cougar came along, as gladly as ever. The dog still seemed to hope that their control would snap, and they would get into a tangle of arms and legs that rolled helplessly down the hillside, leaving their clothing stranded at the top of the slope, as was reported to have happened on occasion to other couples.

She danced at the brink, taken by the glory of the ancient music, but still she could not reach the Players. Then something else came, something weird and wonderful and alarming. What could it be, if not the Players?

She broke step, retreating to make way. But she saw nothing. It must have been her own desire manifesting as a kind of illusion.

Exhilarated but disappointed, she turned to join Stave. She remained unwilling to admit it, but she enjoyed her sessions of pseudo-love with him as much as the dancing now. It would be so easy just to forget her destiny and take the safe way. In fact, recently he had been firmer about this than she; he did want her, but he wanted her destiny to be realized first. He did not want to divert her from it. That was part of what she had come to appreciate in him.

But he was gone. Perplexed she looked around—and spied him far to the side, with the dog. Cougar had run after something, evidently, and Stave had gone to investigate. They would return in a moment.

Then Nona felt something strange again. She heard the music, though she was not dancing. In fact it had not stopped; she had merely been distracted from it for a moment. The Megaplayers—could they be coming after all? She turned to face the cliff—and there was a shimmering there at the verge where she had just danced. She *had* tuned in to something!

Four figures appeared. They did not walk in from the land, or fly down from the sky, or climb up the cliff. They just were there, an instant after there had been nothing but her feeling. They must be the Players! .

But they were small—on her own scale, not giants who could wield the mighty stone instruments. There was a man, and an old woman, and a girl, and a horse. The man was looking down toward the sea, evidently appraising the monstrous dulcimer. The girl was looking right this way.

The man turned to look at Nona. So did the horse.

Then the girl's voice was in her mind. *I am Colene.*

I am Nona, she replied in her mind, amazed. What kind of magic was this?

Hello, Nona. We are friends. And the thought was so sincere that she believed it.

CHAPTER 2

COLENE

COLENE gazed at the young woman. She was lovely, in a red dress, no, a knee-length tunic, with thick black, no, dark brown hair. She was the anchor person, obviously. What a relief! Colene already knew this was a nice woman, because her mind was nice.

The language was unfamiliar, of course. But that didn't matter, with Seqiro's telepathic ability.

However, that did not necessarily mean that this reality was safe. They had to learn more about it, in a hurry. They had just escaped an awful situation in another reality, and had some real problems to work out between themselves, and some significant unwinding to do. New trouble was the last thing they needed—but they had to be prepared for it.

Nona reminded Colene of herself of a few weeks before. That was funny, because Colene was fourteen and Nona was evidently several years older. It was the naïveté and hope and underlying desperation of her situation, all coming through as background emotion: Colene had been that way, and Nona was that way now. So it was as if the four of them were on a fantastic roller-coaster ride, without seat belts, hanging on as the ride became impossibly wild—and now suddenly a fifth passenger had dropped into the car.

Are you the Megaplayers? Nona asked.

The whats? What was this? Oh, Nona thought they were

godlike figures, because of their sudden appearance from seemingly nowhere.

We are travelers, Colene clarified. *Not gods. Just three people. A suicidal girl from a science world, a decent man from a magic world, and a woman who remembers the future and not the past. And a horse. He is Seqiro, and he is telepathic.*

What?

He can read minds. That is how we're talking. We're bypassing language. That is, what I think is being translated into your language by your brain, and what you think is being rendered into my language. That's how it works.

This is amazing magic!

"I can remember it better if you speak aloud when possible," Provos remarked.

"And this is Provos," Colene said immediately, projecting the thought to Nona. Seqiro cooperated so well that it was just as if she herself were telepathic. But without the horse, it would not have been possible.

Nona faced the older woman. "Provos," she agreed.

"And Darius."

Nona faced the man. "Darius." She had no problem with speech; it was just that she spoke a different language.

Then Nona turned and gestured toward a man of about her own age who was approaching with a nondescript white dog with a yellow collar. His clothing was solid blue. "Stave," she said. She indicated the dog. "Cougar."

Then she faced the man and dog and spoke in her own language. Colene listened just enough to verify that it was completely alien, as she had expected, then tuned in on Nona's mind again.

". . . and when I turned back, they appeared from nowhere," Colene translated. Seqiro could send to them all simultaneously, if Colene asked him to and focused on it, but this was easier now that the introductions had been made. "They say they are not the Megaplayers, and their size suggests that this is true. But they must have remarkable magic, because—" She hesitated, and Colene caught the fringe of a complex network of concerns.

Colene stopped translating, intent on the thought. There was danger of some kind, she realized, but she couldn't pick up its nature. Nona meant them no harm, but someone else might. Not Stave, not the dog, but someone.

"I think no one here can understand us," Colene said for herself. "Verbally, I mean. So we might as well talk freely. But someone else may. I'll ask as soon as she stops explaining to Stave."

Stave was looking duly amazed. Now Colene touched his mind. *Hello,* she thought.

His gaze shifted from Nona to Colene. His jaw dropped. *Mind-talk magic!* he thought.

Nona evidently was telling him the same thing. No, she wasn't; she was saying that she was guessing about the visitors. Why was that, since Colene had explained about Seqiro's mental ability?

Then Nona paused, and Colene asked her: "What danger?"

Now it focused. Nona answered directly and silently, but Colene spoke the words again for the benefit of the others. "The despots rule here. They take whatever they want. I must take you to them, or my village will be punished. They will treat you well, until they know how they can use you. But you must not let them know about your mind-magic, for if they knew you could fathom their minds, they would kill you instantly."

There it was. "Why?"

"Because there is no magic of that nature here, and they will fear it. It is their great power of magic that enables them to hold us in thrall. They destroy any theow who evinces magic other than illusion." Theow was an obscure word meaning peon or peasant; Colene dredged it out of her memory because it fit. Nona's concept had nuances of servitude, poverty, and horror; it seemed that the common folk suffered here as they did elsewhere, while those in power exercised their prerogatives ruthlessly.

"But you have magic," Colene said, reading this ability in Nona. There had been a time when she did not believe in magic, but she had experienced too many strange things recently to doubt it any longer. She had had no personal experience with it, but Darius was a magician in his home reality.

"I am the ninthborn of the ninth generation," Nona thought and Colene spoke. "I have the magic of the nines. I can conjure, float, attract, transform, and heal. But only my mother and Stave know, for it must be secret until I find the Megaplayers. The despots would kill me. They would know that I seek to overthrow them and restore grace to our world."

And so Nona had become an anchor: one of the five people who defined the slice of reality that crossed an infinite number of other realities, enabling them to travel to completely strange worlds. She had sought the Megaplayers and inadvertently tuned in on a Virtual Mode. She was surely a special person, with one terrific surprise coming.

But could Nona's access to the Virtual Mode help her solve the problem of her world? Perhaps only if the mystic folk she sought were on one of the realities this Mode crossed.

"What are we going to do?" Darius asked Provos in his own language. Colene picked up on it because Seqiro translated the thoughts to her mind.

"We visited the despots, where Queen Glomerula sought to seduce you and Knave Naylor sought to rape Colene," Provos replied promptly in the same language. She did not know more than a few words of Colene's language, but with Seqiro present it made no difference.

Colene jumped. She had not had a lot of experience with Provos, but understood that the woman remembered backwards: she knew her future but not her past. Suddenly Colene appreciated how useful an ability that could be.

"You seem very sure," Darius said wryly.

"I am. My memory is quick when we spend enough time in a single reality."

Do they succeed? she thought to Provos.

"No." But the woman smiled obliquely, almost before the question.

Colene was relieved. "Then let's go to the castle and get this over with," she said. "We'll be moving on through the Virtual Mode soon, but Nona deserves to know her role in this."

Darius was more cautious. "Why do we spend much time in this reality?" he asked Provos.

"Because we were blocked from the Virtual Mode." She had evidently waited before answering, considering the question.

"What?" Colene had jumped again.

Provos spoke, and Seqiro brought the meaning to her mind. "There is a magic spell which prevents us from passing back through the anchor. We think it is because of the animus."

"The what?"

"It becomes complicated to explain. You have done a better job of it."

Meaning that in due course Colene would figure it out herself and explain it to the others. Maybe that was best. Anyway, they could use some rest in a single universe before tackling the rigors of the Virtual Mode again. "So take us to the castle, Nona," she said.

"Maybe I should do it," Stave suggested, his thought similarly translated. "I have less to hide from the despots."

Nona considered. "Would you, Stave?" And from her came gratitude bordering on love.

Stave looked at her, startled. He had a similar feeling for her, but had not realized that it was so strongly returned. They had never been telepathically linked before.

"We will keep each other's secrets," Colene said.

They walked down the hill, away from the sea. The landscape was spread out before them: walled fields, patches of trees, a sprinkling of houses, and the escarpments leading up to the castle. Down in a hollow was a village, and now there was a path leading to it. It was quite pleasant, to Colene's taste.

Nona separated from the group and went toward the village, while Stave led the way in the other direction, toward the castle. There seemed to be no mechanized transport for theows, or any other kind; people walked. Yet the houses did not look primitive. Archaic, rustic, minimal, perhaps, but not the type she would have expected on a world without heavy transport.

"The despots use the horses," Stave explained, responding to her thought. "They control everything." Then he had another thought, which Seqiro duly transferred: "This mind-magic—the despots will guess, if I respond to your thoughts. I must say I know nothing of you, but led you here."

"That is true," Colene agreed. "You do know nothing of us, and are leading us there."

He smiled. "But I hope to learn more, if we meet again."

Colene glanced at Provos. "Some of us spent much time with him, and liked him well," the older woman said. "Perhaps too well. He is much a man."

That future memory was unnerving at times! But also frustrating. How were they going to experience Stave's manliness? "Then maybe I should explain a bit more to you," Colene said to him. "We are from another reality. The world you know is only one of many."

"Of course," he agreed. "The despots try to hide the information from us, but we know that there are worlds beyond counting, if only we were allowed to walk to them. But the despots control the filaments, so we can not."

These folk knew of alternate realities? That was surprising. And what did he mean by filaments? So she sought a clarification of his concept of worlds—and got only a mental picture of planets strung together like beads, the string between them winding in fancy patterns. Obviously not the same thing. Primitive mythology, perhaps.

"You do not understand?" Stave asked, picking up her return thought. "How can you not, since you come from another world?"

"My world is the same as yours, only not the same," she said. "It is in a different plane of reality. So it has different people, and maybe different geography, and different laws of nature, but it is not removed in space or time from yours, exactly. We have established a Virtual Mode, with Nona as an anchor person."

He shook his head. "That is beyond my understanding!"

"Just as your concept is beyond mine," she said. "Later on we'll get together and hassle this out. For now, just accept the fact that we are stranger to you than we look. We'll just follow you up to the castle, and you do your duty and turn us in, and go away. We'll get in touch with you later."

Stave wasn't satisfied with that. "The despots may mean you ill. They treat everyone with contempt. Do not trust them."

"We don't," she assured him. "We can read their minds."

Only if they allow it, Seqiro reminded her.

Oops! She had become so accustomed to the free expression among the four of them—herself, Darius, Provos, and Seqiro—that she had forgotten this was because they were all willing. A person could close his mind, if he knew how, and strangers tended to be closed anyway, because they were apt to be suspicious or hostile.

"But they will want to communicate with us, to question us," Darius said. "Therefore they will open their minds as we become responsive."

She nodded. That made sense. "But how do they treat horses?" she asked Stave.

"Well, if they are docile. But once they take your horse, they will not give him back unless you satisfy them that you are despots from another center."

"Another center?" Darius asked.

"There are hundreds of despot territories, all across the planet," Stave explained. "All oppress their theows similarly, and though they may contest with each other for dominance, they are united against theows. Only a despot has any rights, in his home territory or when traveling through others."

Colene patted Seqiro on the shoulder. "They will not take this horse." Nevertheless, she suffered a qualm. She had had some experience with a despotic regime.

Provos laughed. "They try!" she said.

"Do they take Seqiro?" Darius asked Provos.

Colene had not gotten used to the business of Provos sometimes answering questions before they were asked, but it made sense in her terms.

"Yes," Provos said. "All seven."

"So we will escape as a group," Darius said. "But not through the anchor. But do we get through the anchor eventually?" This was the question Provos had just answered.

"So we'll just have to play it through," Colene said. Given the assurance that they would get away, she preferred to avoid further confusing hints of the future. What was this "seven" business? Only five could use an anchor. It was complicated for any others.

A blackbird flew toward them. "Stop talking," Stave said quickly. "The minions of the despots can hear and comprehend, and if they think we understand each other, there will be much mischief. Pretend I have tricked you into following."

Colene liked the way his mind worked. He might be a peasant, but he was no fool.

The blackbird circled them, then flew on toward the castle ahead. "They can see things from a distance," Stave murmured almost inaudibly; the telepathy carried his thought. "But they usually need a familiar to hear. They have surely seen us coming from afar."

They came to the castle. It had seemed small from across the valley, but it had grown inversely as the distance diminished, and now was huge. In fact it seemed more like a massively walled city, with the turrets of many buildings within its compound. Colene realized that either the theows had to work here in great numbers, or there were many more people in the ruling class than she had thought.

Stave approached the guard at the gate, a man in a black tunic who carried a formidable sword. "I found these three people and their horse near the sea," he explained. "I brought them here to you, as is proper. They don't seem to speak our language."

Before the guard could answer, the castle gate opened. A grim contingent of interior guards marched out. They approached the party, orienting on Stave. "What is this, theow?" the head guard demanded. Seqiro picked up the thought from Stave's mind; the guards were hostile, so their minds were closed.

"I found them in the countryside," Stave replied. "They are strangers, so I signaled them to follow me, and they did. I thought the despots would want to see them."

The guard faced Darius. "Who are you?" he snapped. Again, the message was from Stave's mind.

Darius looked blank. "Are you speaking to me?" he inquired in his own language, which Colene could not understand; this time it was Darius' thought Seqiro relayed.

The guard seemed taken aback at the unintelligible speech. Satisfied that these were indeed strangers, he pointed to the gate.

"Go there?" Darius asked. He took a step, hesitantly.

The guard turned and walked ahead, leading them in. Stave stood where he was, ignored. *Go with them,* he thought, his face impassive. *They have no interest in me, and that is best. I will tell Ana, whom you know as Nona, that you are here. I will come if you call me, if you can mind-talk from a distance.*

We can, Colene thought. She wished Stave had come in with them, however, because then they would have had a far easier time understanding what was going on. As it was, she was nervous, despite Provos' assurance that they would get through satisfactorily. How accurate was the woman's memory of future events? It couldn't be perfect, because sometimes their actions changed their future.

The gate did not lead straight in. Instead they had to mount a long, steep ramp which seemed to go to the top of the wall. But it didn't; perhaps three quarters of the way up it turned away from the wall and deposited them on a slightly sloping platform, an interior glacis. Apparently the wall surrounded a steep mountain ridge, and the castle proper was at the top of that. This would be some redoubt to storm!

Inside, it looked even more like a city. The outer wall did not connect to the interior structures; there was a wide space between them. That way the inhabitants could defend against an enemy who breached the outer ramparts; he would have to expose himself to further fire before reaching the inner compound.

They were led to a chamber just inside the wall. The head guard barked a command, but this time they really did not understand it.

Then an old man appeared, also in black. He did not walk in, he appeared in the chamber. He smiled. He spoke in more gibberish, addressing Darius.

"I do not understand what you are saying," Darius replied in his own language.

The man lifted his hand, and a doll appeared in it. The doll looked much like Darius. The doll reached out, and in its hand appeared a cloak similar to the one the old man wore, but green. Then the cloak was on the doll.

"An icon!" Darius exclaimed. "My kind of magic!"

"Not necessarily," Colene said. "Guess something else, just in case." Because Nona had not mentioned that type of magic.

"You want us to change clothing?" Darius asked.

The doll was suddenly wearing the cloak. The implication was clear enough. Colene's caution had been justified. Darius might have given away his magic, if it worked here.

"But we need a private place to change," Darius protested.

"Oh, forget it," Colene said. "They don't care about our bodies." She extended her hand toward the man in white, and immediately a green cloak landed on it. She stepped out of her clothing, except for her bra and panties, and dropped the cloak over her head. It was light and silken, pleasant enough to wear, and had a green sash she tied around her waist. Green slippers appeared before her, and she donned them too. The cloak seemed designed for a larger person, as it reached right down to her ankles, but she was satisfied.

Darius had averted his gaze as she changed; it was one of the little ways he had about him, both frustrating and endearing. That was more than could be said for the black-clad old man; he had stared at Colene's body. She wasn't sure whether to be angry or flattered.

Now Darius changed too. On him the cloak reached to the knees. The man stared at him too, so at least it wasn't sexual.

Provos was in between, the tunic falling to her midcalves. The man stared at her body too, or as much of it as showed around her long, loose green corset. What was it about their bodies the man found so odd?

For Seqiro there was a double collar, yellow and green. Colene put it on him. *They'll probably separate us,* she thought. *But we'll be in touch anywhere in the castle.* For his telepathy could reach her anywhere on a planet; they were attuned to each other. That gave her great comfort, especially in a strange situation like this.

Appropriately garbed, they were conducted across the open section to the inner gate. Here another black-cloaked man came to lead Seqiro away, surely to a stable. They had been through this before; it didn't bother the horse to be considered an animal, though it irritated Colene.

The three were admitted to an interior court. Here several men and women sat in comfortable thronelike chairs. All the men were in black tunics, and the women in white tunics. Color coding, Colene realized. Stave had worn blue, and Nona red, which could be the colors for the theows. The green was probably reserved for visitors of either sex. It made sense, for a highly regimented society: nobody had to think about status.

The old man came to stand between them and the seated despots. He gestured. A picture appeared in the air over his head: himself. "Hobard," he said, and the figure glowed momentarily. He touched himself. "Hobard."

That was clear enough. It was his name. Seqiro was making progress on getting into the man's mind. Colene depended on that; she would have been suicidally tense without the assurance of the horse's ability and support.

A picture of Darius appeared. "Darius," Darius said.

Then pictures of Provos and Colene, both of whom gave their names. This was an efficient introduction!

But there was no picture of Seqiro. Evidently they didn't think the horse was important. How little they knew!

A picture of the man on the largest throne appeared. "King Lombard," Hobard said. The word for king was foreign, but Seqiro translated it. Maybe it was dictator or monarch or muck-a-muck or chicken-manure; it didn't matter. This was the head despot.

Lombard? Colene stifled a giggle. There was a special lexicon of colloquial acronyms, back in her subculture on Earth, and one of these was LOMBARD: Lots of Money but a Real Dickhead. Well, maybe that was the case here. Lombard was also a Germanic tribe that invaded Italy after the fall of the Roman Empire. That, too, might fit.

Then the chief woman: "Queen Glomerula." Colene kept a straight face; this was the one who was going to try to seduce Darius! Was it her imagination, or was the woman a nymphomaniac? *She enjoys playing with unfamiliar men,* Seqiro clarified. *This is the impression Hobard has. She seduced him some time ago, then lost interest. The king is tolerant, since his own interest is in helpless theow girls. The king and queen consider it bad form to be stuck with each other for entertainment.* The horse was merely reporting Hobard's private assessment, but Colene found it hilarious, except that the queen's next target was Colene's man. She also found it funny that the queen's name in translation sounded something like an aspect of a kidney. She'd love to give the queen a kidney disease!

Finally "Knave Naylor," the one who was going to try to rape Colene herself. Colene kept her face straight. He looked sinister to her, a knave indeed. But he was going to have a rude surprise when he tried to tackle *this* supposedly innocent visiting maiden.

Hobard appeared again in the image. Beside him formed a picture of a neat house on a hill. The picture drew away, and landscape appeared between the house and the man. Hobard spoke, saying his name and several other words. *He is from Hillside Acres, some distance west of here,* Seqiro clarified.

Now the group of them appeared. "Darius, Provos, Colene, from where?" Hobard asked.

They pretended to be slow to understand, which was reasonable enough, while they consulted mentally with each other. This was a straightforward question, but difficult to answer, assuming they wanted to give such information. How could they clarify that they were not only from three different places but from three different realities, and the horse from a fourth? That they had traveled through the Virtual Mode, which was a kind of temporary reality anchored at each of their homes, crossing other realities at ten-foot intervals, so that things could change abruptly with a single step forward? That the people, geography, and fundamental natural laws changed with each reality, so that in some animals were telepathic while in others there was super-science that allowed gravity cancellation or travel at many times the velocity of light? That Darius could perform a kind of magic in his reality, while Provos remembered the future and not the past? That each of them was associated with his/her anchor, which was both place and person, and that they could get off the Virtual Mode only through one of the five anchors that held it in place? That Nona and the place of the huge stone musical instruments had just become the fifth anchor?

No, even if there were no language barrier, they could not blab all that to these grim strangers. So what could they say? They didn't really know what kind of a world this was, apart from the facts that it had magic and a strong upper-class/lower-class social structure. What would satisfy the despots without giving away too much?

We have come from afar by virtue of a spell, and wish only to return, Darius decided. That did seem to be the best answer.

So Darius used gestures and pointings to images to try to get that across. It turned out that the despots already knew that, they thought; they had a concept of interplanetary travel that was weird, and assumed that the party had somehow *walked* from one planet to another. They wanted to know the origin planet.

Colene and the others were baffled by this. How could anyone walk between planets? Even if the force of gravity did not prevent this, Earth's moon was so far away that it would take thirty years to walk there, and the other planets were much farther away. Were there seven-league boots for this purpose?

The despots were skeptical of their confusion. It was almost as if the despots believed the visitors knew all about it, and were playing ignorant. "You are human," Hobard said, making a number of pictures to get the concept across. Because Colene and the others were genuinely curious about the nature of this world, they drew on Seqiro's telepathy to clarify it. The minds of the other despots remained opaque, but Hobard was trying to establish a liaison, and his mind was opening so that they could start to receive his more complicated thoughts. This was especially true when he focused on a specific thing. "You came from a human world." World was not exactly the concept, but the exact one was not quite fathomable. Planet? Aspect? Subdivision?

"From a human world," Darius agreed, by indicating the correct pictures. "Far away."

Now a diagram appeared, with what might be the wires and resistors of a weird radio set. There was something naggingly familiar about it, but Colene couldn't place it. "Which one?" Hobard demanded. One bug in the picture glowed, and then another.

Maybe we had better try to tell a bit of the truth, Colene thought to Darius. *They'll know if we claim a planet that is wrong; this is their territory.*

Darius agreed. "Far in a different way," he tried to clarify. "Not in distance, but in mode."

But this was lost on the despots. Evidently they had no concept of the Virtual Mode or alternate realities. Indeed, their own reality seemed quite strange enough to hold their attention.

Hobard generated another picture. In its center was a shape like a hairy roach, or perhaps a hairy fat-bodied spider, for it was at the center of a weblike structure of lines. Upon the main lines extending out were smaller bugs, with finer lines radiating from them. Yet it was not a spiderweb; the lines were jagged, and took funny turns.

Then Colene placed the image. "The Mandelbrot set!" she exclaimed.

The others looked at her. Then Seqiro's thought came, warningly: *I have gotten farther into Hobard's mind. Beware asserting yourself.*

Colene was irritated at this interruption to her revelation. *Why not assert myself?* she demanded. *I'm an assertive person.*

Because they judge men and women differently, he explained. *Here men are dominant. Elsewhere women are. The two cultures are enemies.*

Oh. The last thing they needed was to be considered

enemies before they knew their way around. *Take it, Darius,* she thought.

But what is this Man's-brow set? he thought.

I'll explain while you dominate. Tell me to shut up.

The mental exchange had been swift, but things were getting somewhat strained. Darius frowned at Colene. "Silence, girl," he snapped.

Colene hung her head, her gesture confessing that she had spoken out of turn. Darius faced Hobard. "Where?" he asked.

The old man seemed to have lost some of his own concentration. It seemed that Colene's outburst had held considerable significance for the despots. Since they couldn't have understood the meaning of the words—Darius himself didn't understand them, and he had a working knowledge of her language—it had to be because of the thing the remarkable horse was warning them about. Men and women were not equal here. A woman who asserted herself was in trouble.

Yet Nona the peasant girl had been assertive enough, and Stave had not taken offense. Did a different rule apply to the theows?

The magic image had faded. Now it reappeared. The small bug on a webline above the upper leg of the bug glowed.

Hobard pointed to the glowing bug, and tapped his foot on the floor. "Here," he said, using his word, but the translation came through. This was where they were.

Meanwhile Colene's mind was racing through what she remembered of the Mandelbrot set. It was named after the man who had done a special computation involving a complex equation, and plotted the result on a graph. A simple equation was something like $X + Y = 10$, and if X was 10, then Y had to be 0 because there was nothing left for it. If X was 9, then Y was 1, and so on until X was 0 and Y was 10. Those answers could be plotted on graph paper, with X representing up and Y the side: go up ten and across none and place a point. Then up nine and across one, and set another point. A line of points formed, and all the possible answers to that equation were on that line. Simple.

Colene had quickly gone beyond that, and used squares of X and Y to get curved lines. $X^2 + Y^2 = Z^2$ made a perfect circle with a radius of Z. Sine waves were trickier. But a complex equation was something else.

She had been fascinated by the new concept of fractals, which were like fractional dimensions. They enabled a person to take a simple figure and elaborate it infinitely, without taking up any more space. For example, one could start with an equilateral triangle, every angle and every side the same, then put a little triangle in the middle of each side, so that it became a six-pointed star:

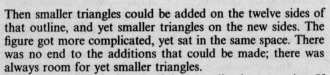

Then smaller triangles could be added on the twelve sides of that outline, and yet smaller triangles on the new sides. The figure got more complicated, yet sat in the same space. There was no end to the additions that could be made; there was always room for yet smaller triangles.

Meanwhile the length of the outer line kept growing. If the initial triangle was three inches on a side, it was nine inches all the way around. The six-pointed star added an inch to each side, so was twelve inches around. The eighteen-pointed figure that resulted from the next round of additions was sixteen inches around. And so on; each step added more sides and points and length, yet the figure could fit on the same sheet of paper. It was an infinite process, with a finite boundary.

Colene got hazy on the technical aspects beyond that. But she knew that a man named Benoit Mandelbrot had coined the term "fractal" for this type of figure, considering the process to be like a fractional dimension. A triangle was a two-dimensional figure; a fractal based on a triangle was a two-and-a-half-dimensional figure. There were implications for the ultimate nature of reality—and, it seemed, for the Virtual Mode. Because they seemed to have stepped into a fractal reality.

Benoit Mandelbrot had plotted his complex equation, and come up with a fractal figure that was a good deal more complicated than a triangle or circle. In fact it was deemed to be the most complicated object in mathematics. It had buglike shapes, and shell shapes, and seahorse-tail shapes, and separate "floating molecules" connected by "devil's polymer," an intricate web of invisibly fine filament. No matter how much the magnification was increased, there were always more and smaller bugs and shells and tails. Colene had been fascinated by the Mandelbrot set, but had thought it had no immediate relevance to her life. So she had watched a video tape showing the Mandelbrot set and what were called Julia sets, which she understood were two-dimensional aspects of the larger set, and let it fade from her thoughts.

Well, that had changed. Because Hobard was telling them that this was not the planet Earth, but a Mandelbrot bug. That just might make this a Julia universe. The implications were mind-blowing.

While she worked this out, Darius was coming at it in a less theoretical manner. He was not burdened by her awareness of the mathematical aspects. "So we are here," he was saying. "On the planet Oria. And we are a satellite of this larger planet Jupiter. And you want to know whether we come from Mercury, Venus, or Mars." He was speaking in his own language, using different names for things, but this was the way the thoughts came to her.

She focused on this confusing alignment. In this fractal universe, it seemed that Earth did not revolve around the sun, but around Jupiter, and so did the other small planets. Each planet was a Mandelbrot bug, and Jupiter was a big bug. The webwork of lines connected the four smaller bugs to the big one; apparently gravity didn't do the job here. Okay, if that was the way it was, that was the way it was. In some realities science worked, and in others pseudoscience like faster-than-light travel worked. Where Darius came from, a kind of sympathetic magic worked, buttressed by emotional telepathy. Here on Oria—their name for Earth—magic worked. And astronomy was weird. But at least she had a handle on it, because of her experience with the Mandelbrot set.

"We come from none of these," Darius said. He illustrated the statement by pointing to each of the other three bug-planets in turn and shaking his head no.

Colene was sent into another bypath of realization. The Mandelbrot set was portrayed two-dimensionally, but this was a three-dimensional world. Her pictures had shown small bugs of similar size to the north and south of a large one, because the south was the mirror image of the north. The north curlicues wound clockwise, the south ones counterclockwise. The Mandelbrot set was excruciatingly well organized, on its own terms. The image Hobard generated was three-dimensional. In fact it wasn't a picture, it was a hologram. It showed four orbiting bugs: North, South, Toward, and Away. The Mandelbrot bug was always represented as pointing its snout to the west, with its babylike bottom toward the east, so those directions weren't available for this. So Oria was north, and Mars south, with Venus and Mercury this way and that way. All of them tiny compared to Jupiter.

But of course they weren't from any of the other planets. They were from Earth, which was the same as Oria. But not only would this be difficult to explain, it might not be wise. Their party of four had gotten trapped in an alternate reality in which a galactic emperor intended to use them to begin his conquest of other realities. Colene had worked a trick to free their anchor in that reality, and the Virtual Mode had found a new anchor here. If these despots caught on to that, not only would Nona be in trouble, the four of them might be similarly trapped here.

But Colene knew that Darius wasn't going to lie about it, if asked directly. He had a thing about integrity. She loved him for that, but it was now a bad problem between them. As was the matter of women: he didn't have a thing about being limited to one.

"None?" Hobard was amazed, and King Lombard was plainly skeptical.

"From a more distant planet?" King Lombard asked. Colene got the gist from Hobard's understanding of the question; the king's mind remained opaque to the horse.

We're wasting time, Colene thought to Darius. *We need to get settled with these folk and get by ourselves, so we can figure out how to get back through the anchor.* Because this was a temporary stop; they were on their way back to Darius' reality, where they would be together, once they worked out their problems.

To her relief, Darius agreed. "It is hard to explain. We have come a long way, and we are tired. May we eat and rest?" He did this by spreading his hands in bafflement, then letting his shoulders slump, then putting a hand to his mouth as if eating. Seqiro buttressed these signals with projected meaning, so that Hobard interpreted them correctly without realizing the source of his understanding.

Hobard translated for King Lombard. The king nodded, then gestured. Red-and-blue-clad theow servants entered, gesturing to the three visitors to accompany them.

The king is in doubt about your nature, Seqiro thought to them. *He wants to know whether you are of the animus.*

The animus. Provos had mentioned that, but the rest of them hadn't yet found out what it was. That was frustrating.

Then Colene had a bright notion. *Seqiro—can you reach Nona and ask her about the animus?*

Yes. But I will lose touch with you while orienting on her.

We can handle that for a while. See what you can get. It may be important.

She felt his presence leave, and knew he was seeking out Nona. She should be well within his range.

Meanwhile the servants were taking them to separate chambers. Some distance apart, by the look of it. She didn't like that, and not because of ignorance: the despots were doing it so that Darius could be seduced and she could be raped. But they were not in a position to protest, and Provos had indicated that those efforts would not be successful. Provos had also smiled mysteriously, as if there were more to it than showed. Provos wasn't worried, of course; not only was she unlikely to be a target, not being young and innocent, she had her memory of the future.

Well, Colene was not about to let any man rape her. She had been through the experience on one occasion, and thereafter become not only smarter about situations but militant. She did not want merely to foil a rape attempt; she wanted to foil it in such a way that the man regretted ever having the notion. What could she do to Knave Naylor that would have the desired effect?

She knew what she wanted to do: fix it so that he was the one who got raped. But she saw several problems with that. The man was likely to have potent (no pun) magic which she could not counter, and if she did counter it, that would only show that she had strong magic too, and women didn't here. In fact, it could be real trouble if she was even assertive, because women weren't supposed to be. So she couldn't fight him; all she could do was hide and whimper like a properly docile girl. That would get her nowhere.

She reached her chamber. It turned out to be well appointed, with running water and a big stone bathtub. What delight, in the midst of quandary.

So she ran the water, and it was hot, and she found some powder that made it bubble, and she soaked herself, truly enjoying it. It had been no lie about their being tired.

Colene. It was Seqiro's thought.

Hey, what kept you, horseface? she replied. *I missed you.* Indeed she had, she realized now; there had been a lingering tightness which now faded.

I am not conversant with Nona as I am with you. It took time to gather the concepts, which she understands well, and I understood when with her mind, but feared I would not retain them.

Well, I have a rape to avoid. Give with the background.

There are two forces, perhaps opposite directions of the same force from which they draw their power of magic, he thought. *The animus and the anima, the male and female principles. Here the animus governs, and the men dominate. But if the current were to change, the anima would dominate, and the female principle would govern.*

It came clear as she reviewed it with him. When the men dominated, they had the strong magic—or perhaps it was the strong magic that enabled them to dominate. The women had status only up to a level below that of the men they married. Any man had power over any woman, but a low-level man knew better than to mess with the wife of a high-level man, because her man would enforce respect. When the anima came, however, the women had the magic and power, and the men served them.

The despots were simply the descendants of the leading men: the firstborn of the firstborn, as it were. The theows were the descendants of men of low status. Theoretically a despot man could marry a theow woman and elevate her status, but this seldom happened; they preferred the daughters of ranking men. If a despot took a liking to a theow girl, he simply hired her for his household, and she was his to use as he wished. Since every theow had to work for a despot, the availability was broad. This was Nona's concern: that she would have either to marry and bear babies, which would deplete her magic, or become the plaything of a despot. It could be a liability to be beautiful, because by the time the despots tired of a theow woman, she might be too old and worn to attract a good theow man, so would be unable to marry and have a family of her own. That would mean, in turn, that she was nonproductive, and a burden to society, and she would disappear.

But with the coming of the anima, the women would have the magic, and the lastborn females of the lastborn females would be the inheritors. The status of men would derive from that of their wives, and their children would have status via their mothers. In effect, the theows would become the rulers, and the despots the servant class. So it was to the interest of the despots, including their women, to maintain the existing order. The change of animus to anima would lead to an immediate political and social and economic upheaval.

But how does it change? Colene asked.

That was where Nona came in. She was the ninthborn of the eighthborn of the seventhborn, all the way back nine generations to the common ancestor with the despot king, who was the firstborn male of the firstborn male back a similar way. The last change had occurred nine generations ago. There was a special power of nines here, or rather of a nine that followed an eight that followed a seven and so on. This was because of the nature of the planet Oria itself. Thus Nona was the one who could reverse the animus and overthrow the despots.

So what does she have to do?

That was the problem: Nona didn't know. Only that she must seek the Megaplayers, the giants who had played the gigantic stone instruments, and gain their help. She had thought the visitors might be from those godlike folk.

And instead they were coincidental travelers on the Virtual Mode. Nona had been opening her mind to that Mode, and tuned in to it, and become an anchor figure, thinking she was doing something else.

They would be unable to use Nona's anchor to depart this universe of Julia, unless Nona succeeded in her quest to bring the anima. Colene had no better idea how to do that than Nona did. Instead of being the creatures who could help Nona, they needed Nona's help.

We have a problem, Colene concluded.

CHAPTER 3

DARIUS

DARIUS felt better after cleaning up. Now he was hungry. He had been checking in with Colene every so often, via the telepathic horse. That remained a novelty; he had learned only just before their arrival at this world that Seqiro was a very special animal. It seemed that in Seqiro's reality, the horses all were telepathic, and governed the human beings. In other realities, other animals had that power. It had been Colene's fortune to encounter an animal who liked human girls, and who wanted to travel the Modes, and who had the power to do so. Now it was the fortune of their group.

For Darius knew enough of the transfer of human emotion to grasp what the transfer of human information could do. This was a powerful tool, and would help them greatly. It was already helping them, because the horse could fathom the minds of these people, regardless of their language, and know their motives. It took a bit of time, of course, because strange minds could not be plumbed any more than a strange terrain could be understood at a glance. But Seqiro had related quickly to Nona and Stave, and was now tuning to Hobard, the translator. It was a great advantage to fathom the motives of their hosts, without the despots knowing.

We have a problem, Colene's thought came.

Quickly she filled him in: Nona had supposed their party to be the Megaplayers she sought. She now knew better, but that left her in difficulty, because she alone could help her people, the theows, and her only avenue for help had been taken by their party's coincidental arrival. Not chance, really; Nona merely had not realized that it was the Virtual Mode to which she was relating, or that she would become an anchor person. In fact she had no notion what either was.

So we have to help her, Colene concluded. *Because we messed up her effort.*

Darius did not necessarily see it that way. But since this animus was blocking their use of the anchor, they had to deal with that, and Nona was the one who could change it. So they had to help her, not because of any moral obligation, but from self-interest.

That, too, Colene thought with mental humor, and he realized that she had been teasing him slightly; of course she had understood their need. *But she doesn't know how.*

We have a problem, he agreed.

THEY joined the despots for the evening meal. They understood, now, that the despots had not decided whether they were despots or theows. If they were the latter, they would be immediately killed, because it would be an embarrassment to treat theows as if they were human beings. But if they were despots, the case would be more chancy. Despots should be allies—but might be seeking conquest. Especially if they were of the anima, and enemies not only of the governing class but of the entire animus.

How did King Lombard propose to ascertain the status of his guests? There were several ways, Hobard's mind suggested as Seqiro quietly explored it. First, despots of the animus were male-dominated. For a moment it had seemed that Colene was the leader of the group, but then it turned out that Darius was. But that wasn't certain, because a group from a world with anima might try to pretend to be animus. Second, the males of animus had the magic, and the females of anima had magic. Illusion was common to all, and was discounted. Who had the magic here? None of the visitors had shown their magic yet, which might be a matter of courtesy or might be suspicious. If none of them had magic, they were theows, and could be dispatched after suitably entertaining their hosts. Entertainment, by despot definition, ranged from sexual exploitation to outright torture.

So the issue would be forced, tonight. Queen Glomerula would try to fathom Darius' nature, evoking what magic he had. If she did not come to a conclusion, King Lombard would arrange to discover the tryst, and would challenge the interloper to a duel. That would bring it out, certainly. But it had its risk, because if Darius were a ranking despot he might have stronger magic than the king, and would kill him and take over his throne. So it might be better to avoid that chance. Unfortunately, Darius thought, he did not have magic in this reality, and in any event it was not the same type.

How do you know?

Darius paused, surprised. The horse was merely curious, but it was a seminal question. Darius had become so used to lacking his magic in other realities, except sometimes his ability to project emotionally, that he had just assumed this was the case here. Yet this was definitely a magic reality, and perhaps more than one kind of magic worked.

He had two types of magic, in his home reality. One was common to all people there, known as sympathetic. The other was unique to him, at least in degree. As the Cyng of Hlahtar—or, as Colene termed it, the King of Laughter—he could draw emotion from a subject person and rebroadcast it, multiplied a thousandfold. That way every person within range achieved the joy of the one. That made everyone happy for several weeks, until the emotion gradually leaked away. The chief liability of this ability was that he needed a subject from which to draw, and this was by custom the wife of the Cyng, who was gradually depleted until she was an emotional husk and had to be discarded. Distressed by the prospect of doing this to a woman he loved, he had sought through the Modes for a woman who could handle it. That was how he had found Colene—only to learn that she, instead of being full of joy, was secretly suicidal. That would be disaster! But he loved her, having foolishly committed his emotion before properly understanding.

Meanwhile he had found another woman, Prima, whose power was similar to his own, who would marry him and enable him to perform his necessary role without being herself depleted. It would not be a love match, but she desired the position rather than love, and would allow him to love Colene as a mistress without hindrance. It was an ideal solution to his problem, except for certain technical factors. Such as the fact that he and Colene had not yet been able to get to his reality, and were currently somewhat estranged. Oh, they were working together, because they had to, but they had to have a settlement when they could, and it was not possible to know what the result of that would be.

But that was all conjectural. Right now he needed magic. Was it possible that he had it? If so, he could readily deal with the queen. He could drain her of her joy, stopping her in the middle of whatever she had in mind.

That left Knave Naylor's effort. The man would simply go in and seduce the girl, and rape her if she proved to be diffident. If she were anima, she would not submit to that; instead she would flatten him with her magic. But if she were animus, she would make only token protest before yielding. Of course then there would be Darius to deal with; as animus he would not take kindly to having his woman used by force. But Queen Glomerula would simply accuse Darius of raping *her*, and the matter would be open to negotiation. It was, it seemed, axiomatic in this culture: one rape canceled another, as far as any onus went. It wasn't as if women had rights or feelings that mattered.

Darius had to admire the directness of it. These folk mixed their pleasure with business, with the business paramount. They expected to take the measure of their guests without delay. If they lacked a certain finesse and took certain risks, well, that was evidently the way of their kind. It was not an attitude he liked, but at least now he understood what was in store.

However, he suspected that innocent little Colene was going to surprise them. She could, he had discovered to his chagrin, be as devious as anyone. Provos had assured them that the planned malice would not be successful, but they still had to find out exactly how they would foil it.

A theow girl led him down to the banquet hall. As he saw the king, queen, and knave again he was struck by the fit of their clothing. The theows had somewhat shapeless general-purpose tunics, salvaged from disaster mainly by their sashes, so that even a man as handsome as Stave and a woman as lovely as Nona looked somewhat awkward. But the despots had perfectly tailored tunics, enhancing their bodies. The king looked regal despite his masked paunch, and the queen looked sexy. The knave looked both, and suitably sinister as well.

The meal itself was good. The despots lived well. Darius and Colene watched the manners of their hosts, and emulated them, while Provos proceeded confidently from future memory. They ate slices of roast animal, and squares of assorted fruits, and drank excellent wine. *One glass only,* he warned Colene. It turned out to be unnecessary; the mere thought of an alcoholic beverage made her stomach tighten, and her revulsion came through to his stomach. She had had a bad experience whose nature he did not know, but it had turned her off this particular business.

So he made it easy for her. "No wine for my woman," he said in peremptory fashion. "Water is all she deserves." After an exchange of signals, Hobard understood, and Colene's privilege of wine was removed. But King Lombard, though appreciative, was not convinced: this was Hobard's opinion.

Darius, concerned about the coming night, tried to focus on the minds of the king and queen. And especially the mind of the knave, who was watching Colene with disturbing directness. But Colene's horse was unable to penetrate any of these; only Hobard was at all open.

He reflected again how this business of informative mind contact was almost as new to him as it was to the folk they had met, Nona and Stave. He had little idea how to take advantage of it. Fortunately Colene was used to it, and she was happy to handle this aspect of their situation. So he merely let her know his concern, and let her work on it.

Indeed, she was up to something. There was a power and deviousness to her mind-set that he had not before been aware of. This precious little girl he loved became more complicated as he came to know her better. So he focused on the amenities of the meal and let her work it out.

The queen was watching him with much the same interest as the knave watched Colene. He felt like a bug under her glass. She was using the standard mechanisms of women with men: a low, loose décolletage that proffered frequent and profound glimpses of her breasts, and glances which lingered just a bit too long. She was not a young woman, but neither was she old; she was at that age at which a woman was capable of the maximum exploitation of her body. It was interesting.

Oh, it is, is it? There was Colene's angry thought.

To be used and thrown away, he thought back, trying to mollify her. But for some reason she seemed unmollified.

Then he had a notion. *I have not tried my magic here,* he thought to Colene. *Give me tokens of your essence.*

What? It was incredulity.

I can be close to you, when apart, if you give me of your solid, liquid, and gaseous essence, he clarified.

The hell I will!

She was misunderstanding. *A hair of your head. A drop of your saliva. The touch of your breath.*

She considered. Then, her curiosity overriding her anger, she quietly plucked a hair from her head, lifted a cloth napkin to her lips, spat into it, and then breathed on it. She wadded it up and passed it to him under the table.

Thank you, Colene. If my magic works here, this will give me great power over you.

She sent him a dark glance. Yet again he seemed to have angered her. But he had the things he needed. This could be very important. He stuffed the napkin into the band of his underwear, and proceeded as if nothing had happened.

Finally the meal ended, and servants guided them back to their chambers. Now the real adventure was about to begin. He wondered what Colene had in mind, since he understood that the male despots could use their magic to incapacitate a woman and make her helpless.

His chamber had a large bed with several covers ranging from a voluminous quilt to a square hardly larger than a towel, and a similar assortment of pillows ranging from huge to tiny. These folk liked freedom of choice! He used the sanitary facilities, stripped, and was in the act of considering pillows when he heard a quiet knock. He got up and went to answer it, holding a medium-sized pillow in front of him.

Sure enough, Queen Glomerula was making her appearance at his door. She was in a sheer white tunic, whose purpose was obviously enhancement rather than concealment, and white veil, evidently intended to indicate anonymity. An officially surreptitious visit.

He stepped back, and she stepped in. She closed the door. Then her cloak and veil faded away, leaving her naked. They had been illusion, and she wore nothing beneath. This woman was all business.

Actually, more of her body could be illusion. He judged her to be about forty years old, and it was an unfortunate fact that few women were outstanding in body at that age, mainly because they didn't seem to care to work at it. Did her illusion extend to touch as well as sight? If so, did it matter? What a man perceived was what he got, generally.

In this case it was quite a perception. In Darius' world, women wore thick diapers around their posteriors, under their skirts, whose purpose was to mask the feminine contours. Breasts were normally concealed by loose blouses over sturdy halters. Only married women or mistresses, in the privacy of their homes, allowed themselves to be seen in less. The sight of such body parts was highly suggestive to men, and care was normally taken to prevent accidental exposure. He had had a problem with Colene, who tended to wear clothing that made her feminine contours too evident. She was young, but that did not detract from her physical appeal. Now they were promised to each other, so her apparel could be tolerated; still, he didn't like it when other men saw her dressed that way. Perhaps that aspect of their relationship was even; she didn't like the way he reacted to other women.

So the queen's exposure had an immediate effect on him, and he desired her body despite his resolve. Fortunately he had the discipline of his profession. He would let her believe that he was captivated by her aspect, but in the end it would come to nothing.

He tossed aside the pillow and stepped toward her—and suddenly she was across the room. Magic, of course—except that he understood that the women here did not have true magic, only illusion. So what was going on?

Maybe the horse knew. Seqiro might not be able to get into her mind, but he surely knew where it was.

It is illusion, Seqiro confirmed. *She has made an image in one place, and covered her actual body with the image of an empty spot in the room.*

An illusion of nothing! That was an aspect he had not anticipated. So she was challenging him to find her. Surely a despot male's magic could readily cut through such pictures and locate a woman immediately, so she was exploring his magical ability. It was necessary that he demonstrate it, to confirm that he was of the animus and therefore to be respected, along with his women and animal.

Queen Glomerula appeared before him, within reach. "Yes?" she inquired, using one of the few words they had been able to identify.

He did not want to admit that he had no intention of indulging her whim, so he acted. He grabbed for her. And missed; the illusion faded, leaving him embracing air. Her laughter sounded behind him.

But this was not a matter for laughter, for she was testing him. If he could not use his magic to capture her, he would be deemed a theow, and would be killed. In this realm only the men had true magic, and only the despots had strong magic.

Where is she? he asked the horse.

I will mark her place. A glint of light appeared, and then another beside it, at about head height. In fact they were her two eyes, perhaps easiest to fix on because a person's consciousness tied closely in to sight.

Darius strode toward the glints. They floated quickly to one side. He veered and intercepted them. He reached out and caught her body, drawing it into himself. It was after all only sight the magic affected, at least in this case. Perhaps touch as well, not to make an image tangible, but to make her genuine body seem more appealing. It certainly was that; one of his hands had landed, perhaps by her design, on what seemed to be her invisible right breast, and the other on her left buttock. Both were extremely female.

He oriented and put his lips to the place her mouth should be. He found her lips and kissed her—and she kissed him back. Seqiro had enabled him to prevail. He had proved his magic.

But now what should he do with her? He did not intend to indulge in sex with her; Colene was the one he wanted for that, and only when the time was right. Yet it might not be good form to reject the queen. He needed a legitimate distraction.

Colene, he thought. They might be privately estranged, but they had a common purpose here.

I thought you'd never ask, she replied. *The knave is about to arrive, and I want you to see what I do to him.*

But I need a pretext to ignore the queen.

What, with one hand on her boob and the other on her ass and your tongue in her mouth?

She is not easy to ignore. Please, a pretext!

You've got one: your magic shows you that I am being threatened. Tell the queen you have put a chastity spell on me. Tell her to show you what's going on here.

How can she do that?

Illusion. These folk are good at it—awful good, Seqiro says. You'll see. Make her show you. It'll be a good show.

He cooperated. He paused as if suddenly realizing something, listening. He disengaged his mouth, but not his hands. "Glomerula!" he snapped. "My woman is being approached. Show her chamber."

But the queen did not understand; there were too few common words. He needed a way to get through to her.

He cast about, and saw the pillows on the bed. He bore the queen back authoritatively and plumped her down on the bed. Her body came into view as he did so, marvelously formed and almost glowing; she was ready for the next event. This was obviously both business and pleasure for her.

But instead of proceeding, he took the smallest pillow and squeezed it into a crude approximation of a human torso. He took the smallest cover and ripped it in half. One half he formed into a wraparound skirt for the pillow; the other half he tore into several shreds, which he tied around the waist and neck and attached in lieu of arms and legs. It was not by any means a great figurine, but he thought it would do for his purpose.

He held it up. "Colene," he told the queen. "Show."

The queen's face brightened with understanding. She knew what was to happen in Colene's chamber. She gestured to the far wall, not only to do magic but to indicate where to look.

Darius looked. The wall became seemingly transparent, and beyond it was Colene's chamber, showing her bed. Colene sat on it in her underclothing, brushing out her hair. He realized that this was illusion, for the girl's chamber was nowhere near his own, but that it reflected reality. Colene was right: these folk had impressive powers of imagery. The picture was so realistic that he reacted to the undiapered body. He hoped Glomerula would believe that it was the queen's body that continued to excite him.

Glomerula seemed surprised about something, but neither he nor the horse could fathom what at the moment. Could it be that some detail of the illusion she was crafting did not match her expectation? That suggested that it was a true picture, not a pure invention.

It's me, Colene's thought confirmed. *There's precious*

little real privacy in this castle. The king's making an illusion picture of his own, Seqiro says, and he's watching what you're doing with the queen. I think he gets his jollies more from watching her with other men than with doing it with her himself.

Then I'll give him something to see, Darius thought. He sat beside the queen, extended his left arm to draw her in beside him, and fondled her right breast with his right hand. It felt like as good a breast as the left; it had appropriate heft and contour. He tried to imagine that it was Colene's breast, but it didn't work, because Colene had less mass in that region. Too bad he was not in a position to explore the matter more thoroughly.

And I'll give you *something to see,* Colene thought viciously. He kept running afoul of her sensitivities, thoughtlessly.

But he had more to do. "Colene is mine," he told the queen. "My magic secures her chastity." He used the doll to indicate the forbidden area. "No other man—" He thrust with a finger to illustrate the forbidden action.

That turned out to be clear enough. Glomerula smiled. She gestured again toward the wall: wait and see. The challenge was on, and the queen seemed as satisfied with that as with her own involvement.

Then he remembered the other thing he wanted to check: his emotional magic. This was the ideal situation to test it, because he had to be quite close to a woman to draw out her joy. As it happened, he was close to the queen.

The door to Colene's room opened and Knave Naylor stepped in. Colene looked up, saw him, and her mouth opened in a soundless scream. This illusion couldn't handle sound.

The knave threw off his cloak and approached her, naked. There was no subtlety: if she didn't find a way to stop him, he would ravish her immediately. That was the point: only a woman of the ruling class of the anima could have any power against a man of the animus, and if she turned out to be such a woman, she would be deemed an enemy, and the despots would do their best to kill her immediately. So her choice was between rape and death, as the knave saw it. Rather, *Darius'* choice was to watch or act; he wasn't sure the anima could work here, on an animus world. Still, he wasn't sure what to do, because he had no certainty that his magic worked here.

But these folk had not encountered the like of Colene. Darius smiled, giving the queen's breast a squeeze to make her think that was the cause of his emotion. The queen seemed to be enjoying both the show and the handling.

Darius drew her as close as possible, squeezing her breast as if turned on by it and/or the scene they watched. But his intent would have horrified her had she fathomed it. He exerted his magic and drew on her emotional vitality.

Nothing happened. His magic did not operate in this reality; there was no doubt now. That was disappointing, but perhaps not surprising. At least he had not had to alert the queen to what he had attempted. She had been saved by the underlying laws of her universe.

He relaxed, but did not let go of her breast, lest she become suspicious. *Oh, sure,* Colene thought witheringly. However, Colene now had a situation of her own to attend to, and couldn't continue to focus on him.

Naylor came to the bed. Colene screamed again and started to get off it. But Naylor made a negligent gesture, and abruptly the girl's feet left the floor. She was floating, her moving legs having no purchase. Then she was borne to the bed, to land on her back, her feet still kicking.

The knave stared at her in much the way Hobard had. Darius followed the specific direction of his gaze, and finally understood: it was her underclothing. It was as if the man had not seen this before. Could it be that these folk did not wear underclothing? That would explain Hobard's interest, and the queen's too. The queen had not come to him naked under her cloak of illusion merely to seduce him; she never wore such things anyway. That made sense at last.

Naylor shook off his surprise and concentrated. Colene's undergarments seemed to catch fire. Flame and smoke puffed around her body, and dissipated, leaving no burns. Now she was naked. There was no doubt about the power of the man's magic; he was controlling her body against her will without touching her.

The knave gestured again. Colene's legs still moved, but now they seemed to be constrained. They spread, her knees lifting, the feet kicking in a futile pattern, well apart. This man seemed to be experienced in this act, for even magic required expertise, and it was just as if invisible hands were placing her legs safely out of the way.

Glomerula's face turned to him. She was smiling. She

was waiting to see how he was going to handle this assault on his woman. To see whether he *could* handle it.

Darius smiled back at her. "You will see, skeptic," he said. "I do not allow trespassing." But he wished Colene would get on with her plan, because he had no idea what it might be, and it was certainly time for it.

Naylor put a knee on the bed, orienting for his business. *Now, Seqiro!* Colene's thought came, so strong that it was as if she had shouted in Darius' face.

The man's face froze. His mouth dropped open. It was as if he saw something horrible, yet there was nothing.

Queen Glomerula's body tensed. She did not understand what was happening. Neither did Darius. *What?* he thought to Colene.

Show him, Seqiro.

Then it was as if Darius were looking through Naylor's eyes. Suddenly he understood.

From the region between Colene's legs a viscous mass was rising. It flexed, and part of it separated from the main mass. It was the head of a large snake! A cobra, with spreading hood and elongating fangs from which glistening poison dripped.

The serpent's eyes fastened on Naylor's genitals. The head moved back, then struck forward.

Naylor screamed and threw himself off the bed, grabbing at his crotch.

Queen Glomerula stared. She did not see the snake, which was an illusion projected only to Naylor's mind. She saw the man reacting to nothing more than the sight of a helpless girl's spread thighs. What was the matter with the man?

Darius took advantage of her distraction to do some more work on his pillow figurine. He rolled up more cloth to form fuller arms and legs, and used a brown fragment to represent hair on the head. It was coming to look more like Colene.

He reached across to where he had set the bundled towel with Colene's essences. He wrapped the single hair in place around the figurine's head, and pressed the damp region where her saliva was to the figure's body until some dampness soaked across. Then he pressed the napkin to the face of the figure and breathed into it, pushing her breath through with the force of his breath. The queen, fascinated by the scene in Colene's room, had not even noticed that he was no longer fondling her breast.

Colene, freed of the spell of immobility, got up and pursued the man. Now she looked like an even larger serpent, one whose gaping jaws could bite great chunks out of the flesh of a man. But to the queen, she looked like an ordinary bare girl.

Why did such illusion work against a man who was surely well experienced with all kinds of magic? Darius realized that it was because it was illusion infused with belief; the horse was projecting the certainty that this was real, and Naylor had no way to resist. Seqiro must have been concentrating on penetrating the man's mind, so as to be able to do this.

Naylor fled. He charged down the hall, heedless of his nakedness. "Anima! Anima!" he cried.

The picture faded as the queen lost her concentration. "There was no anima!" she said, her thought plain despite her unfamiliar words.

It was time to try his magic. If it worked, Darius would have proved that he was of the animus. If it didn't, he would let his supposed chastity spell make the point.

He concentrated on the figurine. "You are Colene," he whispered to it.

He felt a tingle. The magic was working!

Now at last the queen was paying attention to him. She looked with surprise at the figurine.

"Watch," Darius said. He leaned down to draw a square in the slight dust on the floor before the bed. "You are there, Colene," he said to the figurine, setting it down inside the square. "In your chamber, having routed the rapist." Then, through Seqiro, he thought: *Be prepared, Colene; I am about to conjure you with my magic.*

Fat chance! she thought back.

He lifted the figurine and set it carefully in his lap. "Now you are here."

Suddenly Colene was sitting in his lap. She was naked and he was naked, but for once neither paid much attention. "You did it!" she exclaimed, amazed. Then she leaned over and vomited on the floor.

"Uh, conjurations can disturb a person's equilibrium, resulting in a nervous stomach," he said as he deactivated the icon with a negative thought. It was not safe to leave them activated, because then any careless treatment of the figurine affected the subject.

"Now he tells me!" she gasped. Then she sat up straight, twisted, and kissed him hard on the mouth.

Queen Glomerula, still beside him, laughed.

Colene became aware of her. "Shut up, bitch-cow, or I'll kiss you too," she snapped. "Even if it makes me upchuck again."

Darius, wiping the spread vomit from his lips, had to smile. This was Colene, all right!

"And what are you doing with this slut naked on your bed?" Colene demanded of him.

"Demonstrating my magic," he said. "I am of the animus: a magic-wielding man. You wish to make something of it?" That was a colloquialism he had learned from her; it was a kind of challenge to evince disapproval.

"Yeah," she said. "But not in the same bed with Queen Nympho here!"

Darius turned to the queen. "I have decided to play with my own woman. You may go."

The queen assessed the situation, picking up enough of his import to know that she was finished here. She shrugged; there would be another day. She stood, clothed herself again with illusion, and departed the chamber in good order. She had ascertained what she sought: Darius really did have strong magic, and was well able to protect his woman. He was animus.

"Okay, I'm here," Colene said. "Play with me, you macho animus man."

"You need to rest, and to eat something," Darius said, sliding her off his lap.

"I'm not hungry, and I'm not ready to rest."

He glanced at the vomit splattered on the floor, then took one of the larger quilts and used it to mop up the mess. "And put on some clothing," he added.

"Oh, come on, I'll do that," she said. "It's my mess." She got down and nudged him aside.

He glanced at her naked body. "At least don a diaper."

"A diaper!" she exclaimed. "I got sick, not incontinent." Then she remembered. "Oh, that's right—the women of your reality wear big diapers, so no one can see their stuff. But that's when they're in public. They take them off for sex, don't they?"

"Yes. But that is not the case here."

"Stop treating me like a child, Darius! I know what sex is. And by the look of you with that slut queen, you had it in mind." She bundled the quilt and carried it to the bathroom. *Show him, Seqiro,* her thought came back.

Immediately, Darius felt the heat of her love. Colene was raging with emotion, and desired him in a way which belied her youth.

He fought back his response, lest he be overwhelmed by his answering desire for her. "But you *are* a child," he said. "You are fourteen, which by the standard of your culture is below the age of consent. It is not proper to indulge with you."

She emerged from the bathroom, still defiantly naked. "Aren't we in love, Darius?"

"Yes. That does not change your age."

"But according to you, it's all right for you to have sex with nympho queens, meanwhile?"

"Yes, if I choose. But I do not respect Glomerula, so sex with her is not an option."

"If you did respect her, then you would have sex with her?"

"Yes, ordinarily. However—"

"And do you respect me?"

He hesitated, then answered. "Yes."

"And you want me?"

"Yes." He knew this was mischief. The queen's challenge had been replaced by the girl's challenge.

"So by your code, it is all right to have sex with women you don't love, but not with the one you do."

"It is an irony," he agreed. "Now put on a diaper, or I will put one on you."

"Oh, cut the hypocrisy," she snapped. "You won't have sex with me because you say it's against my culture, but you want me to wear a diaper when you know that's no part of my culture."

He was taken aback. "That is true. I can not dictate your mode of dress."

"You can't dictate my mode of sex either!" she flared. "I had it with four men before I ever met you!"

Darius felt his jaw drop. *Can this be true?* he asked Seqiro.

It is true. And the horse opened up the memory to him: Colene at thirteen, on a date with a high school boy she hardly knew, who took her to a private party where they plied her with alcohol and then raped her. Unable to resist, she had gone along with it, and been too chagrined to tell. But she had felt unclean ever since, and carried a brooding, helpless anger. That episode had been a significant step toward her obsession with self-destruction. But along with the shame, she had developed a secondary fascination with sex: to flirt with it, to see how close she could come to it without getting caught again by it. As if a close escape somehow alleviated the disgust of the sex she had not escaped.

"So now you know," she said, watching him as he assimilated the memory. "Why I cut myself, and why I risked having you rape me. Sex and death: they are allied. So you see, anything you are saving me for was lost before you ever met me. Do you hate me now?"

"No," he said, appalled.

She stepped toward him. "So will you—?"

"No."

"What *is* it with you? You know it's pointless, when I'd much rather you did it with me than with some slut like the queen, and there's no reason not to."

"There is reason not to. I am not those men, and you are underage."

"This damned idiotic moral code of yours! It doesn't make sense!"

"It makes a sense you do not appreciate."

"Is that a cut?" she demanded. "When I asked if you respected me, you hesitated. Why? Out with it."

He did not like this, but it was a valid issue. "You deceived the Emperor of the DoOon, in the other reality, and tricked him into terminating his anchor."

"It was the only way to save us and all the rest of the realities! He was going to conquer everything!"

"True. But you prevailed by trickery, violating your honor, and causing me to violate mine."

"I may have saved us and every other universe—and you condemn me?"

"No. You have a standard other than mine. But it is a taint on my love for you."

"I don't understand you!" she exclaimed. "I did what had to be done. You know that. It was the only way. Tell me: how can you blame me?"

He suspected that it would not persuade her, but he tried to clarify it. "The Emperor had made captives of us all, though he did not treat us badly in the direct sense. He proposed to confine us to his reality until he had what he wanted from us, which was a Chip to enable him to cross realities. He threatened to kill Seqiro if you did not cooperate, so you cooperated. He threatened to destroy you if I did not cooperate, so I cooperated. What he did was wrong. But that did not justify wrongness on our part. When I agreed to help him—"

"Under duress!"

"I became bound by my word. Whether given freely or under duress, it was my commitment. He trusted me because he knew I would not break my word. Then we came to the anchor, and you had Seqiro, whose power I did not then know, get into the Emperor's mind and make him free the anchor. That cut us loose from his reality, and we spun through the realities until we connected with another person who formed a new anchor. Now we are in Nona's reality. That may be better for us and for the realities the Emperor would otherwise have invaded. But it was accomplished by a betrayal of trust. I promised to help the Emperor and not to seek harm to him. Instead I led him into betrayal. Because I depended on your word to buttress mine, and your word was not good. For that I must condemn you. How can I love a woman who can not be trusted?"

She was hurt. He saw it in the way her body shrank into itself, and felt it in the roiling darkness of her mind, which remained connected to his. For the first time he felt like killing himself, and knew it was her feeling. His own power of emotional projection might be void in this reality, but that of the horse remained. If only he had understood this aspect of her nature before he loved her! But she had betrayed him in that too, though unwittingly. She had not understood that he needed a woman full of joy, not pain. Had he known, he would have avoided any relationship with her, especially love.

Then her pain turned abruptly to fury. Now her rage beat at him. "Oh, you would have, would you? You didn't care about me or anything, just about a vessel full of joy you could empty, so you could do your job at home. It was all strictly business. But you made a mistake. You got emotionally involved before you were sure. Too bad. Well, let me tell you some things you maybe didn't think of. Here you're so damned concerned with your private personal code, you're not looking at what's best for everyone else. You think your given word is more important than the rest of the universe, literally? You're crazy! The universe doesn't give a wormy horse dropping about what goes on in your head. You think it's better to let billions of people be enslaved and maybe die than to break your word, when you only gave it to save me? *I'm not worth it!* Your word isn't worth it. You have no right to impose your foible on the rest of everything."

He tried to answer, and could not. Never before had she assaulted him like this, with her grief and her fury, and it was devastating. She refused to heed his logic. She continued, her emotion so strong that he was helpless.

"And even if you did, you still have no call to condemn me for doing what I had to do. Maybe you had to keep your word. I had to save our realities. I don't have the luxury of your kind of integrity. I never was able to impose my standard on anyone else. Not when my family started breaking up, and it tore me up more than it tore up my folks, but they were the ones doing it and I was the one who suffered from it. Not when I got raped by those four horny freaks who didn't care who else they hurt, so long as they dipped their sticks. The only real choice I ever had was surviving, any way I could—and I'm not sure I want to do that. So don't tell me you can't love me because I'm not what you thought I was. If you want to love me, it better be for what I really am. You can trust me to be what I am, and that's all. And what I am is in love with you, and you're the greatest thing that ever happened to me, and without you I'd be dead by now, and if you're in trouble I'm going to save you some way, and if I have to kill someone to do it, then I will, and if I have to break my word, then I will, and if I have to hate you for not loving me back the same way, then I will."

She stopped speaking, overcome by emotion. Her face was slick with tears and her hair disheveled. Darius stared at her. As she spoke, something had been occurring in his mind, a subtle but painful change, and now he realized what it was.

It was the realization that he was wrong. That he had judged her by the wrong standard. She was beautiful in her own way, mentally as well as physically, and he did love her for what she was, and he desperately craved her wild and total passion.

He owed her a phenomenal apology.

He started to speak, but she had his thought before he could formulate the words. "Oh, Darius!" she cried, and flung herself into his embrace, her forgiving as abrupt and total as her fury.

He kissed her and held her, feeling her love coming back at him with the cutting edge of her suicidal nature. She did not do things halfway; when she gambled, she gambled everything. When she loved, she loved without restraint. Perhaps he had somehow known her nature all along, and been attracted to it. She was almost completely different from him, but he needed her and could not give her up.

They lay together on the bed, their bodies pressed together. Her damp hair fell partly across his face. "Was that our first?" she asked.

"We didn't do it," he said.

She hit him gently on the shoulder with her fist. "I know we didn't do *that!* I mean, our first knock-down, drag-out fight?"

"May it be our last!" he said fervently.

"No, folk can fight if they want to. It's fun making up, after. Now we can do it." The reference needed no clarification; her mind made it compellingly plain.

"No. Just let me love you, with understanding." It was his mind's turn to make it clear: he did not want to follow after callous young men who had sought no more than her body. Her body was unimportant compared to her feeling.

"That's the nicest thing anybody ever thought about me," she murmured, satisfied.

So they slept, their passion spent in a way the despots would not have understood. Indeed, the despots were probably watching, not understanding their words, mystified by the whole business.

IN the morning they had breakfast with their hosts. King Lombard looked amused, and Queen Glomerula looked grim. Knave Naylor was absent. Provos kept to herself, unworried, as became one who had no need to be concerned about the future. Obviously the despots were satisfied that the visitors were of the animus, but not satisfied about their purpose here. It might be dangerous as well as unethical to murder visiting animus, but might also be dangerous to let them stay. Or go.

Hobard continued working on common words. Communication, aided by Seqiro's hidden assistance, became better. But they were at cross-purposes. Darius and his retinue, as the despots thought of it, wanted only to return through the anchor and travel the Virtual Mode, going home. The despots wanted only to find out enough to exploit the visitors, or to kill them. It was pointless to remain here much longer.

But there were guards throughout the castle, and it was obvious that it would not be possible simply to walk away. Darius disliked the notion of sneaking out at night, and wasn't sure that would work either. So he would have to use magic. That would mean making figurines of all of them, so that he could conjure them to another place. Assuming that the despots had no way to stop his particular type of magic.

He sent a mental message to Provos: *I need solid, liquid, and gas of yours.*

Yes, I gave you those this evening, the woman returned.

That left the horse. How could he get the necessary essences there? If he sought to visit Seqiro, the despots might be suspicious. He wasn't sure how much of his magic Queen Glomerula understood. He had shown her the figurine of Colene, and used it to conjure Colene to him. Conjuration did not seem to be a type of magic these folk used, but he couldn't be sure.

Well, he might conjure himself or Colene to the horse tonight, to get the essences. Then he would be able to complete the icon.

The day passed pleasantly enough. The despots were reasonably gracious hosts, until such time as they came to their decision. Communication was getting easier as a basic vocabulary grew. Queen Glomerula, evidently hoping that Darius might like to conclude the business they had only started the prior night, was attentive. Colene was studiously neutral, as befitted the place of a woman of the animus.

They went to Darius' chamber together in the evening, to the queen's disappointment. Colene chatted about this and that and did an impromptu striptease dance, not for Darius' sole benefit; she was doing it to distract those who were surely watching via their magic. That gave Darius the chance to make three more icons without, they hoped, being observed.

After a reasonable time, they settled down to sleep, Darius showing his seeming contempt for his woman by not bothering to use her for sex.

In due course Seqiro notified them that no one was watching them any more; they promised no further entertainment, either in what they might do with each other or in what the queen might do with Darius if he conjured his woman to her own chamber. The castle slept.

Now we can go to Seqiro, Colene thought.

I will conjure myself there. You may remain here and pretend to be both of us.

Like hell I will! How will I know you're not conjuring yourself to the queen?

For a moment he was irritated. Then she laughed, mentally, and he realized that she had been joking. But she also wanted to come with him, even if the conjuration made her sick again.

Darius didn't argue. He set up for his conjuration. First he used his finger to sketch a square between the two of them, on the bed. *We are here. This is my chamber, our starting point.* Then he sketched another square below it. *Seqiro is here. It is his stall.*

Um, should we go direct? Colene's thought came. *They might be alert to contact between any of us and Seqiro.*

That was a good point. Not everybody in the castle was asleep; some night-shift guards remained alert. He erased the stall square, physically and mentally, deactivating it. Then he made another: *This is the chamber where we donned Oria clothing.* That was reasonably close to the stalls; they could walk across the court to reach Seqiro.

He took the figurine of Colene. *Colene,* he thought firmly, activating it. Then without moving, he addressed his own: *Darius.*

Now they were ready. *We are here,* he thought. *Colene is stepping there.* He moved her icon from the first square to the second—and she disappeared. *I am stepping there.* He moved his own, and the wrenching took him, and he was there beside her. Both of them lying on the floor in their nightclothes.

He deactivated the icons and they got to their feet. Colene did not vomit this time; she had been prepared and exerted her will to keep her stomach in line. He gave her a silent squeeze of approval around the shoulders.

He could make a light magically, but decided not to; it

was better to use the starlight, which was so bright that it shone in through the doorway. Their eyes were already adjusted to the night.

They stepped out—and stopped, amazed.

There was light in the sky, all right, but it wasn't exactly starlight. It was a series of connected patterns, as if each star had several glowing moons, which in turn had a number of moonlets, which in turn—there seemed to be no end to it. Furthermore, these stars seemed *close,* because beyond them they saw the larger glow of Luna. Yet this great moon was not exactly the same. For one thing, it wasn't round. It was crudely shell-shaped. For another, it was surrounded by curlicue patterns of stars, some of which passed behind it and some in front of it. One pattern seemed to dance its way directly toward this planet, before getting lost in the patterns of closer shell patterns.

The Mandelbrot set! she thought, remembering her revelation of the prior day. *It really is true! We're in a fractal universe!*

Like the one they showed in their image? he inquired. *With all the planets and stars connected together?* He was as amazed as she.

Yes! I recognize it now. The shells and seahorse tails, all linked in intricate patterns. This is it!

They looked down at the dark surface of the planet Oria—and the patterns extended all the way to the ground. In fact, there were tiny whorls of light right at their feet, rising from tiny irregularities on the ground. The stars weren't just in the sky, they were everywhere, and they weren't distant and large, they were close and tiny. They were like cobwebs, except that their feet passed through them without effect.

Illusion, Darius decided.

I don't think so, Colene responded. *I think they're real, but phased out, so we can't interfere with them.*

But they couldn't remain indefinitely to stare at the effects. They had a horse to rescue. They resumed their walk, guided by Seqiro's thoughts.

They reached the stalls without interference, and Darius obtained a hair from the horse's mane, a drop of saliva, and the breath on the icon. It was complete.

One thing, the horse thought. *I have discovered that my power is limited in this reality. I did not realize this at first because I had no reason to reach minds beyond this region. But I can communicate completely only at close range. Because I came to know Nona, and her mind is open to me, I can reach her at the village, but it is a strain. I can reach no other person there, and fear I would not be able to reach even you, Colene, at farther range.*

Colene looked at Darius. They both knew that this was a serious limit. But it aligned with Darius' own ability to do sympathetic magic and not emotional magic. The reality was hostile to mind-magic, and perhaps only the horse's great power enabled him to retain even a limited proficiency.

Then Colene patted Seqiro's shoulder. *We won't let you get out of range,* she thought reassuringly. *We haven't been paying you much attention recently, but that's because we don't want to give away your importance to us. I love you, horseface.*

Don't fight with me! Seqiro thought, alarmed.

Darius had to chomp on his tongue to stop from laughing out loud. But Colene took it with good grace. *I can love without fighting,* she thought, burying her face in the horse's mane. *You never oppose your will to mine.*

Darius saw that the bond between girl and horse was as deep as that between girl and man. He felt Colene's love of Seqiro, unconsciously relayed to him by the horse, and understood it. He felt himself loving Seqiro similarly, and didn't fight it. The horse was worthy, and a phenomenal asset to their group. And it had been Seqiro's power that enabled Colene to rescue them from captivity by the Emperor. He now accepted the necessity of that action, and was relieved that it had happened.

Colene turned to him. She hugged him, wordlessly but not thoughtlessly.

"But where are his supplies?" he asked after a moment. For the horse had been burdened with all of their spare food, clothing, and tools.

The despots took everything away.

"My bike!" Colene exclaimed aloud, then covered her mouth as if to silence herself. She was referring to her bicycle, an instrument with which she could travel with greater speed and ease than on foot. It also had been part of Seqiro's load.

That, too. I think they locked up what they did not understand, and they thought that to be part of a wagon.

Colene made a wry face. She did not like losing her

things. But they had no effective way to recover them; any attempt would alert the despots to their effort to escape.

Then Darius conjured himself and Colene by turns back to his chamber. They had the wit to lie down first, so that they would not arrive standing on the bed.

Now that I'm getting to know your magic, I like it, Colene thought. *Though it does make me want to retch.*

This is only the lesser part of it, he replied. *Everyone in my reality has this much.*

So I understand. Say—do you ever need to make folk unhappy? Then you could draw from me, and I'd get happier while they all got suicidal.

The notion seemed preposterous. Then he realized that if they ever got stranded in a reality in which evil folk held them captive, and his cyng power worked, her offer would make sense. She could be dangerous indeed, in certain circumstances.

Thanks, she thought. Then she climbed half on him, kissed him, and went to sleep.

CHAPTER 4

NONA, trying to guide a clumsy pupil in the ways of harmony, jumped. It was the visitor-girl, with her strange mind-magic!

Nona! We need your help!

Nona disengaged with the pupil as expeditiously as she could, and retreated to the personal-needs chamber. *Are the despots trying to kill you?* she thought, uncertain what she could do. She had magic, but had to keep it secret, and in any event she could not match the power of the despots.

No, not exactly. They're taking Seqiro away!

Seqiro was the beautiful horse. Now Nona received his thought directly. *The despots are taking me out of the stall. They are putting paraphernalia on me.*

Then Colene's thought resumed: *Provos told us that the despots would try to take Seqiro. She also told us that the attempt was not successful. But that merely means that Provos remembers us doing something to prevent this. It's up to us to do whatever it is now. And we're stuck here in the castle with the king and queen, who are being very nice to us while they do their dirt behind our backs, stealing Seqiro. We can't do anything without showing our hand.*

So they needed someone else to rescue the horse, before he was taken to another castle and hidden so that he could never be found.

No, the horse's thought came. *I can commune with them if they come within my range, and they will find me. But they will not be able to travel freely. The despots are seeking to take me away, and to kill me if they can not control me. They do not know my mental nature; they see me merely as a fine beast of burden. I do not wish to be that, except for Colene. It is time for us to escape from the despots, but best to do it without alerting them to the extent of our powers.*

Now she understood. Separation from the horse would be a serious problem for the visitors, who depended on his marvelous mind-magic. It gave them the chance to learn the motives and plots of the despots. Nona's own destiny was surely linked with theirs, for they had come in seeming answer to her attempt to contact the Megaplayers, and they knew her secret. Her mental contact with Colene had been so sure and good that she knew the girl was to be trusted.

Now they needed her help. She also needed their help. If they worked together, they might accomplish both their destinies. *What can I do?*

Can you rescue Seqiro?

A theow take a horse from a despot? It was unthinkable!

Oh. Um. I see. Well, see if you can get close to him, and then tell him to throw his rider.

Nona shook her head. *That would not be effective. Despots can float and fly. So can I.*

Colene pondered a moment. *How fast can they fly?*

Not fast. It's as hard to fly as to run, and as tiring. We draw on the magic current, but that gives us ability, not energy.

So this magic isn't something for nothing, Colene concluded. *Suppose Seqiro gallops away?*

Then the despot would follow, and summon others, and they would surround him, and then kill him.

There was another pause. *Well, maybe we can hide him somewhere. You get to him, Nona, and get on him when he moves the despot off, and get out of there. He will accept you because he knows you.* Another pause, during which Nona felt Seqiro's confirmation. *Um, you do know how to ride a horse?*

No.

Brother! Well, rendezvous with him anyway, and float with him or something, and meanwhile we'll get away from here, and then we'll see.

Nona was not sanguine about this plan, but did not

know what else to do, so she agreed. She made an apology to the teacher, explaining that something extremely pressing had come up, and hurried away. Because she was a good worker, and trustworthy, the teacher agreed.

She remained in touch with Seqiro, which was just as well, because soon the horse informed her that he had gone out of range of Colene. He was being ridden past the village toward a more distant village.

Can you reach Stave? she asked the horse. *So he can help?*

Seqiro tried, but discovered that Stave was busy on a carpentry project for a despot and could not get free. So it was up to her alone.

She took a shortcut, where there was no path, just a series of gullies and pools that were hard to cross without getting dunked. Also the myriad smaller rads, which were like boulders of every size arrayed in patterns all across Oria. In the village and castle and the cultivated fields most of the smaller rads had been removed, so that only their faint filaments remained, visible by night. In the unsettled countryside the rads remained natural, and Nona preferred this. She tried not to step on the more delicate ones, though since they ranged all the way down to too small to see, this was impossible. *Is anyone near me?* she asked the horse.

He was not able to get into the minds of despots, but he could tell where they and theows were. *No.*

So she used her magic to float up over the rough terrain. Then she oriented on a tree ahead of her and drew it in, which meant that instead of moving it toward her, she moved herself toward it. In this manner she gained on the horse's progress along the winding road, and came back to land almost in sight of him. It was nervous business, because despite his reassurance, she feared being seen.

She heard the clip-clop of his hooves on the road, and forged on toward him. Then she realized that she was actually ahead of him; there was no need to hurry. *Buck off the despot, and gallop here to me,* she thought to him. This mind-magic was wonderful!

There was a sound. Then a man in a black tunic sailed up in the air beyond the bushes, and hovered there, surprised. He had made himself float rather than crash to land, but meanwhile the horse was galloping swiftly away.

The despot was facing away from her, having gotten

turned when unseated. Nona gambled, and floated up herself, drifting over the road. When the horse caught up with her, she conjured a large rad ahead of him violently toward her. Since the rad was well anchored and far more massive than she was, the effect was to move her forward with a burst of energy to match the horse's velocity, and dropped down to his back. She grabbed onto his mane and hung on.

He slowed immediately. *Guide me,* he thought, now walking swiftly. She discovered that it was not hard to stay on him, because she was in touch with his mind and knew what he was doing; there was no conflict between them. She sat in the saddle the despot had placed, and felt almost confident.

That way! she thought, making a picture in her mind showing where there was an old path through the rough land. She had used that path as a girl to go berry picking, and suspected the despots didn't know about it. The ploy was effective; the despot floated on along the road, assuming that the horse was still running ahead. Despots had much magic, but could use only one type at a time; otherwise the man would have made a picture of the road ahead, and realized that the horse was not there.

So her little trick had worked. Nona followed up by using her magic to scatter the sand and dirt the horse's hooves had printed, so that no sign of his recent passage remained. Unfortunately this path went nowhere useful to them at the moment; it wound down to the shore of the sea. They would have to turn and go along the shore, and the despot would soon find them. It was possible to search a wide area, with the command of illusion that a despot had. Their time was limited.

Then she had an idea. *Seqiro, do you mind the water?*

I like water.

Suppose I weight you down with rocks, so you can stand under the water, and I make a hood with a tube so you can breathe? I think the despot will never think to look for you there. His image will not work well under water, even if he tries.

Seqiro understood her concept immediately, for her mind was open to him in image as well as word. *Yes.*

Now she used her magic to fashion the hood. She summoned a stick of wood from the ground, held it in her hand, and changed it into a hood that would fit snugly over the horse's head, with transparent places so he could see out. It had a long flexible tube projecting from the top. The end of the tube widened out into a twisted shape resembling driftwood. "Now let me put this on you," she murmured. She had forgotten to focus her thought, but realized that the act of talking did that automatically; he still understood her.

Because he knew her mind, the horse did not flinch as Nona reached forward and worked the cumbersome device over his head. When the thing covered his eyes, he saw through hers. Then she got it down, and tied it under his chin, firmly. It looked weird, but she thought it should work.

"Now let me weight you with stones, so you can walk into the water," she said. She used magic to make a harness that fitted before and after the saddle, and floated heavy rocks into it. The work was tiring, for magic was merely another way of doing what a person could have done by hand, as far as the use of energy went, but she didn't stint. She was afraid that at any time the despot would discover his mistake and fly down the side path and find them.

Seqiro walked into the sea. The descent was moderate here, so that he had no trouble with the footing. Nona knew that the waves of the sea had battered the smaller rads of this region into sand. Man and nature kept changing the virgin world, and that was perhaps inevitable, but also sad. Weighted by the stones, Seqiro moved deeper, until the whole of his body was below the surface. Nona had to conjure additional stones to weight herself down, so that she would not float, and make a hood for herself: a detail she had almost forgotten.

The water was cold: another detail she had not thought of. Fortunately she was able to take a strand of seaweed and transform it into a thick warm suit for herself; she was plastered-wet, but the suit kept her warm. Then she made a similar covering for Seqiro, in patchwork pieces, until he said he felt comfortable.

They stood under the sea, their breathing tubes reaching up to their driftwood floats. The air did not taste good, but it sufficed. They seemed to be safe; all they had to do was wait.

"Is the despot close?" she murmured into her hood.

He is close, but ignorant; he is on the path but not at the shore.

Good. He was just casting about, with no idea where they had gone. Probably he hadn't even sent a picture back to the castle to explain the situation, because he didn't want to have the blame for losing the horse. He hoped to find and recover the horse and complete his mission in good order. If so, that was also their fortune; there would be no immediate large-scale action by the despots.

Still, the situation was bleak enough. The loss of the horse would soon be known regardless, and Nona's absence from the village would be suspicious. She had committed herself the moment she came after Seqiro, and would not be able to return to her prior life. Now she had to press forward to victory for herself and the visitors, or to disaster.

She would have preferred that it had not happened. She was not, it seemed, as adventurous a girl as she had thought. Right now, the prospect of settling into a comfortable life with Stave strongly appealed. But she had always known that it was not her destiny to be a wife and mother, and that she would save her people if she could. In fact now, when she was in danger, was the only time she reflected with favor on married existence. It was, she realized, not adventure which made her nervous, but danger. If she could go to far places, and explore strange lands, and meet unusual people, with little actual threat to herself, then it would be ideal.

You belong with us, Seqiro thought.

"But I don't even know who you are, really," she protested. "Just that you came from places I can't fathom, and have powers no one here does."

I will tell you about us. We are each from a different reality. The laws of the universe are different in each one. I am from one in which the horses are telepathic—

"What?"

This is what Colene calls it. You call it mind-magic. The horses use it to control the human beings and make them do the necessary chores. Human beings are useful because they have versatile hands.

"But why did you leave, then?"

I was dissatisfied with that life. I wanted to explore new frontiers and gain new understandings.

"So do I!" Nona exclaimed.

So when I became aware of the forming Virtual Mode, I took it, and found Colene.

"The what?"

The Virtual Mode. One of the humans could explain it to you more effectively than I can, because they have the minds for it.

"But you have a good mind!" she protested.

No. I borrow from the mind of the human being I am with. That is why it was necessary for me to achieve rapport with you before getting out of range of Colene's mind. I did not want to revert to animal intelligence, and be at the mercy of the despots, to whose minds I have not attuned. Now I am borrowing from yours, and you lack the concept of the Virtual Mode, so it is hard for me to explain it. But I can tell you my experience, from memory. I stepped through the anchor with Colene, and we crossed into a new reality every few steps. The worlds changed around us, until they were like nothing we had known. We walked where a sea had been, but no water remained. Until we came to a reality where an Emperor made us captive. Then we escaped from him by freeing his anchor, and came to you, because you are the new anchor person.

"That I don't understand at all! I am not an anchor! I am a person."

This too is not easy for me to explain. Darius and Colene understand it, but we are not with them now. They say that it requires five points to fix four dimensions, and so our Virtual Mode has five realities and five people. You are the person who makes it possible for us to enter your reality. You can enter the Virtual Mode with us, but no other person here can unless you touch that person constantly. Except that something is wrong, and we can not use the anchor to return, because of the animus.

"Now, that I understand!" she said. "The animus gives men the power of real magic, leaving women only the power of illusion, which everyone has. But if I can find out how to reverse it, and establish the anima, then women will have the magic and men will be subservient. The despots will fall, and Oria will be the wonderful world it once was."

Would that affect the anchor?

"I don't know. But it would change the nature of our society, so maybe it would. If the anima came, I would be the queen of Oria, and I would do anything I could to help you."

Provos believes that it does have something to do with the animus.

"Provos, the old woman? I hardly know her, or any of you, yet, and would like to."

She remembers what is yet to happen, but nothing of what has happened. She remembered that we were not harmed by the despots, so we went there. But she does not communicate much, and Darius believes that if we listen to her too much, what she remembers will change. In his presence I understand this.

Nona considered. "Does she remember my association with you? I mean, beyond now?"

Yes. It has passed through her thoughts. We travel far, and you are with us. Finally some of us pass back through the anchor. I do not know why we all do not go, and Provos does not remember what those ones do away from the others, but they do return.

"Does she remember whether the anima comes?"

She does not seem to. But that may be because no one has asked her.

"Could it be that some of you travel because the others are captive?"

It could be. I am not apt at conjecturing.

"Well, maybe you will help me to bring the anima, because then you will be able to return to your Virtual Mode. Then I will be queen of Oria, and I'll have to marry and bear children who have great magic. I dread that."

Why would you be queen? I understood from the thoughts of my friends that this office was inherited.

"It is. Under the animus the firstborn son of the king becomes king after him. Women do not rule, as none of them have magic stronger than illusion, and theow men have similar weakness. It is the power of magic which governs, and it follows the firstborn. But under the anima the magic flows the other way, through the women, and the lastborn. So the lastborn woman of the lastborn woman has the greatest magic, and must therefore rule. But to bring the anima, there must be a special pattern of births leading to a woman who matches the magical nature of our world. That woman is me. Because the world is now governed by the animus, I am the only woman with significant magic; I am the channel. But with the anima, all other women after me would have magic, according to their lineage, and all men would be reduced to illusion. Everything would change."

As a horse, I am indifferent to rank and power of the human type. But most humans seem to desire it. Why do you dread it?

"Because it's just another kind of captivity. I would have to marry, and have babies, and though with the anima these would add to my power rather than deplete it, I would not be free. I want to explore, to see new things, to act without regard to responsibility. I don't want to exchange one form of oppression for another."

This is the way Colene feels. But she also desires love.

Nona considered. "I don't desire love, for that, too, is captivity. Yet I may not be able to avoid it. When I get close to Stave, and pretend to be loving him, so that the despots won't know what I'm really doing, the pretense wears thin and I begin really feeling it. He feels the same for me, I know. It is a trap, but an alluring one. I don't know what to do about that."

Colene also has mixed feelings about Darius. She wants to marry him, but perhaps can not, because he must marry a woman with much joy, and drain that joy from her. She has no joy to spare; she has depression instead. So she must be his mistress only, and let him marry another, and she doesn't like that. He has interest in other women, and she is jealous of them. She wants to breed with him, even though she is afraid of it, so that he won't do it with someone else. He says she is young, and she doesn't like that either.

"How old is she?"

Fourteen years.

"In my culture, that is too young for that kind of activity."

In hers too. But in his culture it is all right, if both people have desire and understanding.

"But then he can—"

He honors the convention of her culture, because she is of it.

"He must be a good man."

Yes. I believe he is correct. But Colene is my girl. I must go with her, however she feels, and help her in what way I can, even when she goes wrong.

"Yes, of course." Nona wished she had a companion like that, because her own situation was precarious.

You are not excluded, Seqiro thought. *I like you too. While we are here, I will help you, as you are helping me. I would be lost without a sympathetic human mind.*

That was a wonderful relief, for the big horse had magic like none other known on Oria. "Thank you, Seqiro." She leaned forward and hugged him as well as she could. She began to believe that she had a chance to accomplish her destiny.

There was a pause in their communication. Then the

horse thought again: *The despot is gone. He is beyond my range. It is safe to emerge.*

"But *is* it?" she asked. "The despots have much stronger powers of illusion than the theows do, and can make pictures of scenes this far from the castle. They may be waiting for us to come out of the water so they can spot us."

How do they do this? I saw the illusion pictures they made, but did not understand how that was done.

"They use their creatures," she explained. "They see through the eyes of animals who serve them, and craft illusion pictures from those images, which they project for anyone to see. This is beyond the powers of theows, but ranking despot women can do it, and all despot men."

So when the queen showed Colene with the knave, there was an animal there?

"Probably a spider in the corner. Once a despot trains a familiar, that creature serves the despot loyally, and the despot makes sure it is fed and cared for. When a familiar is killed, the despot who has it is most annoyed, not because he cares about animals, but because it requires considerable effort to train a replacement. Only the despot who trains a familiar can draw on its images, because animals do not see or hear the way we do, and each is different, and that information must be interpreted. I could train a familiar, but seldom do, lest my ability be discovered. I keep only a lizard near my house, whose perceptions will tell me whether anyone strange has come there."

Then I am a familiar.

She laughed. "I suppose you are, Seqiro! But you are to an ordinary familiar as a king is to a theow child."

Perhaps so. I can see the similarity in the magic. But I can not relate readily to unfamiliar creatures, and have extreme difficulty getting into the minds of strange human beings.

"The despots can't get into human minds at all! Only animals, and only with patience. Then it is mostly a matter of controlling their movement and reading their senses, not truly relating to their thoughts. However, we can never be sure which animals are theirs, so we must always be cautious. When a blackbird watches us, we know it is a familiar, but when a fly buzzes near we have no way to tell. However, I doubt that they have many night creatures; usually they use flying animals to spy away from the castle."

He saw the situation in her mind, and agreed. *We must*

remain hidden until darkness. Unfortunately I am growing hungry.

"But I can make food!" she protested. "All I need is something organic to transform. What do you prefer?"

Oats.

She took one of the smaller stones and transformed it into a bucket. Then she found a loose hair on his back. She held it and concentrated. It became a mass of oats, which poured though her hands and floated up to the surface. "Oops!" she exclaimed in dismay. "I forgot where I was; I meant them to fall into the bucket."

She fashioned another stone into a tight-fitting cover for the bucket, then transformed another hair into oats inside it. She passed this container around to Seqiro's nose. But he couldn't eat it, with both the oats and his nose encased. She did some more magical shaping, and finally got a hood which had a feed bucket at the base.

This is nice magic, the horse thought as he munched.

"So is yours," she said. Then she made some food for herself from a spilled oat, and ate it.

Lend me your mind.

Nona found this request odd, until she fathomed his reason. Seqiro was a horse, with the mind of a horse; he could remember very well, but could not reason in the human fashion by himself. But with the mind of a human being, he could think as well as that human could. He had something to work out.

So while they ate, they thought, and Nona became a viewer of that thought. It was as if she were thinking, but she was not; she was merely watching.

Seqiro drew on his memories and limited understanding of the situation of Colene and her companions, and on Nona's experience of Oria. When the two meshed, it became apparent that three abilities were needed to escape capture by the despots: Nona's magic, Seqiro's mind-talk, and Darius' conjuring. These meshed abilities would enable them not only to escape the despots but to reach the Megaplayers. The Megaplayers were the ones most likely to be able to reverse the animus, establish the anima, and so change the culture of Oria and free the anchor of the hostile spell which prevented the main party from returning to the Virtual Mode.

"It is true!" Nona exclaimed when the horse finished and returned her mind to her. "We must work together, for otherwise we all are lost, and if we succeed we all prevail. You *are* the folk I needed to reach at the instruments."

Or at least we are folk who may be able to help you. Our arrival here was coincidental.

Nona now understood the concept of the Virtual Mode better than before. "It was not coincidence that I came to that place and sought contact. I thought it was the Megaplayers, but it was for a Virtual Mode—and yours was the one I encountered. Perhaps some groups could not have helped me, but yours can, so I was lucky I connected with you."

Perhaps so. But much remains in doubt.

"Much remains in doubt," she agreed. "But I'm glad it was you, Seqiro, and your friends."

The horse did not send a direct thought, but she felt his mental warmth. He did like her. He liked human girls, and she was one, but he also liked the type of girl she was. Just as she liked the type of horse he was.

After eating, they slept, for they knew that they would have little rest once they left the water. They would have to locate Seqiro's friends, and try to find the Megaplayers. Nona found it comfortable, for though she was awkwardly perched on the back of the horse, under water, with a complicated head-hood, Seqiro sent a pleasant mind message of relaxation.

NONA woke from a pleasant dream which quickly faded. Her legs were feeling stiff, because she was not used to remaining on a horse, but in a moment Seqiro's mind caused that discomfort to fade. It was a continuing comfort to be in his company; he knew how to make a human being feel better.

It is a skill we require in my reality, he explained. *There we control the humans, and require them to do our bidding, but we prefer them to be satisfied. Most would have trouble functioning without horses. Colene is more independent, as are you, but the techniques remain helpful.*

"They certainly do! Are there other things you can do for our kind?"

I can make you perform beyond your normal level. But this would be a stress on your body if used too often.

"Beyond my normal level? You mean I could do better magic?"

No. Your magic is beyond my scope. You could run faster, lift a heavier weight, or act with improved coordination. You could be more effective in combat with another of your species, or could accomplish some necessary task with better dispatch.

"So if a despot catches me, I might be able to twist out of his grip with unusual strength, and escape," she said. "But that would not affect his magic. I would have to counter that myself."

Yes.

"Still, it's probably going to be helpful, because our chances of hiding long from the despots are small. We had better hurry to join the others, and start our journey to the Megaplayers."

Seqiro made his way up the slope and out of the water. The lights of the night were bright, helping to clarify the ground so that he did not stumble. Nona had always liked the night as well as the day.

She changed the hoods and hoses back into innocuous objects, and did the same for the stones which had weighted the horse enough to enable him to remain below water, freeing them of encumbrances. "But before we go farther, I must get down," Nona murmured.

Seqiro did not need to inquire why; he knew it from her mind. *You could have done that in the water.*

She realized it was true: she was wet through anyway. The currents would have carried the fluid away. She just hadn't thought of it. So she got down and squatted by a bush, then returned. She preferred to walk beside the horse, getting her legs back into shape.

"Where should we go?" Nona asked.

You must work out a procedure, for I am not an original thinker.

"But you have been thinking original thoughts for hours!" she protested.

No. I have used your mind to think them. Now I am merely in contact with you, and you must do the original thinking. We know that we must work together, but you must decide how we shall get in touch with the others.

Nona realized that this did make sense. The horse had never claimed to be other than a horse, except in the matter of mind-magic. "Then I think we must get close enough to your friends so that you can talk with them. I hope this is not close enough for the creatures of the despots to spot us."

I will try to explore the minds of the creatures we encoun-

ter. If I practice, I should be able to attune more perfectly as time passes.

They walked on toward the castle, the ground illuminated by the tiny filament curls. Then, suddenly, they were in range, for Nona heard Colene's voice in her mind.

Seqiro! Is that you?

I am with Nona, who kept me safe.

That was a considerable exaggeration, but Nona was so glad to have made contact that she didn't protest it.

Darius has a plan. He will join you, while Provos and I hide.

Then Darius was there with them. He had conjured himself there. Nona was amazed, until she remembered what she had learned of his magic from the horse. Just as Seqiro's magic was far superior to that of the despots, so was Darius' magic. Despots could conjure only small objects, nothing living. Nona was the same; any object that was too large simply caused the conjurer to be drawn in instead. That was useful for flying, but not nearly as good as Darius' instant self-conjuration. King Lombard must be fascinated by, and afraid of, the visitors. With excellent reason.

Yes, Seqiro replied. *It was time for them to depart the castle.*

"All right," Darius said, speaking in his strange language, but his thoughts coming through to Nona in hers. "We believe that our chance of escaping unobserved is slight, but that Nona's knowledge of the planet should help. So we have split our parties, and when Colene and Provos are safe, we will join them. Seqiro, have you learned enough to enable us to lead the despots astray?"

Yes. Nona has told me how they use familiars to spy on others, and that these creatures usually fly and seldom go out by night. Talk with her.

Darius faced Nona in the filament light, and she realized how handsome he was. "We fear you can not return to your village, now that you have helped us," he said. "You must hide with us. Colene says that this planet should have many projections, some tiny, some large, and some like other planets. Is this true?"

"Yes, Oria is shaped the way all worlds are," Nona agreed. "Except that much of it has weathered down, so no longer shows clearly. But the filaments remain. You can see their lights." She gestured around them.

"We were amazed when we saw these," he said. "Some extend far into the sky."

"Yes, they are all sizes, and of course the stars are merely the joinings of larger filaments. Is this not true in your own world?"

He smiled. "Hardly! Now I propose to conjure us to different sites, staying ahead of the despots. But I can conjure a person only from me or to me, and only one at a time, safely. As far as I can tell, my range is not limited here, but it is not wise to conjure into a strange place. So one of us must go first, taking the risk, and since Seqiro represents our communication, it must be—"

"I'll go first, of course," Nona said quickly.

"That was not what I was about to say. You are our liaison with your people, and you know this planet. So I will—"

"But you must not risk yourself either," she protested. "You are the only one with the conjuring magic."

He considered. "All of us are necessary; none can be risked. We must find another way. But I do not think it will be safe to walk; it will be slow, and they will follow our tracks."

"Maybe I can train a familiar," Nona said uncertainly.

"A what?"

I will explain.

So while Nona cast about for a suitable animal to train, though she was in grave doubt that she could either find or train it in time, the man and the horse communed.

Then Seqiro's thought came again. *I can find a creature for you, and perhaps enhance your training of it. What is best for your purpose?*

"A bat," she said immediately. "But I would have to hold it in my hand, and they are hard to catch."

There are bats here. If I can get into the mind of one, I will stun it for you.

Then, to her amazement, he did so. A bat fell to the ground not far from them. She hurried to pick it up, guided by the horse's continuing contact with its mind.

It was a grown female in good health. This was ideal! Nona held the bat in her hand and exerted her magic. She felt Seqiro enhancing it. *Lady bat, I call you my familiar,* she thought. *I will help you and you will help me. Give me your senses.* And, thanks to the great added power of the horse's mind-magic, the bat responded almost immediately. It became Nona's familiar in a brief time instead of a day.

Nona flipped the creature into the air. *Find a safe place for us to come,* she thought to the bat.

The familiar flew into the night. But now Nona flew with it, borrowing the perception of its eyes and especially its ears. She saw, through its ears, the dark trees and clearings and gullies, until it came to a place in the lee of a mountain. This was suitable.

"Now I will go," Darius said. "Then I will conjure the two of you to me. How far is it?"

Beyond my range, the horse thought.

Darius paused. "But then if I join the bat, I will not be able to tune in to you for the conjuration. You will be lost to me."

"Then I should go first," Nona said. "So you can remain in touch with Seqiro."

"But then I will have no contact with the bat," he pointed out. "I will not know where to conjure."

They considered the matter, and realized that there was no easy way to do it. Seqiro could be conjured to join the bat, but then Darius and Nona would not be able to communicate with each other. Nona could be conjured first, but then Darius would not be able to move either of the others to join her. If Darius went first, Seqiro and Nona would be stranded behind.

"You say it isn't safe to conjure more than one at a time," she said. "But is the risk that great?"

"The risk is unknown," he said. "In my own reality, with well-established settings, it could be done. But here it might lead to disaster. We might arrive far apart, or one might drop from the sky."

She had to agree that it was best to avoid such a chance. She could float gently down, but neither Darius nor Seqiro could.

"We shall have to make shorter hops," Darius concluded with regret.

But then Nona had another notion. "Could you conjure yourself—and carry me? So that I maintain contact with my familiar, guiding you?"

He looked at her, judging her weight. Because their

minds were connected, she understood that in the process he took note of her appealing figure. Her tunic was still somewhat plastered to her, making her apparel wretched but showing very well the underlying contours. "Yes, I could do that. But it would be an unsteady ride for you, and we might fall when we landed."

"Then we should try it once, and not again if it seems too awkward."

They did it. Darius brought out several little dolls he had made, and took material from Nona's wet dress to make a doll resembling her. He added a hair of her head to it, and a drop of her spit, and had her breathe on it. This was interesting magic! Then he made circles on the ground, identified one as where the three of them stood, and the other as where the bat waited, and invoked the cute horse doll. He moved that doll from one circle to the other—and Seqiro vanished.

Nona had known what was coming, yet not quite believed it. No despot had power like this! Yet Darius was an ordinary man in other ways, not arrogant at all.

Now it was the two of them together, and when Darius spoke it was unintelligible. "I don't understand," she said, showing by her words how it was, because he could not understand her language either.

He smiled. He spoke to the girl doll, and as he did so she felt an odd shiver. The doll had become her, or she the doll, in a weird way.

He approached her. She thought he was going to pick her up, but instead he moved the girl doll into the arms of the man doll—and Nona sailed up and into his waiting arms!

But now his arms were occupied, and he could not move the dolls. He spoke to the girl doll, and she felt its power leave her; then he spoke to the man doll, and stood there somewhat helplessly. She realized what was needed. She reached to his hand and took the embraced dolls from it, very carefully. Then she looked at the far circle, leaned as far as she could toward it, and moved the dolls to it.

There was a horrible wrenching, and the scenery changed. There was a jolt, and Darius fell, and she fell on top of him.

Disoriented, Nona reacted in a manner that had become almost automatic. She put her head down and kissed him on the mouth.

Almost immediately, she realized her mistake. This was not Stave, this was a different man. They were not pretending to be lovers in case a despot familiar was watching, they were magically traveling to another spot on the planet. She felt the flush forging to her face.

Then perhaps you should stop kissing me, the man's thought came.

Oops! Nona jerked her head away, her embarrassment doubling.

But Darius laughed, outside and inside. "Don't worry; I knew what you were thinking," he said. "You forgot who I was."

She felt his understanding. It had indeed been a mistake, no ill intended, and the ambience of the horse's mind-magic made that clear. But her blush did not clear immediately.

"So should we make shorter hops?" Darius asked.

Nona tried to quell her embarrassment enough to think logically. The shorter the hops, the slower would be their progress, both because of the need to set them up more frequently and because they would be making three conjurations instead of two. It seemed to make better sense to make them as long as possible. It wasn't as if it was unpleasant being in Darius' arms.

Once more she was embarrassed, remembering that her conscious thoughts were being shared. This was another woman's man, and she had no business thinking of any personal relationship. The problem was that she wasn't used to this mind-magic, and her thoughts tended to run around like field mice, poking into everything. He seemed to have the same problem, for he had noted her figure, and there had been a whiff of sexual desire. It was odd, feeling what the man felt, but also exhilarating. What could two people do, when one was an attractive man and the other an attractive woman and their secret thoughts were open to each other?

"They can limit it to thinking," he said. "If I followed up on every sexual thought I had, I would be in trouble, and not just with Colene."

That had to be the answer. Nona belatedly remembered to send the bat out again, to find another suitable spot.

They made several more jumps, gradually extending the range and gaining confidence. They should be able to get away from any despots they might encounter. Darius was tired, for he had not had the chance to sleep during the afternoon. So they found a place under a large mountain and settled down for the rest of the night.

Nona made food for them: more oats for Seqiro, and bread for the human beings. Darius was amazed. "You need never go hungry!" he exclaimed.

"That would be true, if I dared show my ability," she agreed. "But it would be death if the despots knew."

He just shook his head, impressed. Nona was quite pleased, knowing that his reaction was sincere.

Then she made some pillows and covers for each of them, perversely enjoying the demonstration of her power. She had never dared do this at home, but these folk already knew, so it made no difference.

Darius lay down and went instantly to sleep. She had half expected him to—but of course he had a woman of his own. She was relieved and just a trifle disappointed.

Nona let the bat go to forage, for it was not right to deprive it of its feeding time. She would be able to summon it when she wanted, now that it was her familiar.

She really wasn't that tired. But it would be best to get more sleep while she could, so—

SHE woke by daylight. Seqiro must have helped her to sleep, for it had never before happened that suddenly. Darius was already up, doing whatever men did in the morning.

She was about to use her magic to make more food. But Seqiro's thought came: *A hostile mind approaches.*

Nona looked up. There on the horizon was a blackbird. "A despot familiar!" she exclaimed. "They have spotted us!"

"Then we had better move," Darius said. "Where's the bat?"

She sent her perception out and found the mind of the bat. "She returned to her cave for the day," she reported. "It is far away. Even if she could perform well by day, it would be too late."

"Is there room in that cave?"

She made the bat open its eyes and look around. "Yes, but it isn't nice, because—"

"We must go there, then." He drew two circles. Seqiro stepped into one, and disappeared when the horse doll moved across to the second.

Then the two of them stepped into the circle. The black-bird was now looming close. It dived down toward them.

Darius picked her up in his strong arms, and she moved the embraced dolls to the other circle. There was the wrenching.

They landed. Darius' feet slid out from under, and they fell in their usual pile. Probably it was because she handled the dolls clumsily, so that they did not land properly upright. But the landing was soft.

Because they were in a mound of guano at the base of the bats' cave. That had been her objection.

They struggled up, horribly soiled. But at least they were not hurt by the fall, and had escaped the eye of the despot's familiar.

No, Seqiro thought.

Then she saw the head of one of the hanging bats turning to gaze at them. The despots had familiars here! Why hadn't she realized that this would be the case?

"Where can we go?" Darius asked, controlling his revulsion of the dung in much the fashion he had controlled his appreciation of Nona's body before.

Colene is now in range, Seqiro thought. *The despots seem not to know her location.*

"Then take us there!" Nona exclaimed. She didn't even wait for him; she climbed sloppily into his embrace and moved the dolls, which she still held.

Nothing happened. Darius smiled, then drew two circles. Oh. Of course. The magic hadn't known where to take them. Where would they have gone, if it had moved them to no specified destination?

The second try was successful. First Seqiro went, then the two of them.

They were in an embrace on a beach, still caked with bat dung. Colene turned from her embrace of the horse to see them. "Now, that's what I call a dirty scene!" she said, wrinkling her nose. She was not entirely joking; a jealous rage was forming like a flash storm.

"Well, it's dirty business, being with other women," Darius replied.

Colene stared at him as he disengaged from Nona. The girl did not like the physical closeness of the two of them at all. Then something changed in her mind, and the rage dissipated.

Darius' joke was registering on another level. She burst out laughing.

Nona did not quite understand the laughter, but realized that it meant that the situation was all right. That was a relief, because she didn't want trouble with these new friends and their marvelous forms of magic. All she wanted was to get this awful manure off her body and out of her hair.

CHAPTER 5

COLENE had to laugh, because it wasn't the time to cry. She knew Darius hadn't been doing anything with Nona, because Seqiro was reassuring her on that. Even if Nona was a luscious young woman closer to Darius' age with, Seqiro said, formidable powers of magic. Certainly she wouldn't be rolling in the hay with him when the hay was reeking bat droppings.

Darius took a step toward her. "Get away from me, you stinker!" she cried. "Get into the water and wash up." She glanced at the horse's feet. "You too, horsehead."

The three of them marched to the water. Seqiro stepped in, but the other two hesitated. "Yes, take off your clothes," Colene said. "Wash them too."

Guided by that, the man and woman pulled off their clothing. Colene watched, feeling less threatened because she seemed to be in charge. They were doing it at her direction. So it didn't matter that Darius was a handsome man and Nona a beautiful woman. That he had one terrific kind of magic and she another. It was all under control.

Yet somehow little boxes were forming in the margin of Colene's mind, reproducing themselves and extending down the page. She drew boxes when she was upset; they overran some pages of her diary. It was written in the form of letters to Maresy Doats, her fanciful equine companion and best friend before Seqiro came into her life. But the boxes told the story better than her written words.

Each box was really a representation of the real box she kept at home on Earth. In it was a small collection of significant things: sleeping pills, razor blades, and her Will. The Will might not be legal, but it was real. It told how to dispose of her things. She knew the box would be found after her death, and hoped that the Will would be honored. Meanwhile, while she lived, the box retreated from her awareness when she was undepressed, and loomed in close when she was normal. It multiplied, trying to surround the page. If the boxes ever succeeded in completely encircling her words, then she would be confined, and would have to lift the lid of the real box and eat the pills and slash open her wrists and let the rich red lifeblood pour out, and sink slowly into oblivion and be gone. She didn't believe in hell, and hoped she wasn't mistaken, because otherwise she was surely going there.

Colene blinked. Three faces were staring at her from the water. Seqiro, standing only ankle-deep. Darius, waist-deep. And Nona, also waist-deep, her bare breasts exactly the kind Colene longed for, remarkably full and firm. The three had been receiving her thoughts.

It was funny: they had no clothing, but she was the naked one.

"They have magic, but you are the remarkable one." It was Provos, whom she had forgotten for the moment. "You do not die in my memory."

And Provos remembered the future. She *knew*.

Colene turned and hugged the older woman.

AFTER that things improved. The soiled clothing was beyond salvage. Nona and Darius donned new tunics Nona made magically from chips of wood: green for him, red for her. Neither wore anything underneath, as was the custom in this reality. They ate a meal Nona made from horsehairs. It was good, and the woman assured them that the food would not revert to its original form once it was inside them. Colene could appreciate how handy Nona would be to have around.

"What next?" Colene inquired.

"We must go to Jupiter," Darius said. "For this must be where the Megaplayers live. We can ask them to help Nona change the animus to anima, and then the despots will fall and we'll be able to go back through the anchor and travel the Virtual Mode again."

"To Jupiter!" Colene exclaimed. "That monstrous planet Hobard showed us? How can we get there?"

"By following the filament," Nona said. "All planets are connected by filaments; we can reach any, if we have the time and the magic. I think Darius' magic will enable us to travel along it."

"But Jupiter's huge!" Colene protested. "Its gravity would crush us!"

"Gravity?" Nona was baffled.

They went through Seqiro to clarify the concept: the force that held people to the ground.

"Oh, but that is the same everywhere," Nona said. "People change size with their planets, but all stand with equal force."

"People change size?" Colene feared they had another confusion.

"So I understand," Nona said. "I have not been away from Oria, but our myths tell of great folk and little folk. The Megaplayers are great folk, as we can see by the size of their instruments."

"Okay," Colene said dubiously. "If gravity doesn't crush the giants, it shouldn't crush us. Magic is wonderful stuff! But how do we get to the filament? I see from Seqiro's mental picture that it connects to the planet under the East Sea."

"We can go under the sea," Nona said. "Just as Seqiro and I did." She sent a picture of horse and woman standing under the water, with weird air tubes leading up.

Colene nodded. "We'll have to have something better than air tubes, because that sea will get deep in that crevice. But I guess we can try it. Let's go."

Then Provos spoke, and they listened, understanding her thoughts if not her words.

"The despots are searching for us. They were looking for hoofprints, but realized that we are together. Their minions spied us by midmorning, and they came in force to capture us. We were traveling under the water toward what Nona calls the East Filament, but they dived down and intercepted us. They had thought that Nona was our captive, but she showed her magic in her effort to save us, and they knew her for what she is, and killed her."

Colene looked at Nona, who was staring in horror at Provos. Any resentment Colene had had of the lovely woman evaporated. Colene thought of killing herself—but Nona faced involuntary death. That was worse.

Darius looked thoughtful. "This is not what must happen," he said. "This is a warning. You saved the two of us from similar mischief when we traveled together. Because I heeded the warning, and we changed my future, your past. Then your memory changed."

Provos looked blankly at him. Colene realized why: this was in her past, so it was beyond her memory. But it offered a hint how they should proceed.

"Suppose we do something else," Colene said. "Suppose we don't go in the water? I mean, we just go hide in the jungle, or something?"

Provos looked confused. "We have to be more specific," Darius explained. "And we have to actually plan to do it, so that she can remember it."

They could change the future! But something else occurred to her. "Provos said I did not die in her memory. But if we change it, then I might die."

"We shall find a future in which we all survive," Darius said. "And in which we remain together. Now we must decide on it, for midmorning is not far distant."

They decided to make short hops up toward wild country halfway toward the head of the planet, conjuring each person individually. Nona would train another familiar, with Seqiro's help. It seemed that she had trained a bat that way before; that was how they had landed in the bat cave and gotten all gunked with guano. Once the despots gave up the chase, they would see about resuming their mission to Jupiter.

But as they reached that decision, Provos spoke again. "The despots searched us out, catching first the laggard ones and then the leading ones, who returned to try to help the others. They killed Nona and Darius, and made Colene and Seqiro slaves. Earlier, when the two almost escaped, they killed the horse also, and the girl killed herself."

Earlier: that meant later, in ordinary time. Colene was catching on to the woman's memory. But it was an unacceptable future, because of what happened to the others.

They tried out other scenarios, and finally found one that worked: Colene would go alone to distract the despots, while the others proceeded toward the filament. Then Colene would be conjured to rejoin the others, and they would leave the planet and be out of range of the malice of the despots.

"But exactly how do I distract the despots?" Colene demanded.

Before Provos could answer, a blackbird flew overhead, peering down at them. "A despot familiar!" Nona cried. "We must go immediately!"

"But it will see us go into the water," Darius said.

That was readily taken care of: Seqiro stunned the bird, and it plummeted into the water. Now the despots had no spy-eye, but they already knew the location. So Colene remained, while Darius conjured the others one by one to some other location. Nona was the last to go. She used her magic to make the footprints they had all left fade out.

"Thank you for saving my life," she said to Colene, with a warm and sincere smile.

"It wouldn't have been threatened if we hadn't come," Colene replied, feeling warmed. But the woman had disappeared.

Colene shrugged, and practiced the smile. If it could warm her, it surely could melt Darius, and she wanted it.

However, she had a more immediate problem: distracting the despots. She must be successful, because Provos had remembered that the plan worked, but it would have been a lot easier if there had been time for that one additional memory. Suppose she messed it up, and changed the future again?

You did a dance and showed them your body, Seqiro's thought came. *Darius was not pleased.*

So that was it! "Well, Darius isn't the one distracting the despots!" she said. "Tell him I'll dance for him, any time he's man enough for it."

Satisfied, she worked out a routine. She wasn't humanity's greatest dancer, but men didn't care how accurate a girl's steps and hand motions were, they cared how her breasts bounced. Nona could have done a better job of that, but this was Colene's show. She had always liked the notion of dancing for a sophisticated audience, and wowing them. Of course she had also always known that it would never happen, and that if she ever did find herself in such a situation she would mess it up. But still the vision appealed. It was part of her suicidal disposition: she always had to flirt with disaster. She felt most truly alive when she did that. She had read somewhere that it was the same urge that led explorers to climb the most dangerous mountains, and drivers to race at deadly speeds. It wasn't just the awful boredom of ordinary existence, it was that they weren't truly alive unless they were near death.

Actually she had come to life when she met Darius. She had played the same game with him, lying virtually naked with him, tempting him to rape her, and he hadn't, and her fascination had quickly turned to love. But she hadn't quite believed that he was from a different reality, and by the time he proved it, it was too late: he was home in his Castle of Laughter, and she was alone in her Hovel of Despair. But then he had made the Virtual Mode, which enabled her to walk across realities as if they were thin slivers of mica, and she had set off in search of him. At first the different realities had seemed much the same as her own, but when she crossed between them, people and animals appeared or disappeared. Then they had become different, with new fundamental laws, such as animals dominating the people and having telepathy. But in one of those other realities had been Seqiro, and she had loved him instantly, and believed in him, and she seldom felt suicidal when he was near. Darius and Seqiro—that was just about all she needed.

Assuming she could survive long enough to enjoy it. What an irony, that when she had the company of both the man and horse of her dreams, so she had no desire to kill herself, she was subject to external threats to her life. And not just her life: Nona was a threat against Colene's relationship to both man and horse, not because Nona had any evil intentions, but because she was what she was: about four years older than Colene, beautiful, and magically gifted.

Still, it was better to have things to fight for than to be without dreams. Even if she died here on Planet Oria, in the Universe of Julia, it would be better than her life had been on Earth.

Another blackbird flew overhead. There was a familiar! Seqiro had learned that the despots worked through animals, using the senses of the creatures so that they could project full pictures on walls or in the air. In fact, Darius and Wicked Queen Glom had watched a picture of Knave Naylor in Colene's room, when he tried to rape her. Colene hadn't fully realized then what had really freaked the man out. It wasn't the illusion, it was the fact that it seemed real to him. The despots were good with illusion, but they always knew the difference between it and reality. So her plan to do exactly what she had done had been flawed; straight illusion would not have done it. Because Seqiro touched the knave's mind directly, getting access to it when the man was all excited about what he thought he was going to do to Colene, the effects had seemed real. He *believed*. Because that was the way it worked, with Seqiro. So Naylor thought that superior magic was protecting her, and that a real serpent was out to kill or castrate him. It was as if a person had a picture of a rattlesnake on his desk, and when he went to pick it up, the snake bit him. But Queen Glom hadn't seen anything, so she figured the knave was losing his mind, and probably they had had him put away privily. A real one-two punch. Anyway, there had been a bug—a literal bug!—in the room that was the queen's familiar, so she had seen through its eyes. The queen had gotten an eyeful!

Still, Colene hadn't much liked the way Darius had hefted the queen's fat breast. The man was just too interested in the flesh of other women, and not interested enough in Colene's. Except when he saw her naked from the waist down, without diapers. She could make him squirm, that way, and she liked that.

There was a noise. Then a blue-clad man appeared up the beach. A male theow, by the color coding. And another, down the beach. The despots must have had some magical ways to ship them, or maybe had just used fast horses, and now they were closing in on her. Well, she hoped the rest of her party had made it to the filament; there seemed to have been time.

She waited while more men appeared and walked toward her. They were looking around, probably wondering where the others were. "Sorry, nobody here but us chickens," she said. And started her dance.

Her first steps were clumsy; she mostly just kicked up sand. Then something seemed to take hold of her, and she became ethereally light and graceful. She whirled, she sprang, she gestured in intricate patterns. How could this be? Then she realized that it was Seqiro's influence: he was guiding her body. It was one of the things he could do.

But horses didn't dance. How could he make her graceful, doing things she had hardly imagined? He might make her move faster or have more power, but this dance was intricately choreographed. The human folk in Seqiro's reality were not given to this sort of thing. He should have no memory of it.

Nona! Seqiro was borrowing from her mind, and relaying it to Colene. It was Nona's ability she was experiencing.

Colene felt another surge of jealousy. *Damn* that woman! She had so much that Colene lacked. But Colene couldn't turn it down; their escape depended on her success.

The men had been moving purposefully. Now they paused. They were supposed to be capturing her and searching out the other members of her party, but she was now acting in an interesting fashion. They probably weren't allowed to rape her, because some ranking figure of royalty had reserved that privilege to himself, and the seeing-eye blackbird was watching. Maybe they planned to kill Darius, so she would have no protector, and then wicked Knave Naylor would dare to return to complete what he had started. But it was okay to watch her. Maybe the despot who was attuned to the familiar was watching too. Men were easy to distract if a woman knew her business.

So she danced, and began lifting her green tunic so that more of her legs showed, and whirling so that the shortened skirt of it flung out, revealing yet more. She still wore the color of the unclassified visitor, which surely enhanced the interest of her person. Ordinary theows would seldom if ever get a glimpse of the private flesh of despots, and she just might be classified a despot; the doubt was there as long as she wore the green. Oh, yes, she was mesmerizing them, and she loved it. Even if it wasn't truly her ability, it was her own little body.

But this would last only so long, and then she had to be out of here. What was keeping Darius? He couldn't have forgotten her!

She hauled the tunic up another notch, giving them a view of her underwear. She had had to tie together bits of cloth after the knave burned her undergarments in heatless flames. Did girls wear panties under their cloaks here? Surely they did—and if not, well, she was an outsider, so she was entitled. What about bras? Well, she'd take those things off too, if she had to. Anything to stretch it out until she was conjured away.

The men were staring. They seemed even more fascinated than before. Were they undergarment freaks? Hobard had stared—maybe that was it! Folk here *didn't* wear anything under their tunics, so she was startlingly different.

Yes. It seemed Seqiro had learned this, but hadn't thought to tell her before. The horse wasn't much for initiating things, and really didn't care much about clothing.

Another figure appeared, this one riding a horse. The garb was black. That meant a despot male. That also meant that the game was over. He would use magic to hog-tie her, and then the conjuration might not work.

She hauled her tunic the rest of the way up and whirled it over her head. "Take a look at this, blackhead!" she cried. Maybe she could wow him too, with her naughty undies, long enough to give her whatever time she needed.

Suddenly she floated, and not by her own design. It was the magic. She was sailing toward the despot. So much for distracting him with her pants. "Damn it, Darius, get me out of here!" she cried.

There was a wrenching, and she landed waist-deep in water. Above her loomed what looked like a transparent bell. It was so large that there was room for Darius, Provos, Colene, and Seqiro, with Nona astride the horse. Several extensions reached down to the sea floor, evidently keeping the big bell stable.

"But what keeps the air fresh?" she asked.

"Nona is making more air from spent bubbles of the old air," Darius explained, handing her a new green tunic. "But she's not used to this, and there are several of us, so it's a drain on her."

She donned the tunic. The bottom of it trailed in the water, but that couldn't be helped. "But if it's magic—"

"Magic takes about the same energy as physical activity," he said. "Unless it's illusion. We don't want her to get overtired. We're pretty deep now."

"But I don't feel any pressure."

"Pressure doesn't build up here. It's no worse a mile down than at the surface. But we'd have a long way to swim, holding our breaths."

And Nona was making it possible to do this. Colene decided not to begrudge her the ride on Seqiro.

Fortunately they were close to the nethermost cleft of the East Valley. The lights of the tiny filament structures became so small that they were no more than a glowing band, and the other sides of the valley appeared. Suddenly they were there: standing over the central dimple. From it extended one straight band of light, which reached right through their bell and beyond without being intercepted. That was the major filament.

"But how do we travel along that?" Colene asked. "It's just a beam of light."

"Nona can tune in to the planetoids along it, and Seqiro can tune me to her, and then I can see to conjure us to them. Actually she may be able to travel along it alone; the theow legends say that those with real magic have this power."

"But this is going to be tricky, one at a time."

"This time we'll travel together. She thinks the despots can do it, so it must be possible for us."

"I hope so," Colene said, liking this less.

Nona sat up straight, extending her arms. Seqiro moved, responsive to her will, until they stood squarely across the filament. In fact it now traveled up through her body and out the top of her head. "Touch me," she murmured.

Darius, Provos, and Colene came close. Nona reached down to take hands with Provos on one side and Colene on the other. Darius reached past Colene to take hold of Nona's knee. Colene wasn't totally pleased with that, but suppressed her objection. She did feel the tingle of magic, as if a trace electric current were running through them.

The magic took hold. Colene's awareness seemed to follow the beam up, up at the speed of light, until it focused on another Mandelbrot bug far away. Darius' free hand moved, holding five doll figures up in that direction.

They shot up through the bell and the water and out along the beam in what turned out to be a zigzag course. Suddenly they were at the planetoid.

It took Colene a moment to get her bearings. They were no longer in the diving bell; that must remain under the sea. They were standing on a bug—but it was only a few miles across. They could step over many of its small projections. In fact, they had to; they were on the tiny head of it, which fastened to a larger head, and a larger one, until the body of it loomed. The head was in sunlight, but the far side of the body was in shadow.

Their own heads towered what should have been miles above the surface—yet they breathed without difficulty. And the gravity was the same as it had been on Oria. Nona had been right: it was the same, regardless of the size of the planet. Julia was a magic universe.

They walked around the body, heading east. The sunlight stopped at about the level of the largest side projections. They continued into the East Valley. Now all around them the filaments glowed, with most merging into ground light, but some rising to head height or beyond. It was similar to what they had seen at night on Oria, only now their heads were in daylight after their bodies were in deep shadow.

They came to the East Valley. This had a puddle of water in it, and Colene realized that it was the same as the sea on Oria. Their perspective had changed. They were like giants on this tiny planet.

"I think I must rest for a while," Nona said.

"I too," Darius agreed. "This is a new exercise for me, and I don't want to go wrong."

There is no danger for us here, Seqiro thought. *It is safe for you to sleep.*

Nona slid off his back, made a huge pillow from a thread of her dress, and lay blissfully down on it. Then, as an afterthought, she made another pillow for Darius.

Colene was tired too, but the evidence of Nona's compatibility with Darius was something she did not want haunting her dreams. So she refused to rest, and turned her attention elsewhere.

This planet was just like Oria, and it helped her to understand Oria's geography. Could there be people on this world, in scale with it? That would be funny!

"Yes," Nona said, picking up the thought. Sometimes Colene wished that Seqiro's telepathic ability weren't quite so comprehensive. Were all her jealous little snits being broadcast to the others?

No. Only the thoughts of normal interest to others, unless you wish it otherwise.

Well, that was a relief! She appreciated the horse's discretion. "There are?" she said, quickly returning to Nona's thought so that her side dialogue with Seqiro wouldn't be noticed. "Little people?"

"There are people on all the worlds, I think. Our stories tell of them. But few travel between worlds, so there is little contact. The ones from Jupiter are the Megaplayers, who left their great instruments by our sea."

"You mean there really are giants to go with those things?" Colene asked, still amazed by the revelation. She knew they were going to see just such giants, but somehow their literalness hadn't registered.

"Oh, yes. Every planet has its folk. But it's hard to know them."

"Now, let me see if I have this straight. Oria is just a little planet out from Jupiter, and there are littler planets along the filament between the two. And the filament comes from one of the projections of Jupiter. So what about the filaments from Oria? Do they have little planets along them, and do those planets have people too?"

"Yes, surely they do," Nona answered. "But those folk are so tiny we can't see them."

Colene shook her head. "I'll just have to see it to believe it. But they would be so small—if this planet's about eight miles in diameter, that's a thousandth of Earth/Oria's size. So to be in proportion, the people would have to stand, oh, under a tenth of an inch tall."

I can improve your sight, so you can see them, Seqiro offered.

Colene remembered how the horse had rendered her into a deadly fast and strong knife-wielder, briefly, as a demonstration of his potential power over her body. In fact he had done it in another way just recently, enabling her to dance effectively. "Okay. Let's do it."

They left Darius and Nona resting, and Provos sitting there with her own future memories, and walked back to the shadow's border. It was good to be alone with Seqiro again, however briefly.

Colene lay down on the ground, realizing that it was furry rather than hard. She had assumed that this was moss. But now she realized that it was something else.

She focused on a tiny clear patch between stands of moss. Her vision became amazingly sharp. It was as if she were using a magnifying glass or even a microscope, and turning up the power.

The edge of the moss resolved itself into a stand of trees. The bare patch became a pasture. To the other side of the pasture, a speck of sand became a perfectly formed little house. This was indeed a landscape!

She squinted, concentrating. The pasture clarified. There

were cows in it. She traced the route of the road passing by the house, and discovered a horse running along it. On the horse was a man.

"Like Gulliver's Travels," she murmured. Then, to clarify the reference for Seqiro, she amplified her spot memory: a man named Jonathan Swift had written a satire of the politics and customs of his time, phrased as Gulliver's voyages to the land of Lilliput with its six-inch-tall folk, and Brobdingnag with its giants. One of the voyages had been to a land of intelligent and refined horses. "I've been there too," she said. "That's where I found you, Seqiro."

The horse (the tiny one) galloped to the house. The man dismounted almost before the horse came to a stop, and dashed into the house. In a moment the tiny door opened again, and the man came out—with a woman. The man pointed—at Colene's face. The two stared up at her.

It was because of her the man had been hurrying home! To these folk, she was a monstrous giant peering down with unknown intent. They were terrified!

"Hey, I'm just curious," she murmured, afraid that her breath might blow them away.

It talks!

That was the man's thought—which Seqiro had relayed to her. She could communicate with them! Their minds must be wide open, or maybe the horse had become attuned to the mind-set of all the people of Julia.

Parts of both, Seqiro responded.

"I'm just a person, like you," she said to the tiny ones, letting her vocalization shape her thought. "I'm just passing through. I hope I didn't step on anyone."

Leave us alone, anima!

Obviously they *had* been doing damage as they tramped heedlessly across this planet! The best thing they could do for these people was to get away and let them repair the damage. Suddenly Colene felt awesomely responsible.

Yet was it any different back home on Earth? All her life she had walked without much regard for the tiny plants and bugs that might be under her feet. Didn't ants care whether they got squished? Now that it was people getting squished, she felt horribly guilty. This was evidently an animus planet, but that did not mean it was right to crush their people.

"I'm sorry," she said. A tear fell and splashed into the pasture, spooking a cow.

She got up, quickly but carefully. Where could she put her great lethal feet, so she wouldn't do more damage?

She decided to put them in her own footprints. That way she would squish only what had already been squished. But she couldn't see her prints in the shadow.

I can tune in to what is there.

"Thanks, horsehead."

Now the impressions of the folk of this world came to her. Surprise. Incredulity. Denial. Horror. Grief.

Every footprint was a disaster area. Trees had been flattened, houses destroyed, people killed.

"Oh, my God!" Colene whispered. "What have I been doing?" But she had the answer. She had been destroying. She had been like an act of nature, wiping out people randomly, not even aware. Gravity might not be any more, for her, but it seemed that she felt exactly like a giant to the folk underfoot.

"Seqiro, guide my feet!" she pleaded, blinded by tears and horror.

They walked back to the others, treading in their own prints. "We've got to get out of here!" Colene cried. Without waiting, she hit them with what she had learned.

"Oh, I never thought!" Nona cried, sitting up. "I knew there were people, but—"

"But you didn't make the connection," Darius finished. "None of us did. It was too far from our experience."

That was true. He was the rational one, Colene remembered. But now they knew, and they could not ignore it.

"How many more of these little planets must we pass before we get to Jupiter?" Darius asked Nona.

"I don't know. Several. Some will be larger than this, some smaller."

"Can we take a longer hop?" Colene asked.

"We can try." Nona walked to the sea, stood in it, and concentrated, tuning in on the filament ahead.

After a bit, she reported that there were two worlds she might reach near the main star. One was larger than this one; the other was smaller. Both were anima.

"Star?" Colene asked.

Nona's thought clarified the concept. A star was not what Colene imagined; it was merely the point at which several filaments diverged. Those on major lines were big and bright; those on minor lines were lesser structures. Those with many rays were brighter than those with few rays. Oria's sun was the nearest large star on an adjacent filament, with ninety-eight rays, closer to them than their own ninety-nine-ray star. But this particular little star had only three rays, so was hardly recognizable.

Darius cut directly to business. "If we take the smaller world, we will risk treading on many more little folk, unless our feet touch only the tops of mountains and they are safe in the valleys."

"No, folk live on mountaintops too," Nona said.

"If we take the larger world, we will have a better chance of seeing where we put our feet."

That seemed to be the better choice. Nona changed the pillows back to threads so they wouldn't suffocate any little folk, and they got together for the jump.

Colene thought she was used to it, but this one turned out to be more dizzying than the last, because it covered considerably more distance. Now she was aware of the complicated convolutions of the filament; it was not jagged but infinitely curved, dancing this way and that as it wound through its intricate patterns. Throughout these patterns were tiny bugs, too small to step on or even to see, yet each was part of the route. Did all these have people too? At least they were not getting tramped on.

They arrived at the planetoid. This one was over ten times the diameter of the last, according to Nona's thought, or about a hundred miles. Colene couldn't see much of it, because the curve of its heads obscured the body. Was it large enough?

They stood astride the diminishing heads, as before, but the progression was longer. They were sliding off a boulder about thirteen feet in diameter, give or take five feet—in her dizziness she didn't care much about accuracy—to land on one about a hundred and fifty feet across. They walked around that, their heads pointing away from the surface of the head they were on, not away from the body beyond, so that they didn't have to jump down. Even so, it might have been easier to have Darius conjure them, but that magic had to be saved for the next effort.

The next head was about two miles in diameter, and felt more like a planetoid in itself. Now she remembered to watch for the works of people, and she saw them. Their houses were about two inches high, and the people themselves about one inch in stature.

"Stop here," she said. "I'll ask them how we can get through without hurting them."

She squatted, and brought her hand down carefully to point at one tiny man who defended his barn bravely with a pitchfork. Her vision sharpened so that she could see his face clearly. "You," she said for Seqiro to forward. "I will talk to you. We are traveling through from a larger world. We don't want to step on any of you. Can you tell us a way to go so that we can put our feet down safely?"

Perhaps the man had had experience with travelers. Maybe that was why he lived here near the point of arrival. At any rate, he did not freak out. "Animus or anima?" he demanded.

That set Colene back. Which force did they represent?

"Anima," Nona said.

"Anima, hiding from animus," Colene told the farmer. "Going to bring the anima, if we can."

The farmer smiled. "Then pass with our blessing. There is a path by the south side." He gestured, pointing the direction.

"Thank you." Colene stood carefully. She did not need to repeat the information; the others had received it too.

They stepped carefully to the south, setting their feet down in empty pastures or barren areas. They found the path; apparently there had been a blight in this region, leaving a depopulated strip. They walked along it, alert for healthy sections, which they avoided by moving to the side or by simply stepping over. Colene was glad she had fashioned underclothing, because she was wary of what little folk might see as she stepped over them.

Now the projections of the planet were plain. They ranged in height from about five hundred feet down to unmeasurably small. This was the way of these fractal worlds, Colene knew; it hadn't been evident on Oria because they hadn't traveled enough on it by day. Also, people had plowed out most of the knobs, near the village, so as to use the land for crops. Man always did mess up the scenery. Here the mountains were shaped like boulders with smaller boulders perched on them, and smaller ones on the smaller ones, and so on without end. It was weird—but also true to the Mandelbrot set as she remembered it. True to the entire science of fractals and Julia sets.

They came to the next larger head, which looked to be about ten miles in diameter. Now Colene saw that there was a river or lake filling in the crevice between the small and large heads. Naturally the water of the planet had to flow somewhere, and since down was toward the center of each head, there was a section between heads where the attraction of both applied. That would be where the water collected. This would be a donut-shaped lake, technically a torus, circling the planet at this narrow section.

But the path did not extend across the next head. They had to hail another farmer. But Colene was getting experienced at this; she sent reassuring, friendly thoughts ahead, so that the man had a notion what she wanted before she actually broached the subject. He directed them to the north, where there had been extensive strip mining, and the land had been left mostly barren. Even some of the larger projecting spheres were gone, leaving the land oddly naked. "They are messing up their planet the same way we did Earth," she muttered.

By the time they made their way to the lake that demarked the next head, they were all physically tired except Seqiro, who seemed indefatigable. Ten miles was ten miles. "Say, you could have floated," Colene said to Nona.

"That would have taken similar energy—and depleted the magic I must save for the next conjuring," the woman replied.

True. There was no easy way across for any of them. "Actually we're not on a schedule, are we?" Colene asked, pursuing another thought. "We can take an extra day if we want to?"

"We can," Darius agreed.

"So why don't we rest the night, then conjure ourselves to the East Valley, and rest again until we're ready to make the long hop?"

They considered, and agreed. They camped by the lake, and stripped and washed themselves, then had a good meal. Nona looked so tired that Colene was hardly jealous of her fine body. Especially since Darius was carefully not looking. Then Colene thought of something else.

She walked to the nearest community of natives. "We

thank you for letting us cross your world," she said for Seqiro to relay. "Is there anything we can do in return for your hospitality?"

The little folk were taken aback. Then they rallied and decided that yes, there was something. They had a construction project that required the filling in of several large mine pits, and it was hard to spare the manpower for that. They had only recently thrown off the yoke of animus despots, and had little new magic, and there was much planetary damage to be undone.

Colene looked at Darius. "Can we move their earth for them, magically?"

"We don't need to," he replied. "We can shovel it physically, if we make big enough tools."

"We can make them," Nona agreed. "That's not the same magic as travel-conjuring, and I am not as fatigued by it."

"Tomorrow," Colene told the little folk. "Mark the earth you want moved, and mark where you want it moved to, and we'll do what we can."

"Agreed," the little folk said appreciatively.

This planet was oriented so that the light of the same great star that brought day to Oria slanted across at an angle to the head. Now dusk came, and then darkness, and the air cooled quickly. Nona had to make blankets for them all except Seqiro, who was satisfied to walk around grazing on the patches of grass and saplings.

"Come here, you little bundle of warmth," Darius told her. "I remember you from Earth."

She joined him and slept in his chaste embrace, delighted.

In the morning Nona floated up and spied the earth mounds and the pits beyond. Everything was marked; the little folk must have labored through the night. She returned to make shovels for the human folk, and a harness and drag for the horse. Then they marched to the first site and started shoveling and dragging, each of their giant shovelfuls the equivalent of ten thousand or a million native shovelfuls. Colene tried to work it out mathematically in her head, cubing one hundred, because each dimension was about a hundred times that of the equivalent for the little folk, but realized that this wouldn't work. It was science-reality figuring, and this was a magic reality, where the square-cube law did not hold and gravity was more or less independent of mass. At any rate, they were doing the job a whole lot faster than the little folk could.

Still, there was a lot of earth to move, and none of the three women were in physical condition to maintain such effort. In the end it was mostly Darius and Seqiro, both sweating profusely as they labored. By the close of day, the job was done. The formerly mounded and pitted terrain had been rendered into a level field.

The little folk were delighted. "We did not think you would do all of it!" their spokesman exclaimed. "We must reward you, O giants of another world."

Colene tried to demur, knowing that there was nothing the local folk could do to repay such heroic effort. "It is merely our thanks for your hospitality," she said.

"We still have the rest of the planet to traverse," Darius reminded her. "We can't walk it all; we'll need to conjure ourselves there. If they can show us good locations to land—"

"However," Colene continued smoothly, "we could use the favor of some information. We are afraid we will accidentally step on some of your people as we travel the length of the planet, so we prefer to conjure ourselves there. But we need to have a series of clear landing sites, lest we do harm arriving blindly. If you could provide information—"

"In the morning!" the spokesman agreed eagerly. "We are amazed that you possess such exotic magic." That reminded Colene that Darius' ability to conjure living folk was unknown in this universe; she would be more careful what she said about it henceforth.

Meanwhile, the natives put on a show for the entertainment of their giant guests. Their material magic remained weak, for their new generation of women were still girls, but their illusion was strong. They generated huge pictures (for them) against the backdrop of night, making images of their dancing—and it was truly evocative dancing. It was a costumed re-enactment of their overthrow of the despots across the world, after the animus had changed. It showed the despots, deprived of their magic, bowing down, and the theows assuming the mantle of dominion. The women performed a symbolic finale that suggested the magic their daughters would have, but was incidentally quite sexy. Especially when they threw off their red tunics and danced naked. She could feel Darius' appreciation. He did not regard the illusion pictures as real, so felt free to watch them intently. She would remember that; would he watch her dance naked if he thought she was an illusion image?

So they slept again. Colene was getting to like this little planet. It was remarkably similar to Oria, except for size; it would not have been possible to tell that its size differed had the five of them not been there for contrast. The proportions of the people were the same, and when they jumped, they took the same amount of time to land. There simply was no change because of the scale. This was just not a science reality.

In the morning the little folk had the information. There was a suitable site beside the lake that separated the main head from the body, forty miles away, and another near the East Sea. They could do it in two hops, if they wished, or one.

"These are longer jumps than we did before, on Oria," Darius said. "The filament isn't the same. Better to try the forty, then the hundred."

They set up for it. It was clear that the little folk meant well; their minds were quite open to Seqiro. The site was described as completely accessible, and Provos remembered no difficulty here. So Darius conjured Seqiro there first, then used his linkage with the horse's mind to conjure the others in turn to the vicinity. Colene was the first to follow Seqiro; then came Nona, Provos, and Darius himself.

Now they stood at the edge of the much larger lake separating the head from the body. It was quite similar to the one they had left, in all respects apart from size. That was the nature of this fractal universe: *everything* was self-similar.

They made a similar series of conjurations to the East Sea. This was just like the one they had left on Oria, only much smaller. But they decided to rest one more day before making the final conjuration to Jupiter.

RESTED, they used a new weighted diving bell to march down under the water. This time the journey was brief, and soon they stood astride the East Filament.

They joined together, in bodies and minds, and sailed up along the filament. This time Colene saw even more: how they zoomed along at lightspeed (or magic-speed), down into the juncture of three rays, and indeed it seemed like another dimension, for she felt as if they were accelerating toward infinite velocity while traveling a path extending toward infinity. Then suddenly the infinities met and canceled, and they were zooming out of the well and toward Jupiter, which now loomed awesomely huge.

They landed on the smallest feasible head of the head of one of the major projections on the side of Jupiter. The connected heads became much larger than Oria, and Jupiter itself was almost unimaginable.

Now there was no concern about stepping on the natives. Rather, they would have to be concerned about being stepped on by the natives. The tiniest head might be small, but Jupiter was large, so the natives would be Jupiter-scale. This was certainly the home of the fabled Megaplayers; the size was right.

But first they had to rest, for Darius and Nona were exhausted by their joint effort of travel. Colene decided to make herself useful by harvesting a berry or grain of wheat and making a nonmagical meal for them. However, she needed water, and wood for a fire. So she and Seqiro got busy.

Provos joined her without being asked. They had camped at the edge of a forest of what appeared to be literally mile-high trees; there was plenty of wood in the form of fallen twigs, which were full-sized logs to them.

There was a lake nearby. Colene headed for it, but Provos held her back. "There is a bad memory," she explained.

So they took another path. Colene looked to the side, to see what might be on the one she would have taken.

She saw an ant. It was a foot long. Suddenly she realized that their most immediate danger was not the Megaplayers.

CHAPTER 6

DARIUS nodded, watching. He was tired, but he still did not care to let Colene go into a strange world alone. An ant, twenty times the size of what he had known. That would be the least of it. What about the birds and snakes?

"Seqiro, can you stun animals?" he inquired, not raising his voice. He had found that it was not the sound, but the thought that counted; the speech tended to focus the thought suitably. The horse was with Colene, but well within mental range. Darius wanted their dialogue to be private, and the horse could pick that up too, and would honor it.

I can, if their minds are not closed. Human minds tend to be guarded, even in realities where telepathy is not known, but animal minds tend to be open. I have been fortunate in my ability to attune to the minds of the smaller folk, perhaps because some of these are anima, like Nona.

"Then you may be our main protection against monsters, as well as our main means of communication with the human giants here."

I will do what I can.

He turned to Nona. The young woman was spread out on her magically made pillow-mattress, attractive though she wasn't trying to be. "Can you conjure weapons?" Again, Seqiro could pick up both the thought and the person for whom it was intended. Also, which thought was to be relayed, and which was not. Darius was really coming to appreciate the horse's ability.

"Yes," she replied, in her own language. "But I am not expert in their use."

"Some weapons do not require expertise. Colene has told me of guns."

"Of what?"

"Colene, describe a gun for Nona."

Colene, now dipping water from a pond that was probably no more than a puddle to this world, obliged with a mental picture of a small metal object with a short tube projecting.

"I can not fetch such a thing, for I know of none," Nona said. "I can make something that looks similar, if you wish."

"That won't work," Colene said. "They have to be made exactly right, and have bullets."

"Bullets?"

"Little bits of metal that shoot out."

"I do not understand how that could be a weapon."

Darius sympathized, for he found the notion confusing too. "No guns," he said. "Knives, spears—they should help."

"Illusions can be effective too," she said. "Often they can fool the animals, so there is no need for violence."

"Yes, Colene used an illusion to thwart Knave Naylor," Darius agreed with satisfaction. "Seqiro can do that, in a fashion. But his illusions are strictly in the mind of the person he touches, no one else."

"Yes, it is a marvelous power," she agreed. "My illusions are visible to everyone; I can not limit them like that."

"The two of you, working together, should be able to discourage almost anything."

"It is nice to be with Seqiro," she said.

Darius realized that Nona, despite her powers, was basically an innocent woman, lacking some of the hard edges Colene had. She hardly seemed the type to change a world. Perhaps it was just as well that she had fallen in with their party, because things were bound to get un-innocent soon enough. "Yes, it is nice," he agreed.

Colene and Provos returned with water. "But I could have conjured that," Nona protested.

"You're supposed to be resting," Colene reminded her. "I'm going to forage something to cook."

"But I can transform—" Nona started. Then Darius'

warning thought registered: it was a thing Colene needed to do. So she compromised by transforming a hair into a fine tuber, then floating it quietly to a place where Colene would soon find it. Darius did not protest; he was in doubt about the safety of natural food here. It could be spoiled or poisonous, despite seeming all right.

They made a meal from the tuber, and this worked well, because it was by no coincidence of the type that became delicious when boiled. Then they formed a barricade-shelter by the base of a towering tree, walling the huge world out. It was large enough to include Seqiro. It seemed snug and safe, but Darius knew that any large animal could crush it with one foot. He still felt insecure.

Then he had an idea. "Nona, can you make an illusion that will remain without further effort?"

"Yes, as long as I am near it."

"Can you make an illusion of the base of the tree covering this shelter, so that it seems to be part of the tree from outside?"

"I can do that. Do you want it to smell like the tree also?"

"Yes! Excellent. That will camouflage us, so maybe we won't be bothered."

Even so, they decided to take turns awake, watching. There were peepholes in the shelter facing in four directions: east, south, west, and up. If there was anything suspicious, Seqiro was supposed to be awakened first, and if he verified hostility or hunger near, he would alert the others.

Fortunately there was no emergency, and they were able to get a fairly good night's rest.

Darius had the first watch. The others settled down, but Colene remained awake. It seemed she wanted to talk to him. Probably the horse remained awake too, connecting their minds. "Why were you hugging Nona?"

Oh. He should have known that she would not forget that detail, from the time he had been with the woman and horse. "I do not care to conjure more than one person at a time, so I had to carry her."

"Why not?"

"That is the natural safe limit of sympathetic magic," he explained. "A person can conjure himself or another person, but it is not wise to—"

"Back in your home reality, maybe. But here maybe things are different. Did you ever try more than one *here?*"

He was surprised. "This is possible. I shall have to try." He marked two circles on the ground, almost touching because there was little room. Then he brought out the Darius and Colene icons. "If you will—"

"Gotcha." She moved so as to stand wedged beside him in one circle.

He invoked the two icons, then moved them toward the other circle. He moved—and so did she. Now they were wedged together in the other circle. "It *is* different here! I can not transfer joy, but I do seem to be able to conjure simultaneously with assurance." He could tell by the feel of it.

"So now you won't have to hug Nona any more."

He looked down at her. "That is unfortunate." Then they laughed.

Nona took the next watch, and Darius lay down. But Colene remained awake. Darius could sleep when he chose, but was curious about Colene's next move. Was she going to tell Nona what she had told him?

Not so. "You don't wear anything under your tunic," Colene said.

"That is true," Nona agreed. "No one does, unless it is cold."

"Men don't either?"

"It is unnecessary. The tunic covers everything."

"What about when the wind blows hard?"

"It is not hard to keep a tunic in place."

"But don't your breasts sag?"

"Sag? Yes, with age. That is natural."

"Well, I have news for you. They look better and last better if they are supported. The flesh doesn't get pulled out of shape. Here, I'll show you." Colene pulled off her tunic, revealing her crudely torn and tied halter and pants. "See, I don't have nearly the stuff you do, but when I have the right uplift, it looks almost as if I do. And if I wear the right kind of pants, my tummy looks better too."

"That is true!" Nona agreed, intrigued. "And such a garment prevents the deterioration of age?"

"Sure. Let me show you the design, and you can make me a good bra and panties."

"Yes. Then I will make them for myself."

Darius knew that Colene was doing this so that Nona would no longer expose her torso when she changed tunics, or bounce as obviously when she walked. That was just as well; he had found Nona's body to be most distracting, whether viewed from a distance or held close. He had tried to do the proper thing, and not look, but the responsibility to hide her private flesh was really the woman's. It would be better yet if both of them wore full female diapers, but he knew it would be useless to suggest that. The women of other cultures simply lacked the appropriate modesty of those of his own reality. Colene exposed herself deliberately, to taunt him, and Nona did so because she felt it was all right when washing among friends; both were driving him moderately mad.

He allowed himself to drift to sleep, while Nona used her magic to make the type of garments Colene wanted. He was glad that Colene was taking a positive approach. He did not care to risk her negative approach.

When he woke, he found a pair of undershorts beside him. Colene had arranged for him to be clothed under his tunic too. He put them on without comment.

NEXT day they set out for a suitable Megaplayer. They did this by helping Nona to gain a local familiar, which was a large (to them) bird, then conjuring themselves as a group to the promising sites the bird spotted. Several such jumps took them onto a larger head of Jupiter, where farms were spotted. Nona had a certain sense about which native person might be amenable to their approach, and Seqiro verified this. But it was Provos who was decisive: she did not remember the first prospect, or the second, or the third. Darius trusted her memory, so they kept searching until Provos acquiesced. So it was that they came to the house of an artisan who lived alone.

This was an older man garbed in green who carved intricately in wood and stone. Plaques, statuettes, and linked figures filled his shelves. There were several musical instruments of exactly the type and size they had seen by the seaside cliff on Oria. The giant's mind was open; he responded immediately to Seqiro's first questing thought. Just like that, they had communication with a Megaplayer.

"We need your help," Darius said to the man.

"I hear you, but I do not see you," the giant responded, looking around.

"We are from Oria, a smaller world. We seek to bring the anima."

"Then show yourselves."

Nona made an illusion picture, so large that the man could see it without difficulty. It showed the group of them.

"A man, three women, and a horse, all in little-world scale," the giant said. "This is not the way the animus passes."

Nona stepped forward, in the image. "I am the ninth of the ninth," she said. "I can bring the anima—but I need the help of the Megaplayers."

The giant considered the image. Darius, viewing it with a man's eye, knew it was impressive; Nona was about as pretty a young woman as could be found, in form and feature. Colene's advice about the supportive undergarment now caused Nona's bosom to manifest magnificently despite the unflattering tunic. She was also nice, and Seqiro was sending the impression of that niceness to the giant. Even though there was such a disparity in size that she could never be a romantic prospect for such a man, such an image and impression had to be highly conducive. It was for Darius, who was as surely barred from her as was the giant, for different reason.

But the man waggled a finger at them warningly, now looking directly at them where they stood on the sill. "Do not seek to use your magic on me," he said. As he spoke, he floated up, not far, but it was clear that his feet no longer touched the floor. A knife appeared in his hand, became a hammer, and floated back to its tool-box.

"You are a despot!" Nona exclaimed, astonished and dismayed. "But you are not in black!"

"I am a man," the giant replied. "Call me Angus. Not all of those with magic choose to be despotic. Some prefer to be creative. I wear green because I am uncommitted to any class or creed."

That was evidently true. This man lived alone and was a craftsman, though he was not compelled to do or be either. He had no concern with status; that was why Seqiro had not picked up on it. But his magic and his mind made him dangerous. He could destroy them in an instant, if he chose.

"I am Nona. How can I convince you?"

"I know something of this matter," Angus said. "I have no special commitment to the existing order, and am willing to see it change. But the man could be doing the magic, and you may be a pretender trying to deceive me. You must demonstrate your special power of anima."

Nona hesitated. "But I do not know what this is," she said. "That is why I have come to you."

Darius hoped that this confession did not destroy her credibility. It was true that a despot man would have all the powers of magic Nona could show, so that only in the absence of the others could she demonstrate it. But it would not be wise for them to separate. The giant might simply make her captive in a cage secured by magic, and none of her talents would free her then. Of course Darius would be able to conjure her out, but that would prove only his magic, not hers.

"The true harbinger of anima will have the power of music," Angus said.

"I can play!" Nona said. "All my life—"

"This is more than training," Angus said. "This is the most subtle but powerful magic, apart from the invocation of the anima itself. It is the power to persuade any person of any world to do your will. To serve you voluntarily, and never betray you. Play that music for me, and I will serve you. I will not do so otherwise."

"But I can not—would not want to compel—"

"You would give up your destiny?"

"No!"

"Then put it to the test, little woman. Play."

"But I did not bring my instruments!"

Angus arched a brow. "You lack the magic of compaction?" The hammer reappeared in his hand. Then it shrank, becoming a miniature of itself. When it was so small it would fit Nona's hand, it floated to her at the sill.

She caught it, surprised. "I can't do that." She reconsidered. "That is, not that way. I could transform it into something else which is larger or smaller, of a different substance, then reshape it, but it would not be exactly the same in detail."

"Try it, Nona," he said. "Restore it to proper size."

She looked doubtfully at the hammer, and concentrated. The hammer expanded.

Nona was so surprised she dropped it. But it hovered as if caught by an unseen hand; Angus had used his magic. It remained as it had been when her hand left it, about twice its prior size.

She took it again, and it resumed its growth. It became

as large as she was, and larger, so that she no longer supported it; instead she merely touched it while it floated. When it was a monster four times her body length she removed her hand. She had done it.

"So you have that magic," Angus said, as the hammer floated back to him. "But is it yours—or the man's?" He glanced at Darius.

"My magic differs," Darius said. He brought out his icon, marked two circles, designated them in his mind, and moved the doll from one to the other. In this manner he conjured himself to the sill on the opposite side of the room. "I am here," he said from behind the giant.

"That was not illusion," Angus said. "Now I am impressed. There is no magic of this nature on this world."

"I am from another reality. Our magic is sympathetic."

"You also have the mind-talk?"

"No. That is Seqiro, the horse. He is from still another reality."

"And the old and young women?"

"From two other realities," Darius said. "One remembers what is to come, and the other deals in science, which is another specialized form of magic."

"You are a remarkable group!" Angus exclaimed.

"But we need your help, for our separate reasons," Darius said.

"Let Nona play, and I may be persuaded," Angus said.

"But I have no dulcimer," Nona protested. "I can not make one that would work; I lack the craftsmanship. Had I realized that I could do the magic of compaction—I did not know it was possible—I would have brought it along. Do you have one that—?"

"I do not," Angus said firmly. "But if I did, I would not lend it to you. The instrument must be of your world, for your magic to work with it. All folk are linked to their worlds, and draw on the magic of their worlds, even when on other worlds. If you are anima, you are anima for your world only; the rule differs for my world."

Darius realized that that made sense. Nona was magical because she was the ninth of the ninth, and that surely was the requirement for Oria. It would not be for Jupiter.

Nona was appalled. "But to go all the way back for my dulcimer—"

"There may be an alternative," Angus said. "I am something of an archaeologist, my interest being in tracing the routes of the diaspora of original mankind. On occasion there are items left behind. There is a site not far from here which I have worked intermittently, as my interest allows. There may be a suitable instrument there, in the section I have not yet done. My illusion pictures are indistinct, but I think there is a dulcimer. If you can fetch it without disturbing the rest of the site, you can use that one."

"Why not just conjure it here?" Darius asked.

"Because the site would collapse into the hole left by its vacancy," Angus said. "That would not be expedient excavation."

"What does a collapse matter?" Darius asked, perplexed.

Colene interceded. "It matters," she said. "I was on a dig once—it was only a one-afternoon class, sort of, but I learned some things. They don't want to disturb anything until they survey it in, or it messes up the tally. They can learn things from the context, like what's above and below it. But if things get hopelessly jumbled, that's no good."

"The one from the science world," Angus said approvingly.

"Very well: no disturbance," Darius said, still not quite understanding the importance, but pleased that Colene had made an impression. "Where is this place?"

"Follow me," Angus said, floating toward the door.

"Wait!" Darius cried. "Only Nona can fly. The rest of us have to conjure."

"Then come here," the giant said, holding out his hand.

Darius looked at Provos. She was already nodding, anticipating his query in the way she had. It was safe.

He conjured them in turn to the waiting hand, stepping each icon there: Provos, Colene, Seqiro, and himself. He might have done them as a group, but he remained in doubt just how safe that was, and there was no need at the moment. Nona floated independently, ready to follow.

Angus closed his hand gently about them. They each stood the height of one of his fingers: Darius matched the middle one, Provos the index, and Colene the little. Nona would have matched the next smallest finger. The horse's head was higher than any, but that didn't count: Seqiro had the giant's other hand to himself, being too big to share the first one.

Angus floated out and up, with Nona trailing. They flew over the tremendous trees. "Like an airplane," Colene breathed, unafraid. Provos also seemed to be enjoying the experience, remembering its safe conclusion. Seqiro could tell from the giant's mind that no harm was intended. That left only Darius nervous, though he tried to conceal it. The travel along the filaments had been like icon conjuring, under his shared control, but this was different. If he should fall—

He felt a hand take his. Colene, offering comfort. As she had when they had first met, in her reality.

His love for her manifested explosively. She was young, and often hard to adjust to, but she was the one. Once they made it back to his reality she would not be his wife, but she would be his love. What a blessing that would be!

He felt her love returning. They were connected, by Seqiro's ability, and she had received his feeling. That was all they needed.

Angus descended. The flight was ending, and Darius had entirely lost track of it.

They settled by an overgrown hillside. The mountain was honeycombed with caves, many far too small for Angus. It was becoming clearer why excavation was no easy matter; the giant would have to remove everything from the front of a cave to get at the back of it. But they, being so much smaller, could enter and go directly to the spot they wanted.

"I used an insect as a familiar and verified that there were small-world artifacts within this cave," Angus said, setting them down before it. "I believe they are from your world, Oria as you call it. But I had no immediate need to excavate here, so left it undisturbed."

Colene assessed the situation. "We'll have to shore it up where we dig or take anything," she said. "So it won't fill in. We'll need planks or something."

"That did not occur to me," Angus said, surprised.

"That is because your magic is not science," Colene said smugly.

"I can make planks," Nona said.

Colene peered into the cave. It was originally larger, but the base had been filled in by refuse so that only the top of it remained open. A man could walk inside if he stooped. "We can't all go in there," she said. "We'd just make a traffic jam."

"A what?" Nona asked.

Colene made an image of metal boxlike objects with wheels at their bases lined up on a road, just sitting there. This evidently made no sense to Nona, but Darius was able to fathom it, having seen such vehicles in Colene's reality. It seemed that at times there were too many of them for the road to hold. "We would get in each other's way," he explained.

"Then I will go in alone to fetch the instrument," Nona said.

"No." It was Provos. She indicated Darius.

"I'm to go with her?" he asked, but was receiving the affirmative before he finished speaking.

Darius looked at Colene. "The rest of us will stay out here and talk with Angus," Colene said.

So it was decided. "Light," Darius said, not liking the darkness in the depth of the cave. He had saved some of Colene's matches, which were little science-sticks for making fire, but Nona made light simply by fashioning an illusion of a lamp.

Darius thought about that as they moved in. An illusion which cast real light. Wasn't it then a real lamp? The point of a lamp was to make light; it didn't have to be physical.

The cave wound into the mountain. He had not realized that it would be so deep. He discovered that he did not really like such confinement; he knew that the rock above was unlikely to collapse right at this moment, after being firm for perhaps thousands of years, but somehow he feared it might. He hoped to get the job done and go back out as soon as possible.

Something scuttled ahead. The light moved to illuminate it. It was a roach—half again as long as his foot. Darius was disgusted, and actually a bit afraid of it. It wasn't that he thought it could hurt him, but that he didn't want it to touch him. How could he get rid of it without contact?

"Can you make an image of a roach-eating creature?" he asked Nona.

"I can—but I don't think they use eyes as we do," she said. "It might not work."

Nevertheless, a bird appeared, peering around as if searching out bugs. The bird hopped toward the roach, and its feet made a scritching noise as they touched the floor.

The roach spun about and scooted away.

Maybe it heard better than it saw, Darius thought. But he hadn't realized that her illusions covered sound as well as sight. Queen Glomerula's picture of Colene and Knave Naylor had been soundless.

"Oh, yes," Nona said. "Sight, sound, and smell. But touch is harder to do, and it is more versatile when direct, instead of through a familiar."

That helped explain it. The queen had had to use a spider or insect as a familiar.

They went on. The passage broadened into a larger cavern, with stalactites directly over their path. Darius didn't like that either; they were too massive, too pointed, too close. Surely they would not fall—yet if one did, it would be devastating. They cast gross moving shadows across the cavern and each other.

The two of them came to the end of the chamber, and that was it: the end. There was no way out except the way they had entered.

The lamp brightened, illuminating the whole chamber. The floor was a mass of rubble and dirt and animal droppings. If the nether portion of the cavern had expanded as much as the upper section, the rubbish was several feet deep. How were they to find anything useful in that, without disturbing it and spoiling the giant's archaeology?

"Look," Nona said, pointing. "A psaltry!"

"A what?" But her meaning was coming through; he must have pulled the name out of a forgotten recess of his mind. A primitive type of harp.

Only this was no kind of harp he recognized. The thing was a tall thin wooden triangle, with a circular opening near the base and three rows of pegs below that.

"But it is broken," she said sadly, picking it up. "See, the strings are gone, and most of the pegs along the top, and there is no bow."

"Bow?" But again her meaning was registering: this was an instrument played with a bow across the strings, though it was unlike any he had seen before.

"Where there is one, there may be another," she said. "But buried, out of sight. It may be broken too, but perhaps I can fix it. If only I can find it."

"Could you get a familiar to search it out?" he asked. "I

mean, a small creature, a little mite, something that can go down between the rocks, through the crevices—"

"A gnat!" she said. "There are some in here." She stooped, feeling through the air with her hands. "Help me, Seqiro," she murmured.

Then she had it: she had located and tamed a gnat, just as she had the bat on Oria. "Go down through the crevices," she told the gnat. "Show me what you see."

There was a noise, but not of any gnat. Darius stared back toward the entrance tunnel. A pair of eyes were staring back at him. "Trouble, I think," he muttered.

A rat, Seqiro thought. *I can sense it, but can not enter its mind to control it. That is a vicious creature.*

"A weapon," Darius said. "I need a weapon."

Nona picked up a chip of rock. In her hands it became a great broadsword with a shiny steel blade. She gave it to him. Then she made a long spear with a trident tip for herself. "I have no flair for combat," she said. "But maybe I can at least hold it at bay from me."

"Combat isn't my specialty either," he admitted. He had carried a sword, but lost it when the despots made them change to green tunics. He had not had any skill with its use; it was merely better than bare hands against animals.

He stepped toward the rat. He saw now that the thing was close to the size of a horse, but short-legged so that it could fit through the small tunnel. It must have come in from an offshoot along the way, smelling them. "Back! Back!" he cried. "Away, vermin!"

The rat moved to the side. It evinced no fear, only caution. It wasn't sure about them, and had no intention of leaving until it knew whether they represented prey.

They had to get rid of it. Darius stepped toward it—and his ankle turned on a loose stone, making him stumble.

Instantly the rat charged. Darius lunged with the sword, stabbing it in the shoulder, but its tough hide snagged the blade and wrenched the sword out of Darius' hand. The rat crashed into him, biting at his face, and he fell on his back, helpless.

The rat pinned him to the floor and bit at his left shoulder. He felt the sharp front teeth sink in, slicing through tunic and flesh, but there was no pain.

"Back! Back!" Nona cried, poking at the rat's snout with her trident. The beast made a sound that might have been a squeak had it been small, but was a hissing snarl now. Its head whipped around, and it caught the shaft of the spear between its teeth. The thing was hauled from Nona's hands, and she fell back, terrified.

"Dagger!" Darius cried, still pinned.

One appeared in Nona's hand, then floated across to his right hand, which was closest to her. He clutched it so that it pointed up, moved his hand down under the beast's throat, and stabbed up. He seemed to score only on loose folds of skin, which moved aside without being penetrated. So he moved farther down, trying for the belly as the rat tried again for his face. The mouth opened, and its hot breath came down on his face as his hand rammed up with all the force he could muster.

This time he scored. The blade dug into the soft, tight underbelly of the rodent. Darius hauled it forward, sawing open a gash. He felt blood pouring out, soaking his tunic, but that was good, because it was the rat's.

The rat's head paused. Then the thing scrambled off and away. The dagger was hauled away with it, embedded. He might not have hurt the creature seriously, but he had given it something to think about, and it probably wouldn't return in a hurry.

Now his left shoulder started hurting. His mind had cut off the pain before, but it could do so no longer. He was gravely injured. He struggled to get to his feet, but the pain over-whelmed him.

"Darius!" It was Nona, trying to help him up.

"It's no use," he gasped. "My shoulder—any motion—the pain—"

"I can help," she said. "Let me touch the wound." She kneeled beside him and slid her left hand into his torn tunic, around to his shoulder.

To his amazement, the pain faded. "You have anesthetic magic!" he gasped.

"Yes." She kept her hand on him, but changed her position, sitting down, leaning back against the cave wall, her legs extended beside him. "Let me get you closer." She tried to haul him up with her free hand, but couldn't.

Darius took advantage of the cessation of pain to sit up. Then she put her right arm around him from behind and hauled him back down against her. His head landed on her soft bosom. He tried to protest, but she held him close, reaching farther around him with her right arm until her right hand joined her left inside his tunic. She had him pinned to her, but it was a far different sensation than that of the rat pinning.

Then he realized that not only was the pain abating, so was the injury. He could feel the torn tendons and flesh knitting themselves together, the blood clearing. She wasn't just making him comfortable, she was healing him!

"Yes," she murmured in his ear. "But it works best when I am closest. Please don't move."

He started to turn his head, but that only put his cheek against her breast. He decided to follow orders and remain quite still. It wasn't as if there was anything unpleasant about this position. He was suffering the most delicious type of captivity imaginable. But if Colene caught him like this—

I'll settle with you later, Colene's thought came.

Oh, that mind communication! Sometimes it was downright inconvenient.

Yes, Colene's thought came. But there was laughter in it. She understood the situation. *Thank God I got her to put on a halter.*

Darius thought about that—and decided *not* to think about it. So he thought about Colene instead.

Good.

Which was one of the things about Colene: she really wasn't the jealous type. She got upset when she saw him with other women—there had been one very awkward scene with a cat-woman called Pussy—but that was because she felt he should be paying such attention to Colene herself. He frustrated her by refusing to take advantage of her in her youth. So Colene had reason for her reactions. She did not react from misunderstandings. She would torment him about this present situation, but never lose sight of the reality.

Oh, yeah?

He hoped.

The bosom moved. Nona was laughing now. She had been picking this up too. Damn that horse!

You can not expect an animal to appreciate the nuances of the human condition.

And that was Seqiro himself—who could indeed appreciate such nuances, when in contact with human minds.

"Have your fun, beast," Darius muttered.

In a surprisingly brief time his shoulder was entirely

healed. He flexed his arm and could find no pain, no problem. Now Nona let him get up; she was done with him.

"How can I thank you?" he asked her sincerely.

"You gained your injury defending me from the monster," she pointed out. "It was only right that I help you recover."

She had a point. "Let's just say that I am impressed," he said.

You sure are!

"And I do thank you," he continued doggedly.

Nona nodded, just as if nothing else were going on. "You are welcome."

He glanced down at himself. The blood was caking on his tunic, and it remained torn where the rat had bitten him. In fact the blood had soaked through to his new undershorts. What a mess!

"Change it," she suggested. In her hand appeared a new tunic, generated from a thread of the old. Then, after a pause, a new pair of shorts too. Colene had taught her well.

He did not hesitate. He pulled off his soiled items and used their clean portions to wipe off the blood that remained on him, with the help of some water Nona conjured. Then he pulled on the new clothing. After what she had done for his body, she could see any part of it she wanted to. It wasn't the first time.

Yeah, but I was there, before.

"You are still here," he murmured in response.

Then they resumed their search for the instrument. The gnat had been buzzing through the crevices all this while, and Nona had been receiving its reports. Suddenly she jumped. "That's it!" she exclaimed, clapping her hands.

They used the shaft of the trident to pry the covering rubble up, carefully, and set it aside. In a moment the surface of a container showed. The thing was sealed in its own case! That was a break they hardly deserved.

Darius lifted out the box, and Nona immediately made a similar box of the same size and shape and set it in the hole. Then they replaced the covering rocks. The site had been restored, except for the one borrowed article.

Nona opened the case. There lay a trapezoidal object with a number of strings stretched from pegs on either side across two central bridges. Beneath the strings were two holes decorated by rose patterns.

Darius stared. He had seen something like this before. But where? He had no idea what it was.

"At the cliffs by the sea," Nona said. "The instruments of the Megaplayers."

That was it! Those huge stone devices—one was just like this, only this one was of a size to be handled by a person of Nona's stature. It was ironic that the huge instrument was there on small Oria, while the small one was here on huge Jupiter. Each in the wrong world.

"It is a dulcimer," Nona said, admiring it. "A hammered dulcimer, and here are the hammers. Its magic has protected it all these years, and I will be able to play it once I tune it. This is a beautiful instrument, better than mine."

"A beautiful instrument," he echoed. It was indeed that, physically; it glistened as if made yesterday.

She closed the case. Then Darius led the way out of the cavern, alert for any appearance of the rat, while Nona carried the precious dulcimer.

They emerged to bright daylight; their eyes had become accustomed to the lesser light of her illusion lamp, which she had managed to maintain throughout. Colene was there, as he blinked, adjusting. "What's this about you in the arms of another woman?" she demanded. But she couldn't hold the pose; she hugged him. "I'm glad you're not torn up, you rascal."

Darius decided not to say anything.

Angus flew them back to his home. This time Nona rode too, carrying the ancient instrument.

At the house Nona got to work on the dulcimer, adjusting the strings, making sure everything was sound. Darius learned that the others had become better acquainted during their wait outside the cave. Angus was interested in their world of origin, and especially interested in Colene's statement that all the members of their little party came from different variants of that same world. He had not believed in other realities, but was becoming convinced as Seqiro showed him mental pictures of the Virtual Mode. "I had thought our universe was vast and varied," he said. "I may have underestimated the case."

"The Virtual Mode has been an amazement to all of us," Darius said. "Every layer of it is another reality, each complete

in itself, just as this one is. But they may have different fundamental laws as well as different customs. Colene and I are still
working out our differences, which are mostly cultural."

"Even when there is a common culture, in all the universe, it can be difficult," Angus said. "I have studied the
legends of our people, trying to align them with the evidence I
find in the ground, and they do offer insights."

Nona looked up. "It is ready," she said. She had set the
dulcimer up on a stand she had made, so that she could sit and
play it conveniently. It tilted up and back, the broad side at the
base, the narrow side away from her. "But I do not know
whether I can do the type of magic you suggest. I have
never—"

"You have never played on a magic instrument," Angus
said.

"Yes. Only common ones are allowed for theows."

"Play it, then, little woman," Angus said. "The magic
will manifest—or it will not. Then we shall know."

Nona took her two delicate hammers, which looked like
oversized needles, being no more than delicate little pieces of
wood and felt with needle-eye circles on the ends, and she
addressed the dulcimer. She touched the strings, and the music
began.

Darius had heard and enjoyed music many times, and
was familiar with the sound of many instruments. But he was
surprised by the finesse with which Nona played. Her little
hammers touched the strings so rapidly that it seemed she was
striking randomly, but the tune indicated otherwise. This was
a divine melody. It was so delicate it seemed faint, yet it also
seemed to fill the universe. It touched his heart and shook the
mighty planet with the same refrain.

As he listened, Darius was satisfied that whatever it was
that Nona had to do, he was bound to support it. Her mission
was right and necessary. The rest of his life did not matter.

The piece was all too brief. When it ended, he could
remember none of the melody or harmony. He knew only that
their decision to help this woman had been correct.

It was Angus who spoke. "It is true," he said. "You are
the one. You have the magic of conversion, and I will help you
in whatever way I can, until you have accomplished your purpose."

We all will, Seqiro thought, interpreting the sentiment of the others.

Darius realized that it had been only to enlist the active help of the giant that Nona had played the dulcimer. But the magic had touched them all. They were all committed to her mission.

"Thank you," Nona said. "But I know so little—only that I must enlist the help of the Megaplayers."

"By that you mean those who left the large instruments on your world," Angus said. "I can tell you a good deal about that. But perhaps it will be easier to understand if first I tell you one of our leading myths, which I think is not current on your own world."

"A myth?" Nona asked. "What I want is to bring the anima. How can a myth relate to that?"

"It does relate," the giant assured her. "It concerns the bringing of the animus to Jupiter by a peon named Earle. I believe it will provide insight into a task whose nature you may not as yet perfectly understand."

She considered that. She nodded. "It is true that there is no such myth among my people. We don't even have peons; we have theows. If you believe it will help—"

"I believe it will. Then we shall discuss it, and perhaps come to understand how to accomplish your purpose. Make yourselves comfortable, for the telling will take an hour."

Nona made pillows for them all, and they settled down to listen to the Myth of Earle.

CHAPTER 7

EARLE

IN the early eons, the anima governed our world you call Jupiter, and the women had the magic and ruled the men. Earle was too virile for this, and resolved to bring the animus and set things right. He was the firstborn son of the firstborn son, down through the eight generations since the anima had taken hold. He alone had the power, for the amazons had killed all the other perfect firstborn males on all the other worlds. Jupiter was a tiny world in an almost endless chain of worlds along a filament that went into a dead-end curl. This alone accounted for its being overlooked by the dread forces of the anima. They had killed most firstborns here too, but had been somewhat lax in the outlying provinces, so his family line had escaped.

So Earle had magic, and he dared not show it. But if he could bring the animus, then he could found a new and glorious age of men, replacing the tyranny of women. Yet how could he accomplish his purpose? He didn't know, and did not dare inquire. So to his friends and associates he was merely an ordinary peon with a certain flair for music who might, were he lucky, be employed to entertain the amazons at court instead of having to labor as a weed-chopper. Actually his power of music, too, was greater than others knew; he could hammer the dulcimer so cleverly and sweetly as to charm the very bees of the flower fields into dancing, and the honey in their combs to added sweetness. But he had the caution to mute this ability too.

He reasoned that since he was the firstborn of the first-born, eight times over, his answer might lie at the first world of the first world, which he believed was the head of a chain of eight. That is, the origin world, from which all others derived. So if he went to that world, he might succeed.

How could he travel there? He knew it was possible to travel along the filaments, for his ancestors had done it. But the secret was known only to the red-cloaked amazons, who would not tell any black-cloaked peon. He had to find out for himself.

Yet there were legends that circulated furtively among his people, and they hinted that the right person might be able to do it if he stood in the light of the filament and wished hard enough. Was Earle the right person? He hoped so!

So he buckled on his sword, used a spell to reduce his precious magic dulcimer to pocket size, and traveled to the East Sea. It was a far distance, so when he was sure no one was watching, he used his magic to fly, and this was much faster, though it also tired him faster. He had to rest for a day once he reached the sea. Then he risked using his magic to enable him to breathe the water, and he walked down under the surface until he came to the crevice and the filament. He bestrode it and wished with all his might that he might travel along it to the larger world at its other end.

Suddenly he was flying along the filament, so fast he was amazed. It was working! He shot straight along, passing many smaller worlds whose folk never noticed, and landed at the larger one, called Sol by certain folk. This, by his reckoning, was the seventh world in the chain, his own world of Jupiter being the eighth.

But it was so big! Judging by the height of the trees, which were in proportion, it was about thirty-six times as far across as Jupiter. It had been wearing to fly across part of Jupiter; how could he fly from one end of Sol to the other? And what of the yet larger worlds to come, which would make Sol seem as small as Jupiter now did? There had to be a better way!

So he approached a native of Sol. It was an aspect of Earle's magic that he could tell whether a person was friendly or unfriendly, and he selected the friendliest one in the nearest village of giants.

But when he flew to that house, he was taken aback. It

was a red-clad woman! An amazon! Surely no member of the ruling class would help any man to reverse the anima, especially not one who stood about two of her inches high.

Yet his magic indicated that she was the most likely prospect. So he explored the matter. He flew in a window and sat on the sill and watched her. She was monstrous, of course, but also beautiful. Her hair was dark brown and waist length, her face pretty, and her body marvelously well formed. Had she been his size, he would have loved her immediately. Except that she was a red amazon and he a black peon.

Could his magic be wrong? If it was, then he was lost, for he would never complete his journey without help. So he nerved himself and addressed her. He did not try to use words, knowing that their languages would differ, but illusion was a common mode of communication. He made a picture of himself, greatly expanded, and flashed it before her face.

She paused in her activity, which happened to be making a tasty-looking cake from grains of wheat. She made an illusion of her own, a giant question mark.

Earle introduced himself. "Earle," the image of him said, tapping his chest.

The woman smiled. She tapped her breastbone. "Kara," she said. Then she turned to look at him directly, tuning in on him with her magic. If she turned hostile now, he would be finished, for his magic was no greater than that of an ordinary amazon, and Kara was a big amazon.

Indeed, she caused him to float to her hand, and he knew he would not be able to escape her power. She held him up before her face and inspected him closely. Her mouth opened, and he feared she was going to eat him. She could bite him in two without effort! Then she smiled again, remaining friendly. He was greatly relieved.

Her curiosity satisfied, she sought to put him aside, her interest in this novelty fading. She meant him no harm, but she had other things to do.

This was not what he wanted. He needed her active help, not her mere tolerance. How could he convince her to take him seriously?

His desperate eye fell on a monstrous long-necked mandolin hanging on her wall. Music—she was musical!

He generated a picture of himself playing his dulcimer.

That got her attention again. Her eye went to her own instrument. Then she looked at him, there in her hand.

He brought out his tiny case and took out his dulcimer. He sat and crossed his legs, then used magic to restore his instrument to its proper size. He set it against his legs, which was not the best position from which to play, but would do in this emergency.

He took his two little hammers and struck the strings. The music came out, clear and strong, every note a delight. Now he could let his full skill manifest, and he reveled in it, making music that was almost painfully beautiful. All that was good in his soul was evoked in that sound, as his hammers moved with blinding cleverness across the strings.

Kara listened. At first her eyes widened slightly with surprise to discover that his skill was genuine; then she relaxed and let it carry her.

When he was done with the piece, she set him carefully on a pillow and went to fetch her own instrument. She sat and played it, and the sound came out so deep and resonant that Earle himself was charmed. She was not as skilled as he, but she was good enough. She was also absolutely beautiful herself as she played, her hair rippling in waves as her body swayed to the music, her bosom gently heaving.

Then they played a piece together, his tiny sound magically amplified to match hers, and it was a truly enjoyable experience. Never before had Earle allowed himself to indulge his full proficiency, and this would have been a delight even had he not done it in the company of a lovely giant amazon.

After that, her interest was changed. She wanted to communicate further with him, to learn all about him. He realized that the music had done what his magic could not: it had moved her heart.

They talked, exchanging illusions. He showed a map of his origin world, though that could hardly have surprised her, considering his size. Earle, encouraged by her surprisingly positive attitude, finally made so bold as to show his mission: travel to the center of the universe, where he hoped to invoke the animus.

He waited, knowing that now she would destroy him, if she was going to. But she merely considered. Then she smiled. I HELP YOU, her pictures indicated.

Earle was amazed and gratified despite her consistent

friendliness. Yet also doubtful. Could he really trust an amazon giant? It seemed he had to. Besides, she was lovely.

So Kara tucked him into her breast pocket, and flew into the sky of Sol. She traveled much faster than he could have, because her flight magic was in proportion to her size. Still, it was a long journey, because she lived on the head, at the west end of Sol, while the filament onward connected at the East Valley. He found it a comfortable ride, for her great bare breast beneath the pocket was marvelously soft and warm and supple. After a time he slept, secure and cushioned in the pocket, and that was pleasant too.

He woke as she came to land at the verge of Jupiter's East Sea. She stumbled as her feet touched; she was tired.

"Rest!" he cried, making a picture of a pile of pillows, of a woman lying down, of eyes closing.

She smiled, agreeing. But first she had things to do. She went to squat in bushes, not bothering to remove him from her pocket. Earle, intrigued, peered down as she hiked up her skirt. She seemed to be exactly like a woman of his own planet in every detail he could see, except for size. He began to wish she *were* his size, for though she was an amazon, she was a perfect woman. Indeed, her status as an amazon added to her allure. He had been close only to peon women, intriguing in their white tunics, and had seen amazon women only as imperious members of the elite class. But the amazons, having more leisure than the peons, could afford to make themselves beautiful, and some of them were extremely so. As this one was, in every part.

Kara made herself a bowl of gruel and mug of cocoa and fell to. Earle was surprised again; this was common fare, not the elegant repast expected of a member of the governing class. But it seemed she was too tired to get fancy, and had no need to be artificial. He liked that. He conjured his own gruel and cocoa, and ate where he was, in her pocket.

Then he had a need of his own. He made a picture, getting her attention. It showed the bushes.

She had the grace not to smile, this time. She lifted him out and held him on her flat hand, and he then flew down to where he could do his business in privacy. He could have flown directly from her pocket, but preferred to check in and out, as it were, so that she would always know where he was. This seemed safest, considering that his whole body was somewhat smaller than her little finger.

He returned in due course to her hand, and she returned him to her pocket. Then she made the pillows he had suggested, and lay down on her back. She made a blanket, and when the mosquitoes came, she made a bottle of perfume that seemed to repel the bugs as much as it attracted Earle. He needed no pillows or blanket; he had as soft a mattress as he could wish, and her body warmed him.

But she did not sleep. He understood the problem: she had performed an extraordinary feat of magic, flying the entire length of the planet, and that aspect of her was depleted. It was like having painfully sore muscles, that would not let a person relax enough to sleep.

Earle, having rested and slept during the long flight, had plenty of energy. He decided to try to help her to relax. He brought out his dulcimer and made it the proper size. He sat on her breast, there by the pocket, and played his music.

Kara smiled, appreciating his effort. She relaxed. But not enough. Something more was needed.

So he made a picture for her, angling it so that she could view it comfortably without lifting her head. It was of a fence between pastures, and a flock of sheep in one. But the grass was greener in the other pasture, so an enterprising sheep leaped over the fence, landing with a musical thumping of his four hooves. Naturally it was followed by another, and another, making an endless chain, all of them jumping to the music. It was the standard device used by his folk; his mother had put him to sleep when he was tiny with just this vision. Counting sheep—and soon the monotony of the distraction caused relaxation and dreams.

Kara smiled with wan appreciation, but even so did not relax quite enough to sleep. So he put a goat in the line, and then a deer, and then other animals, until finally he had bouncingly fat hippopotami doing it. They made heavy music as they struggled across. Kara enjoyed the show, but not enough. So he made images of himself, black-cloaked men, hurdling the fence, one after the other.

She laughed, and joined in the picture: red-cloaked women of the same size alternated with the men. The hems of their garments flared as they came down, showing their legs. Each one who landed had her dress rise a little farther, until at last one hem flared so high that her most private region was revealed. Whereupon the man who followed her, staring at the legs and perhaps a bit more, tripped on the fence and fell on his face. Such was his distraction that his smile remained even after his face made a dent in the sod.

The red woman turned back and came to the black man solicitously. She helped him up. The other figures faded out, leaving only those two beside the fence.

Earle was amazed. This was an interactive illusion! He had participated in games and contests in which peons tried to best each other's images, but the only interaction was when one blotted out another. He had known that amazons had superior illusion, and realized that his own facility was equivalent, but had never dared play the game this way. Now, with an amazon, he was doing it, and it was wonderful.

The picture woman did not let go of the man once he was stable. Instead she embraced him. The man looked exactly as startled as Earle felt: just how friendly would an amazon get with a peon, even in illusion?

Well, maybe he should find out. It wasn't as if any of this was real. It was just a game, a distraction from Kara's tiredness, so she could sleep. So he made as bold as he dared. His figure returned the embrace, and moved his face slowly toward her figure's face.

She did not pull away. Instead, her face met his. They kissed. There was a marvelously romantic melody.

Earle's heart was pounding. A peon man was kissing an amazon woman! In fact, an Earle image was kissing a Kara image. That was not only remarkable, considering the extreme difference in their stations, it was wonderful. He wished he could kiss Kara like that. But of course it was impossible. She was playing a game with him, teasing him, as women were wont to do with men.

Her huge real hand came up to her bosom. Earle quailed. Had he taken the image too far, and she was now going to take him out of her pocket and throw him away?

But her hand only touched him, her fingers squeezing him ever so gently in the pocket, then relaxing. It was reassurance, not censure. She liked the image-game.

He put away his dulcimer and wrapped his arms around her forefinger and hugged it. Her hand remained, resting on her breast, no weight on him. She did not object.

Earle had hardly dared believe before, but now he began to. Kara was lonely, as he was, so was willing to play a game with images that she would never have done in reality. Yet how far would she go, in illusion?

The image had frozen in place. Now motion resumed. The woman disengaged and stepped away from the man. But she did not depart. She drew off her tunic and stood before him in her glorious nakedness, except for her slippers. Then she removed these too. Somehow that magnified the effect. She waited.

The image man hesitated, then slowly pulled off his own tunic and stood in his slippers. He hesitated again, but the woman waited. So he took off the slippers too. Earle had to decide in what state the man should be presented, and decided that any man in that situation would be most ardently inclined. So as the slippers came off, the masculine desire of the image man manifested. Certainly Earle himself was in such a state of desire, futile as it might be. How would the image woman react?

She smiled and came to the man. She kissed him again, and pressed in closely, running her hands across his body as eagerly as he was running his hands across hers. Then they were in the throes of the kind of lovemaking that worked best in imagination: no miscues, no objections, no misalignment of actions. Everything was perfect, and her ardor matched his. Despite the perfection, it took a wonderfully long time to run its course, for illusion could endure for inhuman lengths.

Then the woman faded from the scene. Earle found himself embracing and kissing Kara's huge finger. But Kara herself was relaxed. In fact, she had fallen asleep.

The shared image had finally distracted her enough so that she had tuned out her fatigue. That had after all been the point of it. But in the process, Earle had discovered something awesome. He was falling in love with the giantess.

IN the morning Kara evidently felt better, but Earle was nervous and confused. How could he love an amazon giant? The notion was ludicrous. Nothing could ever come of it. Yet his pulse raced as he gazed up at her face, and it raced again as he gazed across and down at her body. She was his ideal woman, in personality, magic, and form—except for her size. To her it had been a game of idle fancy; it should have been the same for him. After all, the same sequence that had aroused his ultimate passion had put her to sleep. That showed that even had they been the same size in life, she would not have taken any such relationship seriously. It was no more than innocuous diversion for her. A harmless flirtation without true emotional involvement. Only a complete fool would see it otherwise.

Earle knew himself for a fool.

She lifted him out of the pocket and brought him past the truly awesome valley between her breasts and on up to her face. She touched her lips to his head, then set him down. Was she deliberately playing with his feelings, as she had with his image? She was after all an amazon; they were notorious for their callousness toward peons. Yet his magic indicated that she remained friendly. He wanted to trust that magic.

They ate their morning meals, then made ready to travel. Kara made the water porous and breathable, and walked down under the sea to the nether crevice of the East Valley. But here she paused, and an image appeared.

It showed a black-clad man riding up along the filament toward the next world of what some call the Milky Way. A larger red-clad woman remained behind.

She wasn't coming? Somehow he had assumed that she was. But why should she leave her world? She had no reason to bring the animus; it would only deprive her of her magic. She had helped him travel, and had played with him in fancy, and that was it. She would see him off, then return to her home.

But he did not want to go without her. His mission remained, but his day and night with her had done more than move his body. It had moved his mind. His heart.

He made a response image: a small black man with a large red woman, both traveling the filament. Then a reprise of their shared image of the evening, the two figures the same size, the man hugging the woman. He was telling her that he cared for her, however foolishly, and wanted her continuing company. That was all he could do. How would she respond?

She smiled. Then she made the effort, and abruptly they were sailing up along the filament between worlds. She had wanted only his confirmation, his invitation! Did that mean that she cared for him too, or merely that she sought a pretext for adventure? He still wasn't sure why she should support his mission, because it would cost her her magic. But after last night he was not inclined to question her too closely about that.

For one thing, this was a much longer and more convoluted ride than the one he had taken alone from Jupiter to Sol.

In fact, it shot right past worlds of Jupiter's size and larger, and in and out of small ninety-nine-ray stars in a seemingly endless progression. This was part of the huge ray structure of the star with which Jupiter was associated, which was not the one closest to Jupiter. That was because Jupiter was near the end of a formation reaching from Star 99 to Star 98. They were moving in toward 99, and it became glorious as they went, though the constant spins into and out of starlets were dizzying. Gradually Star 98 faded behind, and the light of Star 99 dominated. But as they whirled into its mighty vortex, he realized that it was composed entirely of starlets, which were composed of smaller starlets, in turn composed of yet smaller ones. He couldn't focus on them; he had to orient on the larger filament, to stop from getting disorientation sickness. What a contrast to his straight-line travel from Jupiter to Sol!

Into the heart of 99, into a brief eternity where the endless filament met the infinitely small space, just as was the case with the myriad starlets which comprised the larger pattern. Then out again, whirling and whirling, but the larger filament was almost straight to the head of what appeared to be a tiny projection on a truly monstrous world. It was in fact a rad, of the same sort as was on Sol, and on any world: the boulderlike base for an emerging filament. But this rad was perhaps a thousand times the size of Sol, and the world was perhaps a thousand times the size of the rad. Earle simply could not get a proper perspective on it; his imagination was too small. He had not realized that the universe was quite this big.

They landed on the tip of this projection of the Milky Way, a world of mind-numbingly vast dimension. Its surface was rough, and there were no familiar things, just balls and bags and sticklike things. Kara seemed as mystified as Earle was. These worlds were supposed to be similar, differing only in size.

Then they realized that they were so small for this world that they were the size of germs, those malicious little creatures that cast spells of ill-health on whomever they infested. No wonder it wasn't recognizable! But it probably wasn't safe either, because those germs could be as big as Kara, and Earle wouldn't even make a meal for one.

So they cooperated on a vision, magnifying their perceptions until they could see on a scale a million times as large. Now it was apparent that they stood on the tip of the smallest head, looking down toward the main head, and beyond it the body of the rad, which was actually a tiny one deep in the crevice of Seahorse Valley, between the Milky Way's own head and body. It was perhaps the least significant aspect of this world, and their entire system, down along the filament, was so minor as never to have been noticed by the folk here. This was not the most pleasant revelation for either Earle or Kara, but did not entirely surprise them.

Near this rad grew normal trees. It seemed to be regular farmland, with pastures and villages interspersing the forests. But a million times as big as what Kara had known, and even further removed from Earle's experience. How were they going to communicate with anyone here, let alone get help? For it was obvious they would need help; this world was simply too large for them to handle themselves.

But Earle was determined to proceed. He made a picture: the two of them flying to the nearest native residence and making pictures for that person. They themselves might be far too small for the native to see, but their illusion images could be large enough. Illusion could be any size, for it was formed of nothing.

So they found shelter in a crevice of stone and rested for a day and night, because the journey along the filament had tired them both. They made food and drink and had a good meal, then relaxed and shared another same-size fantasy. This time they did not bother with a fence or sheep; his image and hers appeared directly. It was apparent that Kara enjoyed this as much as Earle did, whatever the nature of her underlying feeling. Such a thing was impossible physically, but in the image their representations hugged and kissed, and she ran her fingers through his hair and he ran his hands across her bottom, and their passion mounted to heights like those of the trees of this world, and they proceeded to an act of love whose perfection was limited only by their comprehensive imaginations.

If only it *could* be possible! But she was thirty-six times his height, and he was so small to her that she could have eaten him in one mouthful. So she might as well be toying with his love; it made no difference in any practical way. Their fancies were the only place where it could happen.

•   •   •

IN the morning they made the long flight down to the nearest house. Kara put forth special effort, buttressed by Earle's own effort, and was able to fly much faster and farther here than on Sol. Thus they covered a distance that would otherwise have been unthinkable. By day's end they were at the base of the rad, near the house.

They spent another night, resting physically but not emotionally. Though it seemed that their imaginations had been exhausted in the prior session of shared illusion, they discovered new resources and made another wonderful experience of it. Kara even tucked him into that valley between her gently heaving breasts, so that he could get just a notion of what it might be like in reality. Earle would have forgotten his mission entirely, had he had a way to do with Kara physically what he did in image. But that was a choice he lacked, except to the extent he could stroke a tiny section of her flesh with his hand. She either liked him, or was really teasing him, or both.

Next day they approached the native, in much the way Earle had approached Kara. They perched invisibly on a windowsill and formed a tremendous illusion picture for the benefit of the man as he got up. They decided to use Kara's image, suspecting that this would impress the giant, but Earle's clothing, for the man was a black-clad peon.

It worked. The man was interested. He made images of his own, inquiring who they were and what they wanted of him. They explained that they were explorers from smaller worlds, and that they wanted to go to the center of the universe and bring the animus. But why would Kara, a woman, want this? the man inquired in pictures. Because, she replied in pictures, she believed that the worlds were becoming decadent under the anima, without much vigor, and she thought it would be more interesting under the animus. The situation of many women, she explained, was not much improved under the anima, for only one woman could be queen, and the queen tended to be jealous of her prerogatives. Perhaps if the burden of power was lifted from the shoulders of women, they could revert to their natural inclination to please men.

Earle found this interesting. Was it really the way she felt, or was it merely to persuade the native to cooperate? If she meant it, it was one more reason he wished he could really be with her. She was truly the ideal woman.

The peon decided that this effort was worth supporting. The way his eyes traveled across Kara's image might have had something to do with it. Her image's assumed white cloak, being unfamiliar, tended to fade out when she was concentrating on difficult concepts, leaving the more familiar body exposed. That was enough to make any man amenable.

When the man discovered just how much smaller Kara was, he was disappointed, but he remained interested in the mission. So he joined them, and they flew up to perch on his head. They used magic to clean out the germs near the base of the most convenient hair on his head, and made a shelter there. They stocked it with the comforts of home.

However, the native had no magic other than illusion, because he was both peon and male. He could not fly across the world to the East Valley. But Earle and Kara had discovered how to share their magic powers. They united their wills again, and reached down into the will of the native, and enabled him to draw on the techniques they possessed. Magic was not so much a matter of power as understanding, it turned out, and their understanding was being lent to him.

The man rose up and flew. Delighted, he sailed rapidly across the world, carrying them along. He flew high, so that the amazons of the Milky Way would not spy him, and came down only at the shore of the East Valley Sea.

After resting another night, and sharing delicious visions with each other but not with the huge native man, Earle and Kara proceeded with the giant into the sea and to the filament. Their ability enabled the native to do what he had never before imagined, and he sailed up along the filament toward the next world.

So it was that they went to the fifth of the worlds in the chain, which was so big that they didn't bother to try to imagine it. And the fourth, third, and second, each one equivalently larger, and finally the first. This was the true center of the universe, so extensive as to be beyond comprehension. Yet its people were the same, in proportion, as were those on all the lesser worlds.

They proceeded, in their chain of eight that resembled one with something in his hair, to the East Valley. Here they descended into the sea and stood athwart the filament there— except that this time there was no filament, for this was the origin world, the beginning of the universe.

The monster man of the First World got down so that his head was under the water by the very tip of the crevice. The giant of the Second World in his hair climbed down to be even closer, and put his head farther into that crevice. So it went, until the giant of the Sixth World, the Milky Way, got down with his head as close in as it could get.

Now it was Earle's turn to act. He dismounted from Kara's pocket, as she stood in their house on #6's head. He made his way down to the very focus of the cleft and stood there alone. "Animus, I invoke you!" he cried, exerting his will.

Nothing happened. Could it be that his immense journey had been for nothing? That this was not the way to invoke the animus?

Then he heard the sound of Kara's mandolin. She herself was out of sight in the murk of the mighty East Valley Sea, but her music reached down to him and touched his soul.

He brought out his dulcimer, made it full size, and set it up. Then he played on it, exerting all his skill.

Now he felt it take effect. The music had once again been the key. The world was changing, invisibly, and with it its dependent worlds, as the animus coursed along the filaments, through to the least significant extremities of the universe. It was done.

But there was no apparent change. The giant men did not seem to have magic, and Kara had not lost hers. Had their effort after all foundered?

"No," Kara's picture reassured him. "The thing has happened. The anima now governs the worlds. But its effect is subtle, because your magic remains. Mine is gone, but you are imbuing me with yours, so I can function as before. It is our children who will feel it. Our sons will have magic, and our daughters will not. In a generation all will be changed."

Oh. He had not realized that it would not be instantaneous, for the men. Perhaps that was just as well, for it meant that the worlds they traveled would not be instantly chaotic. At least, not completely so.

THEY made the long journey back. On each dawningly chaotic world they left its giant native, and took the filament forward to the next. So it was for seven diminishing levels. Then they were back at Sol, Kara's home.

Earle suffered agony of heart. "Oh, Kara," his image

said to hers as the two embraced. "I don't want to leave you!
I have deprived you of your magic, and without me you will
have none."

"I would have you remain with me, were it possible, for
other reason than that," her image replied, kissing his. "But
this is no world for you. You must return to your home, where
you will be honored."

"I am uncertain of that," he replied. "The amazons will
not be pleased to know that I have deprived them of their
power, and the peons will not yet have that power. The amazons will take great delight in executing me."

"True. Then I will go with you and protect you from
their malice. As long as I am with you, my power will seem to
remain, and it will daunt them. If it does not, I can simply step
on them."

Earle would have argued, but he now had two excellent
reasons to desire her company, so he did not.

They took the filament together, and arrived at the East
Valley of Jupiter. Kara waded out of the sea.

Then they paused to reconsider. Earle did not want her
giant feet to trample on the peons. Where could they go, where
Kara would be welcome? "I fear you have no more place on my
world than I on yours," his image said sadly.

Then she had an idea. "Is this not close to the origin of
our species?" her image inquired.

"Why, yes, as legend has it. The tiny subordinate world
of Oria is fabled to have been the origin from which mankind
spread across the universe."

"Then on that tiny world must be the secret of size," she
said. "For as we have seen, every world has people and animals
and plants in proportion to itself. Everything is self-similar; it
is a guiding principle of our universe. They must have been
magically changed to fit, and the first people must have known
how to do it. That magic has been lost in the course of the eons,
but perhaps it remains known on that one world, or can be
rediscovered there."

"The secret of size!" he said, excited. "If we had that, we
could become the same in body as we are in image!"

"That was my thought," her image confessed, blushing
prettily.

Now Earle remembered how she had said "our children," perhaps unconsciously, and he understood that she re-

turned his love. She had not been teasing him; she had been giving him all that was possible.

So they flew a quarter circle around Jupiter, treading on no peons, and landed at the tip of the head of the head of the appropriate rad. Then they rode the filament out to Oria.

Oria was tiny. Every step Earle took was like twenty or twenty-five of his normal ones. For Kara, it was worse. To her, the natives stood only about the thickness of the cloth of her tunic in height, and were no more visible than an ant. To avoid squishing folk, she decided to wade at the edge of the water, or to fly, rather than to tread on land.

But where was the place to find the secret? They considered, and concluded that since this was the ninth world in the chain, it must be at the ninth rad. As it happened, that rad was well up toward the East Sea. In fact, it was under the East Sea. It was believed that mankind and all the animals originated under the sea, so this made sense.

They went there, and Kara stood over the rad, and set Earle down on it. They were right at the verge of the sea; the top of the rad formed an island just offshore, large enough for Kara to lie on.

Earle stood on it and brought out his dulcimer. Kara had hers, but it was reduced to the size of his for easy transport, and she saw no need to restore it yet. He was the one with the special magic, and only his music would do it.

He played, and the sound spread out across the sea and made it shimmer, and across the land and made it quiver. It reached into the sky, and the clouds shivered and turned to haze. "I feel it!" Earle cried. "I can change the size of the one for whom I play. I will make me large, to match you."

"No, make me small to match you," Kara said. "We shall still both be large for this world, and we can remain here together in comfort."

Earle agreed. Since he now had the power, and could invoke it anywhere, they decided to get safely to the shore first. She quickly took him up and floated to the shore, where they sat side by side on the edge of the water, she towering over him as he dangled his feet in the water. To her, the bank was merely a rise, and the sea here barely covered her toes.

He played for her, and she began to shrink. It was working! Once started, the process continued by itself, so he put aside his dulcimer and reached up to hold her huge little finger.

It grew steadily smaller, until he was able to grasp her huge hand. The hand became smaller, along with her body, until at last she was his size. She got up and stepped out of the sea to stand before him. She had shrunk entirely out of her clothing and was naked.

Delighted, he embraced her and kissed her on the lips, physically, for the first time.

But she continued shrinking. Horrified, he tried to hold her, but she shrank in his arms. He took up his dulcimer and played, but the spell would not be reversed. It was running its course, heedless of his will. He had invoked a spell he did not properly understand, and now was paying the penalty.

Helpless, he watched her diminish. Her own mandolin, formerly a tiny thing in her huge hand, remained as it was, and now was far too large for her to play. It slid off the bank and partway into the sea. He was now too large to be her lover. She diminished to a quarter his height, to an eighth, a sixteenth. All he could do was shield her with his huge hand, preventing her from falling into the sea.

Then, less than a twentieth of his height, she stopped. She was now the same size as a native of this planet. Their problem of size remained; they had in effect changed places.

Suddenly he understood. "The magic makes a person fit the world!" he exclaimed. "It makes folk grow or shrink, depending on the world, so that thereafter they can reside there in comfort."

She sent up an image: "Then join me, beloved!" the image cried.

Immediately, he played the music for himself. He began to shrink. He set down the dulcimer and the two hammers, for they were not affected, and his own cloak became too large for him. He stepped out of it, and back from the brink of the cliff, which was now quite formidable though it had been no more than knee height to him before. His dulcimer slid off, joining her mandolin, partly in the sea. It could not be helped.

He became her size, and stopped. Again he embraced her, and kissed her, and did with her the things they had done only in image before. Then they made new clothing for themselves and walked away from the sea. They were united at last.

CHAPTER 8

SECRET

NONA came out of the story, the understanding forming. Kara the giantess had looked exactly like Nona herself; she had seen it in the picture in Angus' mind. This myth explained not only the coming of the animus but also the origin of mankind on Oria itself.

"No," Angus said, answering her thought. "Mankind was there on your world and mine long before then. It merely explains the arrival on your world of two whom you call Megaplayers, one of them my size, the other much larger. Perhaps Kara did not look like you; that was my fancy. But it is one of our stories of the way of the universe, and it suggests how those instruments of ours came to your world."

"Must I go to the origin of the universe, as Earle did?" Nona asked, appalled.

"I think not. The animus, as our myth has it, flows from the origin to the smaller worlds. But the anima is opposite. That should flow the other way."

"The other way!" Nona exclaimed, seeing it. "But there are many small worlds, and only one master world. How can we know which one?"

"I suspect that it is no single world, but any world," Angus said. "Each world can be changed from its own proper source. It may be that the animus sweeps all worlds at once, while the anima takes one world at a time, as its folk discover how to do it. Thus we should be subject to periods of complete animus, followed by gradually increasing anima, until some champion invokes the animus again for all."

"The little world we stopped at on the way here!" Colene exclaimed. "They had just converted to anima! They had found the way."

"Perhaps they can tell you, then," Angus said. "It should be simply a matter of standing over the correct spot, playing your music, and invoking the anima. But I must warn you—"

"That it won't change everything immediately," Nona said. "That I now understand. But the power of the despots will be curtailed, and the next generation will be ours."

"Note that in the legend, Earle and Kara did not remain to face their people after the change to animus," Angus said. "Had they done so, they might have encountered unkind treatment at the hands of the amazons, who would have wielded considerable power for a time, even without their magic. So they went anonymously to a new world, escaping that consequence."

Nona considered that. She had assumed before coming here that the change would be instant and complete, with the men losing their magic and the women gaining it, according to their orders of birth. That way she would have been queen immediately. That was not actually a role that appealed to her. She desired to be queen no more than she desired to be a theow housewife; both were confining for life. She was doing this not for any personal gain, but for the welfare of her people. It was now apparent that the anima, when long established, was no better than the animus; both were merely vehicles for the transmittal of power. But it seemed best that they be changed every so often, to clear out corruption and give new folk a chance to do better.

So she would not be queen. She might instead be a martyr, as the despots struck savagely in revenge for their loss of heredity. That was even worse. Still, she had to do it, if only because now that she had come here she was known, and her family and friends would suffer if the despots retained power.

"Not so, lovely little lady," Angus said, receiving her thought. "You will be the only person on your world with full magic. You will therefore be queen immediately, having the power. You will have to organize your people and institute the new order, abolishing the old. Then there will be no threat to those close to you."

"But I am no leader!" Nona protested. "I can not be ruthless!"

"Riding the tiger," Colene murmured. In her mind was a picture of a young woman on the back of a monstrous ugly feline, in control only so long as she did not dismount.

"However, interpretation leads to further insights about the spread of man across the worlds," Angus said. "In the legend, they had the secret of size change, and it was presumed that those who crossed between the worlds invoked that magic to become the appropriate size for that world. But their instruments did not follow; Earle did not think to make them conform. Nothing is said about animals and plants, which must have been brought by the colonizing explorers. But there would have been similar magic for them, for all things are in proportion to the size of their worlds. Yet I know of no such magic. No one in real life can change size. Was the magic lost after the initial colonization? The legend suggests otherwise, for Earle and Kara were different sizes, yet each changed to become another size. Why, then, can we not discover or remember the secret? I have quested through the ruins of past times, and found no record of any such magic. I do not believe that it exists."

"But folk *are* different sizes!" Nona protested. "We differ from you, and from the tiny folk of the little world we passed. We know this is the case."

"Folk are different," he agreed. "But there may be no magic about that."

Nona shook her head, confused. "But there has to be! How else could they become the right sizes?"

Angus glanced at the others. "I wonder whether any of your companions from other realms have ideas on this?"

"Sure," the intense young Colene said immediately. "Evolution." Nona heard the word, but the concept was too complicated to fathom.

Angus, however, was interested. "This is a science concept?"

"It sure is," Colene agreed. "It means that plants and animals change little by little, over the millennia, the fittest surviving, the unfit dying. They grow small or large, depending on what works best. In this reality it would mean that they evolve to fit the worlds they are on; there must be an advantage to being the right size for each."

"Then how would you interpret the presence of small musical instruments here, or large ones on the little world of Oria?"

"Easy. The people brought them along when they settled. But each generation changed in size, while the instruments didn't, so finally the people couldn't play them, and had to make new ones that matched their size. I admit I find the acoustics hard to believe; the longer strings and larger sounding chambers in the large instruments should play deeper notes than the small ones, but that doesn't seem to be the case. But then big people like you should collapse under their own weight—square-cube ratio, you know—but you don't, and Jupiter doesn't have any stronger gravity than Oria; we're the same weight here as we are there. But even so, you should feel twice as much strain on your feet, and you don't, so science just doesn't apply. So okay, the rest of science doesn't work here, but maybe evolution does. That hammered dulcimer Nona just played belonged to your distant ancestors, who were small when they came here. And those big instruments on Oria belonged to folk your size, before they evolved down to regular size for that world."

"I can't make sense of this!" Nona said, her mind awhirl. "There must be size spells!"

"I admit it is difficult to believe," Angus said. "But it is just one of those impossible things we are constrained to accept. The archaeological evidence indicates that Colene is correct. We have found small bones and tools, and larger ones, and larger still, and the smallest are the oldest. It happened gradually, for people and animals and trees too."

"But Earle and Kara—"

"A legend is only a story," Angus said. "A simplified memory, an attempt to explain what we otherwise have difficulty understanding. We see the relics of past times, and they are the wrong size, so we suggest that magic was responsible. But in this case there seems to be another explanation, and Colene's ready appreciation of it satisfies me that she is indeed from a different kind of place."

"But if it happened slowly," Nona said, trying hard to reason out the consequences of this incredible notion, "then Earle—Kara—"

"Did not invoke magic to change size," Angus finished. "True. If they existed at all, it was not in the fashion described. That must be a happy ending put on to satisfy more recent listeners. But it does suggest that there was travel in each direction. Small folk came from Oria to Jupiter, and colonized it, and slowly grew large. Then, later, large folk must have returned to Oria and colonized it again, and slowly grown small. The myth and the physical remnants agree on this; only the particular manner and timing of it remain obscure."

"But then the Megaplayers—"

He smiled sadly. "Are merely your name for ordinary folk like me, on this larger world. I have no magic to help you, pretty little woman. Even if I went to Oria, I would have no more power than you, except that I could step on despots. In fact I would have less, for I can not compel loyalty to your cause by playing a melody, and I could not bring the anima to Oria no matter how hard I tried. None of the folk of Jupiter could."

"But my mother told me to seek the Megaplayers!" Nona was near tears of confusion and frustration.

"Perhaps she spoke wisely," Angus said. "I can not do such magic myself, but I may be able to advise you in such a way as to enable you to do it yourself. Though I believe there is no magic of living size change, there obviously is the magic of animus and anima, and location is surely vital to it. I believe if you ask the folk of the smaller world you passed, they will tell you that they had a woman of the appropriate lineage, and that she stood at the appropriate site and invoked the anima for her world. That is what you must do."

"I can change it right on Oria?" Nona asked, amazed.

"That is my belief. You are the ninth of the ninth. There is surely a corresponding site on your world that will resonate to your magic. Unfortunately I do not know where that would be. There are so many rads on each world, and so many rads on each rad, that a person could spend a lifetime traveling to each one and trying to invoke the magic, and die before finding the right one."

"The ninth of the ninth," Nona said. "That must be the one."

"Undoubtedly. But where does the count start, and in what direction does it proceed?"

Nona was unable to answer. She had no idea how to count rads. She had never thought of such a thing before.

"Maybe the little folk on that world we passed," Colene said. "Since they did do it, they have to know."

"Yes, and they might even be willing to tell you," Angus said. "But their world is not the same as yours, so their site on it would differ accordingly. It would not work for you. And it may be that they did not do it by counting, but found it by chance."

Colene nodded soberly. "Probably wasted effort," she agreed. "What we need is a solid, sensible system of counting, and I guess that doesn't exist in this universe. Otherwise these changeovers would be more common than they are."

"Such a system does exist in your universe?" Angus inquired.

"Oh, sure, it must. They know a lot about fractals. I never got into it deeply, but the library has whole books—" She paused with realization. "I could probably find out, on Earth! If I got to the right library, or maybe found the right person. Only I can't get back to Earth, because we can't use our anchor. That's why we were trying to help Nona, so she could get rid of the animus and it would stop interfering with our access to the Virtual Mode."

"I am not clear about the nature of this anchor," Angus said. "I gather it is a portal."

Nona was glad to hear the question, because the concept confused her too. She had seen the party appear, and understood that they could not go back, but it was alien magic. Seqiro had explained the Virtual Mode to her, but her comprehension remained limited.

"It is a connection to a particular reality," Darius said. "The Virtual Mode is like a slanting ramp, crossing many levels, and each level is a reality—an entire universe. But it has to be anchored in five places, or it spins wildly. Each anchor ties it to one reality, and all of us on the Mode can pass through those anchors and remain in their realities. We came through Nona's anchor, and so we are here. But the animus prevents us from returning through it and resuming our journey to my home reality."

Angus' brow furrowed. "Is this anchor a place or a person?"

"Both. The person makes it, by committing to it when

the Virtual Mode offers. But it is also the place where that person stands when that commitment is made."

"What happens when the person moves away from that place?"

"Nothing," Darius said. "The person can go anywhere in the anchored reality, or in the Virtual Mode, which is like a reality of its own made from thin strips of all the other realities it crosses. Nona could go to any of our home realities, just as we came to hers. But only Nona, of all those native to her reality, can use that anchor, and only she can free it. Except for the interference of the animus."

"Free it?" Angus asked.

"She committed it; she can uncommit it. Then she will be left in her own reality, and the rest of us will be on the Virtual Mode seeking other realities."

"Suppose she frees it when the rest of you are on this side of the anchor?"

Darius paused. So did the others; their mutual surprise was shared by Seqiro, so that all knew that all felt it.

"We could be trapped!" Colene said after a moment.

"I'm not sure of that," Darius said. "It would leave a Virtual Mode with no anchor people on it." But he was uneasy. His memory, now shared by the others, suggested that many people had entered Virtual Modes, and few had returned to their original anchors. Was this what happened?

"I think Nona is more critical to your welfare than you thought," Angus said. "At least while you are in her reality. But from what you say, you are not necessarily safe while on the Mode, because you are always in some slice of reality, and if one of you was killed, control over that anchor would be lost and you would be destabilized."

"It's no safe place," Colene agreed. "Only someone desperate or halfway suicidal should risk it." There was an undercurrent there that appalled Nona; the girl was speaking of herself.

"I have a conjecture," Angus said. "Nona is the key person for the anima. She has full magic, and the ability to enlist others with her music. When she stands on the correct spot and invokes the anima, it will spread across her world. This suggests that she has the power to nullify the animus. That power is normally limited, but can still nullify it for particular people when she tries, as we have seen here. We have all become anima. That may not matter for those of you of other universes, but it does for me. I am helping her now because she has brought me into the anima, at least in spirit. My powers are at her disposal."

"But I seek no power over you," Nona protested. "I only want to make my world better."

"You have it, nonetheless," Angus said. "If you were my size, and wished to marry me, I would marry you, even as Kara married Earle after he brought her into the animus. But that is not my thought. It is that if you can nullify the animus for single people elsewhere, and for the entire world at the nines spot, you must be able to have effect at the site of this anchor. You should be able to nullify the animus and allow the others to return to their Virtual Mode."

Again they paused in surprise. That did make sense.

"We can go back!" Colene exclaimed.

"No," Provos said almost at the same time. "Her power was not that great. She was able to enable only the smaller part of the group to pass."

"She remembers!" Colene said.

"But she has already forgotten mentioning it," Darius added. "She can't remember what she has told us, so doesn't speak often." Indeed, Provos was looking perplexed, catching on that she must have said something, but not yet knowing what it was. It was yet to be triggered by their prior dialogue.

"But that means that only one or two of us can pass through," Colene said. "Which ones?"

"You must be one," Angus pointed out. "Since you alone know the way around your world. You will go and return with the information. Assuming one other can go with you, which should it be?"

"Seqiro!" Colene said instantly.

"Both," Provos said.

"Is that number or mass?" Darius asked, asking the question the woman had just answered. Then, realizing that he would have to say more for her to understand the question, he added: "The people who pass back through the anchor."

"Which means the horse is too big," Nona said, catching on to the peculiarities of this dialogue. "So it must be you, Darius. Unless—"

"I did," Provos said.

"Who else went through the anchor with Colene?" Darius asked, quickly making the question fit the answer.

And that seemed to be it. Colene and Provos would go, leaving Darius and Seqiro behind. Nona realized that one thing was sure: Colene would do her utmost to return, rather than to be cut off from her man and her horse. And Provos, with her memory of things to come, should be able to help her considerably.

Angus had indeed been a big help, not because of his size or any power of magic, but because of what he knew of legend, and his ability to reason.

But the moment they addressed the prospect of a partial return, they realized that there was more to consider. "We can't just go back to Oria, walk up to the anchor, and move two of us through," Colene said. "The despots are out looking for us, and you can bet they have people watching the East Valley. They'll throw us in chains the moment we land there."

Again Angus had a good suggestion. "When you travel the filament, you pass many worlds. Most are so small you can not even see them, but large ones are passed too. If you go to a world beyond yours, then return from there to the head of Oria, you may elude the ambush of the despots."

Colene gazed up at him. "You are some kind of genius, Angus!" she exclaimed. "If you were my size, I'd kiss you."

His image appeared before her, her size. "Really?" the image asked.

Colene tried to kiss the image, but her head passed right through without resistance. The image laughed.

Colene stepped back and reconsidered. "Nona! Seqiro! Give *me* an image."

Obligingly Nona made an image of Colene, standing beside her, and the horse enabled Colene to identify with that image, so that she could control it directly. Now the illusion girl stepped toward the Angus image, embraced it, and kissed it resoundingly. "But I won't go as far as Kara did," her image said, laughing.

The Angus image shook its head. "It is hard to believe that you are unhappy," it said, and faded out.

"It is getting late in the day," Darius said. "We had better rest, and return tomorrow. We will still have an extended job of conjuring to do when we arrive on Oria, to get from the West Spike to the East Valley."

"That should not be a problem," Angus said.

"Not for you," Darius agreed. "You could fly the length of that world in a day. But only Nona can fly, in our group; the rest must walk or be conjured from place to place, tediously."

"No problem for me or for you," Angus said. "Because of course I am coming with you. My service to Nona will not be complete until she ushers in the anima."

Nona turned to stare up at him. "You will do that? Go to Oria and carry us?"

"This is the nature of my commitment," Angus said. "As it was with Kara and Earle. The legend may not be technically accurate, but the substance is correct. I will help you in whatever way I can. So far I have done so with my mind, but I will do so with my body also. This is one advantage of not being your size." He glanced down at Colene as if regretting that advantage.

Nona felt like kissing him herself. His presence on Oria would enormously simplify their problems there.

THEY had a comfortable night in a box with separate chambers for each, including the horse, and abundant pillows. Soon enough the others were asleep, but Nona lay awake. They had accomplished much, but much remained, and she feared that their future course would not be easy.

A man appeared in her chamber. It was the image of Angus. "Since you and I and Seqiro remain awake, let us talk," he said.

Nona was glad for the company. "Sit beside me," she suggested. She was conscious again of the marvelous magic of the horse, which allowed perfect communication between those whose languages would otherwise be a severe barrier.

Angus-image did. "Do not misunderstand my purpose," he said. "I have not come to seek any favor from you, but to broach more serious subjects that occurred to me in afterthought."

"Maybe those are what are keeping me awake," Nona said.

"Your young man—Stave—what do you suppose is his situation now?"

There was the heart of it. Angus must have picked up her suppressed concern from the context of the thoughts the horse relayed automatically. "I fear for him."

"With reason, if your despots are like ours. They will believe him to be guilty, because of his association with you. They may treat him unkindly."

"No!" she said, meaning yes.

"But perhaps they will anticipate your return, having fathomed your nature," Angus continued. "In that case they will keep him captive, hostage to your behavior. This is perhaps your gravest danger."

"How can I do anything if he suffers?" she asked, dreading the answer.

"You can not, for you are of a gentle nature. But if you will consider the advice of one who is conversant with the despotic mentality, I can help you in this too."

"Tell me what to do!"

"It is not for me to tell you, but for you to tell me. Here is my suggestion. Send Darius and Seqiro early to the region you suspect Stave will be held. Let the horse locate him with mind-talk. Then let the man remove him by living conjuration."

"Yes!" Then she reconsidered. "But if I do that, instead of going to the anchor to help them through it, the delay may imperil my mission with the anima."

"This is why I have approached you privately about this matter," Angus-image said. "It is a decision for you to make alone. I will support you in whatever you choose."

Nona considered. "No, I do not have the right. Stave is dear to me alone, not to the others, and they will be endangered. They are helping me to bring the anima, as you are. I can not work against them without their agreement."

"Perhaps I can distract the despots, so that Stave can be rescued without delaying the others."

"It is not right to ask you to endanger yourself for such a thing either," she said. "I—I think I love Stave, but I fear I can not save him."

Another figure appeared. It was Colene. "Don't turn your back on Stave," she said. "Do you think I want you near my man, if you've lost your man?"

"Oh, but I wouldn't—"

"When Provos and I go through the anchor, that will leave you and Darius and Seqiro. Darius notices women. I'd feel a lot better if Stave were there too."

Suddenly Nona appreciated the sense of it. Still, she

wasn't sure. "If saving Stave takes time, you may not get to go through your anchor. Then all will be lost, because we need that information."

"It's a calculated risk," the girl replied. "I take them all the time. Save him."

That seemed to be it. "Then I will do it." Nona reached out to touch Colene, forgetting that she couldn't make contact with an image, however real it seemed.

But her hand encountered a solid shoulder. Colene was physical!

"Seqiro woke me," Colene said. "He figured it was my business, and it was." She walked away, returning to her chamber.

Nona shook her head. She did not properly understand Colene, but she liked her. It was a great relief to try to save Stave.

"There is another matter," Angus said. "In any event, the despots will be pursuing you closely, and their familiars will be watching every likely place. The site of the anchor will certainly be among them, even if they do not understand its significance. It may even be that the rescue of Stave will help distract them from it, as they will think that your interest is only in him. But you are unlikely to be able to gather at that site without very soon being pressed by despots. You may get the two people through the anchor, but then not have time to escape yourselves. Even if you conjure as a group to another place, they will be in hot pursuit. I could carry you away, but I will be plainly visible, and unless I take you off that world—"

"If we get them through the anchor, and the despots see, they'll never stop watching that place," Nona said. "Colene and Provos will be captured the moment they return."

"I fear that is the case. So some other distraction seems warranted."

"You have an idea?"

"Yes. If you can make it seem that the site is of no significance, and that you are merely passing it on the way to some other site, perhaps they will watch you instead of that place."

"But it's right by the sea. There's nothing else there except—" Nona paused. "Except the instruments of the Megaplayers."

"Which you now know have no special significance,

though they may be archaeologically relevant," Angus said. "However, your despots may believe otherwise. They may assume that those are what you seek. If you go to them, and perhaps even enter them—"

"Enter a giant petrified musical instrument?"

"The image in your mind suggests that Kara's mandolin is there, whose hole is at the level of the sea. If you entered that, and then were conjured away, they might assume that that was the anchor. They might destroy it, but leave the real anchor site alone."

"Colene is right!" Nona exclaimed. "You are a genius!"

"However, there remains the problem of hiding until Colene returns with the information. You must keep yourselves safe, or it will still go for nothing. I have one more suggestion, which may not appeal to you."

"I'm sure it is a good one," Nona said. She remained amazed at the intelligence of this giant. Provos had been entirely correct in selecting Angus to convert.

"It is that you go inside the world."

Nona's heart seemed to constrict. "The inner world!" she said. "Where the demons dwell!"

"They are not demons, but the descendants of people and animals and plants that entered that realm long ago," he said. "I have made a study of them too, for they are part of the history of what we are. They exist I think in every world, large and small. They are no longer conventional in appearance, but many do have human intelligence, and perhaps human emotions. They surely do not like the despots, who kill anything strange on sight. They might give you sanctuary."

"It would be a terrible gamble," Nona said, appalled.

"Perhaps it is not a good suggestion. I could bring you back here."

"No, we have to be close to the anchor, because the despots will be near it even if they don't realize exactly where it is, and Colene and Provos will be exposed."

"I will not be able to go with you, inside your world. It is too small for me. But I could carry images of all of you away, perhaps decoying the despots."

"That should be good," Nona agreed. "But Angus, if we are successful, and the anima comes to Oria, what will you do? Jupiter will still be animus."

"I will return to my normal pursuits. My life is not a bad

one. The events occurring on Oria will have no effect on Jupiter, and there will be no onus attaching to me here. This will be merely an interesting sidelight in my life, of no interest to others." He seemed a little sad.

"You don't suppose there could be a woman of the anima on Jupiter, who—"

He smiled. "I doubt it. These are rare occurrences. In any event I would be too old for her. But I thank you for the thought."

"And I thank you for your help. You surely are the Megaplayer I sought."

His image faded. She was alone again. Now she was able to sleep. She dreamed of Kara, looking like herself, and of Earle, looking like a cross between Angus and Darius.

IN the morning Angus carried them to the region of the spike on the rad, and invoked the filament magic. He was larger, and his range was farther, so they went directly to a worldlet in the spike of Oria. This was so small that there was no place on it for Angus to stand; he merely touched it lightly with his hand, the one holding Seqiro. Nona gazed down in the world, and from this vantage it did indeed look like a bug, as Colene described it, with a crude heart-shaped body and a round head and stubby legs of different sizes. Filaments extended out from the head like elaborate feelers, and from the legs like webs. Still, this was a world, surely with its tiny people, its despots and its theows, its families and its children, with their dreams and frustrations. What a marvel of scale this universe was, with worlds and people of every size, and similar cultures everywhere though they hardly communicated with each other or even knew of each other's existence.

Yet by similar token she now knew that this universe was only one of many, and that the others were similar in having their people and dissimilar in having their different rules of magic. So in some, men could conjure living folk, and in some horses could do mind-magic. What an exciting larger framework that must be! If only she could visit it! But of course her place was here in her own reality, on her own world, ordinary as it now seemed.

Angus oriented on the filament, going the other way, and conjured them along it. Suddenly they were on the head of Oria, and everything except Angus was normal. Except that this was the part of Oria Nona had never before seen: the western spike, with its base in the diminishing series of heads. Like Jupiter, only much smaller.

Now they moved into their plan. They split into two groups, with Seqiro and Darius together, while Nona, Colene, and Provos remained with Angus. Nona concentrated to locate and alert her prior familiar, the bat, and cause it to fly out to a spot near the despots' castle. She had never before tried to do this at such a range, but was successful. Seqiro's range was limited, but contact with a familiar was a different kind of magic. When the bat found a glade in the forest that was unoccupied, Darius conjured himself and the horse there. The two disappeared, and would rejoin the others when they had rescued Stave.

Angus floated up high and began the daylong flight across the world. Now it hardly seemed different from their other travels; the forest and fields spread out between the rads exactly as on Jupiter or on the little worlds at which they had stopped. But on this one she had direct personal experience of the human events.

She had time to think during the flight, and that was unfortunate. She was worried about Stave, and Seqiro and Darius. Had they been able to rescue Stave, or had they just gotten themselves in trouble? Colene had told her to go for the rescue, but if it failed, what was Colene's loss? Her man *and* her wonderful horse!

She looked at Colene. They could not talk now, because their languages were gibberish to each other and Seqiro was not here to join them. They were similarly isolated from Angus. They knew what they had to do, but they had been rendered into temporary strangers. The loss of Seqiro was painful.

Colene met her gaze and nodded yes.

Nona was startled. Could the girl have the mind-magic?

Colene seemed surprised too. She held up her hand with her thumb and forefinger almost touching, as if to say "this much." A little bit of mind-magic? The ability to receive a few thoughts, but not to send them out?

Colene nodded. But she seemed unsure. As if it were a talent she was just learning, perhaps from her association with the horse.

Nona had an idea. She made a slate, and a piece of chalk. She showed it to the girl. She drew a circle on the slate, then erased it. Then she held the slate up so that it faced away from Colene, and drew a triangle. She looked past it at the girl.

Colene lifted one hand. Slowly she traced the outline of a figure in the air. It was a triangle.

Nona turned the slate around, showing the triangle. Colene broke into a smile.

Now they had something to do to divert their minds. Nona drew other figures, and Colene traced them with her finger. She was always right. She was picking it up from Nona's mind.

Then Nona drew another triangle, but formed a mental image of a square.

Colene looked perplexed. Finally she drew a figure with seven points, but evidently wasn't sure of it.

Nona turned the slate around, showing the triangle. Then she tapped her head, and drew the square superimposed on the triangle. The two together formed a figure with seven points. Image and thought had merged, and Colene had received both.

The girl looked awed. She really was doing mind-magic! Nona remembered what it had felt like to discover that she had the power of healing, or the power of compaction. It was wonderful, but also somewhat frightening. What did such magic mean? How would it change her life? Was she truly glad to have it?

The answer was yes: the more magic the better. It just took some getting used to.

Colene caught her eye again and nodded. The girl was reassured by Nona's experience. Her power might be slight compared to that of the horse, but it was nevertheless significant, and it might grow.

Provos was sleeping. It seemed best for the two of them to do the same. They might be busy far into the night.

At dusk they reached the East Sea. Angus was plainly tired. He would not be able to do anything more than set them down and move away. But he had gotten them here, and the despots had not intercepted them.

Now it was time to do their routine, to fool the despots about their real purpose here.

Angus came down beyond the castle, well away from the place of the instruments. He stood there a moment, and put his hand down to the ground. A blackbird turned in the air, spying the giant: the despots were being alerted.

Angus straightened up and started walking. He was as tall as the trees of the forest, and he moved rapidly. He was not physically tired, but magically tired; this was a rest for him as well as a distraction for the despots.

Colene!

It was Seqiro's thought, sent to all of them. They had come within the horse's range! Nona's relief was so great she was unable to formulate a thought right away.

"Did you get Stave?" Colene cried.

Yes. He is with us. We are hiding in the forest. We have been moving around all day, avoiding the despots.

"Then come to us!" Colene said joyfully. "Angus, hold out your other hand."

The giant did so. The horse and two men appeared in it. They had been reunited!

"Where are the despots?" Colene asked as Nona waved to Stave.

"Everywhere," Darius replied. "Their familiars are scouting all around, and the despots of the rest of the world are doing the same. They knew you were coming, but not where you would land. They will close in on us the moment Angus slows."

Nona saw that the man held a new little doll figure he had crafted: one which resembled Stave. He must have had to conjure himself into Stave's cell, to get the necessary air, liquid, and solid for the conjuration of the new person.

Angus paused, and bent down again, touching the ground with the backs of his hands. After a moment he stood again, resuming his walk. Now the despots had another site to investigate; their familiars had not been close enough to see whether the giant had actually put anyone down, and there could be people fleeing into the forest.

"We'll have to act quickly, when we do," Darius said. "We don't know how long it will take to get you through the anchor."

Nona glanced at Provos. The woman seemed unconcerned. That should be a good sign.

Angus made two more pauses, roughly circling the despots' castle. Then he came to the field near the instruments.

There were no despots there. They had been fooled into thinking it wasn't important. Angus stopped near the brink.

"Go!" Colene exclaimed, jumping off the hand. Provos and Nona followed her. Darius and Stave got off the other hand and came to join them.

Provos seemed to know what she was doing. She walked briskly to the brink and reached for Nona's hand.

Nona concentrated, trying to will the anima into being. Would it work without the music?

Provos disappeared.

Colene took Nona's hand. "Keep an eye out for our return," she said. "And watch yourself with my horse, woman."

Nona had to smile. She willed the anima again, and Colene disappeared.

They are coming.

Nona ran back to the giant's hand, paced by Stave and Darius. They climbed on, while Seqiro remained on the other hand. Angus stood.

Indeed, horses were galloping toward them from the village. Nona didn't want to find out what mischief the despots had in mind; death might be the least of it.

Angus reached down toward the sea. For him there was no cliff, merely a rocky bank with old musical instruments leaning against it. He put his hand to the huge hole in the mandolin. The three of them climbed into the hole. Then the other hand brought Seqiro down, and the horse joined them.

An image of Angus appeared with them. "If I do not see you again, I wish you success," he said. "Now conjure yourselves away; I will close my hands about images and pretend I am still carrying you."

"Thank you, good friend!" Nona cried as the image faded.

The hand withdrew, pausing only to make a wave with the fingers. Then they felt the shudder of the ground as Angus tramped away.

Darius faced the horse. "Seqiro, can you find any mind near here in the ground? I must see through that mind's eyes before I conjure us there."

Yes, there is one. The mind is open. Here are the eyes.

"Then take hold," Darius said, doing so himself. He held

dolls of all of them, and he was ready to whisper to them, to make them ready for his magic.

Nona and Stave put their hands on the body of the horse.

Darius marked circles, then moved the dolls. There was the wrenching of conjuration.

CHAPTER 9

VIRTUAL

COLENE blinked, looking for Provos. There she was, waiting just ahead. Nothing seemed to have changed, except that all the others were gone. There were no people and no horses, just a sea-edge landscape.

Colene had not seen this place from within the Virtual Mode before. They had been spinning through realities, and stepped out the moment things stabilized. Perhaps it had been involuntary, the result of the spinning; they had been thrown out by centrifugal force. Actually there was no such force, she knew; it was an illusion, an apparent force, the result of inertia diverted. But for all that, it had a measurable effect, just as magic did. Anyway, now the two of them were back on the Virtual Mode, and Colene felt oddly at home here, though she wished Darius and Seqiro were with her.

But it was dangerous too. Fortunately both she and Provos were experienced here, and would not make obvious mistakes. The first of which was to get separated from each other. A person could quickly get lost amidst realities.

Colene closed her eyes and turned around, tuning in on her own anchor, Earth. She could sense where it was, or at least in what direction it was. Provos would be able to sense her own. They could probably sense the other anchors too, if they tried. Without that ability, they could truly get lost.

She felt the direction, and stopped, facing it. She opened her eyes.

She was facing directly out toward the sea.

Oh, no. They couldn't walk that way, and it would be disastrous to try to swim in that cold, choppy water. With magic they had been able to walk under it, but Colene had no magic, and neither did Provos.

Could they make a boat? No, because anything they made would disappear in ten feet, dumping them. The only material that would stay with them would be from an anchor reality—and if they stepped out onto Oria to get it, they would be stuck there again, with the despots waiting. So crossing the sea was out.

But maybe they could go around it. In fact, if they just walked beside it, in due course the realities would change so that there would no longer be a sea there, and they could cross whatever was there. It was frustrating to have to lose time in a detour, but that was just the way it was.

She turned to the other woman. "What do you think, Provos?"

But Provos was already stepping out, knowing where she was going—toward the despots' castle.

Colene hurried to catch up with her. "But that's directly away from—"

She broke off, because the woman had disappeared.

But in a moment she reappeared, as Colene stepped across the same plane of reality. That was the nature of travel through the Virtual Mode: a person saw an entire reality, or at least as much of it as any person saw from one spot, but this was not exactly illusory so much as unapproachable. Because every few steps took the person up another rung of the ladder, as it were, and it was like looking out at another floor of an endless building. Maybe like an elevator with glass walls, which hovered at each floor but gave admittance to none that was not an anchor. That wasn't a perfect analogy either, but would do for now. Each floor was real on its own terms, but might as well be illusion, because the elevator just didn't stop there. And the moment it crossed the line between floors, everything on one floor disappeared, and everything on the next one appeared. The layout of each floor might be almost identical, but the people would change.

Indeed, this new reality looked the same as the last. The castle remained, and the fields and fences. But this was just another sliver of mica in the block, and it had its own identity.

Probably there were despots there, and even maybe a gruff king, a voluptuous queen, and a dastardly knave. But their names would differ, and they would look different. Probably magic worked. But not quite as it did in Nona's reality. And of course no one had visited from the Virtual Mode. No girl from Earth, no telepathic horse.

They crossed the next border between realities, and the next. There was no sensation, merely the spot disorientation of seeing the scenery shift slightly. One reality had a field of sheep; then they were gone and it was an overgrown pasture. The distant castle remained on the top of its hill—actually a fortified rad, but who really cared?—and looked much the same. But why was Provos going there? What did she remember?

In fact, as Colene understood it, Provos had very little memory when traveling through the Virtual Mode, because her memory was of her future in a particular reality, and they were in any one reality only a few seconds. How could she know where to go?

Colene paced the woman, bothered. Obviously Provos did remember enough to make her certain of her direction, but it couldn't be of these transitory realities. Was it of one beyond, where they did stay, so she was merely headed for it? Colene had not had more than passing association with the woman before; Provos had traveled with Darius. But unless Colene had gotten things muddled, Provos' memory did not work that way. She had to be in a specific reality before she started to remember its future.

So why was the woman heading so purposefully somewhere? Colene wished she could at least ask.

Well, maybe she could. She waved a hand, signaling Provos. When Provos looked at her, she asked, "What are you up to?" and plastered a really confused look on her face to get the message across.

"You are tired?" Provos asked. She spoke in her own language, but Colene understood well enough. It really did seem that she was developing telepathy, from her association with Seqiro. It had been wonderful, verifying this with Nona, and it made her feel a lot better about leaving Darius and Seqiro with her. Nona was a decent person. That had come through along with the symbols she had been thinking. So now Colene could understand Provos, but Provos couldn't understand Colene. Because it seemed that Colene's little bit of telepathy was just one-way: receiving. But that didn't matter all that much, because Provos didn't remember the past anyway, so most dialogue with her was truncated.

But she hadn't answered the right question. Colene pondered a moment, then decided that her luck might be better if she *made* it the right question. "I have a concern." That could be taken as an indication she was tired.

"My home," Provos answered.

"Where are we going?" Colene asked, getting the feel of it. She pointed ahead, making her query-face. This was information, but it still didn't address the issue. It was Colene's home they were supposed to go to, and she was sure the woman understood that, because Seqiro's telepathy had made it plain.

"Because we need supplies," Provos replied, touching her back.

It was like an exploding lightbulb. "Why are we doing this?" she asked, spreading her hands in simulated bafflement. Because the despots had taken their supplies. They had had to change to local tunics, and of course Seqiro had been stripped of his burden. Without Nona's magic, Colene wouldn't even have panties now. Since they could not eat on the Virtual Mode, because food, like other things, disappeared with the crossing of the realities, they had to carry their supplies with them, and these supplies had to be from one of the anchor realities. They had headed almost naked into the Mode, and would never survive it—unless they got supplies. So Provos was heading for her own anchor, which must be close, where she could get those supplies. She didn't need to remember the realities they passed on the way; all she had to remember was that they spent a while at her home getting stocked up.

Suddenly Colene was very glad it was Provos she was with. None of the others had thought of this aspect, in their focus on the immediate problems of Oria. Had Seqiro come here, they would have been stuck, because they did not dare return to his reality. They had barely escaped it before, and could not sneak back. Not with unfriendly telepathic horses there. Assuming it was even within reach. But Provos, with her future memory, must have known that her own anchor was close enough, and could be used to solve this problem.

Colene wanted to thank her for that insight and action, but didn't see how she could do it now without confusing things. She should have done it at the outset. So she just kept the pace.

Now the castle was changing, by small stages, as they advanced toward it. So was the landscape. The contours of the Mandelbrot set fuzzed, becoming more like conventional earthly hills and valleys. They were leaving the region of fractals. Maybe that was just as well, because that was one weird universe! If they had gone into anything even stranger, they might have had a real problem getting through.

Provos continued purposefully down through the valley, then on up the hill. The woman was a determined walker! The castle loomed larger, and not just because it was closer. It now covered a more extensive section of the hill, and the walls towered up several stories. Against what kind of enemy were these ramparts intended to defend?

They stepped into one more reality—and there was a dragon before them. A big wingless fire-breathing creature with metallic scales. Both of them abruptly stopped. The dragon was between them and the castle.

The dragon heard them, and turned its head. Its near eye fixed on them.

Of course they could escape it merely by stepping into an adjacent reality. But if they stepped back, the monster might be lurking for them the moment they resumed forward progress. It would be better to step forward, seemingly into it, but crossing to a new reality before reaching it. Except that Colene's logic warred with her common sense. Nobody walked *toward* a horrendous fantasy dragon!

Then the dragon uttered not a roar but a squeak. It turned tail and fled toward the castle. Astonished, they watched it go. It remained visible because it had no reality boundaries to cross; it was in its own universe, and they could see it as long as they stood where they were.

The dragon charged up to the castle—and inside. No one challenged it. The drawbridge cranked up after it.

It was a dragon castle. And the dragons were terrified of people.

Colene exchanged a glance with Provos, who presumably remembered a similar occurrence in the near future.

Sure enough, in a moment another dragon arrived. The drawbridge lowered to let it in, then lifted again.

"We don't want to meet them," Provos said firmly.

"I wonder what sort of people live in this reality?" Colene said musingly. She realized that they must be getting closer to the beginning of the woman's experiences on the Mode, because in the past she had usually managed to wait for a question before answering it. Now she did not, as if she had not yet learned to. Maybe she had discovered, early in the experience of the others but late in her own with them, how to give her answer before hearing the question, just as the others were learning to ask their questions after hearing the answer. The convolutions of such interactions might become as devious and intricate as those of the filaments of the Mandelbrot set.

They resumed their march. The castle shifted several more times, then disappeared entirely before they reached it. They crossed over a wooded hill, and kept going. Colene was getting tired, but did not complain. She wanted to reach Provos' safe anchor before nightfall, if they could. Not all dragons might be chickens.

They trekked into the valley beyond, forging through thickening forestland. The trees had gradually changed, and now they had yellow trunks and blue leaves. Colene didn't worry about it; if that was the only odd thing about this region, they were well off. Trees were trees.

Then they came to it: the anchor. It was no more visible than the one on Oria, but Colene could tell; there was a feel about the region. Provos had oriented on it unerringly, because it was her own, but now that it was close, Colene could spot it also. It was just a place in a glade in the forest.

They stepped through. Colene felt a kind of firming around her, and knew that she had entered the anchor reality. This was where Provos lived.

Provos paused, as if remembering. Indeed, that must be what she was doing: assimilating the future experience she would have in this place she had left behind. Colene would take similar stock of her past experience when she set foot back on her own reality of Earth. Everything was comfortable, for Provos.

But the pause was brief. This meant, as Colene figured it, that they would not be here long. That was the way she wanted it; she hoped to get to Earth, get the information, and return to Oria as fast as possible, because she felt alone and naked without Seqiro, and tense and depressed without Darius. Without them she was incomplete.

Then Provos led the way through the glade, along a path through the blue-trunked trees, and to a cleared region. There was a house. It was odd, by Colene's definition: it seemed to be about ten feet on a side, square in cross section, and reached up six stories. There were guy wires holding it in place against the wind. In the distance were other houses, of similar type.

Yet as they walked toward it, she realized that it did make sense on its terms. On Earth houses tended to sprawl across the landscape; only in cities did they become taller than they were wide. But on Earth much of the natural terrain had been destroyed by man's advance. Here a house took up no more space than it had to, and the trees and other vegetation remained. This was a nice region. The field seemed to consist of cultivated plants of a number of kinds, all mixed in together: wheat, beans, cucumbers, carrots, potatoes, and roses. No weeds. How did they manage that? Did they remember where the weeds would be growing, and take them out before they got started?

They came to the door—and it wasn't a door, but a window, screened by light mesh instead of glass. Provos opened the mesh and stepped inside, and Colene followed.

The chamber was cubical, maybe eight feet on a side, with the furniture set into the walls. There were cabinets and a closet against one wall, a narrow table with built-in chairs on either side against the next, a thin sink and stove against the third, and a thin stairway climbing the fourth. That was all; the center was bare.

Provos went to the stairs and climbed. Colene followed, feeling increasingly out of place. Just how well did any of their party know Provos? Could she, Colene, find herself trapped in this towerlike edifice? But she reminded herself that Seqiro had known what was in the minds of all of them, and had accepted Provos; the woman had to be okay.

The stair was strange. Each step was just about one foot square and one foot high—but the steps for the left and right feet were offset by six inches. It was like two sets of stairs, one for the right foot, the other for the left foot. Each stairway rose at a forty-five-degree angle, so that by the time it crossed from one side of the house to the other it also reached the next floor. But the ascent was not steep, because only six inches separated the height of the alternate feet. This was efficient and effective. But only just big enough; it was essentially one-way. Two people could not pass each other at all conveniently, because the full width of the sides together was only two feet. But then how often did people need to pass on a stair, especially if this was a residence for one person, as it seemed to be?

The second floor was comfortably set up with shelving on three walls, with books, and a thick soft mat on the floor. Evidently the library or living room.

The stair turned the corner and continued on up. Provos showed the way.

The third floor was a bathroom: sink, tub, toilet, all close enough to what Colene knew to be no trouble. That was a relief!

The fourth floor was storage; there were bins and boxes and jars, and what might be a deep-freeze. Colene wasn't sure what kind of technology existed on this world, but surely they knew how to store their food.

The fifth floor was empty. It was a spare room, perhaps available for expansion when there was a family.

The sixth floor was the bedroom: clothing hung on one side, and a cushion bed was on the other.

The stairs continued to the roof. That was a railed platform. From it the surrounding landscape could be seen, forest, field, and houses.

Provos smiled, acknowledging a compliment.

"Oh, I like it!" Colene exclaimed. "This is a nice world." She was not being facetious; she wished her own world were more like this.

Then they returned to the storage room, where Provos fetched what looked like red potatoes and green eggs. Down to the kitchen, where she prepared something like a cross between a green omelet and red mashed potatoes, with pale orange milk. The food was served on square blue wooden plates, and the milk was in a yellow cup which appeared to have been fashioned from a thick, glossy yellow leaf. The stuff looked weird, but tasted good, and Colene ate heartily.

But with this relaxation came fatigue. Colene had known she was tired, and now realized that she had underestimated the case. She was starting to feel at home here, a little, and that meant she could become aware of lesser things. Such as fatigue. She was ready to drop.

Provos smiled. She did not seem as tired. She was old—about sixty—but tough. Maybe because of living in a house

like this, with all the climbing, and walking around the farm.
Or maybe she just concealed her wear and tear better.

As they finished, Provos took the plates and cups. "I'll
wash the dishes," Colene offered unenthusiastically, trying to
do her part.

But Provos was already shaking her head. She set the
dishes in the sink and stepped back. From the screen behind the
sink a vine entered. It curled down among the dishes, dripping
glistening sap and stroking them with little tonguelike leaves. It
was the dishwasher!

They went upstairs. Colene used the toilet facilities, then
followed Provos up to the bedroom. Then she remembered that
there was only the one bed, and had a horrible thought. Provos
had never expressed any interest in men. Maybe she was too
old. But was it possible that her interest was in women? Like
maybe fresh clean young women? Colene had some scores to
settle with men, who could be crude, brutish, and perpetually
sexual, while women were in general more refined and decent.
But that did not mean she had any desire to—

But Provos was already shoving her hanging clothing
over to the center. It slid along wooden rods, making a space
beyond. Then the woman fetched cushions from somewhere
and threw them down. Colene had a separate bed.

"Thank you," she said, for more than just the bed, and
flung herself flat. In an instant she was asleep.

OF course her green tunic was sadly rumpled in the
morning; she hadn't thought to remove it. But she found clothing laid out for her: a gray sweater, black blouse, brown knit
wool skirt, and knee-length black boots. Also green underwear:
a kind of loose corset extending from breast to rump. Surely
the kind of clothing worn by girls of this world. She remembered that Provos had worn similar, and that was reassuring.
It wasn't exactly a familiar outfit, but neither was it totally
alien.

Colene shrugged and put the stuff on. It fit her reasonably well. The sweater was actually a bit tight, because Colene
was fuller in the chest than Provos. This gave her perverse
pride; she had been feeling somewhat inferior compared to
Nona. The skirt reached all the way to her ankles, as she was
shorter than Provos. The boots were loose on her, because her
feet were smaller than the woman's, but she laced them up tight

and it was all right. It wasn't as if the soiled and rumpled green tunic and slippers were any better; that was Oria clothing. She would have to get to Earth to get her own kind of dress.

She went down the odd stairs, winding around to the bathroom, which she used. This time she was more observant, and saw that the toilet did not actually flush; it fed into a chamber which seemed to contain some kind of gray moss. Another hungry plant.

When it came to environmental responsibility, this was one savvy world.

That made Colene think. Provos seemed to have a good life here. Why had she left it? Darius had needed a woman, Seqiro had needed to escape and explore, and Colene herself had needed both the man and the horse. They all had had reason to risk the rigors of the Virtual Mode. But Provos seemed to need nothing. Why should she have taken such a step? It hadn't been just accident; she had sought her anchor, and had been prepared for it. Oh, she had told Darius that she had remembered a mysterious blank in her future, but there had to have been simpler ways to fill that in. A piece of her puzzle was missing.

Colene wound the rest of the way down to the kitchen. There was Provos, with breakfast just ready. Remarkable timing? No, the woman simply remembered when Colene had come down.

This time the meal was a greenish pudding with blue sauce. The blue turned out to be blueberry syrup; the green tasted vaguely like cornmeal mush. It would do.

After breakfast, Provos produced knapsacks and hats. The knapsacks were functional and capacious. The hats looked like insect heads; they were shiny black with two long antenna-like projections that wavered when the hats moved. Colene would have worn such a thing only on a dare at home. Here she knew it would be standard conservative attire.

Provos nodded affirmatively.

"We have to go shopping?" Colene asked. It was mostly rhetorical; she had picked up that message from the woman's mind.

They walked out along the path. Colene's legs were a little stiff from all the walking in the Virtual Mode, but that was working out. They followed a winding, almost invisible path to the woods, and then no path at all, except that Provos knew where to go.

They came to a canal through the forest. It was only a few feet wide, and the trees overhung it; it would not be visible from above. As they arrived, something rushed along it. A monstrous serpent!

But Provos seemed unalarmed. She stood right by the canal as the thing slid up. It stopped, its huge body almost filling the trench so that the water level rose. There was some sort of framework associated with it, a network of wooden bars and fiber cords.

Then the woman stepped onto the snake's back. Colene realized that this was transportation, the equivalent of a boat or bus. Feeling Provos' certainty, she joined her on the creature. There were four seats suspended by cords between side-bars, in tandem. Provos took the first, so Colene took the second.

Provos snapped her fingers. The serpent slid forward. Its coils didn't loop up; instead it nudged the canal on either side, and though the touches hardly seemed strong, it immediately accelerated. Colene had to hang on to the bars as her seat rocked with the swaying motion. They were moving at what seemed like a phenomenal pace, though probably it was only about fifteen miles an hour.

Colene looked around. The trees of the forest were passing swiftly behind, the more distant ones seeming to move more slowly because of the perspective. This was a fun way to travel!

The serpent swung around a turn, and the seats swung out. "Like a roller coaster!" Colene exclaimed. But not exactly; this was smoother, and all on the horizontal.

Then the snake slowed. Two more people were waiting at the next stop, a woman and a boy. The woman had the same kind of outfit that Provos and Colene wore; the boy had shorts and a cap that resembled a squished slug. Slugs and snails, that's what boys are made of, Colene thought, smiling.

The new woman said something to Provos, and Provos replied. Maybe it was the other way around, the reply coming before the remark. Colene gathered from Provos' mind that she did not know the woman, and that she preferred it this way. Because Provos did not want to have to explain her future absence.

Future absence. Of course—these people did not remember the past, so had no old friends. They had new friends, folk they would associate with in the future. Maybe Provos had known this other woman for decades before, but this was at the end of their acquaintance, so it counted for nothing. And it was reassuring to know that Provos would soon be leaving again; that meant that Colene would be too.

It was a bit scary to realize that at this point, Provos did not remember what had happened in the past. The adventure on Oria was lost to her, just as the coming visit to Earth was lost to Colene's memory. Provos knew Colene only from what was to come. Perhaps to the woman it seemed odd to think that Colene knew her only from what was past. Colene depended on Provos to have an accurate memory of that coming excursion, and Provos depended on Colene to help her with past memories. They were a haphazard but feasible team.

Meanwhile the woman and the boy got on the serpent. They had of course remembered that it would arrive at this time with two seats available. Had that not been the case, they wouldn't have bothered.

The snake moved out again. This time the ride was longer, and took them out of the forest and into a town. The buildings were similar in cross section, but much taller; they reached up twelve or eighteen stories, and had stronger guy lines. They just didn't take up any more ground space than they had to.

The serpent halted at a convergence of canals, and they disembarked. There were many people here, all in the outfits of this realm. This seemed to be a shopping center, for the houses had transparent screens on the sides facing the central street, and their interiors had many goods and items laid out.

Provos headed up a ramp suspended between buildings, one floor, two, three, four. Colene followed, content just to watch. When they took a level hanging walk, the open faces of many buildings were available. These had foodstuffs sealed away in packages. There were breads, and jars of spreads, and tubers and bundles of herbs and eggs of all types. Everything packed for traveling.

Colene nodded. Provos knew what she was doing. She probably remembered a need for certain quantities of a number of items, and knew what Colene's needs and tastes would be. Darius had thought or mentioned—in the presence of Seqiro it didn't make much difference—how Provos had intercepted him near her anchor, well prepared for the journey. It had taken him some time to catch on that she remembered the future, but it had turned out to be a literal lifesaver for him. It would probably be the same for Colene.

Provos made purchases. Her money turned out to be beads on a string. Colene thought of wampum, supposedly American Indian money, though it was doubtful whether the Amerinds used money before the white man came. At any rate, it seemed to work here.

When both their packs were full, they returned to the ground, and to the canal. A snake was just arriving with just the right number of seats for those who needed them. Colene reminded herself that this was really like people getting off a full bus on Earth: there was no coincidence that they got off together and went their separate ways, the ride a memory. Here, people came to fill the bus in the manner they remembered.

The serpent coursed out of the town and to the forest. The day was waning; they would make it back just about dusk. Again, no coincidence; Provos probably remembered finishing promptly then.

And so it was. They stepped into the house as darkness closed, and had supper. Colene realized that they had never had lunch; they had been so busy shopping that she had never noticed. She had not gotten hungry; that green pudding had stayed with her. If that was the kind of food they would have while traveling the Virtual Mode, it was good.

They slept. Colene dreamed of Darius, of being in his arms, of tempting him with her body and not succeeding, but managing to frustrate him something awful. It was a fun dream. *The time will come,* Seqiro thought to her.

She woke. Had she really received the horse's thought? Probably not; they were now on different realities, with a slew of intervening realities. She had thought she received him once before, when they had been separated by thousands of light-years in the super-science Mode, but that had turned out to be her own dawning telepathic ability.

Or could it have been some of both? Her just-barely-developing power of mind, and his expanding mature power? How could they be sure of the limits of it? They weren't separated by light-years now, but by realities, with the anchors connecting them. Maybe his telepathy could pass through the one anchor, and cross the realities, and cross the other anchor, and reach her. It was a nice thought.

She smiled in the darkness. That was a pun, maybe: a nice thought of hers, and a very nice and powerful thought of Seqiro's, if it had reached her across those realities.

She drifted back to sleep, satisfied.

THEY wasted no time in the morning. They ate a solid breakfast and headed out to the anchor. They passed through it without difficulty; this one had no animus magic bollixing it. They were back on the Virtual Mode.

Provos lost her certainty. She had remembered the events of the prior day, but now it was past and she had forgotten them. She had no memory of the realities they passed in seconds, and had to enter a reality in which they were going to remain before her memory came. Before, she had known she had to go home for supplies; that had perhaps not been memory so much as common sense. Now she had only memory, and it wasn't enough.

It was time for Colene to take the lead. She knew where she was going: Earth. It was her home, and she could orient on it more readily than Provos could. She had no memory of the trip there, because it was in her near future, but her knowledge of her purpose guided her.

She oriented, and felt the faint rightness that was the direction of her anchor. "This way, Provos," she said, assuming command.

But almost before she took the first step, she paused. If they went directly to Earth, not passing Go or collecting $200, they would walk smack back into that sea that had balked them before. They couldn't go that way.

Colene pondered. There was more than one way to go. They could move to the side, seeking to get around the sea. Or they could circle the Virtual Mode the other way. Any Virtual Mode, Darius had explained, was like a circle, or rather a pentagon, anchored by five connections. The lines of awareness tended to follow the edge of it; maybe it was the edge she sensed, rather than her home reality. If she followed the edge the opposite way, eventually she could complete the circuit and reach Earth. It was inevitable. It might take longer, but it made sense, because there should be no sea. Maybe. She hoped.

She reoriented. She felt a fainter rightness in the opposite direction. "No, this way," she said.

Provos had already shrugged, accepting it. She lacked the memory to argue. Colene had not argued when they were in Provos' world, for similar reason.

They set off, marching through the changing forest. At times animals flicked into view, spooking at the sudden presence of the two human beings, and flicking out of view again as the two strode on across the next invisible boundary. This was a weirdness to which Colene had become accustomed; in fact she rather enjoyed it. But she knew it could be dangerous, and kept alert.

The landscape changed. The hills and valleys became ridges and furrows, crossed by right-angled ridges and furrows, as if some giant cookie-cutter had shaped the terrain. The trees became lumps of colored protoplasm. When some developed tentacles, Colene got increasingly nervous. She had them pause to take out knives they had bought, and they held them in their hands as they walked. The thing was that if a tentacle grabbed a person, that person might not be able to escape it by stepping across the next boundary. Because the tentacle would hold that person right there in that reality. So they needed to be sure they had at least five feet of freedom, so they could reach the boundary forward or behind. A quick cut at a tentacle might make the difference.

The tentacular trees faded, replaced by blocks of wood which then became metal. Colene did not feel easy about these either, remembering what Darius had said about machine realities which had almost trapped him and Provos. Provos would not remember, because that was in her past. Damn!

But the metal lumps diminished in size, and the landscape became a kind of plain, not quite level, with lines crisscrossing it, like a sheet of graph paper or a diagram of stress vectors. Suddenly cubistic creatures appeared—and disappeared as Colene and Provos hastily stepped into the next reality. Nimble feet were a great asset on the Virtual Mode.

They stopped to have lunch. It was safe, because Provos remembered that it was, and the meal was good. The woman might remember backwards, but she was competent. Colene wondered again why the woman had left her home to risk the Virtual Mode, and wished she possessed the ability to ask. But that concept was too complicated to convey. Provos just seemed to be here because she was here.

The graph paper humped and distorted, becoming more normal hills and valleys. Moss appeared, which grew by reality stages into shrubs and small trees and then full-sized trees and then giant trees reminiscent of those on Jupiter in the Julia reality. Then these twisted into tentacular monsters, making Colene nervous again. But they remained trees, not grabbing at anyone, and there were birds' nests in their heights. Big ones. In fact something frighteningly large appeared, with a wing span of perhaps a hundred feet. A reality in which the fantastic roc birds existed? Why not; anything was possible, in some reality.

Colene was interested in the way realities seemed to be contiguous. Adjacent ones were similar to each other, changing by small stages. Such changes might seem rapid when a person was crossing a reality every two seconds, but that meant about thirty realities a minute, and a lot could shift by then. So they had the partial security of seeing new things coming, and if the trend seemed bad, they could go another way and try to avoid it, or slow down and proceed very carefully. So far they had been lucky; the terrain had been mostly innocuous or avoidable.

Then something sinister started. It wasn't anything in the scenery, which was reasonably ordinary. It was something in Colene's feeling. Something ugly was festering. Was she turning suicidal again?

She glanced at Provos—who was already looking at her. Then Colene realized that the ugliness was being transmitted from the other woman's mind.

Provos put her hands to her head as if to squeeze something out. Colene picked up the woman's alarm. This wasn't something in Provos, it was something being forced on her. Something mental, like a nightmare.

Colene took the woman's arm and urged her across the next boundary. It didn't help. Now it was plain that some mental thing, perhaps like a telepathic horse, had fixed on Provos and was turning her mind into horror.

They stepped back into the prior reality, but it didn't help. This was something that crossed realities. Seqiro had been able to do that, when contacting Colene the first time; she had found him physically by orienting on him mentally. There were many telepathic animals, in their various realities. This must be a telepathic slug or mindworm, feeding off the thoughts of other creatures, or perhaps driving them to it so it could feed on them physically.

"We've got to get out of its range," Colene said. She would not have understood what was wrong with Provos if she had not been able to read the mind horror directly. Since Colene's ability was as yet vestigial, it was surely much worse for Provos herself. The woman wasn't used to mental ugliness. Colene had had some experience, because of her own suicidal depression. Maybe that was why she was more resistant to this attack; the monster preferred healthy minds.

They ran on, and the realities changed, becoming crystalline and mountainous, with sharp little crystals underfoot. Colene was glad now for the knee-length boots. But they could not escape the mind predator, whose strength kept growing. Provos was almost unfunctional, responding only to Colene's direct hauling on her arm. Maybe the thing didn't need to bring its victims to it physically; maybe it could just suck out the mind across the realities. This was a new kind of threat, but as bad as any.

The hills became mountains, and the mountains mesas, with flat tops high up. Colene and Provos were in a valley channel, crunching blue, red, green, and yellow crystals with each step. In the sky were pastel-colored clouds. Suddenly Colene recognized this type of scene, from what Darius had told her: this was his home reality! They were approaching his anchor.

"We've got to get out of the Virtual Mode!" Colene gasped. "There's an anchor close by! Come on!" She dragged the woman along, still orienting on the faint rightness that was the route to an anchor. Had the mind-thing been attacking Colene herself, she wouldn't have been able to do it, for the horror would have blotted out the awareness. That had happened to Provos; Colene could feel it.

They ran on. Provos stumbled, and fell, and Colene fell with her, dragged down by her own hold on the woman. Pain lanced through them both: the sharply pointed crystals had stabbed through their clothing and punctured their skins.

Colene scrambled up, cutting her hand in the process, and lifted on Provos, who seemed not to feel the physical pain. Blood was flowing, soaking their clothing, but they couldn't worry about that. "On! On!" Colene cried. And in the back of her mind she realized that this was the first time in a long time that her blood had flowed when she hadn't cut herself. When she wasn't being suicidal.

The rightness became so strong that Colene realized that they must be at the verge of the anchor. But they weren't physically on it; they were to one side. Where was it?

With horror of another kind she realized that it had to be up on one of the mesas. They had to climb to the top. But how could they? The sides were so steeply angled that they were clifflike.

"Come *on!*" Colene cried, hauling Provos after her as she circled the most promising mountain. It wasn't big around the base, but they did cross several reality boundaries in the process.

Then Colene found what she had hardly dared hope for: ladder steps. There were people here, and they did come down off their platforms sometimes, so they had made notches in the stone. In fact there were parallel series, so that one person could climb while another descended.

"Up!" Colene cried, shoving the woman at the right-side ladder and taking the left herself. Colene climbed a few rungs. "Up! Up! It's the only escape!"

Provos stared at her vaguely, preoccupied by the torment within. Colene tried again. She put all her strength into trying to project her thought mentally. *Up! Escape the monster! Up!*

It got through. Provos grasped a rung and hauled. Once started, she moved rapidly; she was used to vertical houses and in good condition for climbing. Colene had to scramble to keep up.

Gasping, they reached the top. The mesa was only a few feet across, roughly circular, and it was empty. Had they come up here for nothing? No, the anchor had to be here.

Colene took Provos' arm. She stepped to the center of the circle.

Reality changed. Not on this mesa, but on the adjacent one, whose top was about sixty feet away across the chasm between them. It now had a house. Or perhaps a castle, girt by a small forest.

Colene stepped toward it, still holding Provos, passing through the anchor. Suddenly the horror in Provos' mind abated. They had escaped the monster!

But that monster would surely catch Provos again if she stepped back into the Virtual Mode. They had to hide here for a while, until the thing lost interest.

Where could they go? They could not reach the larger mesa, unless they climbed down the cliff and walked back through the crystalline valley. They were already bleeding from their prior tangle with those crystals.

But this was Darius' reality. Magic worked here. There would be people who could help. All she had to do was get their attention. She hoped.

Colene waved at the other mesa. "Help!" she cried.

To her gratified surprise, it worked. A man appeared at the brink of the other mesa, looking across at her. He seemed surprised. She could pick it up in his mind as well as his expression.

"I'm Colene!" she cried. Then she had a better idea. "Darius!"

"Darius!" the man echoed. And disappeared.

But in a moment he was back, with a woman. The woman studied them, and Colene felt an odd but not alien touch on her mind.

The woman consulted with the man. Then both of them jumped across the gulf to land on the small mesa with Colene and Provos. Magic, indeed!

"I'm Colene, Darius' friend," Colene said. "This is Provos, also his friend. We are trying to help him, but need help ourselves." Could they understand her? She feared they could not, because that wasn't their kind of magic. But they should know Darius, and know about the Virtual Mode.

"Colene," the woman echoed. She was perhaps forty, but in good condition. She wore a tunic, and under it showed the bulge of her huge diapers. Grown women wore diapers here, Colene remembered, to conceal their sexual attributes. "Provos." She did understand that much. Then she pointed to the man: "Cyng Pwer." And to herself. "Prima."

"Prima!" Colene echoed. The one whom Darius had rescued from the captivity of the dragons, and whom he would marry, so that Colene could be his mistress. Odd as it seemed, this was no rival, but an important and vital friend, for marriage to Darius would kill Colene.

Prima brought out a little figurine that was made up to look like herself. The Cyng did the same, with his looking like him. Then each brought out another doll, a blank one, and quickly doctored them to resemble Colene and Provos. Colene obligingly provided a hair, some spit, and a breath, and Provos did the same. This was a type of magic they understood.

Prima took Colene's hand, and the Cyng of Pwer took Provos' hand. Provos, freed of the attack by the mind-monster, was now remembering her coming experience in this reality, and understood. Perhaps better than Colene did. Prima and the Cyng moved the figures.

There was a wrenching, and Colene found herself standing on the larger mesa. This was Darius' way, all right!

They walked into the Cyng's castle/house. There pretty young women came to attend to the visitors. Colene and Provos were taken into a separate chamber, stripped, washed, touched with unguent, and magically healed of their cuts. Then, dressed in local tunics, slippers, and diapers—Colene knew better than to balk at this, apart from Provos' acceptance of it—they emerged to join their hosts.

Or rather, to separate. The King of Power was seated in a comfortable chair, and Provos went to join him. Prima led Colene outside. Colene glanced once at Provos, saw that she was satisfied, and knew that it was all right. They would rejoin and resume their travel in due course. They were simply being offered separate accommodations.

Prima took Colene's hand and icon, and conjured the two of them to another mesa and castle. "Cyng Hlahtar," she explained.

The residence of the King of Laughter! This was where Darius lived—and where Colene would also, once she and Darius both got here. This was fascinating.

The current King of Laughter was a huge red-bearded man. He was actually the former king, who had returned to take Darius' place while Darius was on the Virtual Mode. His name was Kublai.

Then Colene learned that Prima was Kublai's wife, but not his love. His love was his former wife, Koren, who was a beautiful young woman not a lot older than Colene, and whose barely concealed bitterness immediately endeared her to Colene. Koren had had to give up her husband, whom she loved, so that he could return to being the King of Laughter and marry Prima. This was because it was necessary for the king to deplete the joy of his wife, eventually discarding her when she had no more joy to give. Prima could handle it; Koren could not. Koren thought that Colene was luckier, and she resented it.

That was one thing Colene could deal with. She understood Koren's situation a whole lot better than the other woman thought she did.

Colene approached Kublai. "Please, Colene, Koren, put us together," she said. "Mind to mind." She knew it wasn't the same as what Seqiro did, but there were aspects of similarity. "Show her my joy."

Kublai looked at Prima. Prima said something in their language. She evidently had a notion what Colene was asking.

Kublai nodded. He came to embrace Colene. Colene focused on her internal state, making no effort to suppress the several facets of her feeling: her depressive state, her love for Darius, and her somewhat bitter compromise with her dream: she could love but not marry Darius, for he would marry Prima.

Then Kublai drew from her. It was a terrible, sinking feeling, and Colene thought she would die, literally. In an instant he restored what he had taken, almost. She felt like living again. This was what he did: he took what feeling was in a woman, multiplied it, and sent it out to everyone, including that woman, so that all shared her joy. Except that Colene had not joy but depression to give.

Kublai stepped away from her. That was all. He had done it. Koren understood exactly how Colene felt, because she had received it.

Koren stared at Colene. Now she knew: their situations were exactly similar. Only their men differed—and those men were to have the same wife, Prima, whom neither loved. The two young women were not rivals or enemies, they were victims of the situation. They were sisters in misery and love.

The tears started so suddenly that it was as if someone had dashed a tiny cup of water in Koren's face. Colene held open her arms, and Koren stepped into them, hugging her.

After that, it was easy. They had no common language, but hardly needed it. Colene was able to pick up what she needed from their minds to get along. She made clear by signals and nods, sometimes twenty-questions type, what she was doing: going home to her reality, to get information she needed to rescue Darius from being stranded in yet another reality.

With, she added sourly, a lovely woman and Colene's beloved horse.

Koren became positively friendly. She had not before had any acquaintance who understood her situation so perfectly, and it was a great relief to her. She hoped Colene would succeed in bringing Darius safely back, not just because that would allow Kublai to retire and marry Koren again, but because she wanted to be Colene's friend and companion. Colene liked that notion; it would certainly make her life here easier. But she doubted that anything so nice and simple could come to pass. The Virtual Mode was a sterner taskmaster than that.

But Prima, too, was friendly. She remained most grateful to Darius for rescuing her, and she liked her role as wife to the man she had loved in her youth. That was part of Koren's problem: she suspected that Kublai's marriage was not quite as loveless as it was supposed to be. The whole business of Darius' departure and Prima's return messed up her formerly idyllic life, and she wanted only to get it put back together the way it once had been. But Prima was reconciled to her situation, and knew how much worse it would have been had Darius not ventured on the Virtual Mode. She had wanted to be the King of Laughter herself, having the special ability for it, but had been denied it because she was a woman. Now she had a portion of it, and would retain that portion if Colene came here. Colene, being depressive, represented less of a threat to her than anyone else.

Koren took Colene out to see the sights: the many mesas, with their separate domiciles of all types, and their elaborate gardens, and the colored clouds which came to nourish those plants. The myriad crystals of the lowlands, reflecting and refracting multicolored splays of light up. The forms of sympathetic magic, which enabled the folk to conjure things or themselves to familiar places. The animals and birds peculiar to this region.

"I love it!" Colene said.

But all this was in her future. First she had to return to Earth, and then to Oria. She had to enable Nona to bring the anima. Only then could they all come here to this marvelous magical land and live happily ever after. Who could say that the authorities would not suffer some change of heart, and allow Prima to assume the role for which she was qualified, freeing Darius to marry Colene just as Darius' return would free Kublai to marry Koren? It was worth dreaming about. If she could just accomplish her present mission.

She slept in a pleasant bedchamber by herself, declining the offer of a handsome young man to be her companion for the night. Even this aspect of this society was clarifying for her: love, sex, and marriage were three different things, and not necessarily found together. Colene was Darius' love; neither of the other two changed that. She had met Ella, Darius' bedmate on off nights; she was pretty, pleasant, bouncy, enthusiastic, and not phenomenally smart. So if Darius married Prima and took off Ella's diaper, Colene would still be his love. That was what counted.

In the morning, she bid farewell to Koren. "I hope we meet again," she said. She looked around. "The same for everything and everyone here. It's a better world than mine."

Then Prima conjured her back to the residence of the Cyng of Pwer, where Provos was waiting. Provos was in her normal outfit, but Colene had elected to stay with the local clothing, even the diaper. It made her feel closer to Darius.

They went to the anchor and ventured cautiously through, ready to retreat if the mind-monster still lurked. It was clear. The monster must have given up and sought other prey. It might return, but with luck they would be well clear by then. They were on their way again, this time to Earth.

CHAPTER 10

RABBLE

DARIUS blinked, acclimatizing to the gloom. They were in a cave or tunnel that seemed to be the continuation of the hole of the giant mandolin, leading straight on into the rock. Perhaps they had simply passed through the petrified back of the mandolin, which had blocked the passage.

It was dark, but the darkness was not total. As they walked, the light brightened somewhat, until they had no trouble seeing their way.

"But where is your contact mind?" Darius asked the horse.

It retreated in alarm as we arrived. But there is another approaching. I can not read it, I only sense its presence. It is female.

"Did you read anything in the original mind?"

No. It was stupid. I reached only as far as its eyes, to help you conjure us.

"Keep working on the new mind. First test for hostility, and warn us. We want only to hide safely until Colene and Provos return."

"You must be ready to use your magic here, Nona," Stave said. "The rabble may be dangerous."

"You call them rabble?" Darius asked, not amused.

"That is what we call them," Nona explained. "All the people and creatures who have been banned from the surface because they lack even illusion magic. There are stories that they have an awful society in the center of the world, and live only to break out and slay all those on the surface. Both the despots and theows watch constantly to be sure that there is no escape for them."

"They may not be friendly, then," Darius remarked with irony.

"Yes," Stave agreed. "But there may also be too many for us to oppose physically. Since they do not have magic, Nona should be able to protect us against them."

"I will try," she agreed. "But I depend on Seqiro to alert me to danger."

She is here.

They paused and let the woman approach them. She was young and comely in a belted brown tunic. She smiled and spread her hands, showing by gesture that she intended no harm. Her hair and eyes were the same shade as her tunic, a nice match.

"This is a banished inhuman monster?" Darius inquired.

I can not yet read her mind, but she is alone and seems friendly.

"I had gathered as much," Darius said wryly.

The woman came to him. She said something.

"I can almost make it out," Nona said. "I think she said she loves you."

Darius snapped a glance at Nona. "This is humor?"

"Maybe I misunderstood," Nona said.

The woman put her arms slowly around Darius, embraced him, and tried to draw his head down for a kiss.

"But I don't think so," Nona added.

He resisted. "But I don't know her!" he protested. "And Colene would be upset."

"I will try to explain to her," Nona said. She spoke to the woman, and because Seqiro continued to translate her thoughts, he heard it as his own language. "Woman, this man is taken."

The woman clung to Darius, speaking emphatically.

I can get only a glimmer. The thoughts are not coming through, but the fringe of the emotion is.

"There is no other," Nona said, translating.

"Yes, there is," Darius said firmly. "Her name is Colene, and she is my love."

Seqiro's thought came again, while Nona tried to get through to the woman.

That emotion is not love as you feel it. It is not quite lust. She desires to breed with you, but for some reason other than your physical appeal. She wants to foal your offspring. I can not fathom why.

The horse was not conscious of irony. Seqiro was not insulting Darius, merely admitting that the woman's motive for choosing this stranger was unclear.

Meanwhile the woman was answering Nona. Nona was catching on to the variant of the language.

"She says that when you come here, you are hers."

"She can say what she chooses. I am not hers."

The woman finally let him go. She turned and walked ahead of them down the tunnel. Darius found her retreat as intriguing as her advance. He glanced at Stave and saw agreement there. The brown tunic was as close-fitting in back as it was in front. Whatever the woman was, she was no physical monster.

"Do we follow?" Nona asked. She too was watching the rabble woman, and her expression was just about what Colene's would have been: assessment and marginal resentment.

"There seems little else to do," Darius said.

They followed. The woman rounded a turn and disappeared, but in a moment they saw her again as they rounded the same turn. She was waiting for them, and now stepped forward to embrace Darius again. She said something.

"Her name is Potia," Nona reported. "She says you must breed with her."

This is odd, Seqiro thought. *I thought I was making progress, but it has become harder to reach her mind.*

"She must realize that something is happening, and be closing her mind," Darius said, gently pushing the woman back. "To what I say as well as to your probing."

A second woman approached. She too was in a brown tunic, but her hair and eyes were yellow. She was as pretty as Potia, but in a different way. She approached Stave.

"Hey," Nona protested as the woman embraced Stave.

The woman spoke. Darius was beginning to recognize the patterning of the language. This woman was saying the same thing to Stave that Potia had said to him, Darius.

Stave looked at Nona. "May I tell her that you are my love?" he asked.

"Is there any danger in that?" Darius asked. "Could that woman decide to get rid of Nona, if she sees her as a rival?"

There does not seem to be hostility, only urgency. She is interested only in Stave.

Nona was hesitating. Then Darius realized, as he felt the underlying emotions Seqiro picked up, that it was not just a matter of safety, but of uncertainty. She was not in love with Stave.

"Perhaps I am not," she said apologetically.

Stave spoke to the woman. "I am not looking for love at the moment."

The woman hardly paused. Her name, she said, was Keli. He had to breed with her. She clarified this by taking one of his hands and placing it on her full bosom.

Stave, intrigued, nevertheless demurred. After a moment Keli withdrew, disappointed, and joined Potia, leading the way on around the turn. They disappeared.

"Again we follow," Darius said, somewhat bemused by this pattern.

As before, the women were waiting for them, as if surprised that the party had not kept up. Each embraced "her" man again, despite lack of encouragement.

They are not hostile. But their minds are odd. I have lost progress again. There is something strange about this situation.

Darius and Stave laughed. There certainly was!

Then a young man approached. He was in brown, too, with brown hair and yellow eyes, and quite handsome. He approached Nona.

Both Darius and Stave moved to block him from her. "No, let him come," Nona said. "These folk seem to have their way of greeting us."

They did indeed! Darius and Stave moved out of the way, and the man came to embrace Nona. He sought to kiss her, but she turned her face aside. "I am Lang," he said. "I am to breed with you."

"Not yet," Nona said, disengaging much as the men had. "But thank you for the offer."

He let her go, though evidently disappointed. He joined the two women in brown and they led the way on down the curvy passage, walking quickly.

"This grows familiar," Darius said. But he did not rush to keep the pace, knowing that the three would wait the moment they got out of sight.

So it was. In a moment they rounded the bend and rejoined the three, who were waiting expectantly. This time all three stepped forward to embrace their chosen people, as if long separated from friends. Darius, Stave, and Nona submitted with resignation.

"All we are missing is a mare," Darius muttered as they followed the rabble folk on down into the planet.

There was the sound of hooves.

It was a brown mare, with brown eyes and yellow mane. She nuzzled Seqiro. She seemed to be ready to mate.

Her name is Bel, Seqiro thought. *But her mind is as obscure as the others. It seems to be of similar intelligence. She will soon be in heat.*

"These encounters are no coincidence," Darius said. "They saw us coming. They must be trying to lull us by suggesting that they find us attractive for breeding purposes. But what is their real object?"

I can not fathom that in any of them.

"But as long as we are sure they are not hostile, we can go with them," Nona said. "If they remain friendly long enough, we shall be able to endure until Colene and Provos return with our information."

"I think I would rather have encountered vicious monsters," Darius said. "Then we could have settled with them and known where we stood. These folk may be friendly, but let's not reveal the several powers we have until such time as we have to."

"I was thinking the same thing," Nona said. "They won't expect magic in a woman."

"Or in men who have been exiled," Stave said.

"Or in a horse," Darius added.

Agreed.

"Are we sure we have magic here?" Stave inquired. "The rabble are confined because they are subhuman, having no magic at all, but that might be because no magic works here."

That could account for my difficulty getting into their minds, Seqiro thought. *My ability is limited in range on the surface, and perhaps limited in depth here.*

"We had better test it," Darius said. "The moment the natives give us another moment by ourselves."

"Which is right now," Darius said. He brought out his icon of himself, invoked it, and lifted it slightly. He felt his body being tugged upward. His magic still worked.

Meanwhile a picture appeared on the wall, of the four of them. That meant that Stave's power of illusion was functional. And a loose stone on the floor lifted, hovered, circled, and dropped. Nona's levitation remained.

"Our powers remain," Darius said. "So probably yours does too, Seqiro. After all, you have been mind-talking with us throughout. But the minds here are hard for you to get into. Once you fathom them, they may be as easy to read as ours are."

There is something else, the horse thought grimly. *I start to penetrate the minds, then lose my way. That has never happened before.*

They walked on around the turn. There were the four rabble. The three human ones came to embrace, and the mare to sniff noses. There certainly was something odd; why did they always repeat these actions after such brief separations?

Now the tunnel opened out into a larger system. There was a broad center passage, with many intersecting tunnels. This might be the equivalent of a village.

Still the four who had introduced themselves disappeared and reappeared, just stepping momentarily out of sight as the group walked on. Finally Seqiro figured it out: *They are changing creatures! Every few minutes we are in the company of four new ones who look, sound, and smell like the others.*

"Now, that's interesting," Darius said. "That accounts for your inability to penetrate their minds: you're continually working on new, unfamiliar minds. But what is the point?"

If I could focus on a single mind for a longer period, I should be able to discover that.

"Then we must help you to do that. How can we prevent one of them from changing?"

"By preventing her from stepping out of our sight," Stave said. "I think I could do that, but I'm not sure how you would feel about it, Nona."

"I am nervous about being ignorant in this place," Nona said. "If you can hold yours, do it."

So Stave proceeded to do that. When the next group

came to embrace, he welcomed it, and did not let his yellow-haired-and-eyed woman Keli go. Instead he kissed her again. "Maybe you are right," he told her carefully in her dialect. "Maybe we had better breed."

Nona faced away, protecting her expression. Now she understood why he had thought she might object. Nevertheless, she made a running translation for Darius; she wrestled with the variants of words, and as she managed to grasp them, Seqiro relayed the meanings.

Keli was delighted. "Now!" she exclaimed, tugging at her tight tunic.

"Maybe not right now, for we of the surface have peculiar conventions. We like to be alone for such activity."

"I will take you to a private chamber!" she said eagerly.

"But we also like to get to know each other first," he continued. "We prefer to have an enduring relationship. That takes time."

"But that is not needed for breeding!" she objected. "You cannot remain with me after breeding."

"Now, this is interesting," Nona murmured. "Women who prefer to breed and run?"

"That is not the way the women of my world feel," Darius said.

But it is for my kind.

Both Darius and Nona smiled.

"It is the way it must be," Keli said. "You must not stay with the one you have bred."

"Why not?" Stave inquired. The other rabble folk were moving on ahead, but he held Keli, who seemed quite willing to remain. "I might want to do it again with you."

"Oh!" She was shocked.

Meanwhile the others disappeared. But Keli, despite her distress, remained. She could not change with another who seemed exactly like her.

"I am from the surface, and ignorant of your ways," Stave said patiently. "You will have to explain to me why I can not breed with you repeatedly, if I like you."

"Because you must be shared," she said.

"But I want to share only with you."

"No! With a thousand women!"

This surprised them all. "What?" Stave asked.

"You must breed with a thousand women before you can settle with one," she explained. "It is the Way."

"It is not my way. I want only one."

Their party, still walking, caught up with the other three. They had changed, but Keli had not.

I am getting into her mind, Seqiro thought. *She is not trying to mask her thoughts.*

"I think none of them are," Darius said. "They merely keep changing, for what reason we hope to learn."

Stave embraced Keli as the others embraced their own. "Maybe after the thousand," she said. "Then you will be free."

"I'm free now," he said.

Now her look was sad. "You are not."

"But I am. If I do not like it here, I will leave."

"You can not. You must breed."

She is speaking the truth. She believes we are captives.

Darius looked around. They were coming to a central garden spot, where many men were working. The plants were unlike those of the surface, which had a superficial resemblance to those of his reality and Colene's. These didn't bother; they were weirdly fractal, with branches radiating out into further branches, but no obvious roots or stems or leaves. Some seemed kaleidoscopic, and some like assorted fish eyes, and yet others like bunches of feathers. Some were squares piled on squares, or fragments of squares, becoming crystalline, reminding him of the valleys of his home. There seemed to be an infinite variety, but he could not see how they grew or how they were used.

"That is not a thing that can be dictated by others," Stave said. "It has to be by choice."

"It's nice when by choice," she said. "But it must be, regardless."

Truth.

Darius liked the smell of this no better than the others did. Why was there this imperative for mass breeding?

"I must learn more of this," Stave said. "I am learning your dialect. Let us go somewhere private and talk, and come to a more perfect understanding."

"Will you breed with me?" she asked eagerly.

He glanced again at Nona. "You're a man," Nona said, resigned. "Do what men do. We need the information." It seemed that their normal dialect was indecipherable to the rabble; Seqiro's help enabled them to understand Keli. Thus they could continue to talk among themselves, without giving away the fact of Seqiro's mind-talk.

"I may breed with you if I come to understand the necessity," Stave said.

"Yes! Here!" She drew him into a side passage, and thence into a private chamber.

Darius glanced at Nona. They had been left behind physically, but not mentally, for Stave remained within range. What were they to do while Stave worked on getting them what they needed to know?

Then Stave reappeared, holding Keli's hand. This was not affection so much as making sure she was not switched for another Keli without his knowledge. "My companions," he said. "They must be fed, and have a place to rest, while we talk."

Immediately, the three other rabble folk, who had changed out several times during this dialogue, responded. They led Darius, Nona, and Seqiro to a table where objects of assorted shapes were piled. This was food?

Potia picked up a branching stick and proffered it to Darius. He gazed blankly at it. Then she put it to her mouth and bit at the fringe. It broke off, and she chewed on the fragment.

Darius took it from her and tried a bite himself. The stuff was brittle, but melted as soon as it touched his mouth. It had a sweet aroma and taste. This was indeed food.

There were also vessels of liquid: bubblelike shapes with projecting blisters, which in turn had projections. When a person bit off a small projection, he could then sip the liquid nectar within.

So they ate, and while they did so, they tuned in on Stave's dialogue with Keli. She was feeding him a similar repast, but in a suggestive manner: she caressed him somewhere each time she gave him something. He was becoming interested, for she was a fine-looking woman. But the point of it was what they were saying to each other.

"I do not understand about breeding with a thousand women," Stave said. "On the surface, a man breeds with one woman, and if he considers doing it with another, the first is upset." As Nona would be, if he let this creature seduce him: his thought came through clearly. Darius understood the situa-

tion well enough. He glanced across at Nona, and she met his
gaze briefly. Her thought came through: she and Stave were
close, but not possessively close; it was Stave's right to do as he
chose. Had she wanted to reserve him for herself, she should
have done it before, and she had not.

"We rabble want most of all to return to the surface
world," Keli replied. "But we can not, for we have no magic,
not even illusion. But if we breed with those from the surface,
our children may have magic, and be able to return. So we long
instead for that, and do our utmost to breed with those who are
fresh from there. It is our rule: any person from that realm
must breed with a thousand of our folk before being free to do
what he prefers. His only choice is with whom to breed. We will
not let you go until you have done this."

Stave was beginning to appreciate the enormity of this
requirement. "But Nona—the woman of our party—she could
never succeed in doing this!"

Darius felt Nona stiffen beside him. This was becoming
uncomfortably personal.

"Yes, she could," Keli answered. "She could breed with
twenty men in a day, and finish in fifty days."

Nona did not seem reassured by that estimate.

"But she would not have a thousand babies!"

"But she would have one, and have given a thousand
men the chance to sire that one."

So that was it: a fair chance for every one of the rabble.
It was beginning to make sense.

"But a man could not do that," Stave continued. "He—
maybe several in a day, but not twenty, and not for long."

"We know. So it will be one a day, for a thousand days.
Starting with me, for you."

"But you might not conceive!"

"But I will have my chance. Some will conceive. There
will be some babies who can go to the surface. That is all we
ask. A thousand attempts with a thousand folk. It is not so
much, because we take good care of you."

"Suppose I decide not to?" he demanded.

"I will try my best to persuade you," she said. "Like
this." She drew off her tunic, to reveal a body that struck
Darius as it did Stave. Stave's mind was relaying a mental
picture: perfection. It would be no chore to address that body.

But Stave, like Darius, knew caution. He knew that the

other rabble folk had been changing every few minutes, though they looked the same. He wanted to know why, but hesitated to ask.

I have found it, Seqiro thought. *These folk are form-changers. Each can assume any form, human or animal, though they can not change their body mass, so it is not true magic. Form does not matter much to them; it is a convenience of the moment. They are giving as many of their number as possible a chance to breed: each has a set time to make an impression, and then must give place to another. Keli is the name of that form, not the person; but the person in that form when Stave took an interest is allowed to continue, and to breed with him if she can.*

Darius whistled soundlessly. Form-changing and the desire to breed with the newcomers: that accounted for everything. It also showed an extremely fine-tuned program. Surely these folk did know how to prevent their visitors from departing, and how to force them to breed if they did not do so voluntarily. This was a trap of an unanticipated nature.

Nona, receiving his thoughts, looked pale. How were they going to handle this?

"Could they even assume our forms?" Darius asked.

They could.

"Then we had better develop sufficient mental touch to know exactly with whom we are dealing," Darius said.

I know the difference between your minds and theirs, the horse assured him. *I will keep you informed. They are not aware of my ability, so are taking no precautions against it. My difficulty in reading their minds is purely because they are constantly changing folk, and new minds are hard to address.*

They continued eating, while Stave continued to fend off Keli's advances without actually rejecting her.

Then Nona stood. "Is there a private chamber for personal matters?" she inquired.

"Ah, you are ready to breed with me?" Lang asked, pleased.

Oops. "Not yet," she said. "I meant for—I have eaten and drunk, and—"

"I will show you," he said quickly. Meanwhile Seqiro confirmed that such conventions were similar here to those of the surface realm.

Nona departed. But then things got interesting. *They are trying it,* Seqiro thought. *The woman who returns to Darius will*

*not be Nona, and the man Nona returns to will not be Darius. I
can not be sure, because Keli is not thinking of this, but I suspect
that they believe that Darius and Nona are interested in each
other.*

"A nice ploy," Darius muttered.

After an interval, he saw Nona returning. "Oh, so they
didn't try it," he said.

That is not Nona.

Darius looked again. It *was* Nona! She was identical, and
she moved the same way. She had been a perfectly beautiful
young woman, and she remained so. In fact she came to sit
beside him, and she kissed him on the side of the face, then
caught his head to turn his face to hers for a full kiss.

But Seqiro relayed her thoughts to him, and they were
impenetrable. They were not the thoughts of the woman he
knew, but of an alien. He had been misled by her appearance
despite the horse's warning; without that warning he would
have been entirely fooled. Except for his surprise that Nona
should act this way. She had kissed him once, when confused
after a conjuration, but otherwise been more reserved. Romantic aggression was not her way. In that respect she was quite
different from Colene.

Potia got up and left. Would that have tipped him off?
He wasn't sure.

Then Nona's thoughts came. *Darius? But I was about to
return to the table. Why are you—oh!*

"He's not Darius," Darius muttered.

*Darius? This isn't you? It looks exactly like you, but you
never tried to touch me like this.*

"I'm not your man," he said without moving his lips.
"There's a woman who looks just like you here with me, and
she's kissing me. What's he doing with you?"

He must think we are lovers! she thought indignantly.
That seemed to be sufficient answer.

"Do we reveal that we know their ploy?" he asked
soundlessly. The Nona emulation was now pressing his captured hand against her full bosom. "If we do, they may proceed
to something we like less."

If we don't, we are going to be lovers by proxy, she responded. *I would prefer to be with the real you.* She meant
because she trusted him, but her thought did not exclude the
aspect of love. That startled him for another reason. Her

thought carried an added nuance: the legendary Earle, in the story told on Jupiter, had looked like a cross between Angus and Darius. She had recognized this, and suppressed the realization.

"We had better get together," he said. "But let's not reveal what we know. Seqiro, guide us."

Follow my thought. A picture showed a hall leading away.

He disengaged far enough to stand. The emulation stood with him. She did something to her red tunic that enabled him to see down inside its front. He knew she wasn't the real Nona, and knew that every action of hers was calculated to damp down his logic and fire up his passion, but it remained an effective view. The more so because she did not wear the halter undergarment Colene had arranged for the real Nona.

"A private chamber," he said aloud. "Maybe we can find one." He looked around.

Null-Nona looked also, evidently understanding him well enough. She spied the entrance to a chamber, and urged him there.

"Where are you, Nona?" he asked silently.

"Down the passage." Seqiro renewed the mental map, so that the two of them knew where they were with respect to each other.

"I don't like this one," he said aloud. "Let's find a better one." He headed down the passage toward the real Nona.

Null-Nona caught his arm, almost turning him into another chamber, but he persisted. "Not good enough. But down here, maybe—" He moved on despite her.

Desperate, Null-Nona pulled off her tunic to reveal her naked body. It was a shock; in Darius' culture women wore bulky diapers under their exterior clothing to conceal their alluring contours, lest any male who spied them be overcome by lust. Even his encounter with Colene's quite different attitude had not been enough to reverse a lifetime's conditioning. Occasional glances down necklines or up skirts were one thing, for they never showed as much as they seemed to; the complete array, without warning, was another. He experienced instant desire.

She embraced him ardently, and sought to draw him into another chamber. The irony was that her passion was surely genuine; she wanted more than anything else to breed with him.

But she was not the woman she seemed to be, and he would be in trouble if he bred with either the emulation or the real one. So he resisted, though in other circumstances he would have been glad to cooperate. It was a considerable challenge.

Meanwhile Nona's thoughts were coming to him. *He is trying to get me into a chamber. I can not resist further without revealing what I know. Yet if I enter that chamber—*

"Enter it," he replied. "But guide me in. Then we shall see what we shall see."

Don't take long, she thought urgently.

Now you know what I am experiencing, Stave's thought came. *I, too, would rather be with you, Nona.*

Then have your paramour assume my form! she snapped mentally. *Darius, you must get here immediately, or I must use my magic on your image.*

Which would mean that the rabble would know her power. Darius put aside the irony of her two thoughts involving Stave and himself—in concert they implied that Darius *was* her lover—and hauled her distractingly exposed image along the hall to that chamber. "This one," he said. "This one seems right."

Null-Nona forgot herself to the extent of speaking. "No! No!" Her sentiment would have been evident in any language. She wrapped herself around him, trying to bear him down right in the passage. Anything to gain the breeding before he discovered the truth.

They stumbled into the chamber. There was the real Nona, in a similar state of dishabille except for her underclothing, almost exactly as exciting, with Null-Darius climbing on her.

"Ha!" Darius cried with righteous anger. He threw Null-Nona away from him and clapped a hand on Null-Darius. "Who are you?"

Nona stared at Null-Nona with feigned astonishment. "Who are you?" she echoed.

Darius took a closer look at Null-Darius. He let his mouth drop open, as if just realizing the man's similarity to himself.

"He looks just like you!" Nona said.

"There are two of you!" Darius said. He hoped that his interest in their deliciously exposed bodies would be taken for surprise. They were like identical twins, one half undressed and the other completely so, and he would have loved to dream of a situation like this. Provided either were truly his to dream of.

The two emulations were not stupid. They affected the same surprise as the real ones, trying to confuse the real ones. But Darius cut through that. "Say something in your own language," he told the two Nonas.

That separated them more surely than the partial clothing. Only one even understood his words—though it was the mental translation she grasped—and so only she could answer appropriately. "I am Nona," she declared. Then: "And you must be Darius, because you spoke correctly." The rabble could not distinguish one language from the other well enough to realize that they were being partly deceived.

Darius and Nona embraced. They were now confirming for the two emulations that they were indeed associating with each other, for this was better than being subject to the breeding program of this realm. Darius felt guilty, knowing how Colene would resent this particular byplay.

Then they turned to face the other two, who were embracing each other, still trying to pretend. But their game was lost; they could breed with each other if they wished, gaining nothing. It was clear that they understood that the visitors had stumbled on part of the truth, and needed an explanation.

"Tell us what this means," Nona said to them. "Why did you try to deceive us? Had we not happened to see you together, we might have been fooled." Thus protecting Seqiro's secret.

"You must breed," the man said. "But you may choose with whom to breed. We wanted to be first."

"You can change form!" Nona said as if just realizing it. "You can imitate us!"

"We thought it would make it easier for you," the woman said.

I have stalled as long as I can, Stave's thought came. *Either join me, or let me have her.*

"It is better to maintain a united front," Darius said. "We must protect him too."

"We must unify our party," Nona said, so that the rabble could understand. "We must be together, so that no one can fool us again. Where is Stave? Where is the horse?"

"We must find them," Darius said.

They marched out, followed somewhat helplessly by the

emulations. Apparently it was bad form to change appearance in the sight of others, so they were locked in.

They walked down the passage, peeking into chambers as if searching each for their lost companions. It would have been a hopeless quest, for there were many chambers, had they not been guided by Seqiro.

They found the horse still at the table, with Bel the yellow-maned mare. *I have no objection to breeding,* he thought.

"Hold off for a while," Darius muttered. "We may need your full attention." He put his hand on the horse's back, as if giving a command, and Seqiro obliged by leaving the mare and following him.

They continued to explore chambers, trying to make it seem as if they were about to find the right one by chance. *I have learned that the creatures here are not completely human,* Seqiro thought. *Neither are they animal. They may be reckoned as animal with human intelligence, and the ability to assume the forms they desire. By my definition they are the equivalent of the folk on the surface, and not inferior.*

"Then why are they so eager to breed with us?" Darius asked.

They believe they are inferior, because they lack magic. They do not consider form-changing to be proper magic.

"This is foolishness!" Darius said. "They should be satisfied with what they are."

To a horse, many human conventions seem similarly foolish.

Darius knew better than to argue, but Nona didn't. "What conventions?" she asked, as if addressing Darius.

Confining your breeding to a single stallion or mare. You should breed with the nearest feasible creature of your species, when in season.

"That does seem to be what the rabble want," she admitted. "So it seems that they are as much animal as human in attitude as well as body."

Here is the chamber.

Nona entered it. "Why, Stave!" she exclaimed. "What are you doing?" As if there could be any confusion on that score.

Keli was chagrined, but not because she was naked. "He is breeding with me," she said. Her words were now clear to them all, because Seqiro had penetrated her mind and was translating freely. "Can't your business wait another minute until we are done?"

But Stave, abashed despite his knowledge that this interruption was incipient, was hastily straightening out his blue tunic. In any other circumstance he would have been mortified to have Nona discover him in such state with another woman. In this case he had begged her to do just that. Still, his embarrassment was striking all of them, mentally.

Darius did what he could to restore equilibrium. "We have learned that these folk are able to change form. One assumed the likeness of Nona, and another the likeness of me, so that we were almost fooled." He indicated the two figures behind him, who still looked exactly like himself and Nona. "We decided that we need to remain together as a group, so that we can no longer be fooled this way. Otherwise we might be hopelessly divided, and never be able to leave this place."

Stave looked at the emulated Darius and Nona. He was impressed. "You are right. I might never have found you, if you had not found me."

"Then stay together," Keli said. "But breed me now."

"Much as I would like to, I must go with my friends," Stave told her with real regret. His feelings were still coming through: he very much wanted a relationship with Nona, but knew that this was probably doomed for reasons not related to whatever feeling she had for him. Thus the offer of a beautiful creature like Keli, or of a creature in the exact likeness of Nona, had considerable appeal.

"But they too must breed," Keli reminded him. "A thousand times, each one."

"What?" Nona demanded. This was information they had had only via Seqiro, so it was necessary to establish this independent source of information.

"The rabble has this requirement for visitors from the surface," Stave explained. "Each must breed with a thousand rabble, before being free. This is to enable more children to have magic that will allow them to return to the surface."

The rabble are gathering.

"We had better get out of here," Darius said tersely. Then, to Stave: "We do not accept any such requirement. They can not hold us to it."

"We do not accept this," Nona translated for Keli, with Seqiro making sure the woman understood.

They stepped out of the chamber, and paused.

The passage was now filled with people and creatures. It was apparent that their small group of four was not going to be able to go anywhere unless the rabble allowed it.

CHAPTER 11

SLICK

THE walk was reasonably routine, considering. They did encounter a dragon, but avoided it, and similarly avoided something that seemed to be a crossbreed between a scorpion and a tractor. They crossed a sea made of jelly solid enough to walk on—that was nervous business, because it might change to thin water at any boundary—and passed a region in which the ground seemed wooden and the trees were made of stone and earth. They did not pass any realities with telepathic animals; that would be in the vicinity of Seqiro's anchor, perhaps on the opposite side of the Virtual Mode.

It was, however, a longer journey, requiring several days. Provos' supplies were adequate; she might not remember details of the many realities they would cross, but she had known how long their excursion would be.

Colene discovered that she rather liked being with Provos, who had many sterling qualities despite being hard to talk with and of another generation. Colene wished that her own parents had had more such qualities. Scratch a suicidal girl, she thought wryly, and you found a fouled-up family. Provos seemed to have no evil habits. Had she ever married? It was hard to tell, but Colene suspected not, because her house was too clean and uncluttered.

What would Provos do on Earth? Colene hadn't thought of that, but now it worried her. Colene herself had a home, such as it was, but she couldn't take Provos there. In fact, maybe she couldn't take herself there; she had been away for a month or so, and there might be awkward questions. But what were they going to do—throw her in prison? She could maybe hide Provos in Dogwood Bumshed, her hideaway. It wasn't as if she were going to stay any length of time.

But Provos herself could help. All they had to do was give her time to get her memory straight, and she would know what pitfalls awaited them. That and common sense should get them through, Colene hoped. She really hadn't been thinking of the possible complications of her home reality when she blithely said she could get the fractal information.

ON the fifth day of this leg of the journey the territory began to look familiar. They were coming to the Earth Colene knew. She experienced a certain bitter nostalgia. She had not loved her life on Earth, yet it had had its points. She had gone over some of them with Seqiro, in a fashion expiating emotional events, but there were others. Her feelings were mixed.

She could have used her bicycle here. But that had been lost to the despots, who had surely been much perplexed by it, and anyway Provos didn't have one. So they plodded on along beside the increasingly stable highway.

They found Colene's town, and walked the street toward it. Cars blinked in and out on the road as the two of them continued to cross realities. Colene had left this place at dawn, with little traffic, so it had been some time before she had realized exactly how strange the Virtual Mode was. Now it was afternoon, with plenty of traffic, and the way the cars popped in and out of existence was startling. Trees were stationary, and animals generally slow-moving, so the eye could reorient on them. But the cars were traveling, some of them at high speed— if there was any driver in Oklahoma who even knew what the speed limit was, he concealed that information—so that they shot through the ten-foot section of whatever reality Colene stood in like the proverbial bats out of hell. Provos was alarmed, but adjusted as Colene reassured her; they were reasonably safe on the sidewalk.

Then they reached Colene's house. It was the wrong design and color and had the wrong trees in the yard. But these details kept shifting as they approached, until everything was pretty close.

Colene led the way around to Bumshed, which was where the anchor actually was. Until they passed through it, nothing really counted; even if they saw people, they would not be in the same reality, and a miss by even one thin reality would be a whole lot more significant than a miss by a mile.

They entered the shed and passed through the anchor. Suddenly the things Colene had left behind appeared: crumpled blankets, a covered privy pot, her teddy bear, Raggedy Ann doll, books, and her guitar. And the knife. All the things she had gathered together here when she planned to kill herself. Only she hadn't had the guts to do it—and then the Virtual Mode had come, and she had grabbed the anchor and gone off to seek Darius.

She stood looking at it all. There was her locked box, containing her instruments of death and her diary addressed to Maresy Doats. There was her picture of Maresy, grazing in a nice field. There was the artificial carnation flower saved from the prom. And there, tucked in between the pot and its cover, was her farewell note for her family.

Hadn't they checked here? Hadn't they seen that note? It couldn't be that they had never even missed her!

She stooped to pull it out. She read it. DEAR FOLKS: DON'T WORRY; I AM FINE. I JUST HAVE SOMEWHERE TO GO. COLENE.

The sheet blurred. She was crying.

Provos put her arms around Colene and held her close. It was a comfort Colene needed. Somehow she had hardly thought of this, of what she had left here. It was as if she really had sliced her arms and bled into the pot until she died, leaving all her precious things around her body. Now she had returned from that death, and they had faithfully waited for her.

But she couldn't afford to waste time moping. She had a job to do, so she could rescue Darius and Seqiro.

Even as she came to that conclusion, Provos was letting her go. The woman began to put the shed in order, making room in the center and fashioning a kind of cushion by a wall. She knew she would have to stay here while Colene went out, because there was no way Provos could get by in this reality.

But Colene had to do some organizing of her own. This was afternoon and her folks should not yet be home from their jobs; she had time to get inside and change to local clothing. It would never do to parade around here in a tunic and giant diaper!

She opened the door and looked out. All was clear. Nothing in sight but the house and the little dogwood tree. Was she really in her home reality? To make sure, Colene went out and walked ten feet: nothing changed. But of course it could be a very similar reality. So she picked up a pebble and walked back. The pebble didn't disappear. She might look like an idiot doing this, but she needed to be sure. This was her home, all right.

Everything in the yard looked just about the same as it had been when she had left it. The grass needed mowing, but it always did. Things looked a little browner, but that was because the fall season was another month along.

Provos emerged from the shed. "But you mustn't be seen!" Colene protested.

The woman walked toward the house. Colene realized that Provos' future memory had taken good hold; she remembered that no one was home at this hour, and she wanted to see the house.

Colene ran to catch up. She went to the back door. It was locked, but Provos was already fetching the key from under the mat. She gave it to Colene, who used it to open the door. Then Provos put it back under the mat. Obviously they had done this in the future.

"Well, this is my old house," Colene said, showing off the cluttered kitchen and living room. It didn't seem to have changed an iota. Hadn't her absence made any difference at all? This was weird!

They went upstairs to her room. This too was unchanged. It was as if she had gone out this same morning, and returned routinely this afternoon. As if the entire month she had been away was only a day here, so she hadn't even been missed yet.

Could that be? Could time on the Virtual Mode be different? No, because it had evidently passed in normal fashion for the folk of Darius' reality. Probably for Provos' reality too; the woman had shut up her house for the duration, being well organized, so it didn't much matter.

And there was a signal of her absence: a little pile of letters on the stool near the door. Her parents did not open her mail; they left it in her room for her to handle when she returned from school. None of it was personal; she had learned the hard way not to trust others, and never to put into writing what she did not want widely known. Maresy Doats was her only truly personal correspondent, and those diary entries were kept locked up, and sometimes written in oblique fashion to confuse any possible snooper. So it was all junk mail, both with her name and without, because anything that related to books, records, or novelty catalogs was in her bailiwick.

Provos was looking. "This is mostly Carrot Sort," Colene told her. " 'Cause that's what it looks like: CAR RT SORT. Means they parcel it out to every house on the route. Maresy says maybe they figure there's a big rabbit here. I say that if they drop any more of this junk on me, I'll drop my Bomb of Gilead on them." She touched the little jar of ointment nearby, marked GILEAD. "That's really 'balm,' but I go for the violence."

Provos smiled, but probably not at anything Colene had said, as she wouldn't remember it even if she understood it. The woman was merely curious about Colene's strange residence. She walked here and there, examining without touching, perhaps getting her upcoming memories straight.

"I gotta change," Colene told Provos. She went to her closet and rummaged until she found blue jeans and a dark blouse. Also regular panties and sneakers.

She pulled off her tunic and undid her diaper, while Provos continued to look around, evidently intrigued by this strange house. Colene went to the bathroom and had a quick washcloth and dab cleanup. She got into her home-reality clothes, which fit her perfectly. Somehow she had almost thought they wouldn't. Maybe she had just hoped that her bra would be a little tight, indicating that her breasts had grown. No such luck. It would be a long time, if ever, before she had a tape measurement like Nona's.

Then she had another thought. Provos should change too. Then the woman wouldn't have to hide; she would look like a local visitor. She turned—to find Provos already picking out suitable clothing.

Colene's jeans and blouses didn't fit Provos. Both were too short and loose. When it came to tape measurements, Provos wasn't in it. But a long dress and sleeved shirt adjusted nicely enough.

"But that hat will have to go," Colene said—even as the

woman removed it. Provos located a kerchief, and tied that around her graying hair; it seemed that she did not feel comfortable with a naked head. She looked reasonably normal now.

Then Colene heard something. A vehicle—and it was pulling into the drive! It was her mother's car. "We've got to get out of here!" she cried. "Before Mom comes in!"

But Provos refused to be rushed. She seemed unconcerned about discovery. Colene reminded herself again that the woman remembered the future; she must know it was going to be all right.

Still, there was a protocol to honor. "I've got to face Mom first," Colene said firmly, and hurried to the stairs.

Colene was there in the living room, watching the TV, when her mother came in. Just as it always had been. She would simply pretend that nothing had happened, and see how it played. She hadn't thought about this aspect of her return before.

It didn't work. "Colene!" her mother screamed, dropping her packages. Then she swayed, seeming about to faint.

Colene jumped up and got to her before she fell. She got her mother to the couch, where they both collapsed. "I'm okay, Mom," she said consolingly.

Her mother clutched her, crying. She reminded Colene of herself, in Bumshed with her things and their sudden memories. Suddenly her mother seemed ten years older, and frail, and Colene just wanted to hold her and reassure her. But somehow that wasn't what came out.

"You never checked Bumshed," she said reprovingly. "I left a note."

"We did!" her mother sobbed. "Your note—it said you were fine, and had somewhere to go. But it didn't say where or why!"

"But nothing was touched," Colene protested.

Her mother gazed at her with a tear-ravaged face. "We were afraid you—there was a knife—all your things were—we didn't dare—"

"You thought I—" Colene started. She had never even hinted to her folks about her suicidal nature. She thought she had fooled them completely.

"That somebody had come and taken you from the

shed," her mother said. "Made you leave a note. That you were raped or dead—oh, thank God it wasn't so!"

They didn't know about the rape scene either. "It wasn't so," Colene agreed. "I just had somewhere to go, Mom. It wasn't as if it would matter much here. You have your beverage and Dad has his social life." She was speaking euphemistically. Her mother got drunk almost every evening, and her father had a mistress who monopolized his free time. As families went, theirs was mostly charade.

"Not matter! Oh, my dear, I haven't had a drink since we lost you! And your father has been home—"

Then, seeing Colene's disbelief, she got up and urged her to the kitchen. She opened the cupboards. There were no bottles there.

"You really—?" Colene asked, almost daring to believe.

"My precious child, we did not have an ideal marriage, but we both loved you. That was the one thing we had in common. Didn't you know?"

Colene felt the tears starting again. "No."

Now it was her mother who held her. "You were always so smart, so good, so well adjusted, despite everything. You were our joy. Only somehow we got distracted by things. When you left, it shocked us to our senses—too late."

Good? Well adjusted? Colene had gone through a series of shocks, beginning with the rape, and had sought to kill herself. Her exterior life had become an act, covering her suicidal depression. She had cut her wrists daily and watched them bleed, daring herself to do it, to die. She had been on the verge of it when Darius had made the Virtual Mode and given her a chance to find him.

"But nothing changed!" Colene protested. "You lived the same way without me as you had with me. I didn't make any difference." There was one of the fundamental bitternesses of her existence.

"Everything changed," her mother said. "We—we were so afraid of what might have happened that we denied it. We didn't report you as a runaway, we didn't make any fuss, we just told the school that you had gone to visit relatives in Alaska, that an emergency had come up there and they needed you, and no one questioned it. But between ourselves we denied it. We didn't touch anything of yours. We put the note back and pretended you were still with us. That you were up in your

room, or out in your shed, or at school, or visiting a friend
down the street. Because if we ever admitted it, then it might
become real, and we couldn't face that. We—we pretended to
be the family everyone always thought we were, with you in-
cluded, and neither of us dared to break the spell—in case you
did come back—so as not to drive you away again—"

Colene was appalled. Her departure had reformed her
parents! They had covered for her, and acted perfectly, just in
the hope of having her back. All the rest had disappeared when
she went. They really did love her!

"Now you are back," her mother said. "Our prayers
have been answered! We will be all the things we never were
before, so you can have a family worthy of you. We had to
believe that you would return!"

How was she to tell them that she had not come to stay?
Colene had just walked into a guilt trip she had never anticipated.

So she avoided the issue. "I—have a friend," she said.

Provos appeared. There was no common language, but
Provos had an unerring memory of what was appropriate, and
there were no slips. "She—I traveled to a, a strange place,"
Colene said. "And met several people, and right now I'm traveling with Provos. We have to—to do something here." It was
all awkward, but it didn't seem to matter. Provos, an old
woman, was a reassuring presence. No one could believe that
Provos would ever be involved in anything oddball. In fact,
soon Provos was helping to fix supper.

Then the other car pulled in. Soon Colene's father entered the house.

"Baby!" he cried, spying Colene. There was relief and
gladness in his face, and tears shone in his eyes.

In a moment it was clear that what her mother had said
was true. The family had become normal, cleaning up its act in
a hurry. All because she had gone. What was she to make of
that?

Try as she might to be cynical, she could not deny it: she
did love her parents. Maybe that was what had made her hold
back, and never quite actually kill herself. Maybe she had
known, deep down, that there was after all a foundation, however dilapidated the superstructure.

They had supper together, making a good impression on
Provos, and on each other. Colene explained that she would

have to go into town tomorrow with Provos, to get something done, and this was not challenged. They didn't want to do anything to drive her away.

The guilt was growing. Colene had given her family no consideration at all, deeming it a lost cause. Now she saw how wrong she had been. But there was still no way she could stay here. Not in this reality.

They watched TV after supper. Provos was fascinated by this too, as she was by the purely mechanical cooking and sanitary facilities.

Provos was satisfied to sleep on a mat on the floor of Colene's room. There just seemed to be no problems with her presence, or Colene's return.

Colene lay awake. All this seemed too good to be true. Had she missed something? Was this some kind of a dream? Should she try to penetrate through to the reality?

Then she remembered the guilt, and was morbidly reassured. It *was* too good to be true—because she was the fly in the ointment. She was the one who made it untrue.

Damn! She wished it had been otherwise. She felt like a clod of horse manure.

NEXT day they were ready to get down to business. Colene had enough money for a taxi, and called to have one come. It wasn't as if she would have any use for money later. Provos was intrigued by the bills and coins, which were not her type of money.

They went to a sleazy gaming center known to be the hangout of borderline-criminal types. Now Provos' future-memory became invaluable. Colene, knowing that the type of information she wanted was too complicated to research in the local library, had decided to make a deal with Slick. Slick was a chance acquaintance she thought could help. Chance acquaintance was a good description: it was chancy to deal with him. He was called Slick because he cut throats for a living, slick as a razor. A dangerous man—but she believed he would treat her fairly. Maybe her intuition was foolish, but there had been something about him, the way he had treated her, that suggested that there was decency in him as well as murder.

They walked through the center. This was morning, and there were few gamers there. But there were some. Colene made ready to approach the first one she saw.

Provos held her back. For once the woman's composure was frayed; something truly bad would come of that introduction.

Colene bypassed that one and approached the next. Again Provos held her back. But the third one was acceptable.

This was a burly man who looked as if he would like to chop up young girls for breakfast. But his expression changed when he heard the name. "Slick? Yeah, I know him."

"Will you tell him Colene wants to deal?" she asked.

The man glanced at Provos. "You and who else?"

"It doesn't matter."

The man nodded. This type of answer was acceptable, in this type of company. "Wait." He went to a pay phone and dialed a number.

He returned, impressed. "He's on his way. He says to take good care of you. Come on."

Colene glanced at Provos. Provos was already nodding. So they went with the man. Apparently Slick's word counted.

The man bought them milkshakes. This was one more novel experience for Provos, though she seemed to like hers well enough. "It's maybe not my business," the man said gruffly. "But there's a story about a little girl, real cute, went with five men about a month back, and when they came out, not one would say what happened, but she'd never been touched and they said she showed 'em something they'd never seen before."

"I'm the one," Colene agreed. Real cute? She liked that.

"Listen, I said it's not my business, but—" He shrugged, evidently quite curious. "Those guys must've seen everything about any woman who ever opened her—uh, whatever. So how . . . ?"

"I challenged one to a duel," Colene said, enjoying this. "One on one, with knives. I won."

He nodded. "I guess you did. But you know—well, those guys were good with knives. So—"

"It was a bleeding contest. I cut my arm with Slick's razor and let it bleed into a bucket. All the other guy had to do was cut himself and outbleed me. But he forfeited. I guess he had a generous nature."

The man stared at her. Then he shook his head, not saying more.

In due course Slick arrived. He was a dark man of average height, undistinguished, but the others in the center knew him and turned away. He didn't say a word; he handed a bill to the other man, who departed. Such was the oblique communication between criminals: never a paper trail, hardly even a verbal trail. Just tacit understandings.

Provos stood and walked to Slick. She hugged him. The man's mouth fell open. So did Colene's. What did Provos remember?

Then the woman released the man and returned to her seat. Slick shook off his confusion and took the vacated chair. Perhaps he assumed that Provos was trying to make it look like a family meeting instead of business.

He looked at Colene. "You sure, girl?" he asked. Again, no actual statement; they knew they weren't here for tiddlywinks.

"I have to have help," Colene said evenly. "It's nothing illegal, it's just that I don't have much time and it's sort of technical. Something I have to find out, that maybe a math prof would know. I hope that you know how to get legal things done too."

Slick smiled. He seemed relieved, oddly. "Let's go where we can talk."

He drove them to a surprisingly nice country house. Colene reminded herself that one thing that successful criminals had was money. Slicing throats must pay very well. The funny thing was that Colene sort of liked the man, maybe because she knew something about slicing flesh and making blood flow. She had scratched her wrists rather than cutting throats, but the principle was similar. She had the feeling that Slick liked her too, maybe for the same reason.

Was she fooling herself? She didn't think so, because she was learning to read minds, and even when she couldn't get the words, she got the emotion. The longer she was with this man, the more her conviction grew: not only did he like her, there was something he wanted from her, and it wasn't sex.

"Your friend," Slick said as they sat in easy chairs. "She knows me from somewhere?"

Provos was already moving purposefully to a wall.

"She's from another world," Colene said. "She remembers the future. She doesn't speak our language, but if you signal what you want to know, like maybe a test question, she can show you."

He turned to look at Provos. She put her hands to a framed picture, and pushed it aside to reveal a wall safe behind.

"I was going to ask—" he said, staring.

"Where the safe was," Colene finished. "You open it later in this session, right? While we're here? She remembers. Take my word, Slick—she has nothing to do with this world, and we hope to leave it tomorrow. You can trust her because she'll be gone."

"You're into heavy stuff," he said.

Provos set the picture straight and went to a chair, where she gazed benevolently at Slick. This made him nervous, though he tried not to show it. Colene was an old hand at reading nervousness.

"Look, you don't have to believe me," Colene said. "I've been traveling in other worlds—other realities—and I'm not crazy. My man is trapped on one of those worlds. It's fractal. I need someone who knows how to name the parts of the Mandelbrot set. That's a mathematical construction."

"Let me check," Slick said. "A math prof, you said?" He fetched a cellular phone.

"I think. He's got to know all about the Mandelbrot set, and Julia sets, fractals, that sort of stuff, and be able to explain it to me. And he's got to be right. No guessing."

Slick placed a call. "Give me the prof," he said. "No, no name, sister. Just get him." There was a pause. Then: "You know who. I got a deal. You know the Manbrot—right, Mandelbrot—you can tell all about it? You can explain it to a teenager? Yeah, she's smart. Naming the parts? Okay, you satisfy her, and it's paid. Tomorrow. Day after?" Slick glanced at Colene, who nodded. "Okay. Day after. No, no catch; it's just something I want. I'll bring her to you. Noon." He ended the call.

"Just like that, a math prof?" Colene asked, impressed.

"He owes the syndicate. A lot of good citizens do. I'll have them cancel the balance. It's a good deal, for him."

"And what's the deal for me?" Colene asked, knowing that there would be a real price to pay, and that she would have to pay it. Slick might like her, but this was business.

"Good deal for you too. She's in the same city as the prof. Sis works for the university there." He turned a hard glance on her, and Colene felt a trill of fear. Slick was being nice, but he *was* a killer. "First, you don't tell anybody."

Colene ran her finger across her own throat. No talking. "Who's 'she'?"

"Second, you really have to try."

"Sure I'll try. But what? I don't want to get into—"

"No sex. No blood. Just find out something for me."

"But you're the one who finds things out!" Colene protested.

"Not this time. She's my niece—my sister's child. About your age. Maybe the one good thing in my life, only she isn't *in* my life; Sis won't let me near her. You know why. I think she's going to kill herself. I want to save her. You talk to her. Find out what's with her. Who's making her hurt. Give me that name."

And if that name had to be killed, it would happen, Colene realized. Slick was a professional; he thought in terms of killing problems. So the girl would have no more trouble.

"Slick, I've got to tell you, killing won't solve some problems. If she's suicidal—"

"You know about suicide," he said.

"Yes. But what I mean is, once a girl's been, say, raped, killing the man won't make that rape go away. I might find out something you don't want to know."

"Then find out how I can make it right for her. Anything. That girl's got to be set right. I'm dirty, but she's got to be clean."

"She may be dirty too," Colene said.

"No. She's clean. Like you."

"Listen, Slick, *I'm* dirty! I got had by four men, and I can't ever wash that filth out of me. It's not so much my body, it's my mind. They shit on my innocence."

"I know it. But you're a fighter. Esta's not. You talk to her, help her be clean. Tell me how. How I can fix things for her."

"This may be like fishing a snowball out of hell. I'm afraid of what I'll have to tell you."

"You want that Mandelbrot info?"

Colene sighed. "Well, I warned you. She may be as far into her situation as you are in yours. She may not even talk to me. All I can promise is to try."

"You try," he agreed. "That's the deal."

"That's the deal."

"You may need money," he said. He walked to the picture, pushed it aside, and worked the combination to the safe. Colene saw Provos watching. This was what she had remembered.

He gave Colene a wad of bills. "Save Esta," he said.

Colene stared at the wad, her eyes refusing to focus on the bills. It had to be more money than she had known existed. "Slick, what *is* this? You hardly know me, and—"

"I know you're the gutsiest little girl this side of hell," he said. "The money doesn't matter any more. Just do the job, and you can keep that roll or throw it away."

Colene shook her head. "There's got to be something I'm missing. You could hire an army of psychiatrists for this! You don't need me."

He gazed at her a moment, considering. "I'll level with you, kid. I don't have much time. I made a mistake, and there'll be a contract on me before long. I have to go far away. So I can't mess with others, and I can't stay here to watch my niece. I have to make it right for her now, while I can. Your showing up right now—it's almost like a message from God. Maybe He knows this is my only chance to do some good before I get blown to hell."

Blown to hell. He was not speaking figuratively. He expected to be killed, and to be in hell. His "mistake" must have been to kill a wrong person, maybe a ranking mobster. It might take the mobster's henchmen a while to figure out just which hired hit-man had done it; then they would act, and it wouldn't be pretty. So this really was Slick's last plane out, as far as helping his niece.

It was a motive Colene could trust. She knew about wrapping things up in this life, before leaving it.

"Let's go." Colene hoped that Provos would be able to help in this too, because it promised to be difficult. She knew just how tricky it could be to talk about suicide to a suicidal girl.

Slick took them back to his car and drove for an hour, to the city of Chickasha. "Take a hotel room for the night," he said. "Two nights. As long as you need. Bring her there, if you have to."

"But what about you? Does she know you? I mean—"

"Kid, I'm under court order not to see her. I love her, and I watch her, and I help her how I can. Her bike's broken, so she has to walk home from school, and no one mugs her.

They know. But if I get near her, she's in trouble, and I don't want that."

Colene considered. "Let me make sure I have this straight. You know her, she knows you, you never molested her—"

"I never touched any child," he said. "My business's my business, but I'm no pervert. That's why I was glad to see you get off last month. I couldn't interfere, because it was your challenge, and you showed you were savvy, but I kept thinking of Esta. But my sister—I can't blame her for not wanting her daughter to associate with the likes of me."

"Okay. But maybe Esta would be better off with you than what she's in now."

"Not with my business! She doesn't know about that, and I don't want her to. She thinks I live too far away to see her. And I do—but not in distance."

Colene was intrigued. She suspected she shouldn't push her luck, so she did. "You figure you're not good enough for your niece?"

"I know it," he said seriously.

"But suppose maybe, just maybe, you could, well, take over, and be her parent-figure, and she'd be like your daughter. You'd have to take her to the dentist and foot the bills for her braces and see that she got in from dates by eleven pee em or be grounded and go to PTA meetings and make her keep her grades up—all that dull stuff parents have to do—and finally she'd grow up and get married and move far away and you'd only get postcards from her any more, but her kids would call you Granddad when they visited. How'd you feel about that?"

He spread his hands on the wheel. "That would be heaven. I've never had a life like that, and never will. I'm locked into what I have. I'm good at it, but I don't enjoy it. I'd have quit long ago, if I could." He smiled grimly. "And now I will, only maybe not the way I wanted."

She was surprised. She had assumed that he did what he did because he liked it. Or at least because he liked the money it paid. Yet now it seemed that he envied ordinary people their routine lives. Somehow he had gotten trapped, and could only dream of change. That had been the case with her, before Darius came, and the Virtual Mode.

"Where can I reach you?"

Slick gave her his business card. It had no name or

address, just the phone number. "Just say your name when you call," he said. "They'll put your message through."

Colene realized that any person who had to ask Slick's business wouldn't want his business. The man was a contract killer. Yet she liked him, and if she wasn't fooling herself, she was picking up his sincerity about Esta from his mind. Also, Provos was not protesting, which meant that things would work out okay. In fact, Provos herself seemed to like him. People with what amounted to telepathy and precognition could walk safely through the most hazardous regions and relationships.

Then another thought made her nervous again. This was the science reality. Magic didn't work here. So how could Provos remember the future? How could Colene have telepathy? Were they fooling themselves?

But these things *were* working. She knew it. Provos had proved her ability, and Colene knew the difference between fancy and reality. Special abilities did not either work or not work in different realities; they might be partial or qualified. Seqiro's telepathy was reduced in range on Oria, but otherwise complete. Provos' future memory seemed to be constant no matter where she was, limited only by her time in a given reality. Darius had lost his sympathetic magic in the reality of the DoOon that they had escaped by freeing its anchor, but had retained some of his emotional transfer ability. On Oria he had lost the transfer and recovered his other magic. So it was different for each person in each reality. It just had to be tested. Magic didn't work here on Earth, but the more subtle things might.

The car stopped at a school yard. It was now early afternoon. "She gets out in ninety minutes," Slick said. "You can meet her when she walks home. Maybe she will think you're a new student, or one she hasn't met."

Colene glanced at Provos. "Will this work?" she asked.

The woman seemed to understand her question from her memory of the future. She nodded affirmatively.

Colene returned to Slick. "But if you figure it's this easy, what's this business about money for a hotel room?"

"You need a base. Where you can talk. Maybe not a hotel. I always take a room when I travel. Whatever you need."

Colene brought out the money, which she hadn't really looked at before. The top bill was a hundred dollars. Under it were more of the same denomination. There could be several thousand dollars here! That made her nervous for a new reason. She had never carried such an amount before.

Then she got a notion. "Provos, you carry it."

The woman's hand was already extended. She took the money and put it out of sight.

Colene's mind oriented on the next problem. "Maybe I can walk with her, but I can't just take her away with me. Her folks would miss her and give the alarm."

"Latchkey," Slick said. "She's alone for three hours."

"Then I can talk to her at her house."

"Maybe. Whatever works."

Colene nodded. She could make do. "How close is this hotel?"

"A mile."

She still wondered why he thought she needed a room for the night. But it seemed feasible. "Okay, let's get that room."

He started the car and drove them to the hotel. It was a fine modern building, surely expensive. The need for the money was becoming more credible.

Colene and Provos entered the lobby and proceeded to the desk. Now it was time for some business Darius wouldn't have liked. But Darius didn't know a lot about life in this reality.

Colene spoke to the clerk. "My aunt and I need a room. She's from another country; she doesn't speak English. She doesn't use banks either; just cash. You have any problem with that?"

The clerk took it in stride. He accepted hundred-dollar bills for the double room and gave them change. He did not protest when Colene guided Provos' hand for the signature on the bill. It occurred to Colene that some of the criminal types might use this hotel, so the personnel had learned to cope. Money was money.

The suite was beautiful. There were two big beds, a bathroom fit for a sultan, and a huge color TV set. A picture window looked out toward the school. "Gee, I hope we have reason to stay here the night!" Colene breathed.

That made her think of Darius. How she would have loved to get him into a room like this, all sumptuous and private, and tempt him until he just couldn't stand it any more. Of course if she succeeded in seducing him, she would lose, because it wasn't sex she wanted, but love. Yet she had to keep skirting that thin edge, risking what she feared. It was her nature. So she would have fought to make him get sexual, and been happy in her frustration when she failed.

But the notion of his getting sexual with any other woman was another matter. There was no temporizing there, no confusion of feelings: she didn't want it. That Nona was too damned pretty! But at least her boyfriend Stave was there, and Stave was a sort of handsome, sort of decent hunk of young man. So Colene didn't need to worry about that. And if there were demons in that underworld they were going to, well, demons were ugly creatures. Maybe in fantasy a demoness was luscious and seductive, but she was pretty sure that wouldn't be the case in real life. And even if the demoness was sexy, what would she want with an ordinary mortal man? So Darius would not be facing any temptation there. He might get cut to pieces and eaten for supper, but not seduced. That was a relief.

A relief? What was she thinking of? Darius had had women galore in his home reality before he met Colene. She loved him anyway. She'd certainly rather have him seduced than dead! She knew he loved her, and that was what counted. She could survive her own jealousy and frustration, but she couldn't survive his loss. All the same, she hoped there were no luscious creatures down inside that world.

Provos was already stripping her clothes. "But we have to go see Esta!" Colene protested. "We've used up most of our free time—"

The woman ignored her. Then Colene realized that this was her answer: they would be here for the night, and she would go alone to meet Esta. Provos really had no business on that excursion.

"Okay. I'll see you later," Colene said. "I guess you know how to turn on the TV. And you know not to go outside this room."

She heard the water of the shower running. Provos was handling Earth okay.

Colene went back out to Slick. "Okay, we're set. I'm ready for Esta."

Slick nodded and started the car.

CHAPTER 12

NONA stared at the multitude of the rabble. Directly before her was the one who was emulating her, still distressingly naked. Beside that one was the imitation Darius, looking so exactly like the original that without the help of the horse's mind-magic she would not have known the difference. Indeed, she had *not* known, until it became apparent that the imitations could not talk in the manner of the originals. Beyond these was a massive throng of people in brown cloaks, male, female, and animal. Some of the animals were horselike, and some were doglike, but others were unlike anything seen on the surface. What were the true forms of the human rabble? Were they like those animals?

One thing was clear: a physical escape was impossible, unless certain conditions were met. If the rabble chose to let them through, or if Seqiro penetrated their minds and changed their wills, or if Darius conjured them out, or if Nona used her magic to float them over the heads of the rabble and away. But it was best not to reveal the nature of the assorted powers of the group. Not until it was a last resort.

Keli came out. "We have tried to make you want to breed with us," she said. "It is better if you want it. But you must do it regardless. Please do it with me now, because you would not like it as much if we have to make you do it."

"But surely they can't make us breed against our will,"

Nona said. Yet she feared that something like this was in the mind of the rabble, for attempts had been made to seduce each of the four of them.

Stave glanced at her. "The despots do."

"But even with the despots, a person has to agree, or suffer privation," she argued.

"They can make us suffer privation," he pointed out. "They are many and we are few, and they possess the food."

Nona realized that it was true. If they lacked the resources to escape without showing their powers, they also lacked the resources to maintain their independence. They would indeed be subject to the will of the rabble, in much the way they were subject to the will of the despots on the surface. The rabble did not possess superior magic, but did control the nether geography.

Still she argued against it. "A thousand breedings—I do not want even one! If I did, it would be with Stave, not with any of these creatures."

"Thank you," Stave said, and there was a surge of joy from him that showed how strongly he desired such a union. "But I fear they are about to use force."

Seqiro must have translated that thought for Keli, because she responded to it. "Yes, we shall make you do it now. You must breed."

"You will starve us until we agree?" Nona asked. It would be a while before they grew hungry, during which time they could plan their escape. In fact, she could make food for them out of hairs or fingernails; anything organic would do, to make anything else organic. But if the rabble discovered that, they would take other steps, and those could be less comfortable. The despots, too, had ways and ways, and could break most peons to their will in time without even using magic, if they chose.

Keli looked at her as if she were naïve. So, disturbingly, did both Stave and Darius.

"What am I missing?" she asked, alarmed.

Both men turned away.

"You, Seqiro," she said. "Tell me."

Colene could tell you, the horse thought.

"But Colene is not here. You must tell me, so that I know what we face." She did not like the mood here.

A picture formed in her mind: Seqiro was sending her the

memory of an image. In it was a woman, a girl, garbed in clothing unlike that of Oria: not a red tunic, but a two-part outfit with blouse and skirt. The concepts came to her from the memory, though she had never worn such items. Then there was a man too, closing the door to the chamber. There was a bed; this seemed to be a sleeping chamber.

The girl had no clear image. Nona realized that this was because it was Colene's memory of herself. She did not see herself from outside, but from inside; she was aware of what she wore, but could not see her own face unless she gazed in a mirror. But apart from that, she was somewhat fuzzy in the mind. What could account for that?

Alcohol, Seqiro thought. *It is a drug that deadens the minds and sensitivities, so that human folk may do what they otherwise would not do.*

Someone had given Colene such a drug? Why?

Then the image abruptly clarified. The man had lost his clothing, and he was naked, with his member erect as if about to indulge in sex. There was no memory of his change in appearance; apparently it had happened during the girl's somewhat sleepy study of the room. She was no longer sleepy; now she realized that the man wanted something from her.

She tried to go to the door, but the man caught her and spun her around and threw her down on the bed. She tried to struggle, but was ineffective. He shoved up her dress, tore down her alien panties, and climbed on top of her. It was forced sex: his desire, not hers.

This is what she terms "rape," Seqiro explained.

The memory faded. Nona stood bemused and horrified. She had lived a sheltered life, she realized; it had never occurred to her that such a thing was possible. She knew that men were constantly interested in indulging in sex, but thought that they always persuaded their partners to cooperate. But obviously a man *could* hold a woman down and do it. One of these rabble could do the same to her, unless she used her magic.

"But I am the only one at risk for that," she said after a moment.

"I don't think so," Darius said darkly.

"But a man—his—he has to—if he simply refuses—"

"He can refuse to act, but he can not refuse to react," Darius said. "If he is held down, and a woman then touches him to arouse him, and then—" He did not finish speaking, but the image in his mind made the process clear. Nona realized that there were ways in which a man could be raped too. What bothered her even more was the dark hint in his mind that worse than that was possible. She did not want to know any more.

"Then we must use our powers to escape, immediately," she said. "We can return to the surface and hide—"

"No," Stave said. "The despots now know what we intend to do. They will be watching, and will try to capture us immediately, or destroy us. Even if we hide from them for a while, we will not be able to find the place for the anima. We must emerge exactly when Colene returns, and hope she has what we need."

He was right. But still she could not accept it. "Even if we agree to do what they want, the rabble will keep us for years! Until we have each done a thousand breedings!"

"There must be another way," Darius said. "Seqiro, does Keli's mind show any alternative?"

Yes. Their society allows a person to decline to breed, by dueling.

"Dueling! Do you mean individual combat?"

Yes. But Keli has no direct experience with that; she knows only that such a convention exists.

"But suppose we get killed? How would that encourage breeding?" Darius seemed as perplexed as Nona herself, which made her feel only slightly better.

"Maybe that is how we avoid breeding," Stave said wryly. "By getting killed."

No, there does not seem to be death.

"Then we had better find out about it," Darius decided. Nona could only agree.

She turned to Keli. "We prefer to duel. How do we do that?"

Keli looked so disappointed that Nona felt sympathy for her despite regarding her as an enemy. "I do not know, but I wish it not to be."

"Maybe Stave can duel you," Nona suggested. "So that you retain your chance." It was clear that Keli, whatever her real appearance, was both female and human in nature.

Keli brightened. "Yes! I have the right. I have been challenged."

"Then find out exactly how it is done, and tell us. We will be here."

Keli walked away. Nona watched her go, surprised. Could it be this easy?

They entered the chamber and made themselves comfortable, waiting. The massed rabble did not try to come in. But the two emulations did: Null-Darius and Null-Nona. They spoke but Seqiro could not interpret their thoughts. He had not had enough time with them to get that far into their minds.

However, Nona had a notion. "Every one of these folks wants to breed with us," she said. "They have an elaborate system of changing off so that as many as possible have a chance. Keli—the one Keli that Stave fixed in place—wants to breed with him. Because we said we wanted to duel, and she is the first to hear it, she considers herself challenged. So she will not change off, and Seqiro can continue to know her mind. These two others must want the same. If we challenge them, then they can not be switched out until they have finished the duel, I think."

Yes, I am beginning to get into them, the horse thought. *I do have a head start on them. That is what they want.*

"Are we better off with folk Seqiro can read?" Darius asked.

"Yes!" Nona agreed. "Because then we'll know what they are trying to do, and will be better able to prevent it. The blank ones will find it easier to fool us."

"Then let's make them happy," Darius said. He addressed Null-Nona. "I challenge you to my duel," he said formally.

Seqiro managed to get just enough of that translated so that the woman understood. She smiled and flung herself forward, kissing him.

"Hey, not yet!" he exclaimed. Nona picked up his embarrassment at embracing a creature who looked exactly like Nona herself, naked. She appreciated the sentiment.

Three more figures entered the room: Potia, Lang, and the equine Bel. "You made Potia jealous," Nona said, almost finding it funny.

"Sorry," he said. "But Potia kept changing too fast. It has to be Null-Nona."

His reasoning seemed sound. "My turn," Nona said. She

walked to Null-Darius. "I challenge you," she said. "And don't kiss me!"

He understood enough to smile, and not advance on her. But Lang scowled. He knew he had lost.

"Now pick yours," Darius suggested to Seqiro.

This Bel will do, the horse thought. *I will not mind breeding with her.*

They sat down again at the table where Stave and Keli had eaten. Their chosen opposites, now clothed, joined them. Nona was struck again by the uncanny accuracy of the emulations; Null-Darius looked and moved exactly like Darius, and Null-Nona seemed to be her own mirror image. Without Seqiro, they certainly could have been fooled, as long as no words were spoken. The imitations did not act at all threatening; they seemed like good companions. This could almost have been fun, were it not unfortunately serious.

Before long, Keli did return. She was the same individual; Seqiro verified that. "I have talked with those who remember," she said. "The duels will start immediately. First mine." She advanced possessively on Stave.

"But we must understand the rules!" Darius protested.

"It will be clear," she replied. She did not seem surprised that he now seemed to be speaking her language, because of Seqiro's translation. Probably the horse was also sending a reassuring feeling, so that she did not think to wonder. "Come with me."

They followed her out of the chamber and down the passage. She led them to a truly grand cavern whose ceiling was so high that it was lost in gloom, and whose sides were smooth. Nona wondered what aspect of what Colene called the Mandelbrot set this represented. Certainly it was unlike the surface, though there was enough light from hidden sources.

There was a platform in the center. In fact there were several platforms, rising in a group. "This is like the daises of my own reality!" Darius exclaimed. "Everything happens on a dais."

That was what Nona was afraid of. But they had no choice now.

Each of them was led to a separate dais. They could see each other, but not reach each other, except by getting off one dais and onto another. Obviously each dais defined the arena for its particular duel.

The rabble were pouring in as word of the duels spread. "They do seem to like a spectacle," Darius muttered. "Colene would have loved getting up before this mob and stepping out of her clothes."

"She likes to go naked?" Nona asked.

"No. She likes to make an impression, and to take suicidal risks."

"And you chose this one to love?"

"No. Love chose this one for me, and I am helpless."

"I would like to know what such love feels like."

"You do not feel it with Stave?"

She paused, reconsidering. "I think not. Friendship, respect—he is a good man."

"But no fire," he said.

"No fire," she agreed.

Then they had to separate, to go to their individual daises. Hers was the closest to their path. It was stepped around the edge, so was easy to reach.

Null-Darius mounted from another side, and stood waiting for her. Meanwhile the others mounted theirs, until the four were filled. They were in a rough square, with space inside and the massed rabble outside.

Nona looked around, expecting some sort of announcement, but there was none. "This was supposed to be explained," she said, nettled.

"I will explain it," Null-Darius said. As usual, his meaning was brought to her by Seqiro, so that she did not have to depend on her interpretation of his words.

"But you are my opponent! How can I trust what you tell me?" But she realized that she could, because once the horse penetrated a mind well enough to translate, he also knew the truth in that mind, and would provide her with it no matter what the person tried to say. Nona wished she could always have Seqiro with her, but knew also that this was not destined. He was committed to Colene. As was Darius. Colene was doubly fortunate.

"There is only one way to do a duel, and I have just learned it," the rabble man said as if that decided it. "We have a day and a night from this point to decide. We may eat, sleep, or do anything we choose, but we may not leave this dais until the breeding occurs, and it is witnessed."

"Witnessed?" But the horse was clarifying the meaning already. This assembled multitude would watch it happen.

She had no intention of letting it happen, but she was morbidly curious. "Suppose it happens early. Then what?"

"Then we are free to leave the dais."

"But not to leave this realm," she said.

"I can not, and you may not," he agreed.

"Suppose one of us has to—to—" She did not wish to speak it, so had Seqiro send the implication of a natural function being performed.

"There is a bucket," he said, gesturing to the side. She looked, and saw it. "When one asks, there will be a brief cessation for this purpose."

And in public, she realized. She was not easy about this, but realized that protest was pointless. The ways of the rabble governed here.

"And what is permissible?" she asked. "How much can one be hurt?"

"No hurt," he said. "The one who hurts the other loses the duel."

Now, this was interesting. "But how does one win?"

He shrugged. "We must breed or fail to breed. That is the only conclusion."

"But if you try to breed with me, how can I try to stop you, without hurting you?"

"You can tie me with the ribbon," he said, gesturing to another side. There were coils of light ribbon that was surely stronger than it looked. "And I will tie you with ribbon if I need to."

So that was the way of it! If she managed to tie him, he would not be able to do anything with her. If he tied her, she would not be able to prevent him. The ribbon would immobilize a person without damage.

"When does it start?" she asked.

"It started when we came to the dais."

"But you have not tried anything!" she said.

"There is time," he said. "Perhaps before the end you will decide to do it without strife. I would like that."

"I doubt I will change my mind," she said. "I do not want to breed."

"Perhaps you will reconsider after watching the other duels," he suggested.

"Watching the others?" she asked blankly.

"It would be pointless to have the breedings all together," he said. "People would not know which one to watch."

She still did not trust this. "Then let's watch all the others," she said. "You stay on your side, I'll stay on my side, and no one touches those ribbons."

"I agree." He sat on the edge of the dais, his feet on one of the steps down.

Nona found this awkward to believe, but Seqiro reassured her. *We are waiting too,* he thought. *I will of course lose, by your definition, but it will happen in its turn.*

"Lose?" she asked.

The mare will come into heat, and I will have to breed her. With my species, breeding is too important to be left to individual whim. But I will continue to support you in your foolish resistance, since your human attitude differs from mine.

"Thank you, Seqiro," she murmured. There were indeed differences between human beings and horses.

Darius and Null-Nona were also waiting. The only active dais was the one to her left, where Stave and Keli were.

As if Nona's attention was the signal, the two started moving toward each other. Keli was naked and Stave was clothed; it seemed that this was a matter of individual choice. They met in the center and touched hands.

Then Keli grasped his right hand. Stave resisted, but she was not trying to apply force. She held his hand up and walked into it, causing him to caress her torso. "Can I not persuade you?" she asked. "I almost did before."

"To do what you want would alienate me from my group," Stave replied. "I must support my friends."

"I know you like me," she said. "Can't you see that what I want is right? It would cost you so little, and give me so much."

Nona, watching and listening, began to feel guilty. Not for the watching, because that was part of the duel, but because she understood the position Stave was in. He was a man, and he surely did want to breed with the woman, who was of exactly the contours that men preferred. But he did not want to do it in public, and he did not want to do it if it meant that he would then have no chance with Nona herself. It was not a nice position he was in. She almost wanted to call across to him, telling him to do it. But she feared that the first default to the way of the rabble would begin the unraveling of their group, and then none of them would escape.

"Let me kiss you," Keli said.

He let her kiss him. Nona saw the expertise of that kiss, and saw his hands slide down her bare back; he was indeed tempted. But he had resolved not to do it, and did not weaken. She felt the warring currents within him, relayed by Seqiro: the burgeoning desire and the denial. She was discovering, through this mental contact, how strong the passions of men were. No wonder they tended to be irrational on this subject.

Keli drew back and shook her head with regret. "Perhaps you won't resist too much when I try to tie you," she said. Then she walked to the edge and picked up a coil of tape.

But when her back was turned, Stave began his defense. His body seemed to shimmer. Nona knew what he was doing: he was crafting an illusion of himself, while he crafted an illusion of nothing beside himself. He stepped into the second illusion, leaving the first.

Keli returned with the tape. She took a length between her two hands and flung it over the man she saw—and the tape passed through him without resistance.

"Oh, no!" she exclaimed in perfectly understandable annoyance. "You have magic!" There was a murmur of awe from the watching throng.

"I have magic," the illusion agreed. "I am a man of the surface." It was only technically correct; illusion was not considered true magic, but rather a cheap variant.

Then Keli regrouped. "But that's why I must breed with you. My child must have magic, to achieve the surface and be human again." She now seemed pleased rather than displeased, having verified her rationale. And more determined than ever.

But Stave was now cloaked by the illusion of nothingness and was in effect invisible. Nona had to admire the quality of the illusion; some were better than others at it, and he was one of the best. Perhaps there was a bit of despot blood in his ancestry. Keli had no such magic, and couldn't see him.

"But I will catch you, my rare prize," Keli said. "I will have your seed." She stretched her ribbon out between her two hands and walked forward, seeking the unseen presence. The ribbon looked slight, but Nona was sure that it was strong enough to bind a person securely.

The illusion followed her. "Here I am," it said.

"No, you aren't," she retorted, not looking.

"But I am," it said. "You will never find me by casting at shadows."

Keli ignored him and continued to walk with her ribbon. She moved back and forth, sometimes jumping, so as to surprise an invisible man who might think he was beyond her reach.

When this didn't work, she expanded her effort. Her arms extended, becoming inhumanly long, still stretching out the ribbon between them. She was a shape-changer, and no longer bothering to maintain her seductive appearance, since that wasn't working. As her arms lengthened, her breasts diminished; she was evidently drawing on their mass. Had she had magic, she might have increased her bulk, but as it was she was limited. Still, it was impressive enough, for no one on the surface had such power of self-changing.

When Keli still did not snare the invisible man, she extended herself again. She became shorter and wider, her legs far apart, and her arms reached out almost to the edges of the dais, still holding the ribbon. She no longer looked human at all. It was amazing.

Just how far could the rabble change? Nona had assumed that they could assume the likeness of any human being of their own sex, but this was far beyond that. Was Keli human at all? How was it possible to know?

The rabble are cross-human, Seqiro thought. *I am learning their nature as the duel proceeds and I get farther into their minds. They have evolved not in size but in malleability, and are now as different from ordinary human beings as the despots are from the theows.*

"But despots and theows are both human," Nona said.

Yes. But in magic they are far apart.

"Because of the animus. But when that changes—"

It will not affect the rabble. But the rabble is close enough to human to breed with humans.

Nona remained amazed. Of course she had seen the remarkable changes in size which were possible without loss of the human condition; Angus was certainly human, yet could not breed with the folk of Oria. So now she was adjusting her concept of human; the rabble differed less than the sizes of surface folk.

The Keli creature started at one side of the dais and slowly crossed it with the ribbon. Now there was no way for an invisible man to avoid being intercepted. But Nona knew that this wasn't going to work.

Because Stave had played a trick on the woman. Nona herself, distracted by the other aspects of the contest, had not caught on to it immediately. The key was this: illusion could be visual or sonic or smell. Not all together. An illusion man could look completely authentic, but he would have to freeze in place for a moment in order to speak. Yet the Stave illusion was speaking without interrupting his motion. That meant that it wasn't the illusion; the man had returned to merge with the illusion, and was now being ignored by the creature who most wanted to catch him. As a tactic, it was a stroke of gentle genius. It seemed that Keli did not know enough of the nature of illusion magic to realize the falsity of this particular example.

However, Stave was now in front of the creature, and would soon be caught even if she didn't realize that he was real. How would he escape?

He did have a way. He fetched a ribbon himself and stretched it out before him. "I am going to tie you," he told Keli. "You had better defend yourself, or you will be helpless."

She paid him no attention. She was intent on her sweep of the dais, which she was sure would be effective, and suffered no distractions. She moved slowly forward.

Stave came to stand directly in front of her. "This is your last warning," he said sternly, threatening her with the ribbon.

Keli took another step. Stave reached over her head, which was now at about half normal human height, and made a loop of ribbon. He dropped it on her and began wrapping more of it around her.

It was a moment before Keli realized what was happening. She had become so accustomed to tuning him out that she could not adjust instantly. But as the tape tightened about her, she did catch on. "You're real!"

"You noticed." He was wrapping loops of ribbon around her extended arms now, making spot knots and pulling them tight. Her arms were reaching out so far that she was unable to bring them in quickly to grab him. Then he ducked down to throw a loop around her legs, pulling it tight. He hauled on the ribbon, hard. She had to fall, for her legs were now being bound together and she could not move to recover her balance.

"You are tying me!" she cried, surprised again, belatedly. She contracted her arms, but they remained enmeshed in the ribbon. Like a spider, he took advantage of her struggles to tie her more securely.

She tried to extend her legs, and they lengthened grotesquely, but remained tied together. Her shortened arms were bound to her sides. She could not shape-change her way out of confinement.

"You fooled me!" she accused him, still changing shape.

"You fooled yourself," he replied. "You will not be breeding with me this day."

Now she returned to her original form, naked and voluptuous. "Stave, you have me helpless! You can do what you desire with me. Breed with me!"

The unfortunate thing about it was that he was tempted. Nona felt his desire as he gazed down on her fetching form. Her very helplessness was seductive. She was trying to make it seem that his victory gave him the right to breed, and though he knew better, and had seen how unhuman she could be, he did desire her now.

But he looked across at Nona, and that stiffened his resolve. "No. I will wait until the time has expired."

Nona felt renewed guilt, denying him his desire. The mind-talk of the horse was giving her a new perspective, and now she understood why men sought women so avidly. Their passions were readily aroused by superficial appearances, but were very strong.

"Then let us be together for that time," Keli pleaded. "Keep me tied, but lie here with me, so that I may at least enjoy your closeness."

Nona realized that the duel was not yet over, and would not be over until the time ran out. Keli might yet manage to seduce Stave.

But the main action of the match was over. It was time for the next to become the focus.

That was Darius, against Null-Nona. This one interested Nona for a more personal reason. She wanted Darius to win, of course, but it required some mental adjustment to wish that the image of herself should lose. Despite that image's desire to breed with him, which was not Nona's desire.

Null-Nona advanced on Darius much as Keli had advanced on Stave: naked and inviting. If the creature succeeded in seducing him, would that make Nona herself culpable? Because it was her likeness that accomplished it? She wished the rabble woman had assumed some other form, or had abandoned this one.

Darius accepted the woman's embrace. Nona marveled at that, because she knew that Darius did not have the power of illusion; he could not fool the woman into ignoring him, and he could not render himself effectively invisible. But she surely could extend her arms and legs the same way as Keli had, and could snare him with them. It was dangerous to embrace her. He surely knew that. So why did he do it?

Then Nona saw the doll in his hand. An icon! This was the mechanism of power for his magic. He had made several of them, which he kept with him at all times. This might be the one for Colene, which he could remake to address Null-Nona. More likely it was a new one. He needed to have the body, water, and air of a person for his icon, and he had to get close enough to obtain those things. He was preparing his defense, even as he seemed to yield to her blandishment.

Darius plucked a hair from Null-Nona's head. Intent on him, she did not notice. She lifted her face to kiss him, while he used his fingers to apply the hair to the icon. There was the essence of the body.

Darius kissed her. It was a long, deep kiss, most passionate and moist. She thought he was being affected, but he was not. For when it broke, he lifted the icon and put his mouth to it: touching it with her saliva. There was the water.

"Breed with me," Null-Nona breathed ardently. But all Darius did was hold up the icon so that her breath bathed it. There was the air. He had completed his icon of her, and she did not know its significance. Nona herself would not have known it had she not had experience with his magic. The rabble woman was about to lose this duel, because she thought Darius was just another surface man. She thought his magic was illusion.

Darius put away the icon of her and brought out another. That must be his own. "Let me show you something," he said, lifting his doll.

For the first time, the woman noticed the icon. She gazed

at it with perplexity. A doll was the last thing she had expected
to contend with here!

Darius gestured. He was making a designation: this is
here, that is there. Then he moved the icon—and jumped himself, from here to there, away from the woman.

Null-Nona's mouth dropped open. She turned to stare at
Darius, who now stood across the dais from her. He waved.
"Magic!" she said, in much the way Keli had, and there was a
similar murmur from the audience. That seemed to be so rare
a quality here in this nether world that it awed those who
beheld it. All of them were desperate for some of that for their
offspring, and Nona could not blame them. They believed that
they were subhuman, and that only conventional magic would
enable them to escape their status as well as their confinement.
The truth was that they were bound mainly by their belief; they
had little need to escape.

"Catch me if you can," Darius told her.

She tried. She fetched the ribbon and stretched it out,
advancing on him. She did not look strong enough to tie him,
but the rabble, like the ribbon, might be stronger than their
assumed forms looked.

Darius waited until the woman was almost in reach.
Then he moved his icon again. Again he hurtled from one spot
to another, leaving the woman gazing at nothing. She too
seemed happy to tackle the challenge, for this was the kind of
magic she wanted her offspring to have.

Null-Nona advanced on Darius again. This time he
brought out his icon of her, and invoked it and moved it—and
she found herself back across the dais. This surprised her anew;
his magic worked on *her*. But it did not faze her. She simply
resumed her advance from afar.

This time she threw a loop of ribbon, surprising Darius
and managing to snare one of his arms. The ribbon had not
seemed solid enough to hurl that way; the woman knew how to
use it, so had won the advantage of surprise. Immediately, she
hauled on it, tugging Darius off-balance, as she ran into him.
In this manner she caught him in another embrace, and this
time it was clear that she did not intend to let him go. In fact
her arms were extending into bands that wrapped all the way
around his body and clasped behind her own back, and her legs
were doing the same.

Darius conjured himself away. But when he landed, the

rabble woman was with him: he had in effect carried her along. So he conjured her away—and she carried him along. She had found a way to nullify his magic; he could use it, but it did not free him from her.

Yet merely clasping him was not enough; Nona had learned to her dismay how a man might rape a woman, but that did not seem feasible in reverse. For one thing, Darius was clothed. How was the rabble woman going to proceed?

That was already becoming clear. The woman locked her legs around him, and unlocked her arms enough to manipulate the ribbon. She was slowly tying him up, so as to be free to do whatever else she wished without letting him go. At the same time she was drawing off his tunic. She surely knew how to finish what she had started, now that she had him helpless.

Indeed, her effort was not limited to the physical aspect. "Whom do you love?" she demanded, her thought coming clearly through to Nona.

"I love Colene," he replied. As he spoke, he formed a mental image of the girl, cute and with evident intelligence and drive. Perhaps he thought that this would discourage the woman. But it did not. Instead Null-Nona started to change to someone else. She did not release him.

But Darius was not yet defeated. He struggled to move his hands, and though he did not have a lot of leeway, he did manage to bring up the Null-Nona icon. How could that help? All he could do was move them both together, as he had already demonstrated.

He brought the doll figure to his other hand. Then he seemed to invoke it and touch one of its little arms. What was he doing?

Null-Nona had been busy tying him, ignoring the small motions of his hands. Now she stopped. Then, unwillingly, she began to unwind the ribbon. She was freeing him!

Then Nona understood. The icons had effect on the people they represented when they were invoked. Normally they were used for large movements, such as conjuring from one spot to another. But it seemed that they could be used for small movements too. He was moving her arms and hands, forcing her to do his will instead of her own. He had reversed the ploy.

Slowly the woman untied him, and then tied herself as well as she was able. Darius helped at the end, directly instead of indirectly. She was now helpless.

Almost. Her change of form was now complete. She looked exactly like Colene.

"Come to me, my love!" she cried in Colene's voice. She had picked even that up from his mental image. It was just as if Darius' girlfriend were bound before him. Would that make him succumb?

Darius stared down at her. Then he lay down with her, not putting his tunic back on. He embraced her, both of them naked.

Nona's heart sank. The man knew that this wasn't Colene, yet he was doing it! What was wrong with him? Was the likeness everything, and the reality nothing?

But Darius was not *doing* anything. He merely lay there, embracing the tied woman. She was as confused as Nona was. "But my love—" she said.

"My love is Colene, whom you now resemble," he told her. "I am lying with you as I lie with her."

"But is she not willing?"

"She is willing and eager."

"But—"

"She is underage, by the standard of her culture."

Nona understood the woman's confusion and amazement. She had thought she had won, then lost, then thought she had managed to win another way, and now learned that this too was a loss, for a reason she had not anticipated. It had been a mistake to emulate Colene, for Colene was sexually forbidden by his code.

Now it was Seqiro's turn. The horse and the mare approached each other. They sniffed noses, and then tails.

Then Seqiro turned away. *She is not equine,* he thought. *I have now reached far enough into her mind to learn her nature.*

"Not a mare?" Nona asked. "But isn't she as much a horse as the others are human? Isn't she in heat?"

She is coming into heat. But her species is not mine. She is a horse-dragon crossbreed, assuming the form but not the nature of a horse. I breed only with my own species.

Nona was pleasantly amazed. She had thought this contest lost, and instead it was won. "But how did you not know this before?"

I had not focused fully on her mind while dealing with the others. She seemed like a horse and smelled like a horse. But I require also the mind of a horse, and her mind is alien. Her odor has no further effect.

Bel was not ready to be spurned. She advanced on Seqiro. He avoided her, stepping aside as she came to him. She turned to encounter him again, only to find him moving away again. He could read her mind; he knew what she was doing, and avoided it at the same time as she did it. She could not close with him.

She gave up on the equine form, and shifted to what seemed to be her natural one. It was indeed somewhat dragonlike, with a solid tail, short legs, clawed feet, and a large head with endless teeth. A fighting form.

I can not fight that, the horse thought.

"You don't have to," Nona said. "Call her bluff."

Seqiro was surprised, but then read the concept in her mind. He stopped avoiding the dragoness and stood still.

She came at him with her jaws wide. He didn't flinch, knowing what was in her mind. She stopped, threshing her tail in annoyance.

It didn't matter, because hurting was not permitted in this contest. The visiting surface folk were too valuable. Bel might bite Seqiro to death, but she couldn't force him to breed. She could not tie him up and make him do it, because he would be potent only when the smell and species were right. He had won, really, by default.

But another day they will have a true mare here, Seqiro thought warningly.

"We will tackle that problem when it comes," Darius said. But Nona felt his concern. They were winning today by illusion and novelty. It would not be enough in other circumstances.

Now it was Nona's turn. Unfortunately she could not simply decline the honor. She could use neither illusion nor self-conjuration to defend herself.

But she could use her magic, and now was the time.

Null-Darius advanced on her. She decided to take no chances; once he caught hold of her, she would have to do something desperate to escape, and if she hurt him she would be declared the loser, which would surely mean something she didn't like. Of the several types of magic available to her, most would not be effective here. Transformation of objects would not help when there were no objects to transform. The same went for conjuration of objects, and she couldn't do it with living people. Healing would not enter into it, because nobody was supposed to be hurt. Expansion or compaction—maybe she could do something with the ribbon, then transform it. But for right now, illusion and levitation seemed to be her choices, and illusion probably would not be very effective, because Null-Darius had seen Darius use it.

So as the man reached for her, she sailed up into the air and hovered above him, out of his reach. He gaped up at her, and there was another murmur of awe from the throng. They really appreciated true magic!

But a commotion developed. Surprise was becoming confusion. What was bothering them? They were beginning to look at Darius and Stave, and showing anger.

Then she realized that even here in the nether realm they had to know that only despot men had such powers of magic, not theow women. They thought that a man was helping her to duel. If so, they would declare her to have forfeited. That could not be allowed.

"No," she said. "I am the one. I am the ninth of the ninth. I am hiding from the despots."

The rabble whose minds Seqiro had penetrated understood her. They spoke to their companions, and in a moment there was a babble throughout the throng as the news was relayed. Her secret was out, but there had been no way to avoid it.

Then Null-Darius spoke. "You may be that, but that is nothing to us. The change of animus does not affect the rabble. You still must breed. After you have finished with us, then you may return to fulfill your destiny."

"Unless I defeat you," she replied evenly.

He shrugged. He walked to the edge and fetched a coil of ribbon. He returned, hefting a loop of it. The material looked thin and light, but she had seen how strong it was, and knew that it had enough solidity to be thrown.

He hurled the loop up at her. She flew up higher, avoiding it. He could not catch her that way.

"But how long can you hover?" he asked.

There was the problem. Levitation might look easy to those who had no magic, but it required as much energy as running, and she was already breathing rapidly. Those who had practiced it all their lives, like Angus, could float for a long time, but Nona had not had that opportunity. She could remain up for a while, but not for a day and a night. When she had to come down, tired, Null-Darius would be there.

She could not depend on avoiding him. She had to incapacitate him. That meant tying him up.

But he was larger and surely stronger than she. He would remove any loops she threw about him as fast as they came. Unless she found a way to tie him quickly and effectively.

She considered as she hovered. Then she thought of a way. She was not sure it would be effective, but it was worth trying.

She conjured the other coil of ribbon to her. It was not easy performing two types of magic simultaneously, and it tired her more rapidly, but she could do it. Then she formed a loop and used the expansion magic that Angus had helped her to discover. The loop became enormous and heavy. She could not hold it up, and had to drop it. But she re-formed it into an open-bottomed cage, and guided it to land on Null-Darius.

It trapped him nicely. While he stared at it in surprise she transformed the bottom edges of it into a flat plate that closed it under the man. Now he was sealed in.

She landed, breathing hard. Had this not worked, she would have had to come down anyway, and he would have had her.

The man took hold of the bars of the cage, but she quickly hardened them into steel-like strength, and he could not budge them. He felt all around it, but it was tight, having been adapted from one piece of ribbon. He was fairly caught. She had won.

He took it philosophically. "I would really have liked to breed with you," he said. "Not only are you a real human creature, you are beautiful. But the magic that makes you so wonderful also makes you unconquerable."

"So now we are free," she said, satisfied. "All of us have won our duels."

"Until tomorrow," he agreed.

"Tomorrow?"

"When your next duels begin. You have won only the right not to breed with us whom you have defeated; the remainder of your thousand have not yet been decided."

Nona was appalled, but the confirmation was coming in from the others. The man spoke the truth. Indeed, this had been clear throughout, and others had remarked on it. She just had not let it register for her own situation.

They had always said that the requirement was a thousand breedings for each of them. That meant that they were still trapped here for a long time. They could fight it every day against new opponents, or submit to it without resistance, but they would not be able to leave the nether world to complete their mission. The only way they could have the freedom to leave their duel-daises for parts of the day was to breed early, so that no further contests were necessary. In short, to capitulate.

What were they to do?

CHAPTER 13

ESTA

THEY were just in time; school was letting out, and the students were surging forth in waves. Slick let Colene off on the sidewalk where Esta normally walked alone toward her home.

"I'll be near if you need me," he said.

Colene watched the car pull away. She turned to look at the surroundings. This was a typical suburban neighborhood. It reminded her of her own—and of how she, hardly more than a month ago, had spied a man in a gully, and helped him, and that was Darius. How her life had changed, because of that one encounter! Of course nothing like that was in the offing now, but it did give her a certain perspective.

The girl appeared, crossing the street at the intersection. She was small and thin, her hair reddish and somewhat frizzed. Slick had said she was thirteen; she looked eleven. Youth was supposed to be the time of carefree innocence; Colene knew better than that, and the sight of this approaching girl was further evidence. Esta's head was bowed, her body slumped, and her clothing was careless. A rumpled dark green skirt, an olive-green shirt—a bad combination. This was a nothing girl; it showed all over. She surely had no friends.

Slick thought she was suicidal. He could be right. What reason would such a person have for living? Colene herself had been popular, yet possessed of a deathwish. How much easier it must be to fade away if one's prospects really *were* blah.

The girl passed without pausing. Colene, surprised, hurried to catch up. "I must talk to you."

"No." Esta walked on.

"Look, I know you don't know me, but I really need to—" Colene broke off, because the girl was ignoring her.

This was a problem Colene hadn't quite anticipated. But she regrouped. "I'm not exactly a stranger. I know your name. Esta. Just wait a moment."

"Anybody could have told you," the girl said, not breaking her stride. "Leave me alone."

"Just listen a moment. Are you okay? I mean—"

"Not supposed to talk to anyone. Go away."

This wasn't working. Colene was starting to feel desperate. So she took a chance. "Slick," she said. "Slick sent me."

Now Esta reacted. "Uncle Slick," she breathed.

"Oops," Colene said, with partially feigned chagrin. "I wasn't supposed to say that. He's under court order not to see you."

The girl abruptly halted. "Court order?"

"You didn't know? You thought he didn't care?"

Esta stared at her, and Colene realized that this was exactly it: the girl had not been told. So she rushed on. "He loves you, Esta, but he'll be arrested if he's caught close to you. So he just sort of watches from afar. But none of your folk know me, so I can be with you, if they don't catch on. Talk to me, Esta; I can be awful good company when I try."

The slight humor of her phrasing was lost on the girl. "Why can't Uncle Slick visit me?"

This was definitely not the time for the whole truth. "Your mother thinks he would be a bad influence."

Esta made a sound. It was, Colene realized, a laugh, but it was so forced and pained that it sounded more like a cross between a bark and a whine. Colene had never heard such an utterance before, but she recognized it instantly: it was sheer misery. This was indeed a lost soul, and there was absolutely nothing funny about it.

"Esta, we *really* have to talk," Colene said.

But the girl had recovered her isolation. "No. You're just more trouble. Go away."

Time for another desperation ploy. Colene kept pace, unwrapping the band of cloth around her left arm. She held it up before the girl's face. "See what I am," she said.

For there were the scars of her nature: many thin white welts across her wrist, and one great long one on her inside forearm. The average person might mistake their significance, but Esta should recognize it.

The girl's eyes widened. "But you're pretty!" she exclaimed.

Now it was Colene's turn to laugh. "Do you think that matters?"

Esta shook her head. "I guess not." But she kept walking.

Colene followed up her opening. "Okay, so you're not supposed to talk to anyone. I don't want to get you in trouble. But your uncle really wants to know how you're doing, and now I know he has reason to be concerned. Look, I don't have to go in your house or anything; we can talk outside—no, I guess not, because people would see. I know: your bike! I can maybe fix it. I know about bikes."

"Flat tire," Esta said. "Keeps leaking air. Overnight, or in the day."

"I know something that'll stop that," Colene said eagerly. "Tire sealant. I can get it at a hardware store. Is there one near here?"

"No."

So much for that. But Colene refused to be balked, now that she was making progress. She looked around.

Sure enough, there was Slick's car parked around the corner. He was watching.

She beckoned to him. Meanwhile, to Esta: "Pretend you don't see anything."

The car glided up. The window rolled down halfway. "Bike tire sealant," Colene said. "One package. We'll wait."

The car glided away. Esta's eyes were round. "That was—"

"Remember, court order," Colene said. "You didn't see anyone."

The girl was impressed. "You really *are* from—"

"A friend," Colene finished. "Let's just walk slowly. No one'll care if you have company one day." She realized that this was a good break; it verified her authority.

"Oh, God, I wish—" Esta started, but didn't continue.

"I don't know if I can help," Colene said. "But tell me.

I've got a notion what it's all about." For surely Slick's worry had substance, and this girl wanted to die.

But Esta was silent. Colene saw the fear in her. She didn't dare talk to any stranger about it, however well connected that stranger might be. This was understandable.

"Let's do this," Colene said. "Let's just walk around this block, waiting for that tire sealant to get here, and I'll talk and you listen. Okay?"

Esta didn't answer, but she did turn the corner when Colene did, walking down the block instead of crossing the street. She was listening.

"I'll tell you about Vincent," Colene said. "He's one of my favorites, for all the wrong reasons. He was the son of a pastor, and he was sort of restless and moody, so he didn't succeed in anything. He was a salesman in an art gallery, a French tutor, a theological student, and an evangelist among the miners. All he did was get more depressed. So at age twenty-seven he tried painting. He figured he wouldn't live many more years, so he might as well do what he could while he could.

"The truth is, he wasn't much. His first paintings were dark and somber and maybe sort of crude. He was trying to express the misery of the poor miners he had seen. But he kept plugging away, though no one cared, and he turned out a lot of stuff, something like sixteen hundred sketches and paintings in ten years. But he seemed pretty crazy to the neighbors, and nobody much wanted the paintings. He talked another painter, Paul, into joining him for a while, but then he got mad at Paul and threatened him with a razor. Then he cut off his own ear. No question about it: he was mad, and they put him in a madhouse for a year. When he got out, he painted seventy paintings in seventy days, standing out in the hot sun.

"But he was having hallucinations, and he couldn't stand it any longer, so one day he took a gun out to the field. He went behind a pile of manure and shot himself in the chest, maybe figuring that manure was all he was worth. But he messed up again, and didn't make a clean job of it. He staggered back to the house. He smoked his pipe through the night, then got a bad fever, and the next night he said, 'There is no end to sorrow,' and died. He was thirty-seven."

"There is no end to sorrow," Esta repeated.

Colene glanced at her. The girl was listening, but her

expression was inscrutable. Girls were good at hiding their feelings, when they had reason, even from other tormented girls. Colene realized why her own parents hadn't understood her; she had been too good at hiding. She continued with her story.

"But that wasn't the end of it, quite. Later they figured out that maybe he wasn't mad, he just had a bad ear infection. The pain was so bad he cut off part of his ear trying to get at it. And his paintings really weren't bad. In fact some were pretty good. In fact he was later credited with being the 'Archetype of Impressionism,' which was the idea of being emotionally spontaneous in painting. His paintings made it into the best museums, and finally one sold for about eighty million dollars. So maybe poor Vincent Van Gogh should have hung on a little longer. He wasn't the failure he thought he was.

"I came to know him sort of by accident. There was this print on the wall, titled *Van Gogh in Arles,* and it was like the dabbling of a child. I mean, I'm no painter, but I could do as well as that. I saw the guy had just spread bands of color sideways across the canvas, and then dabbed splotches of color on to represent flowers. He didn't even try to shape them; they were just blobs. He had part of a house to the side, and a tree. I figured he spent maybe ten minutes on the whole thing. But here it was on the wall, so somebody must have liked it. So, well, I'm sort of ornery, and I wanted to know what was in this painting that would make anybody want to hang it on a wall. It's like not getting the joke when everybody else is laughing; maybe the joke's not *worth* getting, but still your nose is out of joint because you don't like feeling stupid."

"Yes," Esta breathed. She was coming to life.

"So I looked at that painting a lot. And you know, it changed. When I caught a glimpse of it from afar, those splotches really did look like flowers; my imagination filled them in the way I thought they should be, and it was better than meticulous detail would have been. And I saw that what I had figured was a supernatural red ocean beyond a white beach with a blanket on it was really the roof of a house, and the beach was the wall with windows. What had looked like a sailboat was a vent in the roof. But I also saw that the tree looked sort of like a monster with a trunk, maybe an extinct elephant. And some of those carelessly scraped lines formed tulips. It was really a very nice garden, and I'd have loved to be there, instead of in my own dingy little life."

"Yes!"

"So I knew I'd misjudged Vincent, and he was a good artist. He just wasn't wasting energy on unnecessary frills; he was going for the essence. Maybe a critic would see only the quickly clumsy brush strokes and the places where bare canvas showed through, but a real person can see the garden and just about smell the flowers. That's the difference between critics and real folk: the critic sees only the hole, while the real person sees the donut.

"But the point is, it was a tragedy that Vincent killed himself. He was a genius in his own peculiar fashion, and no one knew it then, but now they do. I wanted to kill myself, but I hung on just a little longer, and then I got into such a wonderful adventure you wouldn't believe. It would have been a real shame if I hadn't lived for that. And I know your life may not seem like much now, but—"

"I'm not suicidal," Esta said.

"Because you just never can tell what's around the corner, and—" Colene paused. "What?"

"Well, I've thought of it, but I don't want to die, really. I just wish—" She shrugged.

They had completed their circuit of the block, and now the car was gliding up. A hand extended from the window, holding a package. Colene took the package, and the car went on without stopping.

"Let's go fix your bike," Colene said. She realized that she had blundered, going on an assumption. Esta showed all the signs of being severely troubled, but there were other ways to be troubled.

"But maybe the way Vincent thought he was mad, when it was in his ear, I'm like that," Esta said. "I guess it really hurt in there."

"I guess it did," Colene agreed. "I had a pinched nerve once, and it laid me up for three days. If he had something like that in his head, maybe he was hearing things and hurting and getting dizzy, and it was all just that bum nerve in his ear. If it could have been treated, he would have been all right. But they didn't know about that sort of thing, so they just called him mad. Maybe he wasn't suicidal either, but there just wasn't any other way to get away from it."

"Yes. There is no end to sorrow." It was evident that she related well to that thought.

At least she was responsive now. The story about Van Gogh might have been misplaced, but it had evoked several reactions and seemed to have broken the ice. Colene chatted about inconsequential things as they completed the distance to the house. It turned out to be an ill-kept place with an unmowed lawn and peeling paint. Colene knew how it was; her folks both worked, and when they were home they had other—not better, but other—things to do than keep the grounds in order. So they did the minimum to keep up appearances.

The bicycle was in the garage. It was a standard ten-speed model, with a flat rear tire. That was always a mess, because the derailleur got in the way and it was hard to take off, and the adjustments were always out of whack in little invisible but critical ways when it got put back together.

Colene turned it over and spun the wheel. There was no visible damage. "This will fix it," she said. "I just have to take out the valve core, here. Do you have a tool?"

"A what?"

Evidently not. "Then tweezers will do it." The girl found tweezers, and Colene used them to twist the core out of the valve. Then she shook the bottle of sealant, and opened it, and squeezed its thick yellow juice into the tube via the valve. She screwed the core back into the valve and spun the wheel around. "See, this gunk clogs up the pinprick hole, and presto, no leak. It's like magic. Got a tire pump?"

Esta didn't answer. Colene looked at her, and caught a look of horror on her face. What was there about fixing a tire that bothered her? "Got a tire pump?" she repeated.

Esta found one. It was inefficient, but they took turns pumping until the tire was firm. It did hold air now. "And it shouldn't go flat overnight," Colene said. "Mine didn't. It's the easiest leak to fix, and it won't puncture again soon, unless it's really bad."

"It went down in half an hour," Esta said. "I barely made it home from school." She seemed to have recovered from her horror of the tire repair.

"Well, then, you can try it now, and if it's still solid after half an hour, you'll know. You have time?"

"He doesn't get home until five-thirty," Esta said. There was a tightness about her that Colene picked up on. That would be the stepfather, and it was evident that the girl didn't like him.

"Okay, let's try it," Colene said. She wanted the girl to see that the bike really was fixed, because that would indicate that Colene knew how to fix things. Then maybe Esta would tell her what was going on with that stepfather. Maybe it was just firm discipline, which nobody liked. But Colene feared that it was more than that, because of the girl's repressed state and weird reactions. Slick wouldn't have been concerned otherwise. Slick thought that maybe someone needed killing, and he just might know, because that was his business. So the job wasn't done yet.

They wheeled the bike out to the street, and Esta got on and rode. For the first time the girl seemed other than hangdog; the breeze of motion tugged her reddish hair out a little and her green dress too. She almost had a little sex appeal as her thighs showed. A couple years' development and competent makeup might do a lot for her. But first she would need a sizable attitude transplant. The way a girl acted, the way she felt about herself had a lot to do with how she looked. A homely face wasn't necessarily a liability.

"It's holding," Esta called, pleased.

"Well, it's too soon to tell. But it should be okay."

They took the bike back to the garage. "Look," Colene said. "Your Uncle Slick is worried about you. He thinks you're suicidal, and since I'm suicidal, he figured I might be able to talk to you. I guess we missed on that. But I can tell that something's bothering you, and I'd sure like to know what."

Esta remained guarded. "Why are you suicidal?"

Would candor bring forth candor? It was worth a try. "I think I'm just a depressive type. But it got worse once I hit puberty. Maybe the hormones—I don't know. But what happened to me didn't help."

"What happened to you?" This was good; the girl was showing interest.

"I got raped," Colene said flatly. "It was supposed to be a party, but I was the only girl there, and these four guys—I had some of their drinks, and I didn't know how to handle it, so I was pretty dizzy drunk, and they just did it, all four of them. I thought I'd never get the filth-feeling out of me, and I still feel like such a fool. My folks never knew. After that, well, things just sort of progressed."

Now they were sitting on the step leading to the house from the garage, out of sight of the front. It was reasonably cozy. "I heard four men talking, once, about *it,*" Esta said. "I was lying on my bunk in the corner of the room and I guess they thought I was sleeping, but I wasn't. They were friends of *him.*" She didn't identify the last, but it had to be her stepfather. It was as if she couldn't say the man's name.

"Four men," Colene said. "They—how old were you?"

"Six. It was right after Mom married him. She was in town, and he was baby-sitting me. I didn't like him even then, but I knew I had to keep my mouth shut. So I was pretending to sleep. They had been helping him move stuff in, and then they sat down and drank beer and talked, and I just kept on playing dead. He was on the phone, getting something straight, so they were just waiting for him. But it was interesting, I guess."

"You guess? Now *I'm* interested!" Because if Colene's mention of the gang rape had triggered this memory, it might be relevant.

"It was about women. The men were all married, and I guess they didn't much like it. The first one said that his wife was fat, so that the thought of having candy with her turned his stomach. She had been thin when they married, but then she ate herself fat, and he thought she must want it that way so he would leave her alone. So he went somewhere else for it. The second said that his wife picked a fight every time he mentioned it and wound up shutting him out of the house, so he had to go somewhere else too. The third said that his wife always said no, and if he got really tough about it, she suffered through it with such tragedy that he lost his taste for it, so he went away too. The fourth one said that his wife arranged always to be away, busy, or asleep, so he could never catch her, and he had to get it somewhere else."

"I guess that's what men say," Colene said. "But let me tell you—"

"I know. But I didn't know then. I thought those wives must be really stupid not to give their husbands what they wanted. I thought it was a box of candy they meant, and one wife got fat from eating it all herself, and another shut him out of the house so she wouldn't have to share it with him. I thought they should get two boxes so each could have one. I really sort of sympathized with the men, because their wives were all treating them so bad. I knew how good candy was, and my mother never let me have much of it either. So I hoped Mom would let *him* have all the candy he wanted, even if I didn't like him, so he wouldn't be mad about it. Because I knew it wouldn't be any good if he got mad. That was the way it was with Dad, and he finally left for keeps."

"Candy," Colene said with irony. "When did you learn what it was?"

"When I was seven. He—I think she gave him all he wanted, but he got tired of it with her. Then her job hours changed, and she was home two hours after he was. He was drinking—"

"I know how that is," Colene said. "My mother usually gets home after my dad." But the pattern seemed to have changed, because yesterday Colene's mother had come home first. Maybe to spend more time with him.

"I don't think so."

Colene realized that something more was in the offing. "What did he do?"

"He—I can't tell. He'd kill me. He said he would."

Colene already had a notion. The way Esta had reacted to that tire repair—it was that oozing gunk from the tube! Sexual molestation—at age seven. That was something Colene herself had never suffered. This girl had reason to be unhappy! "So you didn't tell your mother?"

"I—I tried to, after a year—"

"A year! This went on for a year?"

"Every day. But Mom said I was making it up, and she would punish me if I ever tried to tell such a lie again. She wouldn't listen."

Colene knew that this, too, was tragically typical. The woman might love her daughter, but she was part of the problem. "Esta, *I'll* listen. Tell me."

"But I don't dare!"

Colene pondered ways and means, and came up with something she hoped would work. "Esta, I heard somewhere that depression is anger turned inward. You're depressed. I think you have reason. I think you're really angry, but you can't let it out, so you just get worse. I'm suicidal. I know how it is. Tell me what it is that is making you so angry you can't even talk about it. Only to me. I promise I won't laugh and I won't be angry. I just have to know. Because I think I can help you."

The girl gained some courage. It was clear that she wanted to tell, and was warring with her fear. "He hurt me—"

"There," Colene said, indicating her own lap.

"Yes, some. But mostly there." Esta indicated her chest.

"There?" Colene couldn't fathom this. The girl had not yet developed in that region.

"Yes. It hurts real bad. And I can't scream, because—"

"Because he'd kill you?" The horror of this was growing.

"Yes. And because I deserve it, because I'm no good."

Emotional abuse. That was in certain ways the worst of all, because it destroyed the victim's will to resist. "You *don't* deserve it!" Colene declared.

"Yes, I do! I know I must."

Pointless to argue that case right now. There were still facts to ferret. "How did he hurt you on the chest?"

"With a—he smokes—it—"

A new horror dawned. "Show me."

Slowly, reluctantly, the girl unbuttoned her shirt. She wore no bra, but did have a band of gauze around her chest. She drew away the gauze to bare her skin. Colene stared, appalled.

There, where the breasts would develop, was a mass of scar tissue. The girl had been burned repeatedly with lighted cigarettes. Some of the burns were ancient; some were recent.

"He's still doing it?"

"Every day."

Every day—for six years. Torture. No wonder Esta had thought of suicide. This was so much worse than Colene had imagined that it took her a while to grasp it. "But why?"

"Because I'm bad."

"Exactly how does he do it?" Colene hated delving into this, but she was afraid she was misunderstanding. She had to get it right.

"He—he makes me take off my clothes, and he says, 'Open up,' and then he does it."

Colene questioned her further, completing the ugly picture. What took shape was an incestuous molestation of such ugliness that Colene found it difficult to keep her face straight. She did not want her reaction to make the girl stop talking; she had to get it all. Esta herself did not realize the full significance of it; she thought she was being punished for her continued badness.

"Didn't you try to tell anyone else?" Colene asked. "What about a school counselor? Didn't they tell you that this sort of thing is wrong?"

"They did, but I didn't know who to believe," the girl said. "Maybe for good girls it's wrong, but for me—"

"Did you ask a counselor?"

"No. I didn't dare."

"So the school never knew."

"No. Only, maybe . . ." Esta did not finish her thought.

"What was it?" Colene asked sharply. She realized that she had assumed the authority of an official in Esta's view; the girl was responding to her tone of command.

"I—I wasn't doing well in school," the girl confessed, ashamed. "My badness was showing. The teacher said I fit a profile. I didn't mean to!"

"Not your fault," Colene said. The profile of an abused child! "So what happened?"

"They made me go to a doctor. A psy—psy—"

"A shrink. And?"

"He was in his office, and so—so—"

"So sure of himself?"

"Yes. And he said, 'Come on, girl, open up.' "

"And you freaked out," Colene said, recognizing the horrible coincidence of words. The abuser had told her to open up, meaning something else.

"I was very bad," the girl admitted. "The teacher was mad. She said I didn't want help."

So it had come to nothing, because of people who were too quick to judge on the basis of too little understanding. Colene knew the type.

A decision was growing in her. "Esta, do you love your Uncle Slick?"

"Oh, yes! He's nice!"

"You know he would never do a thing like that to you? Or even let it happen, if he knew?"

"I know."

"Pack your things. I'm taking you to him."

"But I couldn't—"

"Before your stepfather gets home and does it to you again."

That persuaded her. Esta hurried into the house.

Colene walked out to the street. She peered each way. When she spied the distant car, she beckoned.

It approached. The window rolled down. "Slick, trust me. It's worse than we thought. We've got to take her out of there. Now."

"I can't—I'm not set up to—the court order—"

"Listen to me. Those don't mean anything. You're in trouble anyway, right? You have to go away already. *Take her with you.*"

"But I don't know a thing about—"

"Slick, you're her only hope. Just take her. You can learn what you need. Right now, she can come to my hotel room. Believe me, I'm not joking. You sent me to find out, and I found out."

"What is it?" Slick demanded. "What's with her?"

"I'll tell you when we have her safe. But you decide now: which do you want, vengeance or to save Esta?"

There was a long pause. "Bring her out."

Colene turned away, and the car moved on. Colene knew it would return the moment they were ready for it.

She went to the house and helped Esta pack. "We'll get you clothes and stuff there," she said. "Just take underwear and what you value most."

Esta took a doll and a picture of a man who must have been her father. She crammed them into the suitcase with her underclothing. She seemed eager to get out of the house, as if afraid that something would stop her from escaping, now that she was taking the plunge, or that she would lose her fragile nerve if she paused.

They hurried out. The car approached.

Esta looked around. "My bike!" she cried.

"We can't—" Colene started. Then she reconsidered. If they thought the girl had fled on her bicycle, it might distract them from a more accurate search. "Okay, if it'll fit. Go get it."

Esta shoved the suitcase at her and ran to the garage. Colene went for the car. "Can her bike fit?"

"On the roof." Slick opened the trunk.

Colene tossed in the suitcase. Then Esta came with the bicycle, and Slick heaved that up onto the rack on top and quickly fastened it down with a strap. They piled into the front seat of the car.

"Now explain," Slick said grimly as he drove.

"I don't think now's the time."

"I'm trusting you. Now you trust me. Why am I doing this?"

Colene realized that he was as doubtful about this as Esta was. On her own authority, she was drastically changing both their lives. She had to tell him, without mincing words. She braced herself.

"Her stepfather gets his kicks from making her hurt," Colene said evenly. "He has sex with her every day, but it's not enough, so he burns her on the chest with a cigarette, and when she stiffens in pain, that's what brings him off."

Slick almost drove off the street.

"Maybe you think I'm lying," Colene said. "Stop for a minute, and I'll show you."

He drew to the side and stopped. It was just as well, because his hands were shaking.

Colene turned to Esta, who was to her right. "It's okay, Esta. He needs to know. He won't laugh or be mad at you. Show him your chest."

Esta obeyed the voice of authority. She opened her shirt and parted the gauze.

Slick stared. "Oh, my God, honey," he breathed. Probably for the first time in years, he had been truly shocked.

"No killing," Colene reminded him. "That'd bring them right to you. We have to let them think she just ran away on her own. Anyway, she needs you with her. To protect her. You're the only man she can trust."

"Killing?" Esta asked as she buttoned her shirt.

"Hyperbole," Colene said quickly, before realizing that the girl might not know the meaning of the word. "I mean he's mad enough to kill, but of course he wouldn't do that." It was a lie, and she felt guilty, as if she had betrayed Darius, but it was necessary.

Slick kept quiet. He resumed driving. His knuckles were white against the wheel.

"I don't want to get Uncle Slick in trouble," Esta said.

"You have it backwards," Colene told her. "He's getting you out of trouble."

They arrived at the hotel. "But you know, this is only for one night here," Colene said to Slick. "Tomorrow I have to see the professor, and you—"

"I will get tickets to far away," Slick said. "We'll go right after you have your information." Then he thought of something. "My sister—"

"She doesn't want to know. You can send her an anonymous note or something, saying Esta's all right. Which she will be now. Believe me, your sister can't protect her, and Esta can't go back there."

He nodded, appreciating the cruel logic.

They got out and unloaded the bicycle and suitcase. Colene held up the room key so that he could see the number, then realized that it didn't match the room. Hotels did that to protect their guests from getting robbed if they lost their keys. So she told him the number. "Come see us as soon as you're ready. Esta needs you. Don't go near that house. When the cops investigate the disappearance, chances are they'll catch on to what was going on. Then they'll be on your side, in a way. They'll make him pay."

He nodded. He got back in the car and moved out.

They went into the hotel and up to the room. The door opened as they approached it; Provos had remembered their arrival.

"This is Provos, my companion," Colene said. "She's a little strange, but she's a good person. She—"

But Provos was already embracing the girl, who looked startled but not alarmed. Then the woman led Esta to the bathroom, where new gauze was laid out. Any explanations would have to wait until later, when the woman did not remember the girl.

Colene got on the phone and ordered a good meal for three. She wanted to eat early, in case things got complicated later. She had proceeded as if Esta's presence were routine, but knew that she was technically guilty of abduction. She didn't think that Esta's family would be able to locate her within a day, but it was best not to gamble.

Room Service delivered the meal. The three of them were completing it when Slick returned. He had two airplane tickets to Mexico City. No doubt he had contacts there, and it would be almost impossible to trace his route thereafter. He also had a small collection of comic books. "I thought—I didn't know what you might like, honey," he said to Esta, pushing them at her.

The girl gazed up at him. "Are you really going to take me away?"

"I have to, honey. If you stay anywhere near here, they'll find you and make you go back. I'm breaking the law just being with you now."

"But you live here! You'll lose your job!"

He shook his head, smiling grimly. "Honey, I didn't really like my job anyway. Maybe I can get a better one, and just take care of you, and we'll never speak of the past. Would you like that?"

She stood. "Oh, Uncle Slick, just hold me."

They embraced, somewhat awkwardly. Esta was nervous about being close to a man, even this friend of her childhood, and Slick did not know how to hold a girl who was a relative. But Colene knew they would work it out. Each of them was the one good thing in the other's life. Each could have a better life with the other.

Then Esta looked at one of the books he had brought. She smiled, accepting it. Colene saw the title: *Morning Becalms Electra*. That was probably humor. Better that than horror.

"I have to call my folks," Colene said. "Don't worry, I won't tell them where I am."

She went to the phone. Provos wheeled the dishes out to the hall, remembering how it would be done in the morning. Provos' lack of concern was a good sign; it meant that there would be no trouble in the night. Slick and Esta shared the couch and talked, seeming happy to get better acquainted.

Colene's father answered the phone. That was probably best, because it meant he was home, rather than out with a woman. "Dad, I won't be home tonight," Colene said. "Something came up. But I'm okay, and I'll be back there probably tomorrow afternoon."

"Back to stay," he said.

The guilt welled up again. "Dad, I can't stay. I have commitments. This is just a visit."

He was persistent. "Where do you have to go that's more important than your family?"

"You wouldn't believe it, Dad."

"Try me."

Why try to lie, when the truth would not be believed? "I have to go on the Virtual Mode. That's like a path across realities, and every few steps I cross into a new reality, until I get to another anchor site. I have—I have a man from one of those other worlds, and a telepathic horse. Provos is from one of those realities. But there's trouble, and our friends are caught in a reality where we don't want to stay. So I had to come back here to—to get something. To help them get back on the Virtual Mode. And I'm going back. You and Mom are better off without me anyway. Just forget me."

"How do you get on this path?"

Was he actually believing her, or just humoring her? Did it matter? "My anchor is in Dogwood Bumshed; that's where I step through. That's where I got on the Virtual Mode, and where I came back here. It's my connection."

"You just go in your shed and disappear?"

"I guess I do, really, the way it must look from here. Because I step into the next reality. I know it sounds crazy, but that's the way it works. The next reality looks the same as this one, but the people are different, I think. Some of the other realities are really weird, and some are dangerous. Magic works in some of them. But I don't expect you to believe any of this, Dad. Just take my word that I have somewhere to go, and I can't stay here."

"I understand. We'll see you here tomorrow, then."

Colene laughed. "Yes. I have to go there, to get to my anchor. Bye for now, Dad."

"Goodbye, honey."

She hung up, struck by the similarity between the way her father addressed her and the way Slick spoke to Esta. A girl one cared for was "honey." It meant so little, and yet so much. Why did it make her feel so horribly guilty?

Her father had taken it surprisingly well. He had really seemed to believe her, or at least to accept it for now. He hadn't tried to argue. Yet he had seemed to care. Maybe he figured that he would be able to talk her into staying when she showed up there.

She looked up. The others were watching her. They had overheard her description of the Virtual Mode. Maybe they thought she was crazy. Except for Provos, of course.

"I guess you'd have to be there," she said. "I know it sounds crazy. My father must think I've gone over the edge."

"You're like me," Esta said. "Nobody knows what's in your mind."

"Close enough," Colene agreed.

Slick stood. "I have things to do," he said. "I'll pick you up in the morning."

"Remember, no—" Colene started.

"I have to arrange for funds to be where we're going. And to put my house on the market. You have changed my life, little girl." He left.

"Which one of us did he mean?" Esta asked.

Colene considered. "Both of us. But mostly you. I think you may be doing as much good for him as he's doing for you."

Esta laughed, unable to believe that. But Colene suspected it was true. She remembered her brief dialogue with Slick on the notion of being like a father. Now it was happening, and she knew he wasn't faking his desire for it. There had been truth in him as he spoke. Unless she was fooling herself about her ability to read minds, a little, here in this reality.

There were two beds in the suite. Provos had taken one, so Colene decided to share the other with Esta.

They slept, but in the night Colene dreamed. A balding man was approaching her, taking her onto his lap, telling her to "open up" her legs, and she was terrified of what was coming but unable to resist. Suddenly her chest was bare. Then she saw the burning cigarette. She tried to scream, but couldn't open her mouth. The pain started.

She snapped awake, shaking and sweating. Esta was writhing beside her, making little strangled moans. It was Esta's dream she had shared!

Colene caught the girl's hand. "It's gone," she said, trying to project the thought to Esta's mind. "It's over. Never again. He can't touch you any more. It's just a bad memory, and it will fade. You'll have a normal life."

Esta slowly relaxed. Colene continued to hold her hand and project calming thoughts. She knew that the victims of abuse could suffer post-traumatic stress, much the way soldiers and the victims of torture did. In fact Esta *was* a victim of torture. She had suffered all three forms of abuse: physical, sexual, and emotional. Systematically. Before she was ten years old, and continuing thereafter. She had massive horror to work out of her system. Could just going away with her uncle be enough? Colene herself had suffered much less, yet remained somewhat fouled up; how much worse it was for Esta!

Yet what else could they do? Slick would try his best to make a good life for them both. That would have to be enough.

Colene relaxed herself, still holding Esta's hand, and drifted back to sleep.

Only to have her own bad dream. She saw a wedding, and heard the Bridal Chorus, a piece of music she had always loved; pursuing its origin she had learned of the German composer Richard Wagner, and become a passing devotee of his music. There was something about it that fascinated her, and not merely its beauty. But this was not an ordinary wedding; she knew it. She strained to see the bride, but the heads of everyone else were in the way and she caught only snatches until she was past. Then she watched the bride's rear, noting how beautiful she was, how elegantly slender yet full, her brown/black hair spreading down across her back.

The bride came to the front, and Colene saw the groom. *It was Darius!* He was so sternly handsome it was almost unbearable. Her love for him suffused her heart and burst beyond it, rising up to her stunned brain and forging down to her genital region, infusing both with longing. She wanted him in every way possible, as much as possible, as long as possible.

Then the bride lifted her veil, and Colene finally saw her face, so beautiful that there was a murmur of awe throughout the congregation. She was absolutely perfect, and so was he, and they made the most wonderful couple. They kissed, and it was the fulfillment of the lifelong dream of every man and every woman who had ever lived.

But Colene watched with horror shading into grief. Because the bride was not herself. She was Nona.

"Oh, Colene," Esta said as Colene struggled awake, shaking. She had shared the dream, because of their linkage. "I'm so sorry."

"I've got to get back to the Julia universe," Colene said. "Before it happens for real." But she was afraid it was already too late, because she was so hopelessly outclassed. Nona had everything: beauty, maturity, innocence, and terrific magic. How could anyone compete? "If I could even only play an instrument the way she does," she added wistfully. "But her hammered dulcimer is like the music of heaven, while my guitar is like strictly amateur." She sighed, experiencing a whiff of suicidal inclination. Maybe it had been too late the moment the anchors changed and Nona had appeared. Maybe this was her punishment for getting them out of their prior predicament by practicing deceit. Darius had come to accept what she had done, but did she accept it herself?

"You're such a good person," Esta said.

"I wish," Colene said, echoing the girl's own expression.

CHAPTER 14

DARIUS watched Nona neatly cage the pseudo-Darius, winning her duel. "So now we are free," she said. "All of us have won our duels."

"Until tomorrow," the rabble man said.

Then it was clear: this was not a duel to eliminate their obligation to breed, it was only for the first of a thousand required breedings. They had won the day—and only the day. Nona looked chagrined: a feeling Darius understood. What were they to do?

He looked at the woman he had tied, who now exactly resembled Colene. But she was not, and that made the difference. He had won his own match—but had to endure the rest of the day and night, assuming that they had night here, before being done. He looked across at Stave, who had Keli similarly tied. And at Seqiro, who was now ignoring his dragon. All of them had won—but what difference did it make, with years of similar contests to follow? They couldn't even get free of their four separate daises unless they agreed to breed; only a breeding finished a duel.

If they were to do anything, they would have to do it together. They would have to consult and organize. But they could not get physically together, or have privacy.

But they didn't need to. Seqiro's mind-magic sufficed. All they needed was someone to take the initiative.

"Stave," he murmured subvocally. "Nona. Seqiro. We must consider our options."

"What options?" Stave asked. "We are confined here whether we fight or breed, a thousand days."

"We do not have a thousand days!" Nona protested. "Colene and Provos will return in just a few days, and if we are not there to join them, what will happen?"

"Seqiro can tell them where we are," Darius suggested.

Only if I am close to the anchor, the horse thought. *I can not reach that far from here.*

"I could conjure you to the spot where we entered this realm," Darius said. "But I fear that would not be wise. The despots may have a trap set there, awaiting our return."

"I might verify that," Nona said. "If I could tame a familiar there. But I don't think my magic reaches beyond this place. There is some sort of barrier that prevents the surface folk from seeing into this realm, and surely I will not be able to see out."

"Then we must find some other way out," Darius said. "We must escape the rabble and emerge where the despots are not watching. At exactly the right time."

"But we can not even leave our daises," Stave said. "We will forfeit our duels when we do."

"That is why we need to consult and plan strategy," Darius said. "We must decide exactly what we are going to do, then do it swiftly, so that the rabble can not stop us."

"And with wonderful Seqiro, we can consult without moving," Nona said, momentarily pleased.

"Yes. I think we had better settle down for the day and night, waiting out our victories. We can ask for food, and use the pots." This reminded Darius of his time in Colene's shack, keeping out of sight. He had had to use a pot there and let her empty it. It had been a somewhat humiliating necessity. But she had taken good care of him, and taught him her language, and he had come to love her.

They do not know that we can commune mentally, Seqiro thought. *Keli does not suspect, and so the others do not.*

"And that is our strength," Darius agreed. "They now know of our other powers, but must think they have us isolated, so that in time we must do their bidding."

Yes.

"But even if we can plan, what can we do?" Nona asked.

"It is too soon to return to the surface, and we can not hide from the rabble while we remain in their realm."

"Could we hide farther inside the world?" Stave asked. "Is there any space there? Isn't it solid to the core?"

"Not according to our legend," Stave said. "There should be caves below each rad, extending ultimately to the center. If you can conjure us through the wall, as you did to get us into this chamber."

"But this is a network of chambers," Darius said.

"Oh, it is not," Nona said. "It is one big chamber, which the rabble have adapted, just as we surface folk have adapted the natural contours to fit our needs."

"Like ants making nests?" Now he realized that the small chambers had indeed been artificial rather than natural; there had been no stalactites. "This big chamber is the natural one?" He gazed up at the rounded ceiling.

"Yes. Above it should be the much larger central chamber at the heart of the world."

"*Above* it? Above it is the surface of the planet!"

"No. Our heads are toward the center, not the surface."

"That is not possible! Gravity doesn't—" Then he remembered the other impossible things about this reality: gravity the same no matter what size the world, giants on big planets and midgets on little ones, all perfectly human. Starlight from fernlike patterns that ranged in size from global down to infinitesimal. At the same time he was receiving confirmation from Seqiro: this was the world-view of these folk, and they had more experience with it than he.

He shook his head, bemused. "Hollow planet," he said. "At least that explains why gravity doesn't change with size, by my logic. The mass I thought was there wasn't. This is one strange universe!"

"The one you hail from is different?" Nona asked. "I mean, in the underlying nature, as well as in its magic?"

"More different than I had appreciated," he agreed. He glanced up again, knowing that the watching rabble would not understand why. In fact, most of them were departing, knowing that the excitement was over. But some remained to keep watch. They were not fools.

Nona asked for food and it was brought to her dais. She had them bring food also for her caged opponent, to whom she handed it in. Darius, guided by her, did the same, except that he actually had to spoon-feed Null-Colene. He didn't dare release her arms. Stave did the same with Keli. Seqiro did not need to feed Bel; she was able to feed herself.

Night closed at the normal time. The light simply faded until the cavern was dark.

That was a relief to Darius, who was now able to use the pot in privacy. But he wasn't sure what to do about Null-Colene. He didn't feel right about leaving her tied, but did not dare untie her. Finally he brought the other pot, picked her up, set her on it, and left her there for a suitable interval. His memory of his experience in True-Colene's reality returned, more strongly; this was turnabout.

True-Colene: he missed her, and hoped she was well. They had spent so little time together, since their first acquaintance and separation! Had he been correct to refrain from sexual relations with her? It was true that she was underage by the standard of her culture, but they were no longer in her culture. He would have to ask her how she felt about it, and try to judge the sincerity of her answer. It would certainly be nice if that barrier between them could be abolished. It was not that he desired sex, though he did, but that he regretted any problem between them, of any nature.

He wanted to sleep, but feared that Null-Colene would manage to work her way free in the night and tie him. The duel was not yet over! If he forgot that, he could lose, even now.

The others had similar misgivings. But Seqiro resolved the problem: he was now able to tune in on all their opponents' minds, so that if something went on in the night, he would know and could rouse them with an imperative thought.

The rabble provided blankets and pillows. The duel was not supposed to be an act of privation, merely a contest of wills. The participants could have anything they wanted and agreed on. It was presumed that Darius would not agree to letting Null-Colene have a knife with which to cut her bonds. But he did agree to warmth. He spread a blanket over her and tucked a pillow under her head, then walked to the other side of the dais.

Darius settled down to sleep. "Darius," Null-Colene called in that too-familiar voice. "Sleep with me. I will be soft and comfortable for you."

"And try to tempt me to breed with you," he retorted.

"Yes, of course. But if you can not resist that when I am tied and helpless, then you do not deserve to abstain."

The funny thing was, that logic made sense to him. He knew what she was and what she wanted, and he had her helpless. The horse would warn him if she became a threat. He did not like leaving her tied and alone for the night. She might be a rabble woman, but she had intelligence and personality and deserved better. Also, she did remind him infernally of True-Colene, as she intended, and it was hard to treat her unkindly.

He went to join her. He lay beside her and put his arms around her, outside the blanket. He arranged his own blanket. He closed his eyes and relaxed.

"Thank you, Darius," she said. "You are kind to me." Somehow that made him feel guilty. But he stifled the feeling and slept.

HE woke as the light brightened with his head on her bare bosom. For a moment he was afraid she had gotten free and managed to tie him, but she remained secure. She had merely worked her way around so as to make of herself a pillow for him. He was now under both blankets with her.

"How did this happen?" he asked.

"I am able to move a little," she said. "I am trying to seduce you."

"If you can move enough to rearrange the blankets, why can't you move enough to get out of your bonds?"

"I am not sure," she confessed. "I did want to, and thought I could, but somehow I didn't."

I dissuaded her, Seqiro's thought came. *I dissuaded all of them. I thought it best.*

"You were right," Darius said, realizing that he would indeed have lost the duel had the horse not been on guard. He had been lulled by the rabble woman's affectation of submission, and her Colene aspect. Colene he could trust, to a degree, because he had come to understand her; this one he could not.

"Oh, Darius," she pleaded, tears in her eyes. "I did not do anything to you in the night. We are under the blankets. No one will see or know. It will cost you nothing. Please breed with me!"

This emulation was coming painfully close to the original! She had found the way to work on his desire.

Though he knew better, he treated her as he might have treated the real Colene. "I bear you no malice. I would not mind breeding with you. But I can not commit to a thousand days of this. I must leave this region in a few days, and return to my true friends. Therefore I may not do this with you or any of the others."

"I understand," she whispered. But her tears soaked her face. His feeling of guilt magnified. She was doing an excellent job of that. Had he not known that it had not been her restraint that had prevented her from overcoming him while he slept, he might have succumbed and given her her victory.

And how were the others faring? Seqiro obviously had no problem, and Nona had her opposite securely caged. But what about Stave?

He slept with Keli, as you did with your opposite. He asked me to nullify his sexual interest, and this I was able to do. Even so, it was an effort.

Surely so! Stave was not part of their Virtual Mode group, and Nona did not love him, so he had no special reason to hold out. His passions were those of the normal young man. The temptation of a beautiful and eager woman would be enormous for him. He was holding out only to support the others, especially Nona's effort to bring the anima.

If Keli had appealed to him the way Null-Colene had appealed to Darius—

Darius got up and looked across at the other dais. There was Stave—and there was Null-Nona.

No, it had to be Keli, who had assumed the form of Nona. Just as Null-Nona had assumed the form of Colene for Darius. These folk were amazingly proficient. So Stave had been tempted exactly as Darius had.

How many more days could they hold out, even if they managed to tie up their opponents?

They had breakfast on their separate daises, the three human beings feeding their confined companions. The food seemed to be of vegetable origin, as it had been the evening before, but of no type he recognized. It was a grainy green porridge that tasted better than it looked. But this was routine; they were actually holding a mental conference and planning their escape.

The first element of this was for Nona to find and tame a suitable familiar. That would enable her to give Seqiro a distant pair of eyes, and the horse could show Darius a suitable site to which to conjure them. This system had worked well enough on the surface, and should work here. It would enable them to get away from the rabble folk. But then they would have to go to the inner chamber, across the barrier they assumed the rabble could not cross, to avoid recapture.

There were several key stages. Nona brought up the first: "How are we going to get away from the daises without causing an immediate alarm? We must be conjured away one by one, for we are not a close-touching group, and the moment one of us disappears the rabble will sound the alarm and close in on the others."

"That we can solve," Stave replied. "We can use illusion. I can make illusion figures to take the place of the four of us, so that the rabble will not know we are gone. Nona can make the illusion of nothing, to cloud each of us as we go to join Seqiro. Once we are together, the conjuring can proceed."

"Yes, that would work," Nona said. "If you can maintain the four illusions long enough."

"Illusion is one thing I am good at," Stave said. "I once made ten illusion figures, just to see if I could do it. Of course they were fuzzy and did not move well. I can do a perfect job on only one at a time, but if I concentrate I think I can make four adequate ones for a while."

"If they aren't moving, perhaps," Darius suggested. "If we all sit and wait for the end of the duels, not only will we be still, the rabble won't be watching us closely."

"Yes, that makes it feasible," Stave agreed.

"I can make four nothing illusions," Nona said. "But not while I'm animating a familiar at a distance. It is difficult to do more than one kind of magic at a time."

"Can you hold a familiar once you have tamed it?" Darius asked. "So you will not lose it while you do other magic?"

"Yes, I can do that. It is the taming, and the using of its senses, that require my full attention at first."

"Then our first step must be to find your familiar," Darius said. "What is there that you can use?"

"I need some small creature who can travel readily without being noticed. I need to bring it to my hand, to tame it. But I have seen no small creatures here."

Darius realized that he hadn't either. Was it possible that only the human rabble had come here?

There does seem to be only one variety of life here, Seqiro thought. *I have quested through minds, and though I can not read many, I can tell that all are human variants. Even the dragons have human intelligence, evincing their origin.*

"What about plant life?" Darius asked. "There should be bees to attend to pollination, and other insects with it."

There is no plant life either. No insects.

"Then what are we eating? This is some kind of grain or tuber." Darius took another mouthful of the green glop.

That seems to be yeast or mold. A thing which grows in the dark, and has many varieties.

"Mold." Darius considered, and decided not to argue the case. It made sense; the absence of sunlight—or what passed for it in this reality—down here made such an alternative reasonable. But it did mean that there was no need for bees. That in turn left Nona without any suitable subject for a familiar.

There is small life, Seqiro thought. *The children.*

"The children!" Nona thought, appalled.

Darius tackled this. "We need something, and we are not going to hurt it. A child can go freely around, if it is old enough. Why not tame a child?"

"Because it has never been done!" Nona protested.

"How do you know what the despots do?"

She took further stock. "I don't," she admitted. "Maybe they do use children. I suppose it is possible."

"I think it is necessary," Stave agreed. "Is there a suitable child we can borrow?"

Yes. There is one unattached, watching the duels. I shall see if I can get into his mind.

"But he can't just walk up to Nona," Darius pointed out. "The others would realize that something is going on."

"I can craft an illusion of nothing around him," Nona said. "But he will have to be quiet, and not speak, because the illusion of silence is a different magic."

I can cause him to be quiet.

In a short while the horse succeeded in getting into the child's mind. Darius did not see the child, because he did not look; he did not want to give away what they were doing. Nona looked only enough to craft her illusion of nothingness.

They continued eating, which took extra time because they were feeding their opponents too. There was a certain camaraderie between each person and the opposite. Null-Colene expressed great appreciation for Darius' help, and never asked him to free her, and continued to look amazingly winsome despite her long bondage. It did make him want to pat her on the head and breed with her. He was sure Stave was reacting similarly. Even Nona seemed to wish she weren't treating her opposite so crudely. A lot of interaction, acquaintanceship, and reconsideration could occur in a day and a night together. Friendship could develop, and desire, and guilt. It was perhaps well that the end of the duel was approaching. Darius wasn't sure how much more of Null-Colene's confined niceness he could take. The real Colene had some sharp edges that made her both difficult and intriguing. This one was merely intriguing. While Null-Nona differed from True-Nona in the absence of magic and her desire for breeding. That was surely ever more tempting for Stave.

Darius was not sure when the rabble boy arrived at Nona's dais, because even if he had looked he would not have seen him. His curiosity was considerable. So he worked out a ploy. "Rabble woman, are you ready to use the . . . ?" he inquired delicately.

"Yes, thank you," she agreed.

So he walked to the rim, glancing innocently around and seeing everything including Nona caged and Null-Darius alone on the dais. Nona was looking out over the audience, her right hand slightly extended. "I wish I could see him!" Darius muttered in frustration.

As you wish. The figure of a child appeared in outline beside Nona. She was holding his hand, taming him as she had the bat when they had fled the despots on the surface. She was able to do two kinds of magic simultaneously now, perhaps because they related to the same subject, and he was close.

Darius picked up the pot and brought it back to Null-Colene. He had seen what he needed to; their plan was working. If they could get through the stages of it and maintain their freedom—

"You are very understanding," the rabble woman murmured.

He hadn't even been thinking of her as he automatically lifted her. She was giving him more credit than due, and that gave him another little twinge of guilt. "I have no bad feeling toward you," he said gruffly. "I merely can't afford to do what your people require."

"But it isn't a difficult way," she said. "You can have the whole of your time free, without working, if you just breed one of us at the start of each day. We will take good care of you. And at the end you may choose one of us to stay with, or depart, as you prefer. Can you blame us for wanting to enable some of our number to return to the surface?"

Darius thought of his similarly benign captivity in the reality of the DoOon, just before coming to the reality of Oria. There they had wanted new breeding stock too, though it had been Colene they had proposed to take it from. They had given him a position as a space captain, with three most attentive animal-headed personal servants. The luscious female, Pussy, had had the head of a cat and the body of a perfect woman. At first he had sought to dismiss her, but as he came to know her he had understood that Pussy was a fine person in her own right, a victim of the system. So it was now with Null-Colene.

"Are you able to assume the head of a cat?" he asked.

"A cat? That is a surface creature?"

"Yes." The rabble had lived so long down here without animals that they had forgotten they existed. "With whiskers, and a furry face, and large round eyes." He formed a mental picture, but it was of Pussy rather than an ordinary cat face.

The woman's face changed as he watched, assuming the likeness of Pussy. It wasn't really a cat face, but a human face highlighted by certain feline characteristics. Seqiro was guiding the image, so that she got it right. The body followed. Now it was as if Pussy were bound before him.

He kissed those feline lips. "That's perfect," he said.

She smiled. "It is the first time I have been kissed in this situation," she said, glancing down.

Darius was not given to blushing, but he felt the heat coming to his face. She was still on the pot!

"Oh, I envy your true love," she said. "You are a man like no other."

By the time he recovered normal color, the invisible boy was gone. Nona would let him return to visibility once he was away from this chamber, but would guide him to some suitable place for them to go.

But the period of the duel was ending. "Soon I will go,

and you will have a new woman to oppose," Null-Pussy said wistfully. "I will not be allowed to be with you until all the other thousand have had their turns. I plead with you, Darius, I beg of you—"

"What would you have done had you succeeded in tying me?" he demanded.

"I would have raped you." She sighed. "You have made your point."

But Darius experienced yet another surge of guilt. He knew that he would not be able to endure a thousand days of this. He would soon be broken down, and have to do what the rabble wanted. As the rabble surely knew, having had experience with prior captives. The whole point of this one, who was probably not even at her fertile time, might be merely to begin the process of breaking him down. Once he capitulated, they would match him with those who were ready to conceive by him. It was a practical system.

"The familiar has found an isolated chamber," Nona reported. "We must gather together before the duels end, or we will have to fight again before we can escape."

"None too soon!" Stave breathed. Darius knew exactly how he felt.

Null-Pussy gave him a direct glance. "I have one more ploy, handsome man. I have sharp cat ears now. I can hear you talking to yourself, and it is in no language I can fathom. But when you talk to me, I understand you perfectly, though you speak in that same language. *You have the magic of mind-talk.*"

She had missed her shot, but not by much. Darius did not answer.

"And you do not want others to know," Null-Pussy continued. "Breed with me, and I will keep your secret."

Darius shook his head. "I wish I could make that deal."

She bowed her head, and the tears flowed again. "I will keep your secret anyway."

That destroyed his remaining resistance. Darius took a step toward her.

You must not. Stave is ready to make the illusion of you.
Darius stopped. How close he had been to losing!
Now step quietly away.

He stepped to the side. He saw the image of himself still standing. But he could not see his true body at all; Nona had crafted her illusion of nothingness at the same time. It was as if his soul had left his body.

After a moment, the image-Darius turned and walked away from Null-Pussy. Darius, watching her from the side, saw her jaw clench. It had indeed been another ploy, complete with tears, and it had failed. She was calculating, not submissive. He was glad that he had seen that tiny signal; it made him feel better. But he still wished he could have done what she wanted. She might be indistinguishable in her malleability from any of the other thousand, but she was quite a woman anyway.

He walked slowly and silently to the edge of the dais, and down the stepped tiers. No one saw him. This was amazing! The magic of illusion was a marvelous thing, especially when cleverly applied.

He saw Stave and Nona on their daises, and knew by the somewhat regular manner of their movements that they were illusions too. In fact, the movements of all three images were synchronous; Stave evidently could not handle individuality in multiple cases. But only someone watching all three with that in mind would catch on.

He crossed between his dais and that of the horse. He climbed. It remained eerie, moving invisibly while his apparent self waited behind. He was accustomed to his own magic, but the magic of others brought wonder.

He came to the top. Was this Seqiro, or merely his image?

I am real. Stave will not be able to maintain the images when we conjure away, so there is no point in making one for me. We will depart together.

Darius remembered the complication that had occurred when Nona's bat was out of Seqiro's mind range. Nona could reach farther than the horse could, for this was her reality. But her mind reach was limited to her familiar.

Then something else occurred to him. She had just made a child a familiar. Could she make a grown person a familiar too? If so, that might enable her to establish mind contact beyond Seqiro's range.

If she made me her familiar, we might have considerable range, Seqiro agreed. *Now the others are coming close.*

Soon they were all there, touching hands beside the horse. "The familiar is within your range?" Darius inquired.

Yes.

"Give me the image."

The picture of an empty chamber appeared in his mind. This was what the child was seeing. Nona was looking through his eyes, and Seqiro was relaying the image to Darius. Good enough.

Darius brought out his collection of icons: horse, woman, man, man, woman. He removed the last woman; that was Null-Colene. He held the others together in one hand and activated them. He fixed two positions in his mind, represented by two circles: *here* and *there*. Then he moved the handful from the first to the second.

There was the familiar wrenching. Their surroundings changed. And now they were all jammed together, in the manner of his handful of icons. Darius found himself plastered to Nona, both of them firm against Seqiro's solid side, with Stave on the horse's other side.

"You are the real Nona?" he inquired gravely after he uninvoked the icons.

She laughed. "I hope so. And this is Jud, my four-year-old familiar."

She turned, and there beside her was the boy, now visible. His eyes were big and not quite focused. Darius realized that he remained under control, which was perhaps just as well.

"Go find us another empty chamber," Nona told the child. "Up near the ceiling." The boy walked away.

"So we can conjure through to the central cavern," Darius said, making sure he had it straight.

"Yes. Before the rabble finds us here."

Indeed, now there was a commotion in the near distance. The abrupt disappearance of the four captives had alarmed the rabble. That was actually one real horse and three illusion figures, but the rabble would not know that.

"My opposite, who assumed several shapes, realized that I was using mind-talk," Darius said. "She said she would not tell, but probably she will. They will probably realize that we have a nonverbal way to communicate with each other."

They do. But it makes no difference. They regard us as magical creatures, and the more magic we show the better it pleases them, because of the potential for their offspring.

"But they will be more careful now."

"So we had better not get caught again," Stave said.

They are spreading out and checking every chamber. They

are leaving one person to continue watching each chamber, so that we can not conjure past them.

"So there will be no place here for us," Darius said. "But how are we going to conjure through the wall to another chamber if Nona has no familiar there?"

I will have to find a mind, and we shall have to go blindly again.

Darius nodded. That was the necessity. But it was risky.

"He has found one," Nona announced.

That was good, because the sound of the search-pursuit was rapidly getting closer. They clustered together, and Darius reinvoked the icons. Seqiro gave him Nona's image, and he conjured them to the new chamber.

This was a tiny one, and it did feel high, which meant it was deeper in the planet. It might be one of the last the rabble would check. But the pursuit sounds remained. The rabble would not stop until every chamber was covered.

Little Jud stared at them placidly.

The sound of footsteps grew suddenly loud.

Stave stepped toward the door opening. "I will block the way," he said.

"No," Nona countered. "I can do it better." She stooped to pick up a pebble. She flipped it toward the doorway—and as it flew, it grew, until it landed crunchingly as a boulder. She had used her expansion magic.

"But I can help," Stave said. He concentrated, and a viciously fanged snake appeared on the boulder, facing outward. The rabble might have forgotten what animals were, but they would be wary of that one.

Still, Darius knew that neither stone nor illusion would hold the rabble back long. Even if they did, the group would remain trapped here, and have to make terms when they got hungry.

I have found a mind.

"Then I will move us across," Darius said. "Brace yourselves; we don't know what we'll find."

They braced themselves, and he invoked and moved the icons. There was the wrenching.

They landed, jumbled, in a cavern so awesomely large that it seemed like the surface. Darius did not know how to judge an internal distance like this, but guessed that it was perhaps a third of the planet's diameter across. The ceiling might well be the center of the planet.

They were on a slope that rose into a pointed mountain peak on one side, and into the great curved side of the chamber on the other sides. It seemed somehow familiar, as if he should recognize this vast domain, but somehow he didn't.

"The other side of the East Sea," Nona said.

That was it! This was the inside of the planet. The pointed mountain was the pointed depth of the sea at the base of the planet, viewed from within the planet. What an amazing perspective!

A sudden growl startled them into looking around. *The mind we oriented on,* Seqiro clarified.

It was a small dragon. Nona quickly scooped up a pebble and transformed it into stone ramparts that effectively barred the creature from charging them. But its growl had alerted larger dragons farther away. One of them launched into the air and flew toward the intruding group. It was so big that it might have been a creature of Jupiter, and it looked hungry.

"I fear this is not a suitable place for us," Darius said. The others nodded agreement.

"But if we go back—" Nona started.

"I think we shall have to come to terms with the rabble," Darius said. "What they want with us is not nearly as deadly as what these dragons want. They are not bad folk; they merely have a need they must pursue, and they are doing so in a manner that is ethical by the standards of their culture. If we negotiate again with them, they should do so in good faith."

True. They tried to deceive us, but only to facilitate their desire, not to harm us. They will honor whatever deal they make with us.

To that Nona could not object, though she did seem a trifle doubtful. Her objection to required breeding was more substantial than that of the males. But the approach of the dragon was persuasive.

They gathered into their tight group, and Nona found the mind of her familiar. The boy remained in the small chamber, gazing at the boulder that partially blocked the entrance.

Darius invoked his icons and conjured them back. They landed behind Jud, who heard them and turned to gaze solemnly at them, unsurprised.

But in the interim, the rabble had arrived. Now the four of them were fairly caught.

BACK at the dais chamber, Darius faced Null-Pussy, who was now free but retained her last form. Apparently the rabble did not bother to change forms unless they had specific reason; they simply remained as they were. "I am talking to you because I best know how," she said. "I have not told the others your secret, but have told them I can bargain more effectively with you than another person might."

"True," Darius said. "I shall be glad to talk with you. I am not the leader of this party, but the others will know what I say."

"We have no leaders. We merely follow our custom. We require four thousand breedings from you. We prefer not to have to duel for each one, as it is apparent that we can not either persuade you or force you to breed. We don't want you conjuring yourselves out again where we might lose you."

"We returned because we did not want to die," Darius said. "We would rather settle with you than do that. But we can't remain for a thousand days. Is there any alternative?"

"If you can breed four thousand times in one day—"

He laughed. "We can not! But if we do not return to the surface when we need to, in several days, the point of our retreat to this region will be lost. Could we go, and return to you after Nona brings the anima?"

"If we let you go, you will never return," Null-Pussy said.

"I fear that is true. But we may not find much point in life if we do not. You may hold us here, but you can not keep us alive if we do not wish it."

"If you try to die, you will become weak. Then we can tie you and force you to eat, as we force you to breed. You will not like it as well, and neither will we, but it is a way."

"Unless we die too quickly."

"We do not believe you really wish to die."

Darius knew that was true. "We prefer to find some other way. An alternative that satisfies us and you. Do you have a suggestion?"

"We would rather have you breed voluntarily. If one among you can not find a way to accept it, the others could breed more, to fill that person's quota."

Now, there was a notion. "You don't care who breeds,
as long as there is the allotted number of breedings?"

"The allotted number of breedings by surface folk, who
have magic," Null-Pussy clarified. "To produce offspring who
may return there. We prefer that your males breed our females,
because there will be many more offspring then."

That meant that Nona could most readily be excused.
That would please her. "Then what you really want is to return."

"Yes, but we can not. We are barred."

There was another notion. "You are barred by the present society. By the despots."

"By the animus!" Nona said.

"And the anima. We are barred regardless, because we
lack magic."

"True," Nona agreed.

"Not true! You don't lack magic," Darius said. "You
have a different kind of magic, as I do. I can't do illusion, but
I can conjure. You can't do illusion, but you can change your
shape. The despots can't do that."

"Shape-change is not magic," she protested. "We all do
that. You also mind-talk."

"Seqiro mind-talks. He does not call it magic either, but
you do. It is a matter of definition. All you need is an adjustment of attitude. Maybe because I am not from this world I can
see what you do not. You are being barred for no reason. And
maybe we can do something about that."

There was a murmur of interest throughout the cavern.
The rabble were picking up on this.

"What can you do?" Null-Pussy asked.

"We can change the definition. Nona is going to bring
the anima, and when she does she will be queen, with authority
to do that. Then you can be free to return." He looked at Nona
for confirmation.

"But shape-change isn't magic," Nona said.

"Who says that? The despots?"

Her eyes widened. "If the despots lose their power—"

"Then you will make the definition," he said. "You will
declare shape-changing to be a type of magic, and open the
gates. We have seen that the rabble are not evil folk; they have
treated us fairly by their conventions. They will make reasonable citizens of surface Oria. The rabble have good reason to

help you, and to let you return to the surface so that you can complete your mission."

"You would do that?" Null-Pussy asked.

Nona considered. It was evident that she had never addressed this question before: what she would do as queen. "I don't know. There are so many of you down here, and if you all came out—"

"Free four thousand," Stave suggested. "Instead of the breedings. They will be able to breed on the surface, with anyone who likes their magic."

"Four thousand, spread across the surface," Nona said, appreciating the parallel. "That might be all right."

"Four thousand," Null-Pussy agreed. "Instead of the breedings."

"Then it is agreed," Darius said, relieved. "You will free us, Nona will bring the anima, and will allow four thousand of you to return to the surface."

"Almost," Null-Pussy said. "We must have assurance that this will be done."

"You will not accept her word?"

"We can not accept her word. She may be killed before she brings the anima. She may leave Oria. She may change her mind. The others may not allow it. We must be sure of our breedings if she defaults. We must keep some of you here."

"But Nona may not be able to do it alone," Darius said. "The despots will be after her; they are already on watch. I must go to help conjure her to safety, and Seqiro must go to keep us in mind communication. We can not understand each other without him."

"Then Stave," the woman said. "He must remain to do the breedings."

"I will do it," Stave said, surprised.

"All four thousand?" Darius asked, amazed. "But I thought—"

"Oh, Stave!" Nona exclaimed, horrified.

"We will accept them all from one of you," Null-Pussy agreed. "But it will take longer."

"It will take eleven years," Stave said. "If she does not honor the agreement. But Nona does not want me, and if I can't have her, I might as well do her a favor she will truly appreciate. It is not as if the labor is arduous."

Nona's mouth opened and closed without sound. It was

evident that she did not want Stave to do this, but saw no better alternative. Finally she managed to speak. "I—I had not decided about you, Stave. You are a fine man. I must not ask you to sacrifice yourself in this manner—"

"Beware," Darius murmured. "Three of us free—it's a good compromise."

"But he will have to—it is so—every day a different—suppose I fail to bring the anima? Eleven years—"

She views that much breeding with horror.

Darius realized that some finesse was required here. "Stave is doing this for you, Nona," he said. "To enable you to complete your destiny. Of course you will bring the anima, and honor the deal with the rabble, and he will then be free."

"But the risk—"

"To make it easier for him, the women can assume your likeness," Darius said. "He might almost forget—"

"But I don't want him to forget!" Then, startled by her own admission, Nona tried to come to terms with it. "I don't want to give you up, Stave. But I think I must. If I fail to bring the anima, I will be dead, and you deserve what comfort you may find with women of my likeness. If I succeed, then perhaps we—"

"Of course," Stave agreed, realizing that his best chance to win Nona's love was coming about because of his commitment to breed with other women.

"Then it is agreed," Null-Pussy said. "The three of you are free to go when you choose." She turned to Stave. "You are not. You must breed today, and every day until we know what is to be. You may choose from among us. Will you choose me first?"

Stave glanced at Nona, who averted her face. "Yes, you," he agreed.

"Then come with me," she said, going to catch his arm in almost predatory fashion. She intended to make sure that her chance did not slip away again. "What likeness do you prefer to have me assume?"

"Nona's," he said.

"That is easy, for I have done that one before." She was changing as they left the dais.

Darius took the real Nona in his arms, to forestall her objection to what Null-Pussy-Nona was doing. "It is best this way," he said. He hoped the rabble woman would not think of the Colene likeness; he would feel uneasy about that. He did understand this aspect of Nona's objection.

"I will remember Stave's sacrifice," Nona said, burying her face against his shoulder.

THE next few days were easy. The rabble made no demands on them, and were friendly. Food was provided, and a chamber for them to share. Though Nona showed no romantic inclination toward Darius, she preferred to sleep close to him and Seqiro, to avoid any possible confusion of identities. For now a number of the rabble had assumed the likenesses of Darius, Nona, and Stave, and these were encountered randomly. It seemed to be a passing fashion.

Keli approached them. She had been the one who originally tried to seduce Stave. "I have not been able to get close to him, because of the press of supplicants," she said. "But I feel I have a right to breed with him, because I came to know him first. Will you intercede for me?"

"What?" Nona asked, shocked.

Again, Darius saw that diplomacy was best. "Perhaps Nona will, if you give her something she appreciates."

"I will do anything!" Keli said.

Darius turned to Nona. "You know Stave must be with a different woman each day. It may be better to have him with a known one than an unknown one, to the extent feasible."

"I have nothing to do with this," Nona said stiffly.

"I was thinking that we do not yet know the extent of your magic," he continued. "You have abilities you yourself do not yet know. Perhaps there are new things you could do, if you had guidance."

She looked at him. "You are thinking of something," she said suspiciously.

"The magic of these rabble: that might be an excellent talent for you. Then you could conceal yourself on the surface without resorting to illusion. Since the despots can penetrate illusion—"

"But that is inherent," Keli said. "It is part of us. If it is not your magic, you can not do it, just as we can not do your magic."

"How can you be sure?" he asked. "Nona has very special powers, and Seqiro can link your minds closely. Perhaps—"

Nona's attention abruptly focused. "If I could learn that—"

"I will teach you!" Keli cried. "If I possibly can!"

"And if Nona learns this, she will ask Stave to choose you next," Darius said, sealing the deal.

Nona glanced at him, realizing that he had maneuvered her into it. But her objection was tempered by dawning realism, and a genuine interest in learning the magic.

CHAPTER 15

RADICAL

COLENE and Esta woke together as the first light seeped through the heavy curtains at the window. Provos was already up and repacking their things. She seemed to have taken part of one of the heavy drapes and cut it up; Colene was about to inquire about this odd behavior, but Esta touched her arm.

"Is it true?" Esta asked hesitantly. "Am I really going to go away with Uncle Slick?"

"It's true," Colene said. "You'll go today."

"But Mom will worry."

Colene knew that syndrome. "You'll send her letters that can't be traced. Your uncle will know how to do it. And you'll never mention what has been. In time maybe you'll forget it yourself."

"Oh, I wish!"

Colene ordered breakfast, knowing that they would have time to shower and dress before it arrived. She was correct. Provos seemed surprised when the food came; this was her first experience, in her memory.

As they finished eating, Provos became nervous. She peered out the window. Colene felt a mental *uh-oh.*

Colene picked up the phone and dialed Slick's number. There was no answer; the line merely opened. "Colene. Tell Slick we're ready now. Hurry—and watch out."

There was no response. Colene hoped that she had done it correctly. "Let's get moving," she said. Then, glancing at Esta: "We'd better mask you. In fact, we'd better mask all of us, because it could be my folks tracing my call or something, or yours. They'll have descriptions."

Provos brought out three things. This was what she had made from the drape. She opened one out and lo, it was a sort of cap or wig. She set it on Esta's head and pulled it snug under the girl's chin, and Esta was transformed into a cross between a nun and a foreign dignitary.

"But that will stand out like a sore eyeball," Colene protested. "We'll hardly get through the hotel lobby, let alone travel around town unnoticed!"

Provos came to her and put a similar cap on her head, and fastened it. Colene shut up, having to trust the woman's judgment.

Finally Provos put one on her own head. Then she led the way to the door, carrying Esta's suitcase.

Colene and Esta followed. "Play along," Colene told the girl. "She knows what she's doing, even if we don't." She hoped. This ploy seemed farfetched and perhaps dangerous.

They went down to the lobby, where Colene approached the desk and checked out. A different shift was on, and the man affected not to notice the headdresses.

They walked outside. Police cars were pulling up to the hotel. Colene suffered a start of apprehension. She wanted to bolt and hide in the bushes, but Provos marched right toward the cars. She approached the first cop as he strode toward the hotel, and said something in her own language.

The policeman shrugged her off. "Ma'am, I don't speak your lingo. We're on other business. You'll have to go to your embassy for a translator. Please stand aside." He resumed his advance on the hotel.

Suddenly the sense of it registered. The police were looking for fugitives, not conspicuous foreigners! Provos had hidden them right under the pursuers' noses.

Colene peered around for Slick's car, but didn't see it. He wasn't here yet. But it was dangerous to linger long. What were they to do?

Provos didn't hesitate. She walked right to a strange car driven by a bearded man and opened the rear door.

"Different car! Of course!" Colene breathed. She and Esta piled in after the woman.

Sure enough, the man in the cap and dark glasses and fake beard was Slick. Provos had remembered.

They pulled away from the hotel without event. They had made a clean getaway. "Provos, I don't know what we'd have done without you!" Colene exclaimed. The woman nodded, removing her headdress; it had served its purpose.

"Got your call," Slick said. "You played it close, kid."

"Well, we didn't want to rush breakfast," Colene said. Esta tittered, and Slick smiled.

He drove several blocks, then parked. "Change cars," he said. This was the kind of procedure he was accustomed to.

The other car was a rattletrap with a bad paint job. But when they got in and he started the motor, Colene recognized the sound of a racing machine. This thing could probably break speed records, if it had to.

They drove to a large shopping center. "We have a couple of hours to kill," Slick said. "The plane takes off after your date with the prof. This is a good place to hide, and we can change your outfits while we're at it."

So they went shopping for clothing. Slick and Provos posed as the elders, while Colene and Esta were the school-age girls. They wound up with matching dresses and shoes. Then Provos got a new outfit, a somewhat severe business suit. They had been transformed again.

They stopped for milkshakes, which Provos liked; she acted as if it were her first experience, and for her it was. Then they returned to the car. It was time for Colene's appointment with the professor.

Colene, nervous about what could go wrong, hardly noticed the university layout, despite the fact that she had once hoped to attend it herself. The University of Oklahoma was known as a football school, but this was the separate Science and Arts aspect, which was different. It was ironic that here she was, to see a professor, but she would never attend this school.

Soon they entered a building and found the professor's chamber, which was a cozy den. There was a large aquarium by one wall, but it did not seem to have any fish in it. Colene had somehow expected a classroom, but of course this wasn't any regular class. The professor was Osborne Felix, and what he called recreational math was his hobby rather than his specialty. He made them comfortable in easy chairs, then focused on Colene.

"If you don't mind," he said to her, "please tell me how you came to be interested in fractals. This will help me to orient on your need." He was a man of middle age and receding hairline, but he did not wear glasses. Colene was trying to adjust her expectation; she had somehow imagined all professors with spectacles.

Colene shook her head. "You wouldn't believe it, Prof."

"Still, I would like to hear it."

"I've just come from a fractal universe," she said.

"Unsurprising. This is a fractal universe."

"Oh, you mean the way ferns form the patterns and all?"

"And all," he agreed. "We are constantly discovering new and subtle elements of our fractal existence, from the pattern of the distribution of galaxies in our universe to the phenomena of quantum mechanics. But I presume that is not what you have in mind."

He was patronizing her. That made Colene react. "For sure. I just came from a world which was shaped exactly like a Mandelbrot bug. I need to find out how to find the ninth of the ninth."

"You are referring to a model of the Mandelbrot set?"

"No, a world. The size of Earth. The rads are huge. And it's a satellite of a much bigger world, which is the satellite of a still bigger one, and so on, nine worlds back. And the stars give off light. The whole universe is one monstrous Mandelbrot set."

Professor Felix frowned. "I suspect we have a confusion about the nature of the Mandelbrot set."

"No, we don't," Colene said. "We just need to know how to number the rads."

Provos got up and walked to the aquarium. Felix glanced at her, surprised. "You have heard about my analogy?"

"No," Colene said. "Let's have it, if it helps the numbering."

The professor shrugged. "Perhaps it is best to begin at the beginning." He went to the aquarium and turned on a light. It sent a strong beam down through the water. Then he turned on a submerged water jet, and the water began to circulate. "Note the shadow pattern," he said.

Colene saw that the ripples and swirls on the surface of

the water were almost invisible, but they cast shadows which were quite clear against the white bottom of the aquarium. There were circular patterns with dark centers, the shadow forms of little whirlpools. These drifted outward from the region of the jet of water, becoming smaller and finally disappearing. But new and larger ones formed closer in.

"Note that the entire pattern is three-dimensional, but the shadows show it in two," Felix said. "We can not perceive the pattern as it truly is; we are as it were seeing a mere silhouette. Yet even that is instructive. There is a regular procession of typical shapes, and by observing it we can see the evolution of figures and derive insight into their nature. We can see that these are not fixed outlines, but moving boundaries, guided by specific rules. The currents of water move with certain amounts of force, and friction with the stable water causes these currents to split and curl, forming vortices. We can photograph the shadows, but we know these are not genuine objects."

"But the universe I saw was genuine," Colene said.

"A universe," he said, disdaining her irrelevancy.

"With the equivalent of land and sea and stars and people and laws of nature, which are magical."

The professor continued as if he had not heard her. "Now consider the Mandelbrot set. This is a mathematical construction. It is obtained by plotting vector sums of points on an Argand plane—that is to say, with one real axis and one imaginary axis. It is a convenient way to graph a complex equation. That is, one with a component involving the square root of minus one. In this case—"

"This is more technical than I need," Colene said. Actually she understood him well enough, but she didn't need basic theory, she needed a way to count rads.

"My point is that this is not a physical object," the professor said. "In fact, the Mandelbrot set is not an ordinary graph. It is that portion of the plane for which the sequence of a mapped equation is bounded. So—"

"Professor, it may be just a mathematical construct to you," Colene said. "But it's pretty damned physical to me. All I want is a clear way to number the rads!"

He focused on her. "Would you try to explain color to a man who had been blind from birth?"

That set her back. "You're saying that first we have to understand the fundamentals before we get specific?"

"Yes. And to establish an analogy that will facilitate at least a partial comprehension."

She sighed. "Point made. I can't demand that you name that color if I don't know what color is. But you know, Prof, I haven't got time for a semester course on the nature of light."

"Agreed. Are you conversant with the concept of Julia sets?"

"I named that reality Julia. But all I know of Julia sets is that they're sort of squiggly shapes on the computer screen. I don't know what they mean. I figure that the Mandelbrot set is maybe one big Julia set."

"Not exactly. The Mandelbrot set helps define a particular family of Julia sets. Each point in the Mandelbrot set is a memory location for a distinct Julia set, which can be of any nature, generated by a fractal equation. But all Julia sets will be self-similar in detail, and a change of scale does not significantly affect the complexity of the figure. So it is possible to tell the general nature of a particular Julia set by knowing its placement on the Mandelbrot set."

"Say, I get it!" Colene exclaimed. "Each point on the Virtual Mode is a location for a distinct universe. And you can tell what that reality will be like, in general, if you know the region of the Virtual Mode you're on."

His brow furrowed. "The Virtual Mode?"

"We're on the same wavelength, Prof! The Virtual Mode is to each universe as the Mandelbrot set is to each Julia set. And the universe I'm talking about happens to look just like the Mandelbrot set, but I guess it's really just a Julia set."

Felix frowned. "If you can satisfy me as to your physical set, I will satisfy you as to the designation of its parts," he said. It was evident that he didn't believe her, and also that he was revising his estimate of her sanity downward. Colene had never been one to take that sort of thing without a fight. So she let him have it.

"Okay. Think of our universe as a series of diminishing spheres. There's the 'Big Bang' at the center, and clusters of galaxies flying out from it, forming the biggest sphere. Each cluster forms another sphere, if it hasn't fallen apart. Each galaxy is a cluster of stars and dust surrounding a ravenous black hole at its center. In the early days a lot of matter was being drawn into that black hole, and as it got torn apart at the edge of that maw it gave off a lot of energy, and we call that a quasar. Now that process has slowed, so we call them galaxies. They're still basically spheres with centers, only instead of flying out they're spiraling in. Meanwhile there's a sphere of dust and fragments around each star; those fragments we call planets. They're not flying out or being drawn in, they're in orbit, but it's the same idea on a smaller scale. Then consider the planets: each one seems to be a spherical conglomeration of solid materials, with a molten core. Same idea, again. Then look at the stuff the planet is made of, and we get down to molecules, which are like even smaller spheres, and then atoms, which seem to be spherical shells surrounding spherical nuclei. Down inside an atom we can get into baryons, made up of quarks: maybe more spheres. So each level of the reality we know is similar to each other level, only different too, never identical. Exactly as it is with fractals. This is a fractal universe, in essence."

She paused. She had gotten the professor's attention, and she could see his estimate of her rising again, as if the mercury in a thermometer had dropped with night and was moving up again with the heat of day. But she had only begun.

"Yet out of this assemblage of diminishing spheres comes the world we normally perceive, which consists of solid ground, liquid seas, and gaseous air. Of houses, cars, and next-door neighbors. Of life and death, love and hate, and parents and children, each similar to its origin yet never quite the same. We don't even think of the spheres, we just eat and drink and laugh and cry and wonder about the meaning of life. This is *us*. Even though we are so small, in terms of the universe as a whole, that someone viewing the universe from another dimension, seeing the whole thing, would never even notice us. We're just mold on a fragment circling a star on the fringe of one black hole among billions. We're not important at all, objectively speaking."

She met the professor's gaze. She could tell that he was on the verge of being impressed. Good; she wasn't done.

"Worse yet, the entire universe we know may be only one per cent of the whole thing. You've heard about the so-called Dark Matter, the stuff that no one can detect, yet it's supposed to make up ninety-nine per cent of everything. We can't see it, we can't touch it, we can't catch a sample of it; it just doesn't seem to exist, as far as we're concerned. But it has gravitational effect, and our galaxies are affected by it, so we know it's there.

We just don't know what it is, or why there's so much of it."

"My friends in the physics department say much the same," the professor agreed. "But this hardly relates to fractals."

"Oh, yes, it does! You asked me for a physical set, and I'm setting up for it. Because the way I see it, it's not one per cent of the whole shebang we can see, it's more like a millionth of it. That gravity we see operating is just the trace that leaks through to our reality from the myriad other realities we can't see. Most of it stays in its own slice of reality, but nothing's perfect, and that tiny leakage may account for the special effects which so mystify our astronomers. From one reality there's hardly enough to make a difference here, but from millions of realities it adds up. So I figure they'll never find a particle to account for all of it, because some of it's coming from places that just don't exist for our scientists. Magic places."

"Magic," the professor said, frowning. "I really don't believe—"

"I'm just telling you how there can be a whole lot out there you never dreamed of, Prof," she said. "You don't have to believe it. Just accept it theoretically, as a rationale for how there can be a physical Mandelbrot set, and follow my lead. The way I guess you make your students do."

He nodded. "I think I would like to have you as a student. I can see that you are an unusually imaginative ninth grader."

"That's not the half of it, Prof!" Colene was aware that his comment was not necessarily a compliment. She marshaled her thoughts. "Now picture the Mandelbrot set not as a construct of the mapping of bounded sequences, but as an actual physical reality. With a monstrous central figure looking like a six-legged bug with hairs curling all around its body and a spike on its snout. That's like the sphere of galaxies surrounding the Big Bang. Each little satellite bug is a miniature of the original, like a galaxy. Each tiny satellite bug of a satellite bug looks much the same as its parent, but the pattern into which it fits is always a little different too. Right down to the quark level, and maybe beyond. Assume that in that reality there is a buglet way out on the fringe of nowhere significant that's the same size as Earth, and occupies the same place as Earth, if you superimposed the two realities. That has people on it who look just about like us. If you stood on that planet-bug and talked to those folk, you'd hardly know you weren't on Earth. Only if you had a microscope or a telescope would you be able to see that all the things of this reality, instead of being composed of diminishing spheres, are composed of diminishing iterations of the Mandelbrot set. And because of this fundamental difference, science wouldn't work well there, but magic would, with special rules of its own that might not make a lot of sense to folk of the spherical universe. And one of those rules was that to do just the right kind of magic, you had to find the ninth of the ninth rad. How would you find it?"

It was a moment before the professor spoke. Then he found a new way to approach the problem. "Accepting such a theoretical construct, I would go to the most feasible nomenclature," he said. "Come here." He walked to a table and brought out a small sheaf of papers.

Colene went there. As she did, she saw Provos gesture to Slick. Slick was picking up on the woman's special ability, and joined her, and the two of them left the chamber. Colene wasn't sure what was going on, but she trusted Provos, whose mind she could read a little, and she didn't want to alarm Esta, who seemed bemused by the dialogue and the ongoing patterns in the water tank.

Felix unrolled a large picture of the Mandelbrot set. Every detail seemed to be there, and there were numbers all across it. The black center part of it was divided into sections, as if it were hollow with chambers ranging from huge to tiny. "I think for this you do not want computerized coordinates," he said. "You are not in the business of calculating the set itself, you merely want a way to identify the parts of it in a readily understood manner. As if you were standing on its edge and figuring out exactly where you are."

"Right," Colene said. "Actually it's more complicated than this. The one I'm on is, pardon the expression, spherical. That is, three-dimensional. The rads are on the front and back as well as the top and bottom."

"But there can be no front and back," he protested, "because the figure is in essence a silhouette, a mere shadow—"

"Of the reality," she finished. "The silhouette of a three-dimensional figure would look like this."

He nodded. "In that case there will be a problem of nomenclature. However, let's first define the existing designations." He lifted a stylus and pointed to the main part of the figure. "This is the Body of the Radical Master, or Rad Master, our primary figure." He pointed to the smaller disk on the left. "This is the Head." He pointed to the line extending to the left. "This is the Spike." He pointed to the depression on the right. "This is the East Valley." He pointed to the deep crevice between the body and the head. "And this is Seahorse Valley." He glanced at her. "Are you with me so far?"

"Right with you," she agreed. "I knew those terms. Those crevices are filled with water, where I've been. But it's the rads I need to know."

"We are coming to them. Now for convenience we always orient the Rad Master this way, with the Spike to the west, no matter which way it may be pointed as you see it. Thus the radicals, each of which is a miniature of the Rad Master, are North above and South below. To clarify the situation, we must assign Radical numbers: R1 for the Body, R2 for the Head, and the largest around the Body is the North Rad, which we designate R3. We descend from the larger to the next smaller for this purpose, never skipping down. Thus the only Rad larger than R3 is R2, which is the Head, and the only Rad larger than R2 is R1, the Body. You remain with me?"

"I sure do! This is coming right onto what I need."

"I'm sure it is. Having proceeded east to reach R3, we continue east to reach R4, which is the largest of all the radicals between R3 and the East Valley, here. Then on to R4, R5, and so on, heading into that valley."

"Right down to the ninth, R9," Colene agreed. "But where is the ninth of the ninth?"

"That would be the ninth rad on that ninth rad," he said, pointing to an almost infinitesimally tiny bump on the small R9. "However, I'm not sure that is what you want. Hasty conclusions are often in error."

He was getting entirely too professorish for her taste. "Well, maybe. But I think that's it."

"But you see there are other R9's. For example, if you were to turn back at R3 and proceed west, you would in due course come to R3:R9, the colon indicating the change of direction. We don't bother to mark R1:R2, because every sequence starts with those two. Consider them implied."

"Change of direction," Colene repeated, remembering

the directions of magic indicated by the animus and anima. Her certainty faded.

"Perhaps you should explain why you want this particular designation."

"Okay, you asked for it. But you won't believe it."

"I don't need to believe it. I only need to understand exactly what you want."

"There's this woman, Nona, who can do magic because she's the ninth of the ninth. She needs to get to the ninth of the ninth rad to change things so that women can do the magic instead of the men, only she doesn't know where that is. So I have to find out, so I can tell her."

"She is the ninthborn child, of the ninthborn of her father's generation?"

"Not exactly. It's her mother, and her mother's mother. For nine generations back."

"That is quite a different matter. Nine generations! Those folk evidently run to large families."

"Actually they weren't all large. It was the secondborn girl, and then the thirdborn. I mean, if the secondborn was a girl, and then she had three children and the third was a girl, and then she had at least four, with the fourth a girl, and so on."

"Matrilineal, for this purpose. So your Nona is the ninth child in her family, the daughter of a woman who was the eighthborn in her family, and so on back through the seventh-born, sixthborn, and back to the firstborn."

"You got it. And they align magically with the Mandel-brot bugs, a chain of satellites nine layers deep."

The professor winced when she referred to the forms as bugs, but shook it off. "I believe I have it now. The ninth rad of the ninth rad would indeed be wrong. It would need to be the ninth rad of the eighth rad of the seventh rad, and so on. An entirely different address."

Colene's mouth fell open. "You're right, Prof! You do know where you're going!"

"It is my business to know," he said. He seemed to be better satisfied with Colene than before. "So let's proceed with the denouement. I believe I can give you a specific address that you can show your friend."

"I'm for that!"

He pointed to the Head. "You will note that the Head

has a head, and so on ad infinitum. We now use a slash to designate a rad on a rad: R2/R2 for the head on the head, R2/R2/R2 for the head on that, and so on. Similarly the next largest rad on the head, here, is R2/R3."

"We can make a chain of rads on rads that way too!" she exclaimed.

"Precisely. And this chain more accurately reflects the numbers of the births."

"It sure does. So then we go to the fourth rad on that rad on the head—"

"R2/R3/R4," he agreed. "And so on to the ninth on the eighth. Unfortunately my printed diagram does not have that level of definition. I can use my computer program to amplify it on the screen, if you wish, but this will take some time—"

The door opened. Slick and Provos entered. "Trouble," Slick said. "She put me on to it. The police must've located us. Do you have what you need, Colene?"

"Just about," Colene said. "But—"

"Take this," Felix said quickly, handing Colene an envelope. "This is an issue of *Amygdala* with a good discussion of nomenclature. You now understand the principles well enough to follow it."

"Right," Colene agreed. "You did the job, Prof."

"And your account is quit," Slick said. "I erased it last night. We don't know each other. If anyone asks you—"

"This encounter never occurred," the professor said. "I have spent this hour reviewing fractals alone." He looked relieved. "And I owe no one anything."

"Right," Slick said. He looked at Colene. "Come on." Provos was already hurrying Esta out the door.

Colene followed them out, pausing only long enough to wave goodbye to Professor Felix. He had in the end had what she wanted, and that was what counted. If she had helped him get out of some bad debt, maybe from gambling, she was glad.

Then she reconsidered. She couldn't just depart without more than a wave; anyone could wave. So she indulged her propensity for risk-taking, ran back into the room, caught the professor by the shoulders, and planted a passionate kiss on his surprised mouth. "You couldn't teach *this* ninth grader much, Prof!" she whispered, and stepped back.

He was still staring with satisfying stupefaction as she closed the door on him.

Provos was leading the way out of the building—but not the way they had entered. In fact they used a fire escape. Then she led them to an unfamiliar car.

It was locked. Slick brought out a tool and jimmied open the door. They piled in while he reached under the wheel to hot-wire the ignition. They were stealing a car!

"But my suitcase—all my things are in the other car," Esta protested.

"We'll get you more," Colene said. "It's not like you had a lot to lose."

"Duck down," Slick said, donning some kind of mask. Colene and Esta were in back, Provos in front. Provos did not seem to be hiding. What was going on?

They pulled out as a police car pulled in. Colene caught just a peep of it through the window before she buried her head.

The car traveled slowly, as if the driver were completely unconcerned about anything in the neighborhood. The two in front removed their masks; Slick seemed to have such things with him as standard equipment. The car turned onto a faster highway and accelerated. Then Slick spoke. "No? Damn!"

Colene and Esta lifted their heads. Slick now looked like an old man with a broad mustache, and Provos looked like another. Provos was pointing back the way they had come.

"You better believe her," Colene said. "She remembers the future, and I think you have no future in that direction."

"But I was headed for the Oklahoma City airport," he said as he slowed and signaled a turn. "That's where our plane leaves. I was going to get you and Provos a taxi back to anywhere you wanted to go."

"So they've got the airport staked out," Colene said. "So you'll have to drive instead. It's better than getting caught."

Slick nodded. "She's been right so far. She put me on to the approach of the police, and to the one car that would not be missed for a day. She may not speak our language, but she's one savvy old woman." He lifted his right hand, and Provos lifted her left hand at the same time and touched his fingers. What got Colene was the fact that neither of them looked, but the contact was perfect.

They drove back through town, then southwest toward Colene's home. This was the opposite direction the police would expect. But they would be watching Slick's house too.

"You'd better just drop Provos and me off near my house and go on through town without stopping. We don't know how fast they'll spread the net, once they catch on that you're not at the airport. Sorry you wasted your money on those tickets."

"The money's nothing. I just want to get my niece clear of this country to where she'll never hurt again. Start a new life, maybe, for us both."

Esta smiled. She wanted it too. She probably realized that her uncle was not on the right side of the law, but she believed in him, and so did Colene, in this respect.

A light started flashing behind them. It was another police car.

Provos turned to Slick, making a signal of not-to-worry. But he, conditioned by years of his business, was already cutting over to the right. He swung out of the lane, around the line of cars ahead, and drove with two wheels in dirt until he squealed onto a small road intersecting at right angles. The rear end of the car slewed, giving Colene a scare before stabilizing. This wasn't her idea of fun driving.

The police car spun onto the road behind them. Slick accelerated, but it was clear that this car lacked the power of the other.

Colene saw Provos concentrating, trying to remember what happened next. She knew that Provos' memories were changing; Slick should have pulled over for the police car, and there would have been no trouble. Maybe it was just a bad taillight. Otherwise Provos would have been concerned. Now Provos *was* concerned, and needed to sort out her new memories to see whether they were acceptable.

They were not. Provos pointed to the right, indicating that they should turn onto the next crossroad. But Slick didn't see her. "Turn!" Colene cried, but by then they were past the spot, and Provos was looking confused again.

Suddenly there were two police cars ahead, turning sideways across the road to form a roadblock. "They radioed ahead," Colene said. "They're going to catch us. Because we acted suspiciously when it was a routine check."

Provos got her memories straight again. She jogged Slick's elbow. This time he caught her signal. She pointed to a trail leading off to the left, winding around behind several farm houses.

Slick whipped the car onto the trail. A cloud of dust flew

up. In a moment a police car appeared behind, stirring up its own dust. Worse and worse; this looked like a dead end, so that they would be trapped. Why had Provos brought them here?

Provos pointed to a dilapidated barn. She held up her flat hand in a stop gesture.

"God, I hope you know what you're doing, woman," Slick muttered. He drew up to the barn and stopped.

Provos gestured them out of the car. She herself was the first out. She ran back the way they had come, through the cloud of dust, waving Slick back.

The police car came up—and Provos stumbled directly in front of it. The brakes screeched as it slid to a stop, barely missing her. She fell half over the hood, wailing.

There was only one man in the car. He got out and caught Provos as she started to fall. He didn't see Slick circle the car and come at him from behind.

Then Slick put one hand on the cop's head. He took a handful of hair and hauled back. The other hand held the open razor. It was barely touching the man's exposed throat. "Now, take it easy," Slick murmured in the man's ear. "You better believe I'll use this thing if I have to."

Provos straightened up and walked to the police car. Colene and Esta followed. Then the two men, walking in lock-step, came too. The wicked razor remained poised. "You are going to drive," Slick told the officer. "I have your gun. I will use it on you if you make a peep. You will radio that you lost the car and are searching. You will acknowledge radio contact without signaling that anything's wrong. Do this, and you will get out of this with your life and health and car. Fail, and I will do what I have to do. All I want is transportation. Got it?"

The man nodded, slowly. A bead of sweat was trailing down the side of his face. He did know who Slick was, and what his business was.

Provos directed Colene to the front seat this time. The others got in back, and the cop took the wheel. Slick did have the gun; he lifted it as he withdrew the razor. It was aimed at the policeman, through the seat back.

The man made the report Slick had specified. He did not give any alarm. Colene knew that Provos would have remembered it if he had.

The car started on down the trail, and then onto a better

road. Provos pointed. "Turn left," Slick said. The man turned left.

Provos shook her head no. The man's hand reached for the radio. "Don't touch it!" Slick snapped before the motion was fairly started.

They came to the highway where all this had started. Provos pointed right. "Turn right," Slick said.

At speed, they relaxed, because Provos had relaxed. She did know what she was doing. Occasionally she would signal them to slow, and Slick gave the order and the driver slowed. What mischief they avoided in this manner the others would never know, and that was just as well.

Then Provos signaled a stop. They stopped. She indicated by gestures that Slick should tie the cop's hands behind him. Slick used the man's own handcuffs for that. Then, following her directions, he looped cord through the handcuffs and tied the man to a telephone pole, a short distance from the police car. Then they walked away. True to their word, they had left the man alive and in health and with his car. But without his gun. Seeing that, the man elected not to cry out to any of the passing vehicles.

Provos waved to a pickup truck coming down the highway. It stopped. Provos glanced at Colene.

Colene took the initiative. She flashed her most winsome smile at the driver. "We lost our car, and need to get into town. Can we ride in the back?"

The driver was a youth not a lot older than Colene herself. He hesitated, staring down at her from the cab. Colene realized that he was trying to get a glimpse down inside her blouse. She leaned forward and drew her head back just enough so that he could get that glimpse. "Yeah, sure," he said, probably not even aware that the eyeful had not been an accident. In certain circumstances, men were easy to manage.

The others climbed onto the back, but Colene joined the driver in front. "Gee, this is real nice of you," she said brightly. Indeed, she felt positive; she enjoyed proving every so often that her stuff worked. "We were really in a bind." She snuggled close.

It was no trouble at all to reach her house. "We'll get off here," she said. "It's been great!" She kissed the youth on the cheek, then scooted out. By the time he realized that he didn't even know her name, it would be too late.

They watched the truck depart. "Okay," Colene said. "They don't know about me yet, so my house isn't watched. My folks won't be home for another hour. So you can come in and phone for a taxi, Slick, and get far away. Provos and I will disappear."

Then things started happening. They heard sirens approaching, and knew that the police *had* gotten the word. "Get out of here!" Colene cried to Slick. "They won't know where you are if Provos and I distract them long enough."

But Provos quickly caught hold of Slick's arm and urged him toward the house. Colene was astonished. "But you can't mean—" Yet suddenly it was falling into place. Provos had been helping so actively; surely this was what she had foreseen. There was now little chance for Slick and Esta to make a clean break; the pursuit was getting too close. No chance except the Virtual Mode. "This is awesome," she finished.

A police car appeared. They ran around the house, into the back yard. And Colene paused, appalled.

Dogwood Bumshed was gone.

Suddenly it came together: her father's understanding when she told him about the Virtual Mode and the anchor in the shed. He *had* believed her—and had acted to prevent her from using it. By having the entire shed removed.

The back door of the house opened. Both her parents came out. They hadn't even gone to work! They had set this up, and lain in wait for her return. They meant to keep her here, whatever way they could.

It was frightening, yet also touching. The members of her family did care for her; they wanted her with them. Yet they proposed to do it by force. It wasn't enough that they knew she was well and halfway happy; they wanted her *here*. So they had betrayed her.

But Provos was forging right on toward the spot, seeming not to have noticed that it was gone. Policemen were appearing all around the property; they must have been waiting in ambush. They would not only trap Colene and Provos, they could catch Slick and Esta: disaster for them both. What did it matter on which side of the yard they were actually caught? They were all doomed.

Colene felt tears of frustration and dawning rage coming. She had worked so hard, and come so close, only to be balked right in sight of the anchor. Slick had faithfully performed his end of the bargain, and now he would be locked away in prison, or worse. And Esta would be returned to her stepfather for her daily torture and rape.

"*Damn* it!" she swore. "It's not fair, it's not right! It's not supposed to be this way!"

"Come on, honey," her father called. "We only want what's best for you. That man's a killer, and the girl's a runaway, and the woman is crazy. But you don't have to be. Give up this delusion. We love you."

What could she say? Deep down she did love her folks, but she hated them too, for all the wasted years, and for getting straightened out only in her absence, and for finally betraying her like this. She could never trust them again. She would die in their captivity. By her own hand. She couldn't live without Darius and Seqiro. And what would happen to *them* when Colene didn't return with the rad numbering information?

Now the neighbors were coming, attracted by the commotion. Men, women, and children, staring curiously. None were hostile, but their presence helped seal this little party's doom. There would be no way to break through them all and escape.

Provos reached the spot of bare ground. She clasped Esta by the hand and stepped forward. She disappeared.

The approaching police stared. Colene's parents stared. Colene stared.

Then it registered: Bumshed was gone, but the anchor wasn't. Only Colene herself could free the anchor. They could escape!

But the police were catching on that something strange was afoot. They charged across toward Slick. Provos reappeared, grasped him by the hand, and hauled him with her across the region. They disappeared.

They had made it to the Virtual Mode! But Colene hadn't—and she was too far from the anchor to make it. The police had already crossed that region, and were converging on her. She alone would be trapped here.

Her father strode forward and grasped her arm. "Come on, honey, we'll take care of you. We'll get you straightened out at an institution—"

Colene had an inspiration. Her hand plunged into her purse. She yanked out the roll of hundred-dollar bills. She brought it to her mouth and used her teeth to rip off the band. Then she hurled it into the air.

The roll came apart. Bills started peeling off. They fluttered through the air, drifting to the ground around her.

"Money!" a child cried, diving for a bill.

The policemen stared. "Those are hundred-dollar bills!"

Then there was a melee. Amazed, Colene's father let go of her arm. Everyone wanted the money.

Colene cranked up her legs and ran at top speed for the anchor. One of the few alert policemen made a grab for her, but she banged past him and got through. She dived for the anchor—

And everyone disappeared. She landed on green turf, alone. She was through! But still nervous, though she knew she couldn't be followed. She scrambled back to her feet and walked on.

Suddenly the others were there: Provos and Slick and Esta. "Thank God!" Colene cried, and tried to hug all three at once.

Then she took stock. "What a pass this is! You folk probably didn't even believe in the Virtual Mode, and now you're on it. And I don't know how we're going to get you off it, because they'll be watching the anchor."

Esta fidgeted. Colene looked at her, realizing that she was shy about expressing herself. Thus encouraged, the girl spoke. "Do we have to get off it? This seems nice."

"Well, this is almost just like the reality you've always lived in," Colene explained. "The house and yard are the same, and most of the city will be the same. But there's never been a shed here, so you know there's no Colene here, and probably no Slick or Esta. It's not your reality; you never existed here."

"Then we could go out and establish our identities," Slick said. "I will have no criminal record, and Esta will have no abusive stepfather. We can make it with a clean slate."

"Why, I guess you could," Colene said, surprised. "You won't need to go to Mexico or anything! But won't you have trouble getting your ID papers and stuff?"

"No, I know how to fake ID's." He looked at Esta. "But getting her back into school without records will be harder. We'll probably have to move to another state."

Colene shook her head, disturbed. "I didn't see this coming, but I guess I should have, because now I see that Provos remembered this all along and knew exactly what to do. She brought you both through the anchor. Now that it's happened, I don't feel easy about just dumping you in a strange world and leaving you. Anything could happen, and it'd be my fault."

Provos had been working with material from her pack. Now she approached Slick and proceeded to tie a length of cloth around his left arm, binding it securely to her right arm. Slick, surprised, did not resist.

"I think I have just been answered," Colene said. "When Provos spends any time in a reality, she remembers what will happen there. It seems you are coming with us."

Provos tossed a cloth to Colene. Colene approached Esta. "You see, you folk can't cross realities unless one of us holds on to you. If we let go by accident, you could get stranded, and we might have trouble finding you. So we have to tie you to us, so we can't let go." As she spoke, she bound her own left arm to Esta's right, so that each was clasping the other's forearm and locked in place.

"Gee," Esta said, intrigued. "You told Professor Felix that there was magic. Will we see dragons?"

"We may," Colene said grimly. "This isn't any game, Esta. There's danger on the Virtual Mode. We are traveling a route we know, but anything can happen when we cross boundaries. Let's get moving."

They walked in step, retracing the route she and Provos had used. Thus commenced what would be a journey of several days. It was uncomfortable, but necessary. Provos led the way this time, though her memory could be at best spotty across the realities, and her path deviated somewhat from the one they had taken.

Colene was alarmed, but then she realized what the woman was doing: she was heading directly for Oria. Because they had been away for too much time already, and God only knew what was happening to Darius and Seqiro and Nona. Colene tried not to think about what effect that beautiful woman might be having on that man and that horse. Right now she had to concentrate on getting through the realities safely, and getting around that sea that bordered the anchor at Oria, because they couldn't cross it. Maybe Provos had enough memory of the future to figure that out too. She hoped.

On the way, Colene talked with Esta, getting to know her better. She confided that she had mixed feelings about leaving her folks of the Earth reality. They weren't evil, just wrong for her. So she knew Earth was no place for her to stay, but still she felt guilty about leaving.

"You're so smart and pretty," Esta responded. "But you feel the same as I do."

"I guess I do," Colene agreed. "But you know, where we're going, there are other things. If Provos knows what she's doing, you'll wind up in a reality where you are as smart and pretty as you want to be."

"But I'll always be ugly inside," Esta argued. "Just as long as I can remember where I came from."

Then another revelation dawned. "Provos is taking you to her reality!" she exclaimed. "Those folk remember only the future, not the past! If you get to be like them, nothing in your past will count. And nothing in Slick's past. It will be an absolutely clean slate."

"And I'll always be ugly here," Esta said, tapping her chest.

"No, I don't think so," Colene said. "Because it's a different culture. They don't judge by the same things. And anyway, we'll be stopping first at Oria, where there's magic. Nona will be able to heal your scars, and then later you'll develop and be a woman, and you won't even remember how you are now."

"I wish," Esta breathed.

"We're going to make it happen," Colene said, beginning to believe. Things had been so complicated, and now the future was starting to come clear. Provos must have joined the Virtual Mode for this: to go to Earth and help rescue Slick and Esta, and bring them back to her own reality where they could live in peace. Provos had a spare floor; she'd probably put Slick there, and let Esta sleep where Colene had, up on the top floor. In that manner Provos would get a family, for all anyone knew a son and a granddaughter. It was a nice world, and they would surely like it. It all made so much sense, in retrospect. And Provos had seen it coming, of course. "Sometimes wishes are granted," Colene told her. "In ways we never expected. I think you have a nice future coming up."

But what of Colene's own future? She had no guarantees about that, because she wasn't going to settle in Provos' reality.

She was headed, she hoped, for Darius' reality, and that looked very nice. So long as Darius hadn't changed his mind in the interim about just which girl he wanted to settle down with. If he had, what then would be Colene's fate?

CHAPTER 16

―――――――――― ANIMA

IT was working! Nona was thrilled. When Seqiro linked her closely with Keli, and Keli changed shape, Nona was able to catch a glimmer of what was happening. Day by day she practiced, and bit by bit she learned. It would be a long time before she was as good as the rabble, but in time she would have it.

Then Seqiro's thought came from the chamber closest to the surface. He had been spending most of his time there, questing out through the rock to the anchor, convinced that though his range was limited, he could sense the one he loved from afar. Nona wished he felt that way about her. *Colene! I feel Colene!*

It was time. "We must go!" Nona cried.

"But first we must tell Stave," Darius reminded her.

Oh. Yes. Nona had promised. "Where is he?" she asked.

"I know where!" Keli said eagerly.

They went to the dais chamber. There was one of the Stave emulations, eating a meal. "Are you the real Stave?" Nona asked him.

He snapped his fingers, and a ball of fire appeared there. It expanded and formed a face. The face winked. He was the real Stave. "Are you the real Nona?" he asked.

"Of course I am!" she said.

He stood. "Then embrace me. Kiss me. Strip naked."

"I will do no such thing!" she said indignantly.

He nodded. "Then you are the real one."

That set her back. Of course the Null-Nonas would be happy to do any of that sort of thing he asked; they all wanted so desperately to breed. "Yes. Colene has returned, and we must go. I—I owe Keli here a favor. You must choose her next."

He shook his head. "But that is not the real Nona speaking. You don't even have her face perfect."

"I changed it," Nona said, realizing that she was at this moment almost a parody of herself. So she proved herself: she flew up and hovered a body length above the floor.

Stave nodded. "If the rabble could do that, they wouldn't need us. Very well: Keli it is."

Keli ran to him. "Oh, thank you! I want you so much!"

"You almost had me, that first day," he told her.

"Yes! And now at last it shall be!"

Nona turned away. This business disgusted her. Yet she knew that if Stave had not agreed to do this, she herself would have had to be defending her body from rape every day for a thousand days. She knew she owed him her gratitude. It was just that somehow she did not properly feel it.

"Nona!" Stave called after her. "Don't forget! You must rescue me from this!"

She turned back to look at him. Keli was already out of her brown tunic, a fine figure of a naked woman. Was Stave hiding a smile? "Yes, as soon as possible," she agreed grimly.

THE three of them gathered at a chamber near the surface, but not the one closest to the anchor where Colene would arrive. The despots would be watching the place where they had been. But they should have some brief freedom if they emerged at a new spot.

Nona reached out, seeking the bat she had tamed as a familiar. She had thought that she could not penetrate the barrier between the nether realm and the surface, but had found that with concentration and determination it was possible. She found the bat in the cave. She woke it and caused it to fly to a forest thicket not far from the village. There Seqiro was able to reach its mind.

The bat flew to a glade in the forest. It flew around it, questing for danger. There did not seem to be any person there.

Darius and Nona climbed onto Seqiro's solid back. Then Darius designated the circles, activated the three icons, and moved them.

They landed in the glade. They staggered, getting reoriented. They seemed to have made it without being spotted.

"But the despots' familiars will be cruising everywhere," Nona said. "They may even be watching for daytime bats."

"I know where the anchor is from here," Darius said. "We can go there immediately."

"But if we go too soon, we shall have to wait there, and they will find us."

Colene is approaching the anchor. She has companions.

Darius was startled. "Companions? Plural? Not just Provos?"

Two others. Male and female. Their minds are not yet clear to me, but both seem unusual.

"Is that good or bad?" This was a complication Darius did not seem to like. Nona was not easy with it either. Why would Colene have brought more people?

It seems bad. The female is young, with much pain.

"Colene must have reason," Darius decided. But his unspoken thoughts, relayed to Nona, indicated that he was nervous about the girl's reasoning. It was not easy to bring others through the Virtual Mode; it was necessary to be tied to them at all times, lest they be lost. Whatever Colene's reason, it would have to be very strong. And why had Provos agreed with it? What future had the old woman seen?

Darius' thoughts made Nona just as nervous. She had come to know Colene as an impulsive but intelligent girl. What strange thing was going on?

They are coming through the anchor.

"Then we go!" Darius said.

He conjured them there. Suddenly they were standing by the anchor, on the slope leading up to the sea and the giant stone instruments.

Colene appeared as she emerged from the anchor. Then two other human figures, and finally Provos.

Despots are approaching.

Nona looked around, but did not see the despots. She trusted the horse's awareness, however. They had to get quickly away from here! But how could they do it with four extra people, two of them strangers? It would take too much time just to explain the situation to them!

"Darius!" Colene called, seeing him. "Where's Angus?"

Seqiro sent out a thought: *ANGUS!*

There was a motion high in the sky. It became the form of the giant man, flying toward them.

Meanwhile Darius was forging toward Colene. He swept her into his embrace. She met him eagerly, kissing him on forehead, nose, and eyeball before finding the range. Nona wished she had been able to love Stave like that. "Conjure us out of here, stupid!" Colene whispered, her words carried by Seqiro's mind-talk.

"But Angus needs to be told—"

"Provos is handling that. I have to be with you. Move it!"

Nona hoped the girl knew what she was doing. Darius lifted Colene onto Seqiro's back, pressed close to Nona and the horse, and tuned in to the familiar-bat. It had moved, and now was over a field. He conjured them there.

"Okay, folks," Colene said briskly. "I got the info. I know where it is, I think. The despots'll be hot on our trail, so we'd better move right along. But they don't know where we're going. First, to the head."

"But it will take the familiar time to get there," Nona protested.

Colene frowned. "Damn, that's right! Then we'd better use Angus after all. Can't save him for a decoy."

Angus!

The giant heard. He swooped down again.

"Take us to the head!" Colene cried.

Provos and the two strangers were on the giant's left hand. Darius, Seqiro, and Nona went to the right hand. "No, Nona—you go with the others," Colene said.

Nona did not argue. She went to the left hand and climbed on.

Angus lifted them carefully: four of them in one hand, three in the other, but one of the three was the massive horse. Angus flew up, high into the sky, leaving behind any despot pursuit. Then he leveled off and commenced the flight west.

Colene kissed Darius again. It was almost as if she was afraid he would disappear if she did not constantly demonstrate her feeling for him. "I made icons for my friends, and got their hair, spit, and breath. Here." She handed him two doll figures. "So you can conjure them too, if you have to."

"Thank you," Darius said, bemused. "But why did you bring—?"

"I'll get to that." Colene looked across the hands. "Nona, I'll go over the stuff with you. But first you have to meet my friends, Slick and Esta. Uncle and niece. From Earth. They're going to Provos' reality."

"Hello," Nona said to them, as perplexed as Darius. What a whirlwind of activity Colene was!

Slick nodded, and the girl just looked at her. "They're not up on your language," Colene explained. "And Seqiro hasn't fully fathomed them yet. But you don't have to wait for that. I can translate. Esta needs your help." Then, to the girl: "Es, show her. It's okay."

The girl worked open her shirt and showed her chest. It was a mass of scars. Nona was appalled. How could such mutilation have come about?

"You don't want to know," Colene said. "Just heal her as well as you can."

Nona thought of the memory Seqiro had shared with her, of Colene's experience with rape, and knew that Colene was not teasing. It was best not to inquire.

She took the girl's hand in her own. "I must touch you, to heal you," she said. Colene picked up her thought and spoke in the girl's strange language.

Esta spoke. "Touch me, I don't care," Colene translated. Nona realized that it was not the language the horse understood, but the mind. Seqiro had access to Colene's mind, but not Esta's mind, so Esta's words were meaningless.

Nona sat behind the girl, her legs spread outside, and drew Esta back into Nona herself. This was what she had done with Darius, when healing his rat bite. She reached around and put her hands inside the girl's shirt, against the bare scarred skin of her chest. She concentrated.

"Something is happening!" Esta exclaimed, surprised. This time Nona understood her directly; perhaps their close contact facilitated Seqiro's entry into the girl's mind.

"I am healing you, with my magic," Nona responded.

"I feel it! I feel it! It feels so good!"

"I told you she could do it," Colene said. "She healed Darius."

"The pain—it's going! Can you heal my mind too?"

"No," Nona said sadly. "Only your body."

"But Provos can heal your mind," Colene said. "She will take you back to her reality, where the folk remember only the future. If you can be like them, you will lose your past, and it won't affect you any more. I think it will be that way, because the longer you are in that reality, the more you will become *of* it, at least in body and culture. That's why Provos came for you; she remembered that you needed her."

"That's why she came?" Darius asked, surprised. "But she can't remember in other realities. She has to be in them before she can remember."

"I know. I was with her. We went to her reality—and to yours. She must remember what it will be like in her reality after she gets back. And she remembers Slick and Esta being with her. She knew them both, the moment she saw them. She hugged them like old friends. Like family members." Colene paused.

"Yes, of course," Provos said.

"Isn't that so, Provos?" Colene asked. Nona knew that the girl had deliberately timed it, to let the woman answer before the question came. "That you remember Slick and Esta with you from now on?"

"It is true," Provos agreed.

"Isn't it true that Slick and Esta have a happy life coming in your reality, with him earning an honest living and her growing up and marrying a local boy and being happy ever after?"

Provos smiled, nodding.

"You have a family now," Colene said evenly. "A son and granddaughter, as far as you know, even if you don't remember marrying or losing your husband. But you love them and they love you, and it doesn't matter where they may have come from."

"Yes, my dear," Provos said to Esta.

Esta stared at Provos. She spoke. Colene translated in her mind as she heard the words, so that Seqiro could send the meaning to the others immediately. To Nona, it was as if she now understood Esta. "I will forget how I have lived? I will remember what is to happen?"

The girl looked across at Colene. "It is a nice place? Where she lives?"

"A real nice place," Colene assured her. "The kind of place you'll want to spend the rest of your life." Nona understood from the peripheral thoughts that they had had this dialogue before, but that Esta needed repeated reassurance. The girl was horribly insecure, and afraid that anything good was illusory. She had suffered terribly, and could not quite believe that this was over.

Nona released the girl; her body had been healed. Esta crawled across Angus' hand to Provos, who had already spread her arms. They hugged.

Slick shook his head. "I never dreamed of such a thing. It's like magic."

"It *is* magic, dummy," Colene said. "Get used to it. After flying across a planet on the hand of a giant, you shouldn't find it all that difficult."

"A barber," Provos said, looking up.

Colene smiled. "What kind of job will Slick have?" she asked the woman. Slick choked, and Nona wondered why, until she caught Colene's thought: Slick had made his former living by slicing people's throats.

Slick recovered in a moment. "I wonder whether there will be a woman for me," he mused.

"She is a hairdresser," Provos replied.

Colene smiled. "That's not your answer. Here, I'll do it. Provos, what kind of job does Slick's wife do?"

Nona smiled. That showed how the two would meet.

"Beautiful," Provos said.

This time Slick put the question himself. "What will my wife look like?"

Darius interceded. "You had better leave something to discover, or you will be bored before it happens." Then he turned to Colene. "You visited *my* reality?"

"We sure did," Colene replied, pleased. "I met Kublai, and Prima, and Koren. Koren and I, we really understand each other. And Ella." She fixed him with an irate gaze. "You won't be taking off her diaper any more once I get there, you damned horny man."

Darius looked abashed, but Nona did not fathom the reason. A diaper was for a baby, but Ella didn't sound like a baby. Then Colene laughed, and hugged him. Whatever it was, it was all right, or at least tolerable.

So it was that they passed the time, coming to know each

other better, while Angus carried them west toward the head. After a while Colene settled down to business.

"I have the stuff on the rads," she told Nona. "But it's a bit tricky. Let me see if I can make it clear."

Colene concentrated, and a picture formed in Nona's mind. It was an outline of Oria, with its body, head, and rads. "What we want is R1/R2/R3 and so on up to /R9. Don't worry about what it's called; I figured it out by studying the newsletter the prof gave me in my reality. R1 is the Body, /R2 is the Head, and /R3 is here." On her mental picture the largest rad on the head glowed. "Then we climb onto /R3 and look for /R4 on it." The rad expanded in the image, until it filled the mental screen. The /R4 that now glowed on that was about halfway between the small head of /R3 and the large curve of the surface of /R2. "We'll keep getting farther around on each next rad," Colene said. "But we'll get there. The ninth rad on the eighth rad is going to be pretty small, though."

"Just so long as you know the way!" Nona said, thrilled at this confirmation that the girl's quest for information had been successful. It seemed so sensible now.

"Just so long as the despots *don't* know the way," Colene said. "Because if they do, they'll stop us."

"But we must succeed, because Provos remembers that we do," Nona said.

"I'm not so sure of that. Provos remembers what's in her own reality, because that's where she'll return to settle. But she's just passing by this one, and maybe what she remembers is subject to change."

"But surely her memories of her own world are fixed, because she isn't there to change things," Nona protested, though she wasn't sure of her logic. "So the right things must happen here, so that she and her friends can go there."

"I see Colene's point," Darius said. "Provos, Slick, and Esta may indeed be guaranteed their arrival at her reality. But the rest of us are not destined for her reality, and so her memory offers us no guarantee. She may take them with her after we succeed here—or fail. Nona can pass just the three of them through the anchor, and the rest of us may be bound here, if the animus continues."

That made uncomfortable sense. There was indeed no guarantee for the success of her mission. Anything could happen—including death for several of them.

They crossed the sea that circled Oria between the Body and the Head and flew across the lesser mass of the Head. Nona remembered the story of Earle and Kara, flying similarly across the worlds. Would she herself someday be the stuff of a legend? Perhaps so, if she succeeded in bringing the anima.

Night came, as the ninety-eight-ray star disappeared behind the world. The myriad other stars now showed more clearly, large and small. It was beautiful, as it always was. Perhaps in the pristine early days of the world all of the patterns of glow had been visible all the time, but now much of it could be seen only in the dark.

Angus found an isolated place and came down to the surface. He was tired and needed to rest, and the rest of them needed food and sanitary relief. Nona took the leaf of a plant and transformed it into fruit. Seqiro accepted grain she made for him, then wandered away to graze, keeping in mind-touch. He was alert for other human beings, especially despots. The despots of this region would not be the same as those of Nona's region, but they surely had spread the word. No despot, anywhere on Oria, could be trusted to be other than an enemy.

They settled for the night. Angus stretched out between rads, careful not to damage any trees, while the others formed a cluster in a glade. Nona made material for a tent, which Darius and Colene and Slick pitched with reasonable success. She made pallets and blankets for them each, but Darius and Colene elected to share theirs, as did Slick and Esta. Provos slept alone, and so did Nona. Surely it did not bother Provos, but Nona wished Stave were with her. Yet had he been with her, he would have been interested in sexual expression, and she was not. She could tell from the ambience of their minds that Slick and Esta had no such interest in each other, being blood relatives, and that Darius and Colene did but were not indulging it. So there was closeness and comfort for others, but not for Nona. By her own choice, mostly. Yet it frustrated her too.

The fact was, she realized, that though she had been slow to commit to Stave, she had expected to in time. The overwhelming importance of the anima had governed her emotion; she could not think of settling down with a man until that was done. If she failed to accomplish it, then she might be dead or imprisoned or exiled, and in no condition to marry. So she had suppressed what feelings she might have had. But now Stave

was gone, and she knew that once he had tasted the endless
blandishments of seductive rabble women, he would lose his
interest in Nona. Why should he settle for one when he could
have any he chose, a new one each day, each more eager than
the last? She had realized from the part of his mind that Seqiro
shared that he was as lusty as the next man, and that his
attraction to Nona herself had been at least as much for her
appearance as for her position as the ninth. Were she not
pretty, and not the ninth, he would never have noticed her. He
was a good man, yet she was not satisfied with this.

So it was best for her to break with Stave. They were not,
in the end, right for each other. She needed a different sort of
man. But where on Oria was the kind she wanted? If she
brought the anima, she would be queen, the only one on the
planet with magic. After the visitors from the Virtual Mode
left. Who would care to marry her? Who would she care to
marry? She didn't want to marry at all!

And there was the heart of it. She did want a social life,
but she was not ready to settle down. She preferred to have
freedom and adventure, to experience a mystery of the future.
Marriage, babies, growing old—that did not appeal at all. Not
even if she were queen.

But what else was there? Her fate had been sealed when
she was born as the ninth.

Nona settled into an unhappy sleep.

WAKE. The despots come.

It was Seqiro. Nona struggled awake, and heard the
others stirring. Outside the tent was the noise of Angus getting
up. It was still dark.

"How close?" Colene asked.

You have time to dress and make droppings.

Nona hurried to do those things. Then she transformed
the tent material back to a piece of string, and the blankets to
tiny swatches of cloth. She was ready when the others were,
with a basket of fruit to hand out for them to eat on the run.

Angus squatted and laid his two hands on the ground.
Each person went to the hand used before.

"No, you come with us, Nona," Colene said. "This is
Business Day."

It was indeed! Nona joined Darius, Colene, and Seqiro
on the right hand, while Provos, Slick, and Esta got on the left.

It was crowded, because of the mass of the horse, but Nona really liked being with Seqiro. She was jealous of Colene in that respect: she had the most fabulous companion!

Angus sailed up. As he did, several men rose from the forest at some distance; the despots were flying after them!

But they could not match the range and speed of the giant from Jupiter. Angus readily left them behind. However, several birds maintained the pursuit: the familiars of the despots. How could they escape pursuit by those?

Angus knows how. He can not use his magic while concentrating on flying, but you can use yours and I can use mine. Do you wish me to stun them?

Nona pondered the matter. The despots now knew about her, but should not know about Seqiro. "We must keep your secret as long as possible," she decided. "You may need your magic as a surprise. I will try to divert them by illusion."

So while Colene guided Angus toward what she called /R3, Nona fashioned a massive pair of illusions. One was of Angus, flying with his hands full. The other was of nothingness, where the real Angus was. Stave had shown how effective this ploy could be; now she was doing it on a larger scale. But a large illusion was harder to manage than a small one, because there was so much detail. Familiars would not be smart, but the despots guiding them would be alert for tricks. This had to be right.

She crafted the two illusions, overlapping. Gradually she replaced the appearance of the real giant with the illusion giant, matching detail to detail. She could not see his back, but assumed that it matched the normal male configuration. When she had it as good as she could make it, she caused the Angus illusion to diverge from the nothingness illusion. This was the test.

Slowly they separated. Would the familiars follow the illusion? It was only visual, so if any were using smell, they would not be deceived.

Most of the birds followed the illusion. But Nona saw with dismay that one small hawk was not being fooled. If its despot realized—

Then the hawk dropped. Seqiro had stunned it. The despot would think that the illusion giant had somehow taken it out, perhaps by throwing something at it. They were escaping.

But she could not maintain the illusion indefinitely. Most magic was close and line-of-sight; only the familiars could operate at a distance, because they had identities of their own. Soon she would lose control, and the illusion would dissipate, and the familiars would cast about until they found the smell of the original.

"We need a better decoy," Colene said, grasping the situation from Nona's thought. "Okay, time for Phase Two. Angus, put us down—Seqiro, Darius, Nona, and me—then fly on with the others as if you're going somewhere. So the familiars will think it's the whole party, and will follow them."

A faint illusion image of Angus appeared at the edge of his invisible hand, in miniature. "But where shall I carry them?" he asked.

"Back to the anchor, of course," Colene said. "So they can complete their destiny, even if we mess up."

And there it was, Nona realized with a shock: the manner that Provos' memory of the future would be correct, even if Nona's mission failed. It was coming true.

Colene glanced at her, mentally. All of them were now invisible, so there was no other way. "Right. Our guarantee is zilch."

No guarantee of success. Somehow Nona had always believed that she would succeed, once she had gotten together with the visitors from the Virtual Mode. Now horrible doubt loomed. She shivered.

"Except that Nona will have to pass them through the anchor," Darius said. "She must either succeed or survive."

Bless him for that revelation, mixed as it was! She could not fail utterly.

Angus descended, while Nona continued to concentrate on the distant illusion. If she could only hold it long enough to let them separate . . .

The giant's feet touched the ground, gently. He stood, then bent down. The four of them climbed off the hand.

Nona turned back to embrace a huge invisible finger. "If I don't see you again, friend Angus—"

The small illusion of him returned. "It has been good with you, Nona. I will know if you succeed."

"You will not be able to commune with the three you carry," Nona said. "But you know where to take them."

"I know."

She was out of words and full of emotion. "I wish you had been my size," she said. Then she opened her arms to the little illusion. He met her, and they kissed, in the manner of Earle and Kara.

It was too much distraction. The distant illusion of Angus disintegrated. But Nona maintained the close illusion of nothingness. "Go, friend Angus," she said. "With my thanks, and my love." For suddenly, this instant, it was true: she loved the giant from Jupiter, who had served her need so loyally. She knew it was a transitory emotion, and foolish considering their sizes, but that part of it would always remain with her.

"For that I do thank you," the little image said.

Then the invisible giant flew up, and they were left on the ground. Nona concentrated on the illusion, until he was too far away; then she lost it, and he became visible. But he was at that point in the vicinity of the prior giant-illusion, so that the familiars would assume that he had always been there. He was still holding both hands up, as if still carrying a double burden.

"The legend!" Colene exclaimed. She was visible now; Nona had had to let their part of the illusion go when she focused on Angus. "You replayed it! That was beautiful."

"Perhaps I am destined to love only the unobtainable," Nona said sadly.

"I'm not so sure of that. I dreamed you got married."

Nona looked at her. There was something dark about the girl's thought, but she could not fathom it.

"We had better move," Darius said. "If you can get a familiar, Nona, I can conjure us to where it goes."

"How about directly to the nearest /R3?" Colene asked. "If I make you a map? There are four of those rads, so we must be halfway close to one."

He shook his head. "That would be dangerous. I need to see where I am going, or to know it from prior experience. A familiar could show it much more accurately."

"Okay. But we'd better get moving."

Seqiro searched, but found no suitable unattached birds in the vicinity. The despots seemed to have taken them all. But then he found a fox, and stunned it.

Nona had never tamed a fox before. But then she had seldom tamed any animal, because of the need to conceal her magic. The principle was the same. She touched the fallen animal, and Seqiro enhanced her mental contact. It was more of a job than the bat had been, but she was able to do it.

Then she sent the fox running toward the third rad on the Head. While they waited for it to cover the distance, she picked a berry and magnified it into a giant berry, so that they could all have their fill of it, finishing their meal.

Despots approach.

That galvanized them. Nona tuned in on the fox. It was most of the way there. They clustered around Seqiro, and Darius brought out his magic icons and invoked them. Seqiro connected Darius' mind to that of the familiar. Then they climbed onto the horse's broad back, and Darius moved the icon.

Nona felt the awful wrenching. Then she found herself sliding off the horse. She managed to get her feet under her before landing on the ground.

They were almost at the base of the towering bulk of /R3; the fox had made excellent progress.

"God, that thing must be three hundred miles tall," Colene said, awed. Her mental concept translated into approximately the right amount. "Somehow I didn't think they would get this big, on this little planet."

"Can we see /R4 from here?" Darius asked.

Colene studied the mountainous outline. "Actually we can see one of its /R4's," she agreed. She pointed. "See that twenty-mile-thick wart there? As I make it, that's it."

"Then I should be able to conjure us there from here," he said. "Provided there is a safe place to land."

"There they are!" someone called in the language of Oria. Nona jumped.

"Damn!" Colene swore. "They must have lured the fox, or spotted it. They're on to us."

They ran for the cover of the nearby forest. The man who had called saw them but was slow to give chase, as if waiting for reinforcements. That gave them a brief respite, but was hardly good news.

"They are becoming more apt at locating us," Darius said as they passed beyond the first trees. "They may suspect where we are going, and have many of their number in this vicinity looking for us."

"It may be that they know where the key rad is," Nona

said, breathing hard as she ran. "They would keep it secret from all theows, of course. But now—"

"Can the dialogue," Colene snapped. "Seqiro, you take Darius and gallop the hell out of here. Decoy them away. We'll get together again after."

"But—" Nona started.

"You and I will go alone," Colene said. "Invisible. Do it."

"It is too far for you afoot," Darius said.

"What do you mean, too far? I just walked across whole worlds!"

"If you take too long, the despots will catch you."

"Oh."

"I will conjure the two of you there before we ride away." He brought out his Colene and Nona icons.

"Yeah, I guess you'd better," Colene agreed reluctantly. She came to stand beside Nona.

Darius invoked his icons, and started to move them.

"There!" the man cried, spying horse and man.

Then the wrenching, and the scene was gone.

They landed tumbled on /R4. Colene righted herself, looked around, and suddenly dropped to the ground again. "God! I'm freaking out!" But the alien words meant nothing to Nona; they were not out of Seqiro's mind-magic range.

Meanwhile Nona stood and gazed across at the ground of /R2 where they had been. She did not see any sign of man or horse, but that was to be expected. At least she had the comfort of knowing that the pair would be hard to catch, because the horse could do mind-magic and the man could conjure them away from the threat of capture.

Then she looked down at Colene, and realized that the girl was staring at her. Suddenly it registered: Colene was not used to being on a rad of this size. To her it looked as if Nona were standing sideways on an almost vertical cliff. For of course this rad projected from about the midpoint of the side of /R3, and they were on the side of /R4.

She tried to reassure the girl. "Do not be concerned. A person's feet are always toward the center of the rad on which she stands. We experienced the same thing on Jupiter."

"Yeah, but this is smaller and more intense, and I've been away," Colene said. "I haven't gotten my reactions realigned yet." The words she spoke were unintelligible, but Nona was sure they related to her concern about falling.

"We can not fall." To illustrate the point, Nona jumped. Colene screamed.

But of course Nona landed immediately back on the surface. Colene, seeing that, laughed nervously, then got up the courage to stand. She remained anchored to the rad. Finally she gritted her teeth and made a little jump. She did not fly loose from the rad. She issued a shaky sigh.

Nona was glad that the girl had come to terms with the nature of walking on a rad, because they would be moving to ever-smaller rads to reach the key point. She would have explained about the way of it, before they left Seqiro, had it occurred to her. But now, alone with Colene, and not yet at the site for the anima—they couldn't even talk to each other!

"Can. Some."

The mind-magic! The girl had been learning it. Her power was little compared to that of the horse, but far better than none. "Then we go," Nona said, speaking without vocalizing, to concentrate her thoughts. "Now. To the next rad."

"Go," Colene agreed the same way. "To Slash R Five." The designation was clear, because they both knew it. Colene looked around. "There." She pointed.

Then Nona saw the figure of a man. Was it a despot? She couldn't take the chance. Quickly she fashioned a spell of nothingness to hide them both. She took Colene's hand so that they could remain together without talking.

It turned out to be a fair distance, through fairly rough country, but they had no choice. This rad was tiny compared to its parent rad, and minuscule compared to the one from which they had been conjured, but it was far from the smallest. Nona relaxed the nothingness spell once they were sure they were not being pursued, so that she would be free to do other magic. When they came to a difficult ravine, she held Colene in her arms and flew across it. She could not go far that way, for the extra weight was extremely tiring, but for this short hop it really helped. Mostly they just walked, and talked. Colene was getting better with practice, but Nona still had to interpolate to re-create the full thoughts. The effort helped take her mind off her doubt about her situation.

"One thing I want to know," Colene said approximately, though Nona was sure she had the essence. "This world is in animus phase, right? It's a man's world. So how come you can do major magic? Even considering that you're the ninth."

"It is because of the flow of the current of magic," Nona tried to explain. It would have been so much easier with the horse present! "It originates at the center of the universe and flows out along the filaments to every part of it. It spreads out at each world, in an umbra, a field, with a current which the despot men can tap and adapt. I, too, can tap that current, because of my special nature."

"But when you bring the anima, then what happens?"

"Then the current changes, and flows the wrong way for the despot men. They flow along the lines of the first of the first, but the anima will be the last of the last. The lastborn woman instead of the firstborn man."

"So then why won't you lose your power of magic also, when they do?"

"Because I am the key person, by order of birth and gender. I am *the* opposite, in perfect balance, able to draw on the flow from either side. When the flow changes, that other side will be the primary one. No man will be able to draw on it any more, except when there is a first of the first for nine generations, who will be able to travel to the center of the universe and change it as Earle did."

"Well, maybe," Colene said, evidently not really understanding it. "But shouldn't the reversal point be at the spike? We're headed off to the side."

"It is not really a reversal, but a change," Nona tried to explain. "The main flow remains from the center of the universe to the rest, but the field around our world will be changed, to be somewhat skew, in a manner only the lastborn women will be able to address."

"Like a reversal of the Earth's magnetic field!" Colene exclaimed. Nona found this incomprehensible, so did not argue.

But in a moment the girl had another question. "Angus—he's of the animus. So what happens to him when it changes? Does he pitch headfirst into the sea?"

"Angus is not of this world," Nona explained. "He responds to the rule of his own world, Jupiter. He did not lose his power when we crossed that small anima world."

"Yeah, that's right. I'm glad. He's nice. Too bad you couldn't have been his size."

"A legend can have a happy ending," Nona said.

"You'll have one too. You'll be queen."

"True," Nona said without enthusiasm.

"Well, I'll sure be glad when it's done and you're queen and I can go back on the Virtual Mode with my horse and my man."

The girl was wary of the effect another woman could have on such a horse and such a man. Nona could appreciate why. Nona herself remained upset by the thought of Stave and the rabble women, though Stave would gladly have stayed with her if it had been possible. How much greater must be Colene's concern, for she had truly wondrous companions. Darius was a man among men, with powerful magic, and Seqiro was a horse among horses, wonderful to be with. It had been a great act of necessity and trust for Colene to leave both man and horse behind while she revisited her own world. She surely longed to reach the safety of Darius' world, and to settle there to be one with him and Seqiro. How well Nona understood!

They were near the /R5 rad when darkness closed, but not near enough. Nona made tent material and bedding material and an assortment of foods, and they settled for the night.

"You're so beautiful and so talented and so mature and so nice," Colene remarked. "You have so much going for you. I'm jealous. I really am."

She was jealous of Nona! What irony.

"Because both Darius and Seqiro like you and admire your magic."

"I feel the same about them," Nona said.

"Because you are halfway in love with both of them," the girl continued.

"That's not true!" Nona exclaimed, appalled.

"Isn't it? You know that Earle in the Jupiter legend looks like a cross between Angus and Darius, and Kara looks like you. So it was a simulated romance between you and Darius, since Angus is out of reach."

And Nona realized with expanding horror that Colene was right. Stave—it was not just that he was indulging his masculine appetite with other women. It was that Nona had found a stern, powerful, and magic man, and a completely understanding and mentally encompassing horse, and she longed to be with both. She craved distant adventure and passion, and both man and horse were creatures of exactly that, with their Virtual Mode.

But neither was hers to claim. "Oh, Colene, I would never—"

"I know you wouldn't. Seqiro showed me how you feel and how you are. You're better than me in every way, especially decency. You have the kind of honor Darius has, and I don't. But the choice may not be yours to make. It may be theirs."

Nona felt the tears on her face. "Colene, I—"

"I dreamed you married Darius, and I'm not fool enough to think it can't happen."

Nona stared at her, stricken.

"So I guess you can see why I don't want you on the Virtual Mode," the girl continued relentlessly. "Because if you go there, I'm doomed."

"Of course. I will remain here. I will be queen." But it was grief, not joy, in the decision.

NEXT morning they reached the next rad. This one they would be able to traverse in minutes. It was only, according to Colene's alien measurement, about one mile in diameter. It seemed to be roughly parallel to the hugely looming grandparent rad, /R3, which was itself in a similar relation to R1, the Body of Oria. But their feet pointed straight down toward the center of /R5. Colene seemed to be adjusting, mainly by not looking up.

There were trees and brush here, the same size as on the main planet. The sizes of things were in scale with their worlds, but this was not a separate world, only a projection of a world. They stayed under the trees when they could, avoiding exposure. Then, as they approached /R6, which was about the size of the despots' castle at home, they paused. For there, circling lazily above it, was a buzzard.

"That may be a despot familiar," Nona whispered.

"Well, they have to be watching the sites," Colene said. "Probably just one despot each, so as not to use too many personnel and give away the fact that there's something important there." Nona was having very little difficulty understanding her now, because during their close association of the past day and night their mental rapport had been enhanced. The girl saw them as rivals for a man, but Nona liked Colene as well as she liked Darius or Seqiro. She wished she could have them all for friends. She knew Colene would not understand that, however.

So she addressed the external problem instead. "Yes, of course. But one despot male will be enough to counter me. I had thought at first that Darius would be here to conjure him away, or Seqiro, to give him a bad mind. Alone, I fear I can not accomplish my mission."

"Well, you aren't exactly alone, you know."

Nona looked at her. "I apologize; I did not mean to disparage you. But you lack the magic of the others, and I fear that only strong magic will suffice."

"I have a little magic, remember," the girl said. "We're talking, aren't we?"

"Yes, of course; you are getting the mind-magic. But my mind is open to you, and we know each other; we are attuned. Can you communicate with a strange despot?"

Colene grimaced. "I don't think so. And I sure couldn't stop him, anyway. So maybe I'm not much use. But maybe I can do something. If worse comes to worst, maybe we can get Darius back in here to take out that despot."

"If his coming doesn't bring other despots."

"Yeah. Let me try." She concentrated, evidently reaching out mentally.

Meanwhile, Nona made a new spell of nothingness to cover them. She could have changed her own appearance somewhat, using the magic Keli had taught her, but that would not conceal them. The familiar would be able to smell them, so invisibility wouldn't be effective long either, unless she took out the bird, but it might help against an inattentive despot.

"Good God!" the girl exclaimed. "It's Naylor!"

Nona was surprised. "The knave?"

"I must've tuned in to him, some, before, without realizing! That's one joker I'll never forget. He tried to rape me!"

Nona remembered the memory-vision of rape Seqiro had shown her. "That is horrible, Colene! Then you are afraid of him."

"Afraid, hell! I want his ass on a burning-hot poker!"

The images were obscure, but the emotion came through. It was not fear but anger the girl felt. Unfortunately anger was not sufficient. If Knave Naylor saw Colene again, he would surely use his magic to incapacitate her, and then he would finish what he had started before. And Nona still would not be able to complete her mission, because he would be able to stun Colene and then turn against Nona. "We dare not approach him," Nona said.

Colene was quiet for a while. Then she spoke with a grimness that was almost frightening. "The way I see it, we have to get this job done. Because otherwise you won't be queen, and the rest of us won't be able to get away from this reality. We'll be stuck forever in the universe of Julia, and you will take my man and horse from me, no matter how hard you try not to. So I'm going to have to use my nerve."

"Your nerve? Colene, you may have courage, but that will not stop a despot! And this one—surely he lusts for you yet, and is angry. You must not let him see you."

"You got it backwards, sister. He must not see *you*. So he won't know you're here. He must see me. I'm perfect to distract him, because of his grudge against me. I'll be the last decoy. I'll lead him off the site, so you can go there and do your thing while he's trying to do his thing with me."

"But Colene! He will rape you!"

"I've been raped before," the girl said. "If I can fight enough to take his whole attention long enough, you can finish. Then the power will be yours, and you can destroy him. I won't say it's a way I like, but it's our best bet."

"I could not ask you to do that!" Nona protested. "It was bad enough when Stave undertook my breedings, and he—he really wanted to be with those women. You don't want it at all. You hate rape. Your loathing and rage are coming through to me. It is the worst possible risk for you."

"That's why it takes nerve," Colene said. "Suicidal nerve. The truth is, I have a deathwish, and it drives me to flirt with death and destruction. And rape. Same thing, maybe. I don't like it, but I can't help it. I'm not nice like you. I've got to try this. But you'd better be quick with your mission, because after I lose, you lose too. He won't stop with one—not when the other looks like you. Not when it's the fate of all the despots on the line."

"But—"

"Make me visible. You stay invisible. When I get him off the point, you go there. You don't need me to count off, any more. /R7 will be the seventh around /R6, the way we've been counting, and it'll be only the size of your two hands splayed.

/R8 will be smaller than your little fingernail. /R9 will be too small for you to see. But you'll know where it is. Get on it, woman."

Nona liked no part of this, but was helpless against the girl's determination. It was a possible solution, and if she could act quickly enough, she might succeed.

Colene, visible, walked to the crevice between /R5 and /R6, stopping at the edge of the little ring-sea there. She reached up and touched /R6, then drew up her feet. In a moment she was standing on /R6, her head pointed toward /R5. She had learned the way of it.

Nona, invisible, flew up toward /R7, landing a short distance from it. Colene was right: there was evil Knave Naylor, sitting on /R7 and looking supremely bored. He was using his magic to make ants float away from their nest, struggling, to land in the puddle circling the base of the rad. Every so often his eyes would go vague, and she knew he was drawing instead on the vision of the familiar, searching for anyone who might be approaching. He was hardly working at it, not expecting anything to happen. But the moment he did spy anything, he would be formidable. The knave might not be a nice man, but he did have passions.

There was a noise. Naylor looked, and spied Colene.

"The alien theow bitch!" he exclaimed, amazed. The vulture veered and flew down. "Where is the man?"

"My man isn't here," Colene said, but her words were unintelligible to the knave. "It's just you and me, you misbegotten animal-part!" The last insult was beyond Nona's power to decipher, but she was sure that had Naylor understood it, he would have been enraged.

The vulture flew near the girl, circling her, trying to sniff out any companion. But there was none. Nona was on the other side, hunched amidst a copse of saplings, hoping the bird did not smell her.

Naylor took a step toward Colene. "No man? You're a decoy, then! He's guarding the theow bitch at another site."

Colene's bravado became seeming fright. She retreated.

Naylor strode after her. "You can't escape! You and I have unfinished business."

The girl turned and fled, running around the curve of the rad. Naylor extended his magic and caused her to float up, her feet moving helplessly, and she still tried to run. He held her there, struggling in the air, while he took his time walking across to her. He was still wary of the possible proximity of her man, with his terrible magic.

Nona had her chance, thanks to Colene's suicidal bravery. She walked quietly to /R7. It was a miniature of the rads they had been traversing. Its little head pointed up. She counted off from the head, until she found /R8, which was down toward its inwardly curving base. It was about the size of the head of a fancy ornamental pin.

Colene screamed. Nona jumped, and looked to see the knave's hands on the girl. He was ripping off her odd clothing, exposing her body, and she was unable to move her limbs to resist. Nona had to try to help her.

Stick to your business! The thought came through with surprising clarity. The girl might be screaming, but she knew exactly what she was doing. She was putting on a show for the man, keeping him distracted. There was fear in her thought, but also rage, and determination. She was going to make this scene last as long as she could. Nona could not be concerned with her, right now; she had to get her own business done, in time to save Colene and the world.

But now how was she supposed to find /R9? It was, as Colene had warned, too small to see. Even its extended filament was too small.

But Nona did not have to see it. She was the ninth: she should be able to sense it. She extended her finger to the place it had to be, at the base of the head of the /R8 pin. Then she extended her sensitivity, trying to tune in on it as she would with a familiar.

She felt a tingle. It was there! The key filament!

"Nona!" It was Colene, calling verbally. "He sees you! You're visible!"

Nona glanced back over her shoulder. Naylor had let go of the naked girl and was starting toward Nona. He was about to use his magic on her. She had concentrated so intensely on the key point that she had let her other magic go—and now she could not use her magic in her defense without losing that delicately tingling connection.

But the knave was reorienting his magic too. Colene dropped to the ground behind him. He could not focus his magic on both Colene and Nona, and he knew that Nona was the more dangerous one. But the girl would not let him go. She bounded up immediately and launched herself at the man from behind. She tackled him, causing him to fall.

Naylor cursed and tried to strike at her with his fist. But Colene caught his hand with one of hers, brought it to her mouth, and bit it. He yelled with the pain, for the moment forgetting about Nona. The girl was truly fighting him, with her suicidal fury, tooth and nail; it was impossible for him to ignore her. Colene so desperately wanted to escape with her man and horse to the Virtual Mode, so as to be free of Nona, that she was absolutely fearless and without restraint.

Nona concentrated on the tingle. She sent her spirit into it, and suddenly she saw the key filament, magnified enormously. It seemed to surround her, its power expanding.

A hand fell heavily on her shoulder. "Get away from there!" Naylor cried.

Nona realized that he must have used his magic to stun Colene, and now was free to stop Nona. She might fight him on an almost even basis if she let go of her contact with the filament. But what would be the point? She would have saved herself at the expense of her destiny.

The hand was trying to pull her away. The fingers dug cruelly into the flesh of her shoulder. But his magic was not fastening on her, to make her lose her volition. Because he was using that to keep Colene suspended in air, still struggling; the girl was far more dangerous to him physically than Nona was, because of her determination and courage.

Nona wrenched her shoulder away and reoriented on the filament. But he grabbed at her again.

"You know your family is gone?" Naylor demanded of her. "We declared them nonproductive, a burden on society, and they disappeared. You are alone."

Nona was stricken. Her dear mother and father!

"Don't listen to him!" Colene screamed. "He's trying to distract you without magic!"

Because he was using his magic to restrain Colene. He was using anything he had—and he might be lying.

Nona threw the rest of her being into the connection with the filament. "Anima, invoke!" she cried with her voice and soul.

She felt herself falling into it. She passed into the /R9 filament, and through the /R9 rad, and the /R8 rad, and on through the series of them, so swiftly that it was no time, yet also nine generations. She expanded to embrace the whole world with her being.

Then she was back in her body, at the seventh rad, and the magic was off her. She stood, throwing off Knave Naylor's hand. She invoked her magic, and caused him to float helplessly. He had no magic to oppose her.

The anima had come.

But what was she to do with him? She could not let him go; he would only attack someone again. He was a rapist.

Then she knew. The four of them had visited just one of the many occupied chambers inside the world. There were many others, and surely some were more brutal than others. She had a place for him.

Colene lay nearby, naked and bruised from the fight and the fall when Naylor's magic let her go. Nona went to her and touched her, healing her. The girl sat up. "Did he—?" Nona asked, but already she knew that the man had not gotten that far. How could any man rape a spitfire like that?

"No," Colene said. "Did you—?"

"Yes. It has changed. No man has magic now."

"So the women have it?"

"No. But their daughters will. The age of the despots is over."

"And we can go back on the Virtual Mode," Colene said.

"Yes. But first you must get dressed."

Colene looked down at herself, and laughed.

AFTER that it was straightforward. Angus returned to carry them back to Nona's home village, where the celebration was in progress. The despots were moving out of their castles all across Oria, though they could have defended them. The question was whether it was to be a peaceful transition or a violent one, and the despots preferred to keep it peaceful. That way they would not be slaughtered when the magic came to the daughters and finally overwhelmed them.

Riding for the day on the giant's hand, they discussed what was to be. "What will be your first act as queen?" Colene inquired.

"Oh, of course I will honor the deal we made with the rabble, and allow four thousand of them to emerge to the surface."

"Well, that was easy," Colene said. "What about your second?"

"I will banish Knave Naylor to the nether region reported to have the ugliest and most aggressive women. He will learn about rape!"

Colene laughed so hard she nearly rolled off the hand. "The punishment sure fits the crime!" Then she sobered. "And what about the third?"

Nona considered. "Then I suppose I will have to choose a man to marry. It is expected; there have to be offspring."

"That's easy! You've got Stave."

"I suppose I do," Nona agreed. "I do owe him that. He is certainly a worthy man." It should not be any worse with him than with any other, she thought, considering that she didn't want to marry at all.

What did she want? She wanted an impossible dream. She wanted to go with the bold girl and the magic man and the magic horse, and explore the other universes. To be free, unbound, without obligation to strangers. But she couldn't say that.

"So I guess you wouldn't even want to do anything crazy, like bugging out on it all. Like going on the Virtual Mode, where you wouldn't be queen, and maybe wouldn't even have any magic, and might get wiped out at any time."

The girl's words were in her own idiom, but her meaning was clear, thanks to Seqiro's translation. It was indeed her foolish desire. But Nona knew the girl did not want her along, for excellent reason. So she would not ask. She averted her face, trying to stifle the tears.

"Damn it, woman!" Colene exclaimed. "Not only are you prettier than me, and have way more magic than I ever will, and you can play music the way I never could, you're way nicer too! You're everything I wish I was!"

"No, you have such courage and generosity," Nona protested. "You went back to your world to get the information I needed, and you risked your life to fight a despot to give me time. I owe you so much, and I would trade places with you, were it possible. You are the kind of decisive person I will never be. You deserve to be queen, as I do not." In fact Colene might even like it, as Nona did not. "Perhaps I could teach you some of my music, before you go. I have taught music to a number of students. Seqiro makes it easy to tame familiars, and per-

haps he can help similarly with music. In just a few hours,
perhaps—"

"You're the very last woman I want near my man or my
horse! You could take them both from me, just like that."

"I am sorry," Nona said. "But when you go, you can
close down that anchor, and—"

"We do need to close down an anchor," Colene said.
"Because Provos and I found a bad mental monster near Darius' anchor, and it may be lurking there again, so we won't get
through. If we take out an anchor, the realities will spin until
we latch onto a new one, and then the Virtual Mode will
stabilize again, and it'll be all new paths, but we should be able
to get through. We hope."

"Yes, I understand."

"But it doesn't have to be your anchor. Provos is going
home; she's through with the Virtual Mode, and Slick and Esta
will never want to go back to Earth. So that's the one to dump.
After we go there with her, on the familiar route, to be sure
she's safe. We don't want to change an anchor first, because
there might be a new sea or something cutting her off from
hers."

"I suppose that's true," Nona said. "You must do what
you feel is best."

"So will you come with us?"

Nona blinked. "You can not mean—"

"Listen, I did some thinking, and I realized that I'm sort
of right between you and Esta. You're older and better than I
am, and Esta's younger and suffered worse than I ever did. I'm
sort of helping her to be more like me, to stand up for herself
and know she's worth something, no matter what happened
before. But meanwhile how do I get better myself? And what
I realized was that if I ever want to be anything like you, I'd
better start acting more mature. It's no good to torpedo someone else who doesn't deserve it. I've just got to improve myself.
To damn well learn to be the kind of person I want to be. To
study you. Darius and Seqiro like you, and Provos doesn't
care, and I—I thought you'd *want* to be queen, but Seqiro says
you'd just about rather die, and I know about that sort of
feeling. So I want you too. Maybe it's my suicidal nature again,
my deathwish, forcing me to flirt with the worst possible
threats. I know how there's that attraction between you and
Darius. Because you're both great people, and I do like you

too, and maybe I can learn enough from you to be what I want
to be, and win him fair and square, and if I can't, then I don't
deserve him. And in that case, there's nobody I'd rather have
marry him or whatever than you. So will you come?"

Nona gazed at Colene for a moment, mentally untan-
gling her convoluted logic. She had called the girl brave and
generous. How right she had been! Then her last barrier fell,
and she dissolved into tears.

THE two great red roses of the Megaplayers' stone-ham-
mered dulcimer were glowing. The anima had come, and
changed them, and the way was open.

Nona held the hand of the girl Esta, for Nona was an
anchor person and could conduct another person across the
Virtual Mode. Yet it was Esta who had the greater experience
here, and she was glad to share all she knew of it. Darius
conducted the man Slick, leaving Provos and Colene to show
the way. Seqiro, loaded with the supplies they had recovered
from the former despots, including Colene's strange science-
magic bicycle machine, followed, keeping them all in touch
with each other. There were timid dragons and other oddities.
It was exactly the kind of adventure Nona delighted in.

Then they stood at Provos' anchor and watched the
woman, man, and girl cross out of the Virtual Mode. It was
done, and Provos had already forgotten almost their entire
association. She saw no more than the bright future for herself
and her family. Only Esta turned back momentarily, to wave.
Then Provos did the final thing, and the anchor let go.

The forested world spun around and through the other
forested realm in which the four of them stood. Nona was
awed, though she had been warned. Whole sections of scenery
collided without colliding, and the nature of reality changed
fantastically around them.

Then it stopped. Things stabilized. Another anchor had
been set. A new Virtual Mode had formed. Before them stood
the strangest monster Nona could have imagined.

"Uh-oh," Colene said.

AUTHOR'S NOTE

I had this novel scheduled for writing during the first three months of 1991. But I have hired a research assistant for a year, Alan Riggs, and naturally I want to do my heavy research while I have him, not when I don't. So I set up to do my World War II novel, *Volk,* the fall of 1990. I started *Volk* in 1980, ten years before, but found no market for it. Publishers wanted only science fiction and fantasy from me. They insisted on typecasting me. It didn't matter whether I could be competent in a new genre (I can be) or how good a novel it was (contrary to critics, I do know how to write), or whether I had something original and evocative to say (I did); they were tuned out. I have chafed under this idiocy for long enough, and now I am doing something about it. More on that in a moment.

But I knew that other commitments could fall due in this period, causing *Volk* to run a month or two into 1991. That would squeeze *Fractal Mode,* and the contract deadline dictated that this must not happen. So I moved the novel up to AwGhost, SapTimber, OctOgre of 1990. Better early than late. Then interruptions came, such as a couple of conventions I had to attend to promote my works, and half a spate of interviews, and it ran into NoRemember. I hate to travel, and I'm not all that keen on conventions, and I'm tired of interviews, but such things seem to be the price for what I want to do, so I do them. So this novel ran a bit overtime, but since I did it early, I'm okay.

So how did it go, otherwise? That question reminds me of the sick joke: "Apart from that, Mrs. Lincoln, how did you enjoy the play?" A novel doesn't just go, any more than a marriage does; it's a life experience. It is struggle and frustration and wonder and pain and joy. (Note to Ye Copy Editor: Leave my "ands" alone!) And yes, sometimes I find my fiction becoming reality, in devious ways. At the time I was writing the scene in Chapter 3 in which Darius condemns Colene for her deceit, and she blasts back at him with her statement of desperation, something similar happened to me. It had to be coincidence, because I saw that scene coming before I finished *Virtual Mode.* There are ways in which Darius is like me. Not in appearance—he is young and handsome—or in ability—he can do magic—but in his judgment of people. He has a relatively inflexible standard of honor, as I do, and many folk do not understand this. Those who cross me in a matter of honor might as well travel to some other world, as far as I'm concerned, for they will not be in mine. This applies to individuals and to corporations, to friends and to publishers both amateur and professional, and I have left a fair trail of ex-associates behind me. This does not mean that there is animosity, though there can be, or that I will not do business with them; sometimes I have to. Just that they will never again have my respect. Many do not understand my objection to their ways—and that is the point. Honor is not a thing swine can grasp. But there are different codes of honor, some of which can be respected by those who do not share them, and here is where the interactions can get tricky. Colene is not a bad girl; her code differs from Darius' code, but is consistent to itself. He judged her by his code, and he did not have the right. When he saw that, he apologized, and thereafter did not mention it again. It is to Colene's credit that she did not hold a grudge. Similarly I judged a woman by my code, and hurt her thereby, and then saw that I had erred. Such error is no light matter to me. I apologized, and the matter is at rest. We are in intermittent touch, not close; that's not the point. It is a question not of closeness but of mutual respect. It was eerie, seeing it happen in the novel and my life at the same time.

There was also solid research in this novel. Fractals are simple in theory but can be mind-bendingly complex in practice. The Mandelbrot set exists, not precisely as described in this novel, but it is indeed called the most complicated object in mathematics. I encountered it inadvertently. I saw an article on it years ago and was intrigued, but did not follow up. Then later a correspondent, Dave Alway, introduced me to Ed Pegg, who founded *Centaurs Gatherum,* a magazine for centaurs. Ed introduced me to the artist Kurt Cagle, who founded *Sea Tails,* a magazine for merfolk. You'd be amazed at the varieties of centaurs and merfolk there are! Kurt sent me a copy of *Chaos,* by James Gleick, a fascinating book—and there within it were the pictures of the Mandelbrot set. I had bought a copy of this book on my own, several months before, and hadn't yet gotten to it; it was Kurt's copy that got my attention. So it seemed fated that I would get into fractals; when I didn't follow up, other sources brought them to me again.

It turned out that Ed Pegg, too, was a fractals fan. He offered to get me more information. I accepted. Before I was done, I had amassed a small collection of books on fractals, gotten a computer program to generate them, gotten in touch with Benoit Mandelbrot himself, and subscribed to *Amygdala,* a newsletter of fractals. It was from the last that I got the system of nomenclature Colene encountered. I had also spent many hours entranced by the devious and marvelous underlying order of the Mandelbrot set. I just had to do something with this, and so I made it the setting for this novel. I did my best to simplify its ramifications, because even professional mathematicians can have trouble fathoming aspects of the set, and it can be bewildering for average folk. If you found part of Chapter 15 confusing, that's why. I took significant license adapting it; this is a novel of fantasy with respect to some of the concepts as well as the garden-variety magic. But for those who want to see how convoluted and beautiful the Mandelbrot set is in full color and detail, watch the video tape *Nothing But Zooms* or its longer sequel, *Mandelbrot Sets and Julia Sets,* both put out by Art Matrix. This is where mathematics merges with art.

Now back to what I am doing to achieve my independence from typecasting by publishers. Publishers, like women, are not all alike, but in certain respects they seem so. In fact, sometimes they seem like flocks of chickens, all spooking together at something inconsequential. Sometimes they seem like sheep of Orwell's *Animal Farm* persuasion, defining things irrelevantly: FOUR LEGS GOOD, TWO LEGS BAA-AA-AAD! Sometimes they merely seem like idiots. One publisher, advised that I want my box number used for regular mail so that stray fans won't be able to find my house and drop in on me unannounced, now sends all my regular mail to the house address *except* for an occasional one to the box with the name Piers Anthony deleted and the words "Don't Use Number" substituted. So much for that. (So how come this comment is seeing print? Well, the present publisher, like my wife when I remark on women drivers, knows that I wouldn't dare say anything bad about *it*.) Good books do get denied, and bad ones do get published, and foulups are chronic. So I am going to see what I can do for myself. I can foul up readily enough on my own, and I might as well publish my own bad books.

So I am setting up my own marketing facility, HI PIERS, and if your local bookstore won't sell you an Anthony book, calendar, or whatever, call my "troll free" number 1-800 HI PIERS and we'll sell it to you. If no publisher takes what I write, I will publish it myself, and HI PIERS will sell it. That's how this got started: I couldn't get a publisher for the 1991 Xanth Calendar, despite the fact that it may be the most beautiful calendar extant, so I published it myself. It's easy enough to do; all it takes is time and suicidal nerve about risking money. So maybe I'm a little like Colene too. At this writing we are running TV ads and building up our mailing list, hoping to make this work.

So it was in this period that I had to take time off from writing to go to the TV Channel 6 studio in Orlando, Florida, and speak my amateurish lines under the lights. You would think I would be able to do a professional job of being Piers Anthony, but I found I was capable of fluffing even that. Something about reading from the monitor that makes me lose any naturalness to which I might aspire. Something about speaking for a microphone that turns my voice into duck talk. So I struggled through, constantly being assured that this disaster was great.

But I did get one fun commercial in, in which I pretended *(pretended?)* to foul up, and concluded, "Oh, just buy the bleeping book!" And would you believe it: the cable TV outfits wouldn't run it, for reasons which changed each time we inquired: because of the dirty word "bleeping," because it was facetious, because they were afraid they'd get blamed for running a reject. Publishers' syndrome, again. So we added that to the videotaped *Interview With an Ogre*. That's what I mean: I now have the means to get my stuff to my readers despite whimsical editorial censoring. What a feeling of power!

At any rate, at this writing it remains to be seen whether HI PIERS will turn out to be genius or idiocy. That is, whether it succeeds or fails. But its object is to make my titles readily available to my readers, help promote my works, and make me better known as a writer. The addresses of those mentioned in this Note may have changed by the time you read this, so I haven't run them, but if you call HI PIERS they'll give you current information. If you are curious whether HI PIERS is succeeding or failing, call the number, and if you get a no-such-number intercept you'll know it failed. If you get a response of "Hi Piers" you're stuck; you will be locked onto our mailing list forever.

In this period another venture saw fruition: the ElfQuest folk, Father Tree Press, published *Return to Centaur,* the first part of the graphic adaptation of my thirteenth Xanth novel, *Isle of View,* which was also published at this time. This is the one featuring Jenny Elf, the character made from the girl who was paralyzed by a drunken driver. I told her story and gave her address in the book, and letters poured in to her at the rate of ten a day. They were all nice letters too. At this writing about 350 have reached her, and I think they are like a lifeboat, buoying her, showing how people care.

Jenny herself managed to get in trouble in school. There was a stiff note from the principal. How does a girl who can't get out of her wheelchair and can't speak get in trouble at a special school for just such students? Well, it seems she wore a button in her cap. She had found the button when shopping. Now, why would the school officials get so upset about that? Well, possibly it was because of the nature of the message on it: I'M BAD WITH NAMES. MAY I CALL YOU S——HEAD? (I have edited out part of the original, in the interest of not getting a note from the principal.) Jenny may be paralyzed, but she's full of mischief. She was the same age as Colene at this time, fourteen, which may explain it. But as I was editing this novel in NoRemember she won the school's "Citizen of the Month" award. Right: they didn't remember that button. She is now making a determined effort to walk again. She uses a walker, and has succeeded in making it across a room. There's still a long way to go, but this is significant progress.

I also got into another experiment. Another correspondent—I have half a slew of them!—urged me to try a special line of health foods. These are Oriental herbs refined and concentrated to powders which can be used as supplements and foods. Theoretically great improvement can result. I am a skeptic, but I try not to condemn anything on the basis of ignorance. So I pondered a few weeks, and finally agreed to try it, cautiously. My expectation is nothing; I already have a healthful life, having no "vices." That is, I don't smoke, drink coffee, or use drugs, and while I'm not a teetotaler, I touch alcohol only when social protocol requires, and then quite sparingly. I exercise and sleep regularly, have a consciously healthy diet, and always use a seat belt when riding in a car. I am a workaholic, though; nobody's perfect. In short, I see little to be gained from Oriental powders. But sometimes I am surprised. For example, just before starting on this novel I read a book about the search for the so-called Dark Matter in the universe: *The Fifth Essence,* by Lawrence M. Krauss. The theory is that we are unable to perceive 99% of our universe. Ridiculous, of course; they probably just hadn't thought to check for the amount of matter hidden inside the black holes in the center of the galaxies. But I checked, just to be sure. And that book converted me. I now believe in Dark Matter, and this novel offers a hint about its whereabouts. So I'm giving this diet the same fair trial, and will in due course form an informed opinion. Tune in, next Author's Note, maybe.

I spoke of health. I do work at it, and am probably in the upper percentiles of healthiness for men my age, which at this writing is fifty-six. But there are annoying deficiencies. I remain diabetic—fortunately Type II, the mild type—and can not stand on my feet for more than a few minutes without getting tired. Thus it is true that I can run longer than I can stand; it is as if my engine lacks an idling jet. Every so often a change in weather can bring me a bad fit of allergy, so that I have to stuff tissue in my nose to stop it from dripping into the keyboard. My knees have improved slightly in the past decade, but I still can't quite squat without pain. And remember my tongue? In the Note in *Virtual* I told how it was sore, and the dentist smoothed out a worn onlay. Well, that didn't do it. In the end I had two onlays replaced with smooth new crowns, and still my tongue was sore. After fourteen visits to dentists, during which my mouth was seen by five different ones, I still have only a stop-gap solution: a plastic appliance, or stint, that I put in my mouth to cover the region that makes my tongue sore. It seems that I have an "ectopic" taste bud on the side of my tongue that has become sensitive to something in that part of my mouth. Stop that sniggering, you women; this is nothing like an ectopic pregnancy.

Last time I gave credits to several readers for contributions to the novel. This time there are fewer. In 1989 Hannah Blakeman sent me a package of articles on alcoholism and child abuse. I had intended to use it for *Virtual* but Colene's family didn't turn out that way. You may have heard it said that the characters of a novel sometimes dictate their own story lines. It's true. Colene's mother was alcoholic, but the girl was not directly abused by her family, though the problems of that family surely contributed to the insecurity that manifested as a flirtation with suicide. But this material on alcoholics was eye-opening, and I wanted to use it. It enabled me to recognize in retrospect a situation that had perplexed me in prior years: I had run afoul of an adult child of an alcoholic. That is, a person who had been a child of an alcoholic, and had grown up and left that family. In the ignorance I suspect I share with most folk, I thought that once a person gets out of such a situation, things are all right. That is not necessarily the case. The emotional scars can remain for life. To make a poor analogy: you can not amputate a child's leg, and expect him to win foot races as an adult. You can't abuse him in his formative years, and expect him to be without pain thereafter. You can't force a little girl to have sex several times a day for years and expect her to grow up with a healthy sexual attitude. You can't dedicate years to making children believe that they are worthless and expect them to have good self-esteem thereafter. So just as folk run afoul of me, because of the standards I set to correct the problems of my youth, so also I run afoul of others, who carry their problems out of sight. I am not the child of an alcoholic, and was never abused in that manner, but there are ways I can relate, as you can see by the tone of this Note. One thing you who had secure or happy childhoods should understand about those of us who did not: we who control our feelings, who avoid conflicts at all costs or seem to seek them, who are hypersensitive, self-critical, compulsive, workaholic, and above all, survivors—we are not that way from perversity, and we can not just relax and let it go. We have learned to cope in ways you never had to.

So I pondered the material for this novel, and crafted a bad case: Esta, a girl who had suffered all three types of abuse known in alcoholic families. Physical, sexual, and emotional. Not the skewed definitions sometimes seen, as if physical abuse means one spanking, sexual abuse means someone used a dirty word, and emotional abuse means setting an eleven P.M. curfew. The *real* things, so bad that we prefer not to believe they happen. Esta, thinking herself weak, was strong; she was surviving with minimal apparent damage. Exactly as an unconscionable number of others do. She, at least, will have a chance to recover completely, healed physically by magic and emotionally by the reversal of her life-memories. Those in real life do not have that option.

Rather than try to give a help number which might change by the time this sees print, for those who see themselves or friends in aspects of this discussion, I will try to see that HI PIERS has such information. If you call and say, "Please, I don't want to be put on your mailing list, I just need the number of Sexual Abuse Anonymous," or whatever, we will give you that number. This much I hope I can do to help. There is doubt, however: we are not at this point certain about liability. That is, if someone calls in, and we give a helpline number, and the folk there fail to help, are we liable for a lawsuit? Don't laugh; such things happen. So we'll help if we can safely do so. Actually other folk have problems too; as I wrote this Note I received a letter from a young man who had had intestinal surgery; several doctors had failed to diagnose his malady, and when one did he was dying; they saved him, but now he has $80,000 in medical bills not covered by insurance. Canada has a good system of medical coverage; the United States has deadly chaos. Will it ever change?

Another credit with a story behind it: in the *Phaze Doubt* Note I mentioned discovering the cover of the record album *Heartdance,* with the beautiful picture of the giant musical instruments by the sea, and the girl in red standing at the brink. Well, I set that picture up between my keyboard and the monitor screen as I typed this novel. That's the starting point, with Nona there. In the Note for *Virtual* I mentioned a sketch sent by Oria Tripp, of a young woman in red walking toward mountains: "Someday." I put that beside the computer. Nona again, perhaps. So I named the planet Oria. Thus do little things catch my fancy and become other things. Please don't write begging me to name a magic planet after you; I generally do such things only when the whim strikes.

And one even farther-fetched: as I completed my first draft I received a wonderful letter from Julia. No last name, no return address, just a note of appreciation for my Note in *And Eternity*. She had suffered the loss of three children, and said my comment to the Ligeia girls prompted her to seek counseling, which helped her. I appreciate the letter and the thought, though it often seems to be the nicest letters I am unable to answer, while I am swamped with demanding letters from others. But the thing is, the Mandelbrot set—the *set*ting for this novel—is related to the Julia sets, so it seemed somehow appropriate to receive a Julia letter.

And I heard from Arthur Babick, a man I had known about thirty-five years ago, in college. He had heard a radio announcer praising my books, so he called the station, then wrote me. I wound up doing a half-hour telephone interview for them. It's nice to know that those I knew in a bygone day do still exist. I mentioned to Art that I am doing spot research on consciousness, as I orient on future projects, and he sent several articles on the subject. I see similarities between the problems of consciousness and those of chaos. Which leads nicely into the next novel in this series, *Chaos Mode,* which will also relate to the creatures of the Burgess Shale. That might sound dull to you. Well, let me tell you—no, that had better wait for the next Note.

Meanwhile, my life continued in its petty pace. I use a VGA color monitor, which I have set with yellow print on a brown background. That's fine; I like it, except that I am nervous about reports that radiation from computer monitors may be frying folks' brains. Would anyone notice the difference if my brains were fried? Suddenly my bottom command line disappeared. You know, the line that gives the name of my file, tells where my cursor is, the time of day and whatnot. I depend on that line, because when there's a special instruction, that's where it is. For example, my Control V evokes the message "Don't touch this key again!" and Control Z says, "Help! I'm being held captive in this computer." Would *you* want to live without messages like these? My colors also were shuffled. What had happened? Had I miskeyed in some fatal fashion? Alan looked into it, and concluded that there was no way a miskey could have done it. Apparently I had lost the 23-line display, and it was now projecting 25 lines, with the bottom one showing just below the screen. Thus my command line was literally out of sight. Great! What could I do about it? Apparently the 23-line display was gone; maybe it had existed once, but would not in the future. Finally Alan found a solution: there's a control on the monitor which squeezes the display together. We could cram those 25 lines in! I had my command line back. Once again the fell plot of the evil computer had been foiled.

Well, not quite. We still had not gotten the colors back; it had set itself on half my colors, and the other half on Blink, with the colors I wanted preempted by the Blinking section. Alan got into the works and recovered my slate of colors. But when I printed out the day's work on the laser printer, my 60-line pages had been reduced to 57 lines, with slipsheets inserted to carry the extra 3 lines. Thus my printout was 57 lines, 3 lines, 57 lines, 3 lines, and so on. But we hadn't touched the printer. How did an adjustment to the programming for the monitor do that to the printer? It wasn't my word processing program, Sprint; that was formatting for 60 lines. No doubt a computer expert will tell you it couldn't happen. Just as a dentist will assure you that you don't feel what you feel as he drills into your nerve. Alan finally ran that down too: the system was refusing to read the appropriate formatting file. Alan removed that file, then put it back in the same place. That tricked the system into reading it again, and all is well. There is a certain art to outsmarting a stupid machine.

Letters continued to pile in at a record annual rate; I answered over 500 during this novel, though I can not promise to answer them all. Some of them ask for money, some for free books. I don't want to seem unkind, but I'm not in the business of giving things away. I also continued my internecine war with copy editors; those for my novels have improved, which means they mess less with my pristine text, but one systematically changed all my dashes in a story to ellipses. That is, three dots . . . , thus. The dash is properly used to signal a break in the text—like this—while the ellipsis is properly used to signal omitted words, as the . . . copy eds seem not to know. Growl! And the Post Orifice issued a fiat changing the way we must address letters: HENCEFORTH ALL CAPITALS NO PUNCTUATION. Surprise: I like it; it's easier to do.

I had to sign 1,150 pages for our special limited hardcover edition of *Isle of View*. Have you ever tried to sign that many sheets? My signature has been degenerating over the years, as if there are only so many signatures in me, and later copies get degraded. Now it is illegible, with the last four letters of PIERS condensed into half a squiggle and the I-dot in the middle of the loop of the P. That's to confound the grapho-analysts. I half expect the purchasers of that edition to stare at the signature and say, "Pay fifty bucks for *this?*" I certainly couldn't blame them.

Virtual Mode came back to haunt me too: it had not yet been published, and the routine permission for my use of a few words from a popular song hit a snag. For thirteen words they demanded $450, take it or leave it. That's over thirty dollars a word, for doing the proprietors the favor of publicizing their song. It's a nice song, but not a nice attitude, so I didn't take it, I left it, and rewrote the concluding paragraph of that Author's Note to exclude those words. Now you know why I did not name that tune.

In this period, too, Iraq invaded Kuwait, setting off an international crisis. Sigh; if I had the power to right every wrong in the world, I wouldn't even know where to start. But I wish you folk out there the best you are fated to have.

After I finished the novel and this Note in first draft, at the end of OctOgre, I went to the World Fantasy Convention at the beginning of NoRemember. I don't like to travel, and can live without conventions, but this was for business. A full Convention Report is beyond the scope of this Note, but I'll touch on a few items. I was not listed in advance promotion, at my request, so that few folk realized that I would be there, but I did attend the autographing session and participated in a panel on "The Never-ending Sequel." Others on it were Jo Clayton, Philip Jose Farmer, and Gordon Dickson, so it was a pretty high-powered panel. The moderator, Jack Chalker, wasn't there, which left us headless. We got along nicely anyway, and halfway through Jack arrived, having had a time confusion. The shift from Daylight Saving to Standard Time had occurred just the week before, and for many of us the trip to Central Time complicated it further; I simply left my watch as it was and made mental adjustments, as I knew I'd have to shift back soon. You probably think I said something funny there. Okay: when others remarked on the manner writers like Dickens were panned as hacks in their lifetimes, then elevated to literary genius status after their deaths, I said, "I'd like to know how to go from hack to genius without dying." Because I do expect to have a better critical reception after death; it could hardly be worse than it is in life. A genre newsmagazine once did a survey of the top SF/fantasy writers extant; I came in at #37. Once a review book listed its top forty-three fantasy novels for the year; I had had four fantasies published that year, but did not make the list. I may have had more SF/fantasy genre bestsellers than any other writer, with twenty-two titles appearing on the New York Times and/or Publishers Weekly bestseller lists as of this writing; that's why. The critical assumption is that any writer who is popular with readers can not be worthwhile. So it really wasn't funny, and all other real writers understand, because they get similar critical treatment, but it did get a laugh.

However, our panel did get serious too; it ranged all over. We discussed history, and I remarked how man is currently destroying the world by overrunning it. I feel about that as Colene does, by no particular coincidence.

My business at the Con was with editors and publishers, including Susan Allison of Berkley, who will be surprised to see her name here, and to promote HI PIERS. We were trying to sell my publishers on the notion of cooperative cable TV ads for my books: we would make the ads and the publisher would pay the better part of the cost of running them. We had them in for meals. It is an ironclad rule that the publisher always pays for the author's meal, but I never was much for rules, and it was my treat. Which meant they had to watch our sample commercials, including my "bleeping" one. The publishers were noncommittal; I can't think why.

There was also a cute young woman taking pictures of middle-aged old men like me, which strikes me as a reversal of the natural order. She had us scheduled every twenty minutes throughout the convention. When my turn came, and she was setting up her photographic paraphernalia, I demonstrated the joke we played as children: smile angelically, and just as the camera clicks, make a horrible face. As I spoke, I turned to face the camera, stuck out my tongue, and wiggled my fingers at my ears. FLASH! Perfect messed-up shot. No, she did take others—these folk never leave such things to chance—but I wonder whether that will be the one she publishes?

Meanwhile Jenny was attending Sci-Con, where I had met her the year before. The convention was down to a third of its normal size, because so many of its attendees had been shipped to the Persian Gulf for the crisis. That's one way to stamp out fandom! But I understand that Jenny had a ball. For one thing, our Jenny Elf T-shirts were just coming out, with her face on them.

So I returned from the convention, and set up for the two-hour job of plugging in a few items I had overlooked when writing the novel. That took three days. Then the formal editing, normally done in a week. I started on the 10th—and completed it Thanksgiving Day, the 22nd. Because everything in the world came in to take my time, so that I was operating at about 50% efficiency. I mean that's when my wife bought a new car and I had to go into town to sign papers and drive it home. The second issue of the *Hi Piers* newsletter was getting ready for publication, requiring almost daily long technical calls. There was motion picture interest in my Xanth series, but naturally the purchaser wanted more rights than I could afford to give, leading to Florida/California phone calls going nowhere fast. Assorted relatives visited. My bicycle tire went flat; the first time I fixed it the way Colene did, with gunk, but the second time it was too far gone for that and I'm going to have to get a new tire. I ride my bike a mile and a half each morning, fetching in the newspapers, you see. So I had to use my wife's bike, my knees just about banging the handlebars. Sigh. As you can see, my home life is distressingly typical.

And in this period of the writing and editing of this novel, I had six other novels published: *Hard Sell, Firefly, Isle of View, Dead Morn, Orc's Opal,* and *Balook*. They should all be in paperback reprint by the time you read this. I'm trying to keep up with the demands of my readers, really I am, inadequate as my effort may seem.

NoRemember 22, 1990

The exotic, entertaining adventures of two heroic misfits, by the
acclaimed author of the best-selling Xanth and Mode series.

PIERS ANTHONY

Critically injured policeman Walter Toland faces
a bleak future until he discovers Killobyte, the
virtual-reality computer game with effects so
vivid they are indistinguishable from the real
world. Through the game he meets diabetic Baal
Curran. Fantastic heroism becomes unharnessed
danger when Toland and Baal are trapped in the
game by a deranged hacker who refuses to let
them out, even when Baal's need for insulin
becomes critical.

KILLOBYTE

Coming in hardcover to bookstores everywhere.

G. P. Putnam's Sons
A member of The Putnam Berkley Group, Inc.